DAVID
GILMAN

MASTER OF WAR

SHADOW

⊢ OF THE ⊢

HAWK

HEAD
of ZEUS

First published in the UK in 2021 by Head of Zeus Ltd
This paperback edition first published in 2021 by Head of Zeus Ltd

9 7 5 3 1 2 4 6 8

A catalogue record for this book is available from
the British Library.

ISBN (PB): 9781788545006
ISBN (E): 9781788544979

Typeset by Siliconchips Services Ltd UK

Printed and bound in Great Britain by
CPI Group (UK) Ltd, Croydon CR0 4YY

Head of Zeus Ltd
First Floor East
5–8 Hardwick Street
London EC1R 4RG

WWW.HEADOFZEUS.COM

For Suzy

CHARACTER LIST

*Sir Thomas Blackstone

THOMAS BLACKSTONE'S MEN
*Sir Gilbert Killbere
*Meulon: Norman captain
*John Jacob: captain
*Renfred: German man-at-arms and captain
*Will Longdon: veteran archer and centenar
*Jack Halfpenny: archer and ventenar
*Meuric Kynith: Welsh archer and ventenar
*Beyard: Gascon captain
*Aicart: Gascon man-at-arms
*Loys: Gascon man-at-arms
*Bascon Gâsconay: man-at-arms
*William Ashford: man-at-arms, captain
*Tom Brook: man-at-arms

ITALIAN CLERIC
*Niccolò Torellini: Florentine priest

ENGLISH MERCENARIES
*Ranulph de Hayle/Ronec le Bête
Sir Hugh Calveley
Walter Hewitt
William Latimer
Matthew Gourney

BRETON NOBILITY AND COMMANDERS

John de Montfort: English-backed claimant to the Duchy of Brittany

Charles de Blois: French-backed claimant to the Duchy of Brittany

Lord of Mayenne: Breton regional lord

Bertrand du Guesclin: Breton commander

Olivier de Mauny: nobleman and Bertrand du Guesclin's cousin

Jean de Beaumanoir: lord and ally of Charles de Blois

ENGLISH ROYALTY

Edward of Woodstock: Prince of Wales and Aquitaine

ENGLISH OFFICIALS

Sir John Chandos: Constable of Aquitaine

Sir Nigel Loring: the Prince's chamberlain

FRENCH ROYALTY

Charles V: King of France

FRENCH OFFICIALS, NOBLEMEN, MERCENARIES AND MEN-AT-ARMS

Jean de Grailly, Captal de Buch: Gascon lord

Lord de Graumont: French regional lord

*Godfrey de Claville: captain of Villaines

Simon Bucy: counsellor to the French King

Gontier de Bagneaux: confidential secretary to the French King

Jean de Bourbon: Count de la Marche

Le Bègue de Villaines: French nobleman

Arnoul d'Audrehem: Marshal of France

Eustache d'Aubricourt: Hainault mercenary

SPANISH ROYALTY

Charles, King of Navarre: claimant to the French throne

Don Pedro I: King of Castile and León

Blanche de Bourbon: Queen of Castile and León

Henry of Trastámara: Don Pedro's half-brother and claimant to his throne

SPANISH OFFICIALS

Iñigo Ortiz de Estúñiga: guard commander for Blanche de Bourbon

*High Steward to King Don Pedro

Gutier de Toledo: commander of the royal bodyguard

SPANISH MEN-AT-ARMS, VILLEINS, SERVANTS, MERCHANTS, SURGEON AND CLERICS

*Garindo: heretic priest

*Velasquita Alcón de Lugo

*Lázaro: Queen of Castile's servant

*Halif ben Josef: Jewish surgeon

*Ariz: man-at-arms

*Saustin: man-at-arms

*Tibalt: man-at-arms

*Elias Navarette and Salamon Bonisac: Jewish merchants

*Andrés: guide

*Santos: guide

*Pérez of Burgos: merchant

*Álvaraz: Castilian army commander

Gil Boccanegra: Genoese Admiral of the Castilian Fleet

Suero Gómez: Archbishop of Santiago de Compostela

Peralvarez: dean of Santiago cathedral

*Gontrán: fisherman and pilgrim

Nasrid Moors
*Sayyid al-Hakam
*Abid al-Hakam
*Najih bin Wālid

*Indicates fictional characters

1364–1366

BLACKSTONE'S JOURNEY THROUGH FRANCE AND SPAIN

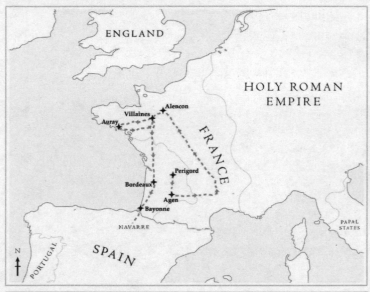

BLACKSTONE'S ROUTE --✦--

A noble man must either live a good life or die a noble death.

Sophocles

PROLOGUE

King Pedro's Palace
Burgos, Castile, Spain

The darkened room bore no sign of evil incantation, even though some deemed the practice of astrology to be against Divine Law. Garindo knew the risks he took if he edged closer to the abyss of necromancy and witchcraft – and it was easily done: the thirst for greater knowledge of the universe could lead a man to embrace the dark arts. However, his own religious convictions kept him on the side of righteousness, even though he had been charged with heresy by the Pope for practising astrology.

The heretic priest blinked in the near darkness. He had been studying for hours and the candles had burnt low. His predictions had come to fruition and he now feared another whose powers were greater than his own. She was Satan's mistress.

He had begged the King to rid himself of this witch, who was always at his side. She lived behind the veil of darkness. So far his own skills had kept her at bay. But for how much longer? Heresy or witchcraft? Who would prevail?

It was God who permitted the devil to exist, cast down from heaven to test men and women, to allow them to choose whether to fight the demonic possession offered by the devil or succumb to its temptation. Garindo's skills came from the great books of the East, from Sanskrit, Greek and the learned writing of the Arabs, the study of which was itself considered a sin, for it implied a forsaking of the belief that it was God who guided and determined men's lives and the fortunes of kings.

The old man sighed, resigned to defying divine power. He would use his skill. He did not like what he saw in the chart that lay beneath his hand. Whom to fear the most? God, displeased that he tampered with men's fate? Or the devil's mistress, who vied for the King's favour? He feared the threat of divine justice less than the magic of the practitioners of witchcraft, whose spells were so powerful they could kill a man. His terror of them overpowered his belief that God would protect him. There were times when God let the devil rampage through men's hearts. Perhaps that was a test of faith.

He closed the thick wooden door behind him. The lock turned laboriously from the weight of the iron key. He wanted his bed. Sleep had eluded him these past days as he studied the charts. The candle he held spluttered and wax stung the back of his hand, but he ignored it. He was deep in thought, seeking the words he must use when he gave his findings to the King, knowing how the man's rage could flare at bad tidings. His shoes scuffed the uneven tiled floor, his old knees complaining from sitting too long at his deliberations. His breath caught as the darkness ahead shifted. His heart tried to burst from his chest, its beats thudding in his ears. He rasped out a challenge: 'Who is there? Show yourself.'

There was no response. He shivered and crossed himself, asking the Almighty to protect him. His spine crawled at the fear of what might lie ahead. Silence. Perhaps it had been a scurrying rat. He listened. The low-burning candle would soon plunge him into total darkness. If he did not move his fear might strangle him. He stepped forward, his hand stroking the wall to guide him and offer comfort.

A cool breeze brushed his face.

A door or window had been left open. Had it allowed night spirits to enter the palace?

He recoiled as something rubbed against his leg. He kicked and heard one of the feral cats screech. He laughed nervously at his own foolishness and shuffled towards his bedchamber, unaware that the darkness moved again behind him. Unaware that the king's favourite was watching.

And waiting.

Everything he had foretold had come to pass. But he had not seen his own death.

PART ONE

DEATH OF AN ARCHER

CHAPTER ONE

France, North of Bordeaux
1364

The rider was frozen dead in the saddle. Snow, and then bodkin-tipped frost driven into bones by a snarling wind, had torn away the man's soul. But it was not the hand of God that led him to Blackstone's encampment. A hardy monk returning on foot to the safety of Blackstone's protection at the Abbaye Notre-Dame de Boschaud had come across the exhausted man, who with his final breaths had gasped for help to find the English King's Master of War. The monk, seeking refuge from the bitter winter that was killing man and beast across the land, had plodded on towards the fortified abbey, deep in prayer and leading the man's suffering horse.

Strong arms, fingers clawing in the biting cold, reached for the dead man, cutting the reins to free his frozen grip. Blackstone saw the satchel bearing the Prince's seal. The messenger's clothing creaked when they eased him from the saddle. The horse faltered, head low. Men guided it towards the stable with a gentleness reserved for a beast with a courageous heart that deserved to be saved. Blankets, deep, soft straw, boiled oats and warmth from the other horses would aid its chances of survival.

They settled the dead man onto a stool, propping his back against the wall. Blackstone looked into his blue eyes. The Prince's messenger had fought against his own death in his determination to deliver the contents of the satchel. Blackstone reached out to close the man's eyes but the lids were frozen open, gazing out from eternity at the gathered men. Some crossed themselves.

'Shall we put him close to the fire?' said Blackstone's centenar Will Longdon.

'Sweet Jesus, you idiot, you want him rotting?' the veteran knight Gilbert Killbere said. 'Get him down to the cellars. He needs to be kept cold until the thaw and then the monks can bury him.'

The veteran archer shrugged. 'We'll put him in the cheese room – then we won't notice when he starts to stink.'

'You're a disrespectful godless wretch,' said Killbere.

Blackstone turned to the gathered men. 'As are many of us, Gilbert, but we will treat this man with respect. The rigor in his muscles will ease. Have the monks wrap him in linen and lay him somewhere close to God.' He turned to his squire. 'John, speak to the abbot, make my request known to him. Ask for a side chapel and prayers to be said.'

John Jacob nodded and gestured to the men to bear the messenger away. As they bent to their task, he glanced at the satchel. 'I'll wager that's bad news, Sir Thomas.'

Killbere closed the door behind them and pushed more wood into the fire; then he tugged his heavy cloak around him. Like the others, he wore strips of cloth wrapped over his boots to help ward off the bone-cracking cold of the stone floors. Monks were not lords of a manor who placed fresh reeds beneath their rugs.

'Worst winter I can remember and this is already spring,' said Killbere, squatting on a stool, pushing his swaddled boots towards the flames. 'Snot drips and freezes like damned icicles. We hack wine casks open and melt chunks of wine over a fire. It's too cold to fight even if we could find a Frenchman to raise a sword against and not a whore or a nun in sight to embrace beneath the blankets. It's not just the cold wind that makes your eyes water. It's the ball ache. We should go back to Italy. South. Naples or somewhere.'

Blackstone held the unopened satchel containing orders from the Prince of Wales. He felt the leather stiff beneath his fingertips. 'Knowing the Prince, he'll find something to warm us.'

'Then open it. It's time we left this place.'

Blackstone took out the folded parchment and broke its wax seal. A loyal messenger had sacrificed his life to deliver the summons. What was so important that he should pay such a price? His eyes followed a clerk's neat hand. Killbere waited, eyebrows raised, questioning.

'Agen,' said Blackstone, his mind's eye placing the ancient city halfway between Bordeaux and Toulouse in the south-west. Close enough to the northern Spanish kingdom of Navarre. 'We travel to meet the Prince and Charles of Navarre.'

Killbere poked the fire in disgust. 'That popinjay. We saved his bastard arse when we fought the Jacquerie. These damned noblemen. Peacocks on the battlefield. All he's fit for is killing peasants. What does he want now?'

Blackstone shook his head and passed Killbere the letter. 'All we know is that the Prince summons us.'

'Two days' ride in this weather,' said Killbere. 'At least. I tell you, Thomas, the King of Navarre is up to no good. I'm not joyful at the thought that we'll be dragged into a fight to help him.' He tossed the folded document onto the table. 'God's tears, our King and our Prince won the damned war thanks to men like ours shedding their blood; if this upstart has ambitions beyond his ability then let others ride to their deaths on his behalf, not us. He should stay in that sliver of land he calls a kingdom.'

The Abbaye Notre-Dame de Boschaud nestled in the heart of Aquitaine between the Prince's palace in Bordeaux and the seneschal at Poitiers. If routiers or the French struck, Blackstone was well placed to retaliate. What prompted this summons south? Defence or attack?

'You wanted a fight, Gilbert, perhaps we are being given one.'

Below the castle walls Agen's honey-coloured brick buildings glowed in the day's late sun, rays of gold enriching the great river that served as the city's trading route and defence. Blackstone's hundred iron-shod horses clattered up the cobbled approach to the castle as guards peered down from the high walls. The Prince's banner furled in the clear air above the white-slaked landscape stretching to the far horizon and Navarre's Pyrenean kingdom.

'Even colder up here,' said Will Longdon. 'I hope there's meat and wine waiting for us. My arse aches and my stomach growls.'

'Pottage and Gascon wine if we're lucky,' said his ventenar, Jack Halfpenny.

Killbere half turned in the saddle. 'If you're lucky enough to be fed you keep your bows with you. We've a Spanish lord and his men inside these walls and what they can't take as a trophy in battle they will steal. An Englishman's bow is a prize.'

'And a Welshman's,' called Meuric Kynith, Longdon's other ventenar.

'Any damned bow, you heathen Celt,' said Killbere. 'Any archer loses his bow to a scab-arsed Navarrese thief, I'll have him flogged.'

Blackstone glanced at the veteran knight at his side. 'Gilbert, our archers wouldn't relinquish their bows even in the grip of death. There's no need to lecture them. Think of the years we have fought together. Not once have we seen any of them cast aside or lose a hemp cord, never mind their bow.'

'They've been wintering these past months, Thomas. You kept them busy, I'll grant you; building walls and exercising horses keep a man's muscles taut, but it softens their brain. They need a kick up the arse every once in a while.' He looked over his shoulder. 'Especially archers.'

'And you kicked my arse often enough when I was a lad and pulled a bow for the King,' said Blackstone.

'You deserved it. And it did you no harm. I take pride that my boot and the flat of my hand kept your senses sharp. How else would you have become the King's Master of War?'

'How else?' Blackstone smiled as the gates opened.

CHAPTER TWO

Blackstone and Killbere stood in the corridor outside the great hall waiting to be beckoned inside. The Prince always travelled with an entourage and his presence in Agen was as well attended as ever. He had been in the city since November, not only to have homage paid to him by Gascon lords but to meet the Pyrenean rulers. It was Charles of Navarre who now commanded the Prince's attention.

Killbere muttered out of the side of his mouth. 'Navarre is odious, despicable and treacherous. Let's be careful, Thomas. This wheedling bastard will have us shed blood for him if we are not cautious. The Prince values us yet we are but pawns in his grand scheme.'

'What scheme is that?' Blackstone whispered back, glancing at the court officials, aides and clerks who jostled along the corridor, any of whom would be eager to hear a note of dissent and report it to their superiors. It was how courtiers gained promotion and favours.

'How in God's name am I to know the mind of a prince? My bowels tell me this meeting will place us in jeopardy. There were two hundred men-at-arms preparing to move in the outer ward. Their horses looked fresh and so did they.'

'They're not troops readying for war, Gilbert, they're the Prince's entourage. I saw William Ashford and his men. I think the Prince is soon to return to Bordeaux.'

A flurry of activity caused a rise in the hubbub of voices. Blackstone was tall enough to see over the surge of courtiers and glimpsed a nobleman wearing an adorned cloak. He came out of a room further along the passage and turned away, followed by his personal retinue.

'What?' said Killbere.

'Navarre. He's just left.'

'Are you sure it was him?'

Blackstone nodded. The man's haughty bearing would have picked him out in a crowd even without the fur-collared embroidered robe.

Before Killbere could say anything more a servant swung open the doors, revealing a vast chamber decorated fit for a king or prince even though the castle at Agen had only been a temporary residence. Richly coloured tapestries hung from every wall. Ornate designs of swans with women's heads hung each side of a centrepiece, black with emblazoned silver ostrich plumes. It was the Prince's duty to administer the Duchy of Aquitaine and every man and woman who had the honour to be in his company loved and admired him. After the privations of years of war, the Prince's extravagant feasts and entertainment had become a byword, serving the dual purpose of impressing those who needed to be impressed and uplifting the spirits of a nation that had endured great hardship. Blackstone knew that this room was where the Prince had governed the duchy over the past months and had accepted the allegiance of a thousand lords. Edward's warmth, conviviality and largesse had brought disparate leaders and their fiefdoms under his control.

Now the Prince stood, one arm leaning against the high mantel above the log fire as he gazed into the flames. Rugs and fresh reeds smothered the stone floor; a table, long enough for two men to lie head to toe, showed an unfurled map in front of the Prince's upholstered chair. Another door led off from the far corner, used no doubt by Navarre to leave the room. Did protocol demand the arrogant aristocrat avoid meeting the scar-faced knight who had been essential to his success years before when he had defeated the peasant uprising?

Blackstone and Killbere bowed.

The Prince, smiling, turned away from the flames and the thoughts that consumed him. 'Thomas, time has healed your wounds?'

'Thank you, highness, yes, I am well. Your physicians were most attentive.'

He faced the Prince whose destiny had been entwined with his own since boyhood, when they had fought at Crécy and Blackstone had saved Edward's life. Their journey thereafter had been fraught, through turbulent years of defiance and disagreement, until finally time and circumstances had healed the rifts. Despite it all, the years had solidified Blackstone's iron-hard loyalty until once again, at great risk to his own life, he had saved the Prince from the assassination attempt at Bergerac the previous August. The attempt resulted in Blackstone suffering near fatal wounds when he fought an old ally. A friend who had become an enemy.

Those events had made the Prince of Wales genuinely concerned for Blackstone's wellbeing. 'I thank God for his blessings, Thomas. We had prayers said for you. So too our father.'

'I am grateful, my Prince.'

'We feel we should have had our priest spend more time at your bedside while you recovered. A psalter read before retiring calms a man's mind. The psalms are words of comfort and wisdom. And your life is spent in the valley of the shadow of death, Thomas.' Edward smiled, knowing the seriousness of his suggestion would not sit well with the Master of War.

'Perhaps the Goddess of the Silver Wheel has more sway over you than we appreciate.'

Blackstone unconsciously touched the archer's talisman at his throat. Arianrhod. The Celtic goddess who protected in this life and carried the fallen across to the next.

'I'll take my comfort where I can find it, lord.'

'And your son, Henry?'

Blackstone felt the pang of separation at mention of his son. 'My Prince, as you know, after his own injuries were attended to, he was granted a scholarship at Oxford by our gracious lord King.'

The Prince nodded 'He has our father's protection. England would seem to be the safest place for Thomas Blackstone's son. We trust you are content with him using his mother's maiden name? Father Torellini advised it would be wise.'

'I am unable to give you enough thanks for his well-being, highness.'

'Thomas, you have saved the King's son's life twice. It is a gesture of gratitude from our King. We hope he is a good student.'

'He's a stranger to England. He was born here and what education he has had was in Florence and Avignon. He has seen bloodshed enough for a boy his age, so I pray he settles and realizes his good fortune.'

'We are certain he will do well. And you, Sir Gilbert, are you as anxious as ever to confront our enemies?'

'I seek only to serve my Prince and my King and kill those who come between us.'

Edward beckoned them to the table. 'Turmoil awaits us at every turn. Our plans for alliances can crumble at any moment.'

'And the King of Navarre is part of that turmoil?' said Blackstone.

The Prince nodded.

Blackstone's life had been as tainted as others by the King of Navarre. 'He's a traitor. As far back as '46, when I was a boy, he drew the de Harcourt family into rebellion against the French royal family. They executed my friend and mentor. Years later we helped him against the Jacquerie. He is a snake, highness. He will twist and turn and inflict his venom.'

'Thomas, you are talking of a King. His father-in-law was the King of France and his mother a daughter of the fleurs-de-lys. He has royal blood. You are disrespectful.'

'My disrespect is well founded, my lord. He will turn on you. The day will come when he will strike a deal with the French. His kingdom is at our backs. He controls the passes over the Pyrenees. Do not trust him.'

For a moment it seemed the Prince might chastise Blackstone. Instead, he nodded. 'I know all of this, Thomas. The politics of Spain are now coiled like the serpent around us. I favour him only so far. He goes to war. He will attack the French army of the north once he crosses the Seine. He lays claim to the throne of France.' He paused. 'Yet again.'

'Highness, we both know how dangerous that is,' said Blackstone. 'The river crossings are few and far between and held by French forces. He cannot win.'

The Prince's finger traced a line on the map south of Paris along the river. 'The town of Vernon commands a bridge across the Seine and Vernon belongs to Navarre's sister, the dowager Queen. That's her domain. That is where they will cross.'

'Navarre is no field commander,' said Killbere. 'We've seen him lead men. Or try to.'

'He will not lead the troops. He has recruited two thousand routiers, Gascons and Bretons and some English, as well as his own Navarrese troops. Our esteemed Gascon lord and friend the Captal de Buch will command them. Navarre will stay...' He paused and smiled. '... at home. That is the most generous way we can phrase it. He stays in his castle at Pamplona.'

Blackstone and the Prince held each other's gaze for a moment. The involvement of the experienced commander Jean de Grailly, the Captal de Buch, was not lost on Blackstone; some of his own men-at-arms were Gascons and one of his ablest captains, Beyard, was a sworn man to the Captal.

'My Lord de Grailly wants my men?'

'Yes.'

'Highness, that leaves me depleted. I have a small command by choice. We are close knit. We travel fast. I can rally a thousand men and more to meet your own demands when the need arises but I need men with me who have fought together. Who know what to expect of the man at their shoulder. At least let me keep my captain Beyard.'

'No. He goes with de Grailly. He needs him.'

Blackstone was about to protest but the stern look from the Prince stopped him. 'Do not challenge your Prince's decision, Thomas.'

Blackstone dipped his head. 'My lord. May I ask for those men taken from me to be replaced from your own?'

'Who?'

'William Ashford from the King's guard and his dozen men. They rode with us when he accompanied Father Torellini to Avignon. He's a man I trust and he would have stayed with us had he not been recalled to accompany you from Bordeaux to Bergerac.'

The Prince seemed uncertain. 'I value him highly, Thomas. I keep him close.'

'Highness, I need a man of equal stature to Beyard. If I am to serve you effectively, then grant me Ashford.'

Edward's reluctance was obvious. 'Thomas, were it any man other than you we would decline such a request. However, it is a fair trade. He and his men are yours.'

'I am grateful, my lord.'

Killbere shuffled. 'Highness, may I speak?'

'You have spent too many years in Thomas's company to know restraint, Gilbert. You see the flaws already in this plan?'

'This matter with Charles of Navarre. It makes no sense,' said Killbere. 'We have a treaty with France. Are the English involved?'

'We are not.'

'Then we are not to fight?' said Blackstone.

The Prince leaned forward and indicated Spain. The different regions defined on the map showed the small but strategically important kingdom of Navarre squeezed between the sea and the kingdom of Aragon to the east and the greater kingdom of Castile to the south. Fewer than a hundred thousand souls inhabited Navarre, but its narrow border with the Prince's Duchy of Aquitaine provided a gateway north into France for the ambitious Pyrenean king.

'The French expect his troops to enter France further east where their southern army of several thousand are waiting to stop him.'

Blackstone's instincts warned him. 'Then you'll let them travel through your territory, my lord.'

'Yes. That is all we will do for him.' He sat in the armchair and fidgeted with his cloak, tugging it across his legs. He looked at Blackstone, waiting for a further response. Blackstone knew there was more to be said. It made little sense for the Prince to help the troublesome King of Navarre. Why risk antagonizing the French? What would cause the Prince of Wales to take such a chance? The previous year Blackstone had secured the loyalty of the Count de Foix, by helping him beat his sworn enemy Jean d'Armagnac. The Count had then demanded a massive ransom on his defeated enemy. The victory and the wealth it subsequently brought had made the Count de Foix a more powerful lord than he had been before the battle, but at least he was no longer a threat to Aquitaine and the Prince. Blackstone ignored the Prince's gaze and stepped to the fire. If the sight of the flames had helped the Prince order his thoughts then they might help him see the truth behind the Prince's decision.

He looked into the smoke as a soothsayer might do, to divine the truth. It curled into misshapen faces as contorted as the politics of Aquitaine and France. Now there was a greater game to be played out.

'There is no reason for you to jeopardize the truce with France,' Blackstone said. 'You need to secure Navarre's seaward ports and have him as an ally because there is a civil war going on in Spain between Castile and Aragon. The treaty England signed years ago with Castile means that if they are invaded you must go to their aide, and if the Kingdom of Navarre is not an ally, then as an enemy he can strike you from the rear. You secure territory for the future because the way into Castile is across the Pyrenean passes and they lie in his territory.' He looked at Killbere and saw that the veteran knight also understood.

'So, your highness, you want us to draw the French away from his flank,' said Killbere. 'To make sure he can march without hindrance. We're to be a distraction. Bait.'

'And that does not implicate the Crown and will not affect the truce between you and the King of France,' said

Blackstone. He faltered. Thought again and faced the Prince. 'But there's more.'

The Prince nodded. 'Agreements are being made and others put aside. Sooner or later you will be asked to fight the French again. Our father must secure Brittany. Charles of Blois threatens us with his claim to rule. Men are already being prepared in the north.'

'By Sir John Chandos?' said Killbere. 'Sir John directs routiers to your cause, thereby denying them to the French?'

'Yes. Using you to shield de Grailly's flanks is a means of sending you closer to our father's choice, John de Montfort, and his bid for victory, without alerting the French to our father's intentions.'

'Chandos subdues the routiers so that the French cannot recruit them against Navarre,' said Blackstone. 'And by doing that he secures the northern border so that when de Montfort goes into battle against Charles of Blois then it's the English against the French.'

'Brittany must be under English rule. A proxy war for the balance of power, Thomas. How else is England to secure territory in France now that we are at peace?' said the Prince.

'Does Navarre know of your plans?'

'He is assured that you will ride at his flank. That is all. The less our Spanish King knows about our intentions the better chance of our success.'

'But we won't fight if Navarre gets there first and wins,' Blackstone said. 'Why does he strike now? King John was dishonoured when his second son broke parole but the King returned into custody in England months ago to reclaim his honour. He still rules France. Even if Navarre defeats the army and rides into Paris, he cannot defeat King John. Highness, this makes no sense.'

The Prince stood and gave an almost imperceptible gesture. A servant came forward and poured wine.

'Thomas, Navarre strikes against the Dauphin before his coronation. The King of France is dead.'

CHAPTER THREE

As Blackstone and Killbere strode through the corridors, armed and intimidating, looking as though they had fought the devil and won, lesser mortals stepped aside. Killbere's scowl aided their decision. The castle's inner ward was busy with men and horses who awaited their orders.

'Jean le Bon dead. The old bastard,' said Killbere. 'Who'd have thought after you tried to kill him at Poitiers that years later he would rot on silken sheets, chewed away by disease in a foreign land. Sweet justice, Thomas. It would be a damned miracle if the Dauphin can be stopped before he's crowned. We should fight with de Grailly and bring his wretched son down as well.'

'Whatever we think of the Dauphin, he's a clever man, more so than his father. He might not be a warrior prince but he held us out of Paris the last time we fought. Navarre doesn't have the skill but Jean de Grailly has. He might yet deliver the crown to an ally of our King.'

'The French won't stop until you're dead and they seize France back from England. You don't believe the scheming rat the Dauphin would stop his vendetta against you?'

'No. But we aren't about to face him on the field of battle. We are not involved in Navarre's conflict.'

'Then why don't we help him and bring the House of Valois to its knees? Even if it means siding with Navarre? At least we would have Jean de Grailly and Beyard at our side.'

'And defy the Prince?'

'You haven't done that before? What's the worst that can happen? He'll banish us again. I keep telling you: we can make more money and live a better life in Italy. Father Torellini banks our money with the Bardi. We have enough to live on. We have fought for so many years we should end it with defeating the French. I would die a happy man.'

'When we fought at Launac I thought you might die a happy man then.'

'I grant you, Thomas, my vitals were stirred at the drumbeat and trumpet and the banners and pennons flashing their colours across the ranks. It was a fight worth having but it did not take us any closer to defeating the French Crown.'

'We do what the Prince asks and give de Grailly and Beyard a chance to go north.'

'Surely you can't believe they can win?'

'The Prince says that Chandos has controlled the routiers, which means the French can't recruit them.' Blackstone stopped before they reached the men. 'What doubts we have we keep to ourselves, Gilbert.'

Killbere spat and wiped a hand across his beard. 'I don't want to see Beyard or any of our Gascons throwing their lives away for a turd like Navarre. They need us at their side.'

'Beyard is de Grailly's captain. He has to go. He has no choice and neither do we.'

Killbere grunted. He knew full well there was nothing either of them could do, but it was worth trying.

'William!' Blackstone called.

William Ashford stood with his men in the yard. Striding briskly across to Blackstone and Killbere, he dipped his head respectfully. 'Sir Thomas, it's a pleasure to see you again. You've recovered, I see.'

Blackstone extended his hand to the man who had served the King, the Prince and then Blackstone. 'Too long lying on my back nursed like a mewling child by the Prince's physicians. After three months we wintered in a monastery until now when we are summoned by the Prince.'

'And we are but one faltering step away from becoming celibate, tonsured recluses ourselves,' said Killbere in greeting. 'A brothel and a raucous tavern are what a man needs after hibernation.'

'Not here, Sir Gilbert,' said Ashford. 'The Prince is a pious man. When he visits a town the brothels close and the taverns water down their wine. No mayor or council wants trouble with drunken soldiers when he's around.'

'And you've fared well?' said Blackstone.

'The Prince did me the honour of allowing me to serve as his bodyguard.'

'Then I hope it will not disappoint you that I requested you and your men join me, and he has agreed.'

'I know, Sir Thomas. The Prince said you would ask for me.'

Killbere grunted. 'Damn, he played us like simpletons. He wanted us to be grateful and in his debt for the favour. Thomas, don't ever play cards with Edward of Woodstock. He will have every silver and gold coin we have saved.'

'That's why he's a prince of the realm,' said Blackstone. 'And we fight and die.'

Killbere grinned. 'Treaties aren't worth the parchment they're written on. Another war for the balance of power. We should thank God that we live a more honourable life than those duplicitous vermin scurrying along the corridors of power.' He shrugged with a sheepish grin. 'Not counting our blessed King and Prince of course.'

'But we won't fight if Navarre gets there first and wins,' Blackstone said.

'And I saw a unicorn in the forest on our way here and a fairy farting so loud it scared the crows,' Killbere said.

'Stranger things have happened,' said Blackstone.

'You're right; I almost married that nun. Did I ever tell you about that?'

'Not more than a thousand times over the years.' Blackstone turned away.

'Where are you going?' said Killbere.

'To speak to Beyard and give my blessings to him and his men.'

'Ah, then I'll tell William about her. He hasn't heard the story.'

CHAPTER FOUR

Blackstone and his men rode for three days within sight of the column snaking across the undulating landscape. Initially they saw distant pennons as a French scouting party shadowed them. Blackstone rode close to the border of Aquitaine and Languedoc, a feint to draw French attention and create uncertainty. When the French saw his column of men with his banner unfurled, they gathered in greater numbers in case the Englishman dared strike into French territory. It gave scant satisfaction to any of the fighting men that they had sown doubt and fear into their old enemy. Their task was to draw men and interest from the French southern army. Their presence taunted the French commanders but neither Englishman, Navarrese nor Frenchman violated the border and the truce.

Beyard and his Gascons were obliged to join their sworn lord but the bond between them and Blackstone's fighters was as raucous and strong as ever. Insults were traded when Beyard and his men rode out to join the gathering army and every man kept any thought that they were most likely riding to their death locked inside. The King of Navarre's ambitions had caused the demise of many a good fighter.

'It would serve the world better if the aristocrats went under the sword instead of good fighting men,' said Will Longdon.

'You think the Jacquerie had the right idea?' said Meulon, the throat-cutter.

'A peasant uprising needs to be planned. Once they slaughter a nobleman's children and roast them on a spit, they lose control,' Will Longdon said.

Meulon snorted and spat. 'You're a peasant. Perhaps you should lead the next revolt?'

'I'd make a better job of it.'

'The noblemen hold the reins, you rump of a pig's arse. They need fighting men and we get paid for doing their dirty work. Kill the aristocrats and we have no work.'

The veteran archer turned in the saddle to where Meulon rode at the head of his men. 'Your brains were left in the dirt when your mother dropped you out of her belly in that turnip field. If there were no noblemen, we would have their money. We would have a life of luxury.'

'Until another greedy bastard came and snatched it from you,' said Longdon's Welsh ventenar, Meuric Kynith. 'You'll not win a country by killing the rich and powerful, you must take it by stealth. Like I seized these boots off a nobleman when he was washing his arse in a river.'

'I don't want a bloody country, you pagan bastard, only a nobleman's money. And if I had a nobleman's money I would have a pair of fine boots like these for myself.'

'But when you have such wealth then you would have to pay the likes of us to protect you,' Kynith said.

'Which is all you're fit for because you haven't the brains to do anything else.'

'That would make you the same as the noblemen we have now,' said Meulon. 'And we would need another revolt to rid ourselves of you.'

Killbere shouted, 'I will send you all to the nearest leper house if your bickering does not cease. I prefer birdsong and horse farts for conversation.'

Killbere's chastisement quietened the instigators. The low murmur from Will Longdon's lips was barely audible. 'I would have knights stand their watch on the wall until their balls hardened like frozen walnuts.'

It was loud enough for Blackstone's keen hearing. 'Then you would live with eunuchs and be the only man left to fight. The battle is lost before it starts, Will. Accept what we are. Fine doublets and silk sheets do not become an archer. Better if such a man takes his pleasure in killing knights.' He turned to Killbere. 'Preferably theirs.'

The slow-moving army eventually passed east of Poitiers and drew up close to the Breton border.

'My Lord de Grailly. I can go no further. I follow my Prince's orders.'

Jean de Grailly watched his men ride past him. 'I begged that you fight with us, Thomas, but the treaty forbids it.'

'I would furl my colours and disguise my blazon and join you but the Dauphin would soon know we stood together and then my fate and that of my men would mean banishment again. I have other orders. My lord, I beg a favour.'

'If it's in my power, Sir Thomas.'

'Whichever way the battle turns, send Beyard to me with news. I ride north to join Sir John Chandos. I will travel slowly. I'll wait three days in the forest at Alençon and then ride on. Beyard knows our strongholds and where we take shelter. If it goes badly for you, send word. We will turn and cover your retreat.'

'And face the Prince's wrath,' said de Grailly.

'Bands of routiers remain on the Breton march. I will smother my blazon with mud and no Frenchman will know the difference. It's all I can offer if the tide turns.'

'I accept. But we won't need you. More men join us at Évreux and then once we cross the bridge over the Seine at Vernon we strike the Dauphin's underbelly. Paris and France will be ours.' His grin reflected his confidence. 'It will be a fight you will regret not being part of. The Prince should have thrown in with Navarre. When he's crowned he will be generous to those who gave their support.'

'My Prince gave you free passage. Seven thousand Frenchmen waited for you to break out through Languedoc. You would not have made a dozen leagues, my lord, and I suspect you know that.'

The sombre look on de Grailly's face was enough acknowledgement of the truth. 'I will see you in Paris, Thomas.' He wheeled the horse and spurred it into a canter. Beyard remained a moment longer, nodded his farewell and understanding to Blackstone.

'Beyard,' said Blackstone, arresting the Gascon's departure. 'Do not die for a worthless cause. Remember what I said.'

'I will, Sir Thomas, and am glad of it. But I fight at his side as I fought at yours. The rest is out of my hands. It is what it is.' He yanked the reins and followed his sworn lord.

'Goddammit, Thomas, I hate to see as courageous a fighter as Beyard ride into another man's self-made hell,' said Killbere. 'I'm pleased you said what you did but Chandos will be grinding what's left of his teeth when we arrive late.'

'Arriving in good time only serves a purpose when a battle is to be fought, arriving late for another month sitting in a cold castle listening to old knights bleating about past glory is a fate worse than death. I wish we were with Beyard and de Grailly. We'll stay at Alençon as long as we can.'

CHAPTER FIVE

Sir John Chandos had stopped routiers raiding across the north by directing them to Navarre's cause and denying them to the French. It was a tribute to de Grailly's reputation that various bands of English, Gascons, Spanish and Germans gathered at Évreux under his command. Two thousand horsemen followed the Captal de Buch east towards Vernon and the bridge across the Seine. It was then that a messenger arrived and told him that Navarre's sister had surrendered the town and the bridge to the French forces and that they had been encamped and ready to fight for days. Before they could reach the River Seine, a smaller river, the Eure at the hamlet of Cocherel, had to be crossed. The French guarded that crossing, determined to halt all attempts at reaching the main bridge at Vernon. It was smaller and easier to defend. The news took a darker turn when de Grailly learnt there were Gascons under contract to the Dauphin on the side of the French.

Beyard saw de Grailly's dismay at fighting his own countrymen. 'My lord, there are men we know ready to face us,' said Beyard. 'We will not be able to distinguish friend from foe. Let's turn back. We must find another way across the Seine. Blackstone will help us.'

De Grailly shook his head. 'I will lose these men who have joined us for booty and plunder. We must take the bridge. It's the only way.'

Later that day, when they crested a hill at Cocherel, they saw the French army already in position.

'They are inferior in number,' said the Captal, his spirits boosted by the knowledge that he had the upper hand. 'They stand in our way of reaching Vernon and we have the advantage.'

Beyard saw the truth of it. The French were dismounted, standing in ranks. They could not attack uphill against mounted troops. Beyard took stock of the massed troops. 'They are only a hundred or so fewer than us, but they have men in reserve at the rear. They're Bretons. They are the danger if they scatter us in the fight.'

'Their men have been here for days. Their supplies are low. They are weak. Now that they see we have the advantage they'll break. Take your men onto their flank,' said de Grailly.

Beyard had learnt lessons of war from Blackstone but to argue with his lord, a man who had fought in crusades and at the great battle of Poitiers, was not something he could do without risk of censure. 'My lord, if I take men and split our force it is we who are weakened. They can turn and hold the ground. Our horses' blood will be up and we might not rein them back in time. The river is beyond their ranks. If we break through and turn, we have the river at our backs. We have no ground to defend.'

The Captal de Buch showed no sign of displeasure at his orders being questioned. Beyard was the best of men and had served him loyally over the years. That Blackstone had given him command was an honour afforded few men. 'Beyard, time is against us. Flank them and stop them using the bridge. They have nowhere to turn. Once we breach their defences, the road to Paris is open. If the Dauphin's army is here, it is not at the bridge at Vernon. Win here and we win Paris. Seize the city and the Dauphin will not be anointed king. It is a risk worth taking. Take heart; let us win the day and then France.'

Beyard's instincts warned him of the danger but the prize was too great. He wheeled his horse and called out to Bascon Gâsconay, one of the men who had served alongside him with Blackstone.

'Stay close to me. If I am killed ride and tell Sir Thomas. He waits at the forest at Alençon.'

Below them, their enemy raised their pennons. A cacophony of trumpets from the French tore the air. Emboldened, they bellowed their resolve, battening down their fear. Beyard spurred his horse, his men galloping stirrup to stirrup. A broadhead thrust into an enemy already milling in disorder. He saw de Grailly lead the main charge. The ground shook. Horses whinnied. The armies clashed. Men screamed frenzied curses. Others pain. Sounds of battle soared. Beyard's horse trampled men beneath its iron-shod hooves. He slashed down and back, cutting a swathe through men who jabbed with lance and spear, while his cavalry crushed men as if they were riding through a field of wheat. Horses came down as Frenchmen lunged spears into their chests. Some carried their riders forward another thirty yards or more and then fell, writhing in agony as the rider fought to free himself before men, hacking savagely, fell on him.

Beyard saw de Grailly in the midst of the battle, wielding his axe, his blood-splattered shield testament to the ferocity of the fight. Beyard heeled his mount, knocking more men to the ground. He felt the first shudder through the great beast's muscles as four opponents struck out bravely at the war horse. Two rammed spears into its chest, another slashed at its legs. The beast's head reared, eyes wide, teeth bared in agony. Beyard was ready for the fourth man who swung a mace at him as he leapt free from the dying horse. Its wildly thrashing death throes kept its tormentors at bay as Beyard, grunting with effort and shaking sweat from his eyes, slammed his shield against his attacker, forcing strength into his legs to push the bigger man off balance; as the man twisted away Beyard slashed down and severed his arm at the shoulder.

He stepped clear and began to attack other men standing in defensive knots. They broke when his Gascons joined him, felling men at the edges, leaving the rest vulnerable. The Gascons pressed on. Their opponents fell back. Some begged for mercy. It was denied. Blood-lust smothered men's thoughts as thickly as bloodstains smeared mail and shield.

Yet the French ranks held. They pushed back as the Bretons held in reserve added their weight. Beyard slithered through men's gore. Dead horses blocked the passage of battle. Beyard turned to the men at his side, shouting above the din, when a crossbow bolt pierced one man's neck. Beyard swung instinctively. The bowman was less than ten strides away. Beyond him was the bridge. They were almost there. A blow from a mace felled him to his knees. Shield raised, he swept his sword back in a scything arc and felt the blade bite into a man's legs. He tried to stand but his head swirled, his eyes blurred and he sank down and fell onto his back. He heard rolling thunder across the clear sky and then realized it was the dull thud of hoofbeats across the wooden bridge. The French had more reserves hidden in the trees across the river. The strength fled from his arms as he yielded to his descent into darkness. They had lost.

CHAPTER SIX

Blackstone walked among the dead.

Horses stood in the midst of the carnage, blood-smeared, reins loose, some grazing. Blackstone's men despatched those limping from broken legs or seriously wounded. Strutting crows pecked at the fallen troops as the men scoured the field for their Gascon comrades. When they found one, they called out his name, their sadness all that broke the silence. It took hours for them to search the hundreds slain. They recovered nine bodies of the twelve men who had served under Beyard. There was no sign of the Captal de Buch or his captain. They gathered the shields bearing de Grailly's blazon of five scallops set against a black cross.

Blackstone bent and eased a body aside, his blazon showing him to be from Burgundy, a French ally. The youth was too young to have more than a few whiskers on his face. He looked no older than Blackstone's son, Henry. The young knight had clearly sought glory and the enemy dead around his corpse was evidence he had fought hard. There was no sign of a wound. His dead horse lay on its side but it wasn't the fall that had killed him. Blackstone tugged the lad free from those around him and saw the tell-tale rivulet of dried blood from a slash in his groin. A sword tip or knife had pierced his mail and cut into the artery that, once severed, meant his life had drained from him: a merciful wound that saved him from the agony of severed limbs or crushed skull. He would have fought on for a few minutes more, feeling the weakness seeping into his body, robbing him of strength. He might even have been unaware that the injury was taking his life.

Blackstone laid a calloused palm on the youth's cold skin. A proud father would put aside his loss and boast of his son's prowess fighting for the new King while a mother grieved, consumed with pain.

'He's not here,' said John Jacob. 'We've turned all the dead and pulled aside the bodies that lie across each other. There must be close to a thousand out here. Beyard and his men would have fought close together. We found half of them lying near each other. Friends in life and death.'

Blackstone stepped over the dead knight. 'Have the men search along the riverbank.'

'Renfred and William Ashford's men have already searched the riverside, Sir Thomas,' said his squire.

The aftermath of a battle lays a sense of loss over men, no matter what victories they have celebrated in the past. Death on such a huge scale, where hundreds of men lay rotting, was sobering even to the veterans.

'We'll take those we find from the battlefield for burial; there's a monastery some miles back,' said Blackstone.

John Jacob acknowledged the order and turned back to the task.

'It was ferocious, Thomas,' said Killbere, tossing aside a bloodstained falchion. 'God himself wept tears of blood here. There's a host of brave men dead on this field. And many a young knight impaled, and others hacked apart and left to die in agony. I'm surprised we didn't hear the clash of the attack where we camped.'

'Any closer than a day's ride and we would not have been able to resist helping them.'

'Aye, more the pity we weren't here. The wolves and wild boar will soon come to feast.'

'If Beyard isn't here then he's captured,' said Blackstone, looking across the field strewn with contorted corpses. They were an hour's ride from the bridge at Vernon. De Grailly had been half a day's ride to Paris. So close.

'Sir Thomas!' Meulon called. He had continued searching and now pointed into the distance, across the wooden bridge. Horsemen appeared from the trees. They showed no sign of advancing but simply watched Blackstone's men. There was little doubt there were others waiting out of sight.

'Gilbert, ready the men,' said Blackstone as he mounted the bastard horse.

'Where in God's name are you going?'

'To find out where de Grailly and Beyard are being held.'

John Jacob rode to his side.

'I doubt they're in the mood to talk, Thomas,' said Killbere.

'Then be ready for an argument,' Blackstone said and set off with his squire.

Two days ago the bent and bloodied Bascon Gâsconay had ridden into the forest at Alençon. His wounds were to prove fatal, but he managed to deliver his message about the battle. It had been obvious when Beyard fell and the French reserves committed that the fight was lost. He lingered for that night and died in the cold hours before dawn. They buried him in a clearing, piling stones on the earth to stop wolves and boar digging up his corpse. By the time Blackstone arrived at the field of slaughter the sun had arced across the afternoon sky. There were enough hours of daylight remaining in the late spring evening for the men to gather their dead friends and enough time for more violence to be committed. The horsemen waiting across the bridge were likely to be the rearguard but if the main force was still close, then they could soon turn back.

Blackstone drew up the bastard horse. He felt its tension beneath the saddle as its withers bristled. It was as ready to fight as its master. 'I am Sir Thomas Blackstone. I am not a part of Lord de Grailly's army. I am here searching for the bodies of my friends.'

One rider urged his horse forward from the others, stopping ten paces from Blackstone. He bore the signs of the hard-fought battle. A dirty rag encrusted with gore bound his thigh. Grime and flecks of blood stained his beard. The man's eyes were weary but Blackstone saw he had the resolve to fight again if need be. 'I know your name. I fought the English with the old King at Poitiers.'

Blackstone remained silent. The veteran would have crossbowmen in the trees.

The man looked past Blackstone and John Jacob to where Blackstone's men formed up ready to fight five hundred yards away.

'We have no argument with you. We've been watching you. There are hundreds of bodies to search. We won't stop you.'

'We're not searching for men from Navarre but the Gascon Lord de Grailly and his captain. You know their blazon?'

The Frenchman grunted. 'I know it. We took many as prisoners for ransom.'

Blackstone studied the man and his dozen companions. He eased the bastard horse a few paces to the side so he could study them. They were common men, not knights or lords. 'We'll pay,' he said.

The man grinned. 'How much?'

'A lot. More than you would see in a lifetime.'

'Even for scum?'

Blackstone leaned forward; his horse shifted its weight. Blackstone glared at the Frenchman, who realized his insult had provoked the scar-faced knight. He saw that Blackstone had shifted his position so that the crossbowmen in the trees no longer had a clear view. He would be the first man to die if the Englishman chose violence.

He recanted, his voice inflected with a note of respect. 'The Captal de Buch is ransomed to the Dauphin, my lord. They have taken him to Meaux.'

There was no hope of venturing so far into French territory and attempting a rescue of the Prince's ally, even if Blackstone had wanted to. De Grailly was imprisoned in the walled city east of Paris where Blackstone's wife and daughter had been murdered years before. A place that haunted him.

'And the other man who served Lord de Grailly?' said John Jacob. 'His name is Beyard.'

The man shrugged. 'I don't know the names of those taken. Breton and Norman lords ransomed those of rank. If he's alive then who knows where he is? We fight and they reap the rewards. All that's left for us is the plunder taken from the fallen.'

Blackstone knew he told the truth. He tugged the reins. 'We take our dead and leave,' he said.

For a moment it seemed the man might attempt to stop him. His hand rested on his sword hilt. The Englishman had money for ransom. His eyes darted from Blackstone to the men in the field beyond. How many men could he stop from crossing the bridge if he attacked and brought the English knight and his squire down? Could he act quickly enough? His hand returned to the reins.

'A wise decision,' said Blackstone.

The man swallowed hard. The Englishman had the eyes of a falcon and the instinct of a wolf.

CHAPTER SEVEN

Blackstone and his men rode west to join forces with Sir John Chandos after they buried their Gascon comrades. The campaign to aid the young John de Montfort claim the Duchy of Brittany from the French King's choice, Charles de Blois, would soon begin, especially now that the threat to the French Crown had been stopped. Smoke billowed above a distant forest.

'The French have the bit between their teeth, Thomas,' said Killbere. 'They'll take back every town and village that Navarre's supporters hold.'

Blackstone studied the ground that lay between them and the forest. Were there men in sufficient numbers concealed in the trees to attack his hundred? 'Take them or destroy them. A storm rages around us, Gilbert, and we may have to fight our way through to Chandos. That forest is dense enough to conceal more men than we have. If the French are laying a scourge on Normandy, then Chandos might be under siege.'

'And there's proof enough lying on the field at Cocherel that he wasn't successful stopping routiers joining forces with the French.'

By the time they had skirted the forest and approached the smouldering town that lay beyond, its palisade walls and timber-framed houses had burnt down to blackened ribs with collapsed roofs. Man, woman and child lay dead along with domestic animals. A dozen heads were impaled on poles.

'What place is this?' said John Jacob.

'Those who know are dead,' said Meulon.

The breeze carried acrid smoke and the stench of burnt flesh.

Blackstone's battle-hardened veterans needed no command to fan out defensively. Death could be a whisper away if rogue mercenary bowmen were hiding within range and a sudden cavalry charge could inflict heavy casualties.

'Survivors!' Will Longdon called as a dozen men and women with children clambered out of a ditch a hundred paces away. They looked as though they had crawled out of a house fire. Their clothes were torn, their faces smeared in soot; blood encrusted their wounds. They held back, fear seizing them, rooting them to the spot. Perhaps they were uncertain whether the horsemen were more routiers or their lord's men finally come to protect them.

'Come forward,' Meulon called. 'You'll not be harmed.'

Blackstone knew how terrifying his men looked to the villeins. He dismounted, handed the reins to John Jacob and walked towards the huddled group. He halted halfway. 'Send one man forward. I serve King Edward and the Prince of Wales and Aquitaine. We are not routiers. We will help you.'

There was a muted conversation and then one man, carrying a child, stepped away from the group. A woman reached for his arm, begging him not to go, but he calmed her and handed her the child. He walked forward, but then faltered, eyes looking left and right at the horseman. Plucking up courage, he got within ten paces and went down on his knees and clasped his hands together.

'I beg you, lord, do not harm us. Much violence has been done to us. We are poor people who offered no resistance but they came from the east and slew everyone except those you see.'

'Get to your feet,' said Blackstone. 'Did they name themselves?'

The man clambered upright. He remained hunched, eyes lowered. He shook his head in answer.

'These men,' said Blackstone, pointing to the heads on poles. 'Who are they?'

'Normans, my lord, men who hold ground for Navarre. They protected us until the routiers came.'

'What lord's manor is this?' said Blackstone.

'He holds it in the name of the King of Navarre.'

'Who?' Blackstone snapped, impatient at the man's slow response.

'Lord de Graumont.'

The name meant nothing to Blackstone. 'Where is he?'

The man looked perplexed and half turned to point at the decapitated heads.

Blackstone knew de Grailly's defeat would have unleashed Breton warlords across Normandy. 'You heard a name?'

The villager thought hard. He shook his head. Then raised it, eyes bright with memory. 'Ronec.'

'A Breton?' said Blackstone. 'Or French?'

The man nodded, his broken-toothed smile showing black stumps, the question unfathomable to him. 'Some spoke a language we did not know.'

'Navarrese? Spanish?'

The man's blank expression was the only answer.

'All right,' said Blackstone. He took in the devastation. 'There is nothing for you here. We'll escort you to the next town or village. Take what you can from the ruins.'

'Lord,' said the man. 'We are in your debt.'

'There is no debt. Decide where it is we must take you.'

The villein's eyes widened, confusion creasing his brow. 'We ... we have no knowledge beyond our commune. Once a year the *bailli* comes and assesses our crops.'

'What did he say?' said Killbere as he joined Blackstone.

'He doesn't know anything. The reeve comes every year for his lord's due. Graumont? Does the name mean anything?'

Killbere shook his head. 'More local lords in France than rats in a sewer.'

'This one sits on top of that pole,' said Blackstone.

The villein's face creased in fear as he listened to the exchange between Blackstone and Killbere. He nodded vigorously. 'My lord. You speak the same language as those who attacked us.'

'Englishmen?' said Killbere. 'Is that what he means?'

Blackstone nodded. 'We've English and Breton skinners ahead of us.' He raised a hand to calm the frightened villager. 'We are not the same people as those who attacked you. Bring your people forward; we'll escort you to the next village. Understand? If we had wished you harm you would already be dead.'

The peasant bobbed, bent like a beaten dog, dignity long since annihilated by a harsh life. He scurried back to the fearful survivors huddled at the edge of the ditch.

'What do we do with them?' said Killbere.

'Escort them to safety.'

Killbere grunted and spat. 'Wherever that might be.'

The men made two litters, poles braced either side of one of the spare horses, and then cross-braced with saplings. They carried two of the injured women and children on the litters as the other survivors trudged alongside the horsemen, bearing what few possessions they could salvage. By the time daylight faded they had picked up four more survivors who had run for their lives when the routiers had swept through their village. Blackstone gleaned fragments of information.

The routiers were Bretons and Englishmen paid by the French. Men who had likely fought at Cocherel.

'The King decreed no Englishman was to ride against the French,' said John Jacob as the men watched the survivors set up camp. Grateful for their lives and Blackstone's protection, they lit fires, prepared food and attended to the men's needs by carrying water and gathering wood.

'They're not fighting the French; they're killing Navarre's men. Norman lords who hold his towns. All of this serves the Breton cause. If Paris commands them to destroy Navarre's towns and lay waste to the domains he holds in Normandy, then they destroy any chance of us using them when we fight the Bretons.'

'Charles of Blois won't be a part of this. It's a separate fight,' said John Jacob. 'Sir John has let them slip through.'

'No, Chandos couldn't stop those routiers already under contract,' Killbere said. 'The new French King will pull together any of these men. It serves him and Blois when the time comes. Thomas, if we find more survivors along the way then we're bringing another problem to his door.'

'Then we must rid ourselves of them before we reach him. We need to find out more about these routiers, especially any Englishmen. Send Renfred and Meulon to me,' he told his squire.

Killbere fussed at the fire. 'It will take us... what, nine or ten days to reach Chandos? Perhaps more with these stragglers. We need to make better time.'

'I know. We'll find another village that doesn't belong to one of Navarre's lords. They'll need their strength so we will let them rest and eat what food we can spare.'

'You know what these villeins are like. They don't welcome outsiders from other villages.'

'I'll bribe them. Money buys lives.'

'A blade to the throat might be more effective.'

'That's the down payment.'

Renfred and Meulon accompanied John Jacob to Blackstone. They squatted next to the fire as Blackstone scratched out a route on the ground for them and made a model of the territory where he had spent his earlier years raiding against enemies and protecting villages. 'Ride south-west. We are here on the edge of Alençon, half a day's ride should bring us on the Roman road to Villaines.' He indicated the rough terrain he had laid out: 'In this forest is the village of Saint-Pierre. Scout the road. See that it is safe. We'll leave the survivors there.'

'We should cut out their tongues,' said Meulon. 'They'll talk. Just because we've helped them doesn't mean they won't tell the French or Bretons where we are or where we're going.'

'And I'm telling them that we are going north not south.'

'And how do we go on from there, Sir Thomas?' said Renfred.

'We skirt Villaines. The town's loyal to the French King. We must get to Sir John.'

Meulon and Renfred nodded their understanding. 'Where do we meet you?'

'Edge of the forest, here.' He pointed with the stick to the rough model. 'Look for a ruined chapel. We'll feed these people and let them rest and then travel by night along the road. It's quicker and there's less chance of an attack. Routiers won't risk an assault against a column of men whose strength they can't determine.'

Renfred tapped Meulon's shoulder. 'There's another hour before it's dark. We'll leave now to give us more time.' The two captains got to their feet.

'Meulon,' said Killbere. 'Don't kill anyone you don't have to.'

The throat-cutter's teeth bared behind his thick beard. To a stranger it was a snarl. To those who knew him it was his attempt at a smile.

Killbere winced as the captains walked back into the forest to gather their men. 'Meulon can turn a man's bowels to water.' He drank from a wineskin. 'And that's before he draws his knife.'

CHAPTER EIGHT

Screams of terror haunted the darkness as flames from the burning village lit the night sky. Meulon and Renfred had travelled across well-worn roads until reaching the cave-black forest, where the pitiful cries of innocents being slaughtered guided them through the trees. They halted at the edge of a clearing, watching shadows flit this way and that three hundred yards away as routiers murdered and raped their way through the undefended town.

Indistinct voices pierced the mayhem. Dogs yelped in pain and then fell silent. A woman broke free from four men who had entered her house and dragged her out. The men did not stop her. They laughed; two of them unsheathed their knives and used her for target practice. Both knives found the woman's back. Then they hauled a child from its hiding place in the bushes nearby as it screamed for its dead mother. A blade glinted blood red in the fire glow. The child dropped with a slashed throat. One man kicked the body and the others turned away to inflict more carnage.

Meulon's grunt was a savage expression of disgust. His hand reached for his knife. 'Renfred, find your way back. Bring Sir Thomas. These bastards will destroy everything before we make another ten miles down the road.'

The German captain placed a restraining hand on his friend's arm, knowing Meulon's intentions. 'You cannot go in there alone.'

They got to their feet. The giant hobbled his horse. 'We have never slain children, Renfred. These men will kill every living creature. We need a prisoner to tell us who these bastards are. Fetch Sir Thomas. Do as I ask.' Without another word, he ran, his great frame hunched as he used the forest edge for cover.

Renfred hesitated. The urge to accompany his friend tore at him. It would take hours to bring Blackstone but they needed men at their back if they were to pursue these killers. His hand smothered his horse's muzzle. The sturdy beast shifted, ready for him to clasp the reins and put his weight into the saddle, man and horse accustomed to each other, ready to ride hard.

Meulon moved quietly for a man his size. He pressed his back against a cob building as desperate sounds came from within. A woman cried out; a man cursed. He heard flesh being struck and the woman's protestations silenced to a whimpering. Meulon stepped into the hovel. A flickering lamp burned, showing one man straddling a woman as another, addled with drink, gloated. The drunk blinked, wineskin half raised as darkness blocked the open doorway. In two great strides Meulon was on him, a knife thrust upwards beneath his throat. The man gurgled and fell but the swift action barely drew the rapist's attention. Meulon clawed his head back and drew the blade across his throat, throwing the writhing man's weight aside so that the pouring blood did not smother the woman. She gazed open-mouthed at the black-bearded monster looming over her. He bent and snatched her up. She was too terrified to scream.

'Stay silent and you will be safe,' he urged her. 'Go from here. Run for the forest. Stay there. Others are coming to help. You understand?'

Fear clouded her reason. She shook her head. The impossible had happened. Meulon pulled her to the door, held her back, checked that the killers were not close. 'The trees,' he said. 'You run, you hide, and you stay there. I have friends coming to help you. Englishmen.'

She trembled. 'English? Like these men?'

Meulon glared at her. 'These men are Bretons.'

She shook her head. 'English,' she said.

'I give you your life, woman. You must run when I tell you. Do not look back. Stay in the forest. I will send others if I can save them. The Englishmen who come are not your enemy. Understand?'

She appeared to come to her senses and snatched at his hand, kissing it in thanks, tears spilling down her cheeks. He glanced once more into the chaos outside and thrust her towards the black wall that was the forest. The moment she'd made her escape he ran for three routiers on the other side of a huddle of flaming houses who were tearing apart the insides. A man and woman lay dead at their feet. Meulon heard them cursing. They were English, without doubt. Blackstone had taught him to speak the language years before but it was Will Longdon who had taught him to curse like an Englishman. It made no difference that these mercenaries were killing Navarre's people, or that Sir John Chandos was supposed to have stopped them from joining the Bretons or the French. It made no difference because they were going to die.

The three killers sensed rather than saw the man surging towards them as they raised their eyes, squinting through firelight. Meulon barged the first man, arcing his knife hand so that the blade cut through the neck of the second man, who fell writhing into flames as the first rolled in agony from a displaced shoulder and broken ribs. Their companion lunged with his sword at the wild giant but where the man had stood a heartbeat before was now space. He saw the blur of an arm and then felt the burning tear across his throat. As he sank to his knees, clutching his pulsating blood, his killer despatched the first routier and was out of sight. There had been no cry of alarm from any of Meulon's victims. None of the mercenaries knew that the flitting shadow that ran among them was a killer exacting his own justice. When his victims saw his blood-flecked bearded face looming from the shimmering darkness, it was too late. That heart-lurching moment was their last.

A dozen men lay dead. Meulon urged surviving villagers to run for the forest as he killed. He had not yet drawn his sword but the tide was turning against him. Men across the village finally realized he was attacking their own. They turned, yelling commands, and ran towards him, blocking his escape.

Meulon backed against a cob-and wattle-hovel. Fire consumed the thatch and walls as he made his stand. He unsheathed his sword and held the killing knife in his other hand. The men were wary, unsure whether to rush him, and Meulon took the initiative with two great strides forward, inflicting vicious wounds on the first man. He used the burning hovel to protect his back as they lunged. He knew they would soon overwhelm him but they faltered as the roof collapsed in a torrent of sparks.

Men behind his attackers began to scream, the sudden commotion causing confusion among those pressing Meulon. He took advantage of it and cut low, taking men's legs from under them, and then saw why the routiers were panicking. Barely a dozen strides away, a shield bearing a familiar blazon forced routiers aside as savage blade strokes maimed and killed. Renfred's attack splintered the group; only three of the ten men survived. They turned and ran.

Meulon's great fist knocked the nearest to the ground. Blackstone needed at least one man alive. One was enough.

Several villagers rushed from their hiding places; clubs and scythes brought down the remaining two. They hacked the killers to death, the routiers' screams satisfying a lust for revenge.

Meulon and Renfred watched.

'It's done, my friend,' said Meulon. 'Death came close for me. I'm grateful you stayed.'

Renfred gripped Meulon's shoulder. 'You gave me no choice. I had a dozen and more survivors running into the trees and routiers were chasing them. I had to stop them. By the time I'd done that it was too late to do anything else but join you.'

Birdsong lilted over the sound of spluttering timbers of the burning hovels. First light cast its dull glow across the tortured village. Bodies lay scattered, little more than crumpled mounds of bloodied rags. Women and children filtered back from the forest, searching for their dead.

Meulon grunted and lifted a bloodied hand.

The light spreading across the sky exposed the blood-soaked gambeson beneath his mail. 'You're wounded,' said Renfred.

Meulon sighed. 'Aye, a knife thrust.' He spat the sour taste from his throat. 'Perhaps death is closer than I thought.'

CHAPTER NINE

The scrawny villager sent by Renfred reached the ruined chapel and told Blackstone that his men and twenty-three survivors from Saint-Pierre waited for him at the burnt-out village. The faint sound of a church bell clanged out the hour for prime, its dull resonance carried on the breeze from miles away. It told Blackstone that they were still in enemy territory. Only the French-held town of Villaines had a church.

Will Longdon joined Blackstone, John Jacob and Killbere. They spurred their horses ahead, leaving William Ashford to bring on the slow-moving column. When they found the charred remains of the village, Renfred hailed them from the forest's edge.

'I fear his wound is mortal, Sir Thomas.'

Blackstone dismounted. The villagers had made a rough shelter and a bed of ferns for the injured Meulon. Fever gripped him. A woman knelt at his side, bathing the big man's forehead with a cloth. She stood as Blackstone approached.

'This man saved me, my lord. Me and many others. He will die if his wound is not cared for. We have nothing.' She bowed her head. 'Only our gratitude. We are praying for him.'

Killbere eased her aside as Blackstone knelt next his injured captain. 'Meulon, we're here now and Will Longdon will stitch and bind you. We have herbs and ointment. You'll soon be back at my side.'

Meulon licked his dry lips. His voice barely a whisper. 'Sir Thomas. I have brought more trouble to your door. We saved more villagers.'

'And that is not trouble, Meulon, that is a duty. You killed enough men to clear our way ahead to Sir John. Now let Will Longdon see to your wound.'

Meulon sighed. 'His hands are as rough as a boar's arse and fingers as thick as dog turds. He'll hurt me more than the damned wound.'

'And I'll take pleasure in having you at my mercy,' said Will Longdon, settling next to Meulon and opening his sack of herbal tinctures and creams, jealously guarded these past few years since inheriting them from a woman apothecary who had sacrificed her life to save Blackstone's.

'Aye, and when I die I shall haunt you at night and plague you during the day.' Meulon whispered, coughing from the effort of tormenting Longdon.

Blackstone went to where Renfred waited with the bound prisoner. The routier glared at the scar-faced man who looked down at him. 'Get him to his feet,' said Blackstone.

Renfred yanked the man up and pressed him back against a tree. The man's misshapen face reflected his brutal life. The flattened nose, and a cheekbone clearly broken years before and never set cleanly, gave his face a lopsided look. What teeth he had were little more than blackened stumps. It was no surprise that lice itched in his beard, making him bend his head to his shoulder to scratch.

'Water, my lord. I am parched. My throat's as dry as the sole of my boot.'

'Your stench offends,' said Killbere. 'You've soiled yourself.'

He nodded towards the prostrate Meulon. 'The fucker damned near broke my neck. That would loose anyone's bowels.'

'You're an Englishman. Who do you serve?' said Blackstone.

'I'm a veteran of the war, my lord. I served the King.'

'The English or the French, you arsewipe?' said Killbere.

'Now, now, sir knight. I gave my blood on the field at Poitiers like many a stout-hearted man from Gloucester. And like many of my comrades I was cut loose when the war was won. I fight so I may live. Rough wine and a piece of mutton is not much for a man to ask for, eh? You know well, my lord, you and Sir Thomas Blackstone here. I know your blazon and your legend right enough. You did your fair share of slaughter.'

Renfred slapped him, splitting his lip. 'We neither rape nor kill women, you whoreson. Do not foul Sir Thomas's name.'

The routier spat blood. The blow meant nothing to a man used to violence. 'Kill me and be done with it. I have nothing to bargain with.'

'I can give you to the survivors and let them tear you apart,' Blackstone said. 'Or you can have wine until you're senseless and then I'll hang you. Choose.'

He bared his blackened teeth. 'A good bargain, Sir Thomas. I'll take the wine and the rope.'

'Then who commands you? Who is Ronec?'

'Ah. You've heard of him?' The routier raised his bound hands and blew snot from his bloodied nostrils. 'Ronec's a clever bastard. How many use another name to bring money into our purse? Ronec is as English as you and me, Sir Thomas. Ronec le Bête, he calls himself. Married a French whore after the truce, sired a clutch of bastards here and there. The "Beast" sounds better in French than English. Puts the fear of Christ into everyone.'

'I have fought across France and Italy for half my life and I never heard of him until yesterday,' said Blackstone.

The mercenary shrugged. 'So what? A man lives and dies and no one knows his name. But he has ambition. Who can blame a man for that? Besides...' He sniggered. 'Shield yourself behind a false name and those who pay for the slaughter keep their hands clean.'

Killbere pushed his knife under the man's chin, forcing him onto his toes as a trickle of blood ran down his throat. 'My lord,' the man begged.

Blackstone pressed a hand against Killbere's arm, lowering the blade. 'I may not save you from the rope unless you tell me his name.'

The routier looked at the blood he had wiped from his neck. 'He's from a good family in Essex. Turned bad. Thieved and killed and was imprisoned by the sheriff but pardoned by the King when he invaded back in '59. He fought in the Prince of Wales's division at Rheims. Ranulph de Hayle. That's who he is.' The killer grinned, his arrogance undiminished, having bought himself a better death. 'Sir Thomas, how about giving me one of the girls before you hang me? I'll take her quick. That one. The youngster. No loss to you and a man can die happy with drink in his belly and his cock pleasured one last time.'

Blackstone and Killbere looked to where the man leered. A girl, no more than twelve or thirteen, offering comfort to the orphaned child she cradled.

Blackstone grabbed him by the scruff of his jupon and marched him into the open. The routier blustered and cried out but Blackstone ignored him as he turned to face the survivors in the forest. 'This man raped and killed. He is yours to do with what you want.' He pushed the terrified man away from him.

The routier stumbled. Got to his feet, clasped his bounds hands in supplication. 'Sir Thomas. You promised me a good death. Hang me, lord, I beg you,' he pleaded as the survivors emerged from the trees and headed towards them.

'We have no rope,' said Blackstone.

The man stuttered, wild-eyed, then turned and ran, stumbling across the open ground towards the burnt-out huts. The villagers cried out, a howl of belly-deep pain for the loss of their loved ones, and chased after him. Fear drove him two hundred yards before they fell on him. Like wolves at a kill they tore him apart.

CHAPTER TEN

Meulon refused any assistance to mount his horse. No words of concern or cajoling persuaded him to accept help in front of the men and surviving villagers. Will Longdon was brushed away. Pride overcame pain.

'There's a piece of the blade in him, Thomas,' said Will Longdon. 'Its tip must have snapped off. I cleaned the wound and pressed plantain into it to cleanse the cut, then crushed wild garlic to make a poultice and keep poison at bay. He's bandaged with a strip of clean linen, but if we do not get the knife point out of him... and... and I cannot tell if it chipped his rib... and if it has, then—'

Blackstone pressed a hand onto his centenar's shoulder. 'I know, he'll die. Will, you have done everything you could. Now we must find a barber-surgeon.'

Killbere pressed his foot into the stirrup. 'And where do we go for that? We're days from Chandos and Meulon will be dead in three if he's lucky.'

'Villaines will have someone,' Blackstone said.

Killbere reached out and caught his friend's arm. 'Thomas! We cannot turn him over to the French. Even if they have a surgeon they have no cause to help us. They would cut his throat rather than attend him.'

Blackstone tugged the reins so the bastard horse did not bite Killbere's mount. 'We have saved French villagers close to their domain. Once they fall under Villaines's protection they will pay taxes. In offering them sanctuary we give the town income.'

'And that is all you are going to offer whoever commands the town? Scrag-arsed, half-starved peasants?'

'I have more to offer.'

'And you're going to share this with me?'

'Not yet.' Blackstone spurred the great beast. There was little enough time to find a surgeon.

Blackstone drove the survivors from the two villages at a harsh pace. Yet they kept up for they knew if they did not they would be abandoned and that meant death from other routiers, and they were determined to remain under the protection of the English knight who had given them life and allowed them to exact revenge. Their sweat and exertion were repaid as they came in sight of the town's castle. It had been damaged during the war but the town's defences had been rebuilt by the capable captain in command.

Meulon's grim insistence on staying on his horse was thwarted when he fell from the saddle, unconscious, several miles along the road. The men fashioned another litter and bore him at the head of the column between Blackstone and Killbere. Meulon's face was drained of colour by the time they reached the fortified town. Blackstone halted the column half a mile from the gates. 'Who commands here?' said Killbere.

'I don't know. This territory falls under the Lord of Mayenne, but whoever it is he's strengthened the town's defences and it looks as though he was in the fight at Cocherel,' Blackstone said, pointing to a handful of abandoned supply wagons that stood in the open fields in front of the gates. 'Those bear de Grailly's blazon.'

'Thomas, he might be holding Beyard as a prisoner. Those routiers at the bridge said he had been taken for ransom by some lord or other.'

'We'll soon find out. Gilbert, spread the men out. I want those in the watchtowers to see us clearly.' Blackstone turned in the saddle. 'John, you will accompany me with Meulon's litter.'

'Once they know who you are, Thomas, your life is not worth a cobbler's boot nail,' said Killbere.

'Gilbert, do as I ask. We have to save Meulon – whatever the risk.'

Killbere nodded. He knew as well as the next man that Meulon might not survive another day without help. He and John Jacob wheeled their horses to follow Blackstone's orders.

Blackstone turned the bastard horse towards the huddled survivors. He pointed to two of the men. 'You will follow me. Bring the woman and the child on the litter. Everyone else will follow. I'll speak to the mayor and the council or whoever commands here. I will bargain for your sanctuary and the care of those who need it. You follow behind me. Do not rush the gates. These people might not accept you. Understood?'

There was a murmur of understanding. Villagers raised their voices in thanks for Blackstone's protection.

Killbere reined in. 'Thomas, those parapets may be low but they're bristling with crossbows. It might not be much of a town but what defences they have look to be effective. Enfilade there and there. And I'll wager they'll have barricades as a second line of defence.'

Blackstone looked at the men, who stood in plain sight. 'If John Jacob and I don't come out by nightfall then choose their weakest place and come at them under cover of darkness. They'll be vulnerable then.'

'I will,' said Killbere, 'and gladly because you will likely be strung up by your ankles wearing your balls around your neck.'

Blackstone led; John Jacob followed, guiding Meulon's litter; the stragglers came behind. Blackstone stopped fifty paces from the town gates and waited. If the command was given for the crossbowmen to loose they were dead.

The gates opened and a stocky man-at-arms strode out, flanked by six more. He stopped thirty paces from Blackstone. It made sense. Standing there, he would not be struck by the lethal bolts.

'You are Sir Thomas Blackstone,' he said. 'I recognize your blazon. I am Godfrey de Claville. I am captain here. State your business, Sir Thomas.'

'We came across two villages attacked by routiers. We saved these villeins and my man here was wounded while killing many of the skinners single-handed. He'll die if I don't find him a surgeon – and these people will die if they are left without protection. I seek help and hospitality.'

The man-at-arms stepped forward, raising a hand to stop his companions from following. The bastard horse dipped its head, ears pricked, hoof scraping the ground. De Claville stopped. 'Your horse is wary, Sir Thomas. I will approach no closer. I've no wish to startle him further and cause any of my men to panic and loose their arrows.' He waited for Blackstone to answer but the scar-faced man made no response. 'We are enemies. You come here expecting me to help you? That I might offer to save one of your men? Why would I – even if I had a barber-surgeon? And why would I take in more mouths to feed? In fact, why would I not seize you now and hold you to ransom?'

'You and your men would die by my hand before your bowmen could loose their bolts. You serve the Lord of Mayenne. This territory is yours to command. Take in these people and offer your protection. Set them to work on the land and they will pay their hearth tax, which enriches your lord. And that raises you further in his estimation. There is a band of routiers raiding this domain, and that is why you have every man you can muster on the walls. And there are scarcely enough to defend the town so you do not have the men to hunt down the skinners.'

Godfrey de Claville swept an arm across the horizon. 'His name is Ranulph de Hayle. He masquerades as Ronec le Bête, a Frenchman, and he is protected by your great knight Sir John Chandos.'

'You're wrong. I know Sir John. He's the most honourable of men. He would not allow it.'

'I cannot stop Ronec because I dare not leave the town undefended. His men kill without mercy. And sooner or later he will come here and he outnumbers us. Villaines will fall but we will die defending it.' He looked up at Blackstone. 'Perhaps you wish to use the pretext of trying to save a wounded man so that you can get behind our gates.'

'I would ride into Villaines and risk my life. I would be at your mercy. You fought at Cocherel,' he said.

De Claville looked puzzled as to how Blackstone knew; then, when he glanced at the abandoned wagons, he realized.

'You defeated men who were my friends, some who served with me in the past. Your part in the victory has already brought you credit and honour. If you gave your word for my safety and that of my squire, I would accept it. I have no desire to cause harm to anyone under your care.'

Godfrey de Claville looked past the villeins to where Blackstone's men were spread out across the meadow. He had too few men to withstand a sustained attack and Blackstone knew it. He could hold off an assault against the low walls and defensive ditches for a short while, but these men would keep pressing until they were within the town. No matter how hard the militia and townspeople fought, Blackstone's men would win.

'I give you my word,' de Claville said.

CHAPTER ELEVEN

Godfrey de Claville ushered Blackstone and John Jacob through the gates. The barricades in the streets would have slowed any assault but Blackstone knew that a determined attack would have broken through. They dismounted in front of a broad-fronted building as de Claville's men pressed curious onlookers aside. There were fewer houses than in many other towns but the streets twisted and tangled along one side and then flared into an open space where sheep and goats grazed. Blackstone saw women drawing water from two different wells and a priest hurrying head down, either in prayer or in hope that the savage-looking men who had come into the town were not harbingers of doom. Perhaps, Blackstone thought, he was in a hurry to hide his brass candlesticks. Blackstone handed the bastard horse's reins to John Jacob as de Claville beckoned men to lift Meulon's great frame from the litter. It took six of them.

'In here,' said de Claville.

Blackstone followed him inside to a cool room with a vaulted roof. The sweet smell of spring grass wafted through an open window. A long table, scrubbed clean, with benches either side, dominated the room.

'My men eat here. There are kitchens in the next room.' De Claville gestured for the litter-bearers to lift the unconscious man onto the table. They heaved him up and were then dismissed to return to their duties at the wall.

Blackstone put a hand against Meulon's forehead, its pallor and his shallow breathing telling him that his friend's life might be forfeit by nightfall.

'I have sent for the barber-surgeon,' said de Claville.

Blackstone nodded. The room would have barely seated thirty men. So that was the town's strength, apart from the town's militia, which would be pressed into service when the need arose. 'You took prisoners at Cocherel?'

'A few. I captured a handful of men and was awarded most of their supplies. We are a small town. It was a generous reward that added to our grain stores.'

'I am looking for a man called Beyard. A Gascon. He fought with de Grailly. I was told a Breton lord captured him.'

'I took no Gascons, only Navarrese. I'll ransom them when the time is right.'

A dishevelled man, his drab cloak stained with what looked to be dry blood, came into the room. He pulled back his cowl with one hand and gripped a rolled cloth to his chest with the other. 'I was pulling teeth,' he said by way of explanation to de Claville, his eyes on the wounded man. 'And him?'

'Wounded with a knife blade. We cleaned the wound and packed it with herbs,' said Blackstone.

'Waste of time. Herbs cause harm, didn't anyone ever tell you that?' said the barber-surgeon. 'Cow dung is what you need to seal a wound.'

Blackstone knew differently. He had seen the curative effects of herbs on his men's injuries, but he remained silent. A battlefield surgeon could act with speed and efficiency if he was the right kind of man.

'Tell me what you plan to do before you do it,' said Blackstone.

The surgeon pulled back his sleeves. His grubby fingers probed Meulon's wound. Meulon's body recoiled. 'I feel the metal,' he said. 'All right, what I'm going to do to him will wake him up. Get men in here to hold him,' he told de Claville and unrolled the bound cloth, exposing cutting knives, pliers and a saw. Their pitted blades were chipped and dull. Cleaner knives would be found in a badly run kitchen. 'I cut here,' he said, showing a lateral and horizontal cut across Meulon's side. 'He's a big man but getting in deep enough and pulling out a shard of a blade, I don't know. I might cut into his rib. I am not responsible, you understand. The body holds many secrets that we do not understand. He'll bleed like a pig,' he said matter-of-factly and reached for a knife.

Blackstone grabbed his arm. 'You will not go near my friend. I would have my own men treat him before I let you rip him apart.'

The surgeon trembled. The man towered over him, threatening violence. 'My lord, he will die anyway. Better that I try.'

Blackstone took a handful of the man's cloak, marched him to the door and threw him into the street. He turned to de Claville. 'He's a butcher. I've seen men die on the battlefield because of men like him. Is there no monk or nun who knows how to heal? An apothecary?'

Godfrey de Claville was no coward but when Blackstone had lifted the surgeon's feet off the ground and tossed him aside as if he were nothing more than a bundle of cloth, he had pressed himself against the wall. 'Sir Thomas, there is no monastery or convent less than several hours from here, but we have a priest who will make sure your friend is shriven before he dies.'

'Merciful Christ,' said Blackstone. 'This man's life is precious to me. Find me someone to help him and I swear to you I will give you whatever you wish – if it is within my power.'

Godfrey de Claville saw the pagan symbol around Blackstone's neck. 'You were an archer, Sir Thomas. I see you wear the Silver Wheel Goddess. Arianrhod protects English bowmen who kill good Frenchmen, but you wear a crucifix as well.'

'Good Frenchmen mutilate archers when they are seized. They need all the protection they can get. The crucifix is my wife's.'

'And which power holds sway over your soul? The pagan goddess or the symbol of everlasting life?'

'I make my own destiny. And I will pray to whoever I damned well please. I made you an offer.'

De Claville saw no reason to antagonize Blackstone further. 'There is a man. They captured him in the baggage train with Jean de Grailly's retinue. But if you are fearful of a Christian God or your man here fears for his soul, then I will not bring him.'

'Speak in plain words, man. Who is it? You bring a sorcerer? If he can help, fetch him. A friend who lives is better than one dead and his soul and mine have long since been ransomed to the devil.'

De Claville turned to the guard outside the door. 'Fetch the Jew!'

CHAPTER TWELVE

Godfrey de Claville's guards ushered in a man older in years than anyone else in the room, who wore a robe that reached below his knees, covered by a hooded dark tan cloak held by a brooch. He seemed to be someone of importance as his shirt was silk and his shoes, although scuffed, were of a quality leather. His cloak and clothing were, however, grubby: witness to his incarceration although there was no sign that he had been injured. Flecks of grey sprinkled his beard, and he was slightly built, his hands as slender as a woman's. He carried a leather satchel and a rolled-up oilskin. He glanced at Blackstone, settled his baggage on the long table and gazed down at the injured man. He did not touch the wound or examine the patient they had summoned him to attend. Satisfied with what he saw, he raised his eyes to Blackstone.

'I am Halif ben Josef. I served Lord Jean de Grailly at the behest of my lord, Charles of Navarre. I am a Jew.'

Blackstone looked him up and down. 'You wear no mark.'

'Yet I am a Jew. My lord, Jews in Navarre are given more latitude than elsewhere in Spain. Your man will die unless I attend him but they do not permit a Jewish doctor to treat a Christian.' The man's gentle voice bore no malice.

'You attend Jean de Grailly,' said Blackstone. 'He's Christian.'

'Even so, I am obliged to ask permission. As we talk your man is dying.'

'Then stop talking,' said Blackstone. 'You have it. There's a broken piece of knife blade in his side.'

Ben Josef dipped his head and turned to Godfrey de Claville. 'I will need two bowls of hot water and clean linen to bind the man's wound.'

De Claville hesitated for only a second as he glanced at Blackstone and then ordered the men at the door.

'Sir knight,' said ben Josef, 'you will help me.'

'To do what?'

'Lift his shoulders. I must remove his tunic and shirt.'

It was obvious no one else had the strength to lift Meulon's weight. He stepped forward but ben Josef raised a hand.

'No. Not on the same side as his wound. Your clothes are rank with sweat and dirt. We must take all precautions: the wound is already poisoned. Do it here on the opposite side.'

The surgeon gave his commands with no sign of deference. He was in control. Blackstone did as instructed and the smaller man tugged free Meulon's garments. The huge man, groggy from pain, groaned and tried to rise. Blackstone's strength held him still.

'Meulon, it's me. I've found help for you.'

Meulon gritted his teeth and allowed Blackstone to ease him down again.

Two men came into the room carrying the water and linen the Jew had requested.

'Put them here,' said ben Josef, undoing the straps on his satchel and exposing a case full of dark glass bottles. He selected four and laid them side by side, pouring measured amounts from each one into a small glass. Loosening the ties on the oilskin, he unfurled the rolled cloth. Slender instruments of polished steel nestled next to each other. They were burnished from persistent cleaning. Halif ben Josef appeared to mutter a prayer before unclipping the brooch that held his cloak. He pulled off his robe and rolled his sleeves above his elbows. He soaked his hands, twisting and turning them, releasing their grime. When he was satisfied they were clean, he wiped them on a piece of linen and then cast it aside so it would not be used again.

'What is that?' said Blackstone, pointing to the small glass of liquid.

'It is a combination of poisons that can kill but tempered with plants that will balance them and render your man unconscious. A man of his strength and size will need a strong potion. I will inflict great pain on him.'

'My men use herbs for their wounds. I've used henbane before,' said Blackstone.

'Yes, lord, but there is opium in this mixture. We physicians learn from the Arabs. There are no constraints on sharing knowledge of healing.' He gestured Blackstone to raise Meulon again and then put the glass to the wounded man's lips. He drank without resisting. Ben Josef nodded, satisfied that the potion would soon do its work. 'Lie him down,' he told Blackstone. 'And then bring me that candle.'

Blackstone reached for the burning candle as ben Josef swabbed Meulon's wound with the clean linen, discarding each bloodied piece until satisfied that the exposed wound was dirt free. 'Here,' he said, beckoning Blackstone to bring the flame closer. Blackstone allowed him to guide his arm until the candle was exactly where he needed it. He placed a hand over Meulon's lower ribs above the wound. 'It is here,' he said without looking up. 'I feel the metal. It is lodged here. Now I must remove it without cutting into the rib.'

He chose one of the instruments laid out on the oilskin. It was tendril slender, a pair of blunt-ended scissors with flattened ends. The small finger holes were barely large enough to accommodate ben Josef's hands. He bent to the task, using his free hand to ease a finger into the wound and get a sense of where to guide the thin forceps. He probed deeply. Blood drained from the wound and he swabbed it with more linen. Meulon flinched. Ben Josef stopped, waiting to see if the pain had penetrated the opiate potion. The big man's breathing settled. Blackstone realized his own breath was held tight in his chest as he observed the Jew's tender skill.

'There is no sign that the blade cut his intestine. God has been merciful: the layers of muscle deflected the blade, but once I secure it, then we must offer a prayer I do not cause damage when I pull the shard of metal free.' Ben Josef glanced at Blackstone and saw the two symbols at his neck. 'God hears prayers no matter to whom you pray.'

Blackstone raised the Silver Wheel Goddess to his lips.

Halif ben Josef staunched a flow of blood and then drew back the blunt-edged clamp slowly.

'It catches,' said ben Josef. He stopped. 'If it is a sharp or ragged, it will tear his intestine or another organ. He has been lucky so far. I tell you this because I cannot be certain what will happen if I continue.'

'Do what you must,' said Blackstone. 'If you leave it in there he'll die anyway.'

The man's delicate hand drew back the blunt instrument and with a gentle turn of the wrist withdrew the metal shard. He examined it against the light. 'I do not think it pierced his intestine. I see no sign of it.' He placed the metal and the clamp onto a piece of linen and after washing his hands again packed the wound with absorbent herbs, threaded a curved needle and stitched the wound. Blackstone recognized the man's expertise. The swift and efficient closing of the wound made Will Longdon's usual attempts seem like a man stitching a coarse shirt.

'Now I shall make a poultice and bind him. He must not ride for five or six days. More if possible.'

'I'll be lucky to keep him out of the saddle for a day,' said Blackstone.

'Then my work might have been in vain.'

'Can you keep him drugged?'

'For a day or two, yes.'

'Then I can ask no more of you, Halif ben Josef. You have my thanks. I am in your debt.'

Ben Josef smiled and applied the dressing. 'I am sworn to heal. How can there be debt?'

'Then how can I repay you?'

The physician wiped his hands and considered Blackstone's request.

'When I was captured these men took two rings from my hand. They were my late wife's and I treasured them with a sentiment only an old man who has enjoyed a long marriage can understand.'

'I am not an old man but I understand, Master Josef. You shall have them returned to you.'

Halif ben Josef bowed his head in thanks. 'That is not all that was taken. Before the battle at Cocherel I was not in servitude nor held under contract. I was a free man.'

The request was a simple one. Blackstone nodded and stepped outside with Godfrey de Claville. 'Give me a small wagon and horses and a straw mattress and I'll pay the Jew's ransom and that of any other prisoners you hold.'

De Claville shook his head. 'The half-dozen others are not worth much but he's worth a lot, Sir Thomas. The King of Navarre will pay to have such a skilled surgeon returned to him.'

'There's a battle coming between those who wish to rule Brittany. Armies are already gathering, you know that.

You serve the Lord of Mayenne and he'll call on you. I will give you two things. A ransom paid and a promise that if I see you on the battlefield I will not fight you. I cannot promise you your life in battle but give my word I will not take it.'

'Sir Thomas, I am a Norman, not a Breton. I don't give a damn about Charles de Blois or John de Montfort. Noblemen squander men's lives as easily as trampling a field of grain. If there is a choice, I will not take my men into the fight, so I will need a ransom large enough to buy me my freedom to choose.'

Blackstone looked over his shoulder to where ben Josef bathed Meulon's face with the tenderness of a woman with a child. He looked back at de Claville. 'You shall have your ransom and I wish you a long life to spend it.'

'I want something more,' said de Claville. 'The man who slaughters innocents has part of his scalp missing here.' He touched above his right ear. 'He wears a surcoat of four upturned daggers against blue cloth. Bring me Ranulph de Hayle's head and rid us of the threat he poses. He is a beast who needs to be killed.'

CHAPTER THIRTEEN

Killbere choked on his wine at Blackstone's answer to his question. He spat it out. 'God's tears, Thomas. Six pounds? For an old man? I could buy several horses for less. And you know how many archers a day we could have at our side with six pounds?'

'How many would that be, Gilbert?'

'At sixpence a day we could have...' He scowled as the arithmetic eluded him.

Blackstone waited as Killbere struggled. 'Two hundred and forty archers,' said Blackstone.

'No matter,' said an irritated Killbere. 'Have you lost your senses? He's a Spaniard. What good will he do us?'

'He saved Meulon's life: that's worth more than any damned horse and many archers.'

'I do not question the value of Meulon's life, Thomas, I ask why you would pay a king's ransom for a Jew who will attract distrust and censure. He will not be permitted to practice, you know that.'

'I don't care whether a man is Christian, Pagan, Muslim or Jew. He stays with us until I return him to Navarre.'

'You mean we don't even own him?'

'When did we ever have slaves?' said Blackstone. 'This man has skills greater than any barber-surgeon I have witnessed and he will stay with us for as long as it takes for us to return him safely. I have signed the promissory note. De Claville will take it to a banker in Rheims and Father Torellini will honour the debt from my account in Florence.'

Killbere sighed. 'Thomas, let us at least turn a profit and sell him to the King of Navarre.'

'Time will tell what favour we might need from him. Until then he is our guest and he rides in the wagon with Meulon.'

'And the Spanish prisoners you paid for? Are they to fight with us?'

'They've sworn their loyalty to me. We'll see how well they fight when the time comes. I have put them under Renfred's command.'

Killbere corked the wineskin. 'And I'll wager that Godfrey de Claville has already sent riders to warn Charles of Blois that we are on our way to join Chandos.'

'It makes no difference, Gilbert. Men are swarming in from everywhere. It's a war between the English and the French in all but name. Their new King will want Brittany under his control, not Edward's. He'll send Normans and men from Burgundy to fight alongside the Bretons. He beat Navarre at Cocherel and now he will want to win against de Montfort.'

'The question is, who makes the first move and where? Do any of those Navarrese prisoners know anything about Beyard?'

'He was taken for ransom on the battlefield by one of the Breton lords. Godfrey de Claville lied to us. Ranulph de Hayle was here. He bought some of the Spanish prisoners. De Claville kept others back. The French have a profitable trade going on.'

'Then you think he had Beyard?'

'No.'

'Why not? The lying whoreson might have made a healthy profit on him.'

'I spoke to the Spanish. One of them thought he might have been taken to the castle at Auray.'

Killbere smiled. 'Now, that's convenient. We are to meet Chandos near there.'

'And all we need to do is ensure that we get de Montfort and Chandos to do as we want. If Beyard's held there, then we need to get inside.'

'Which will be the more difficult? Getting inside such a stronghold or convincing Chandos and de Montfort to let us?'

'That we'll have to see when we get there. In the meantime, we must ensure these newcomers do not cause friction among us. Especially any feeling the men have about the Jew.' Blackstone walked to the edge of the forest where the men were camped. Clusters of them stood around the covered cart that bore Meulon, cosseted on a straw mattress and watched over by ben Josef. Blackstone's men looked warily at the man in his Spanish garb.

'The Navarrese I ransomed spoke well of the Jew. They told me that de Grailly had campaigned with him before as his surgeon. I didn't know that.'

'De Grailly's a Gascon: he probably didn't want the Pope hearing about it. He excommunicated the Castilian King for having Moors as his personal guard. No man needs a religious conflict bearing down on him when there's a war to be fought,' said Killbere.

Blackstone kicked dirt over the fire. 'We'll take no censure about ben Josef. I've told the captains he is under my protection and that if any man falls wounded, then he will treat them. That or they can pray to the Almighty to save them and hope for a barber-surgeon. I know who I'd choose.'

Killbere settled the wineskin on his saddle's pommel. 'Well, I hope you know what you're doing, Thomas, now that we have Spanish prisoners ready to fight the Bretons and French, and a Jewish surgeon honoured by de Grailly and ransomed by an Englishman. Our lads will be wary of Navarre's men, and others will not enjoy having a Jew among us. There could be enough bad blood to start our own war.'

'Then let's give them a battle to fight against the Bretons and remind the new French King that his men face English and Welsh archers and men-at-arms determined to give Edward and the Prince the victory they crave.' He hauled himself into the saddle. The bastard horse fought the reins but Blackstone controlled him. 'Winning wars is what we do best.'

They travelled at a modest pace, stopping where they could at monasteries along the way, seeking comfort to aid Meulon's recovery. Halif ben Josef was not permitted to enter such places and camped with John Jacob and the men outside the walls as Blackstone and Killbere stayed with their wounded friend. All of them ignored Ben Josef except John Jacob, but as word of the surgeon's skill spread among them, some approached with ailments of their own. He offered advice and treatment, giving them herbs and potions that went beyond Will Longdon's knowledge. After only a few days ben Josef's religion was less important to the fighting men than his healing skills.

Blackstone had delayed their onward journey by staying longer at every camp and monastic shelter and, after many weeks, they reached Sir John Chandos north of the Breton town of Auray. By then Meulon could walk and ride, but followed Blackstone's demand that he allow ben Josef to examine and dress the wound every day.

'I've seen Moors and Jews living in the same city in Castile and Navarre,' said Chandos. 'The Prince would do well to consult men like him.'

'He's ill?' said Blackstone. 'I saw no sign of it.'

'There are days he is weak, others when he is not. No one knows except those closest to him. It is a malady that comes and goes and is not understood by his physicians. No one else must know of it.'

'I understand,' said Blackstone. If the Prince was weakened by illness then his rule of Aquitaine was vulnerable. 'I'm looking for one of my captains taken at Cocherel. He's a Gascon who served with de Grailly.'

Chandos unrolled a map of the Breton march. 'He could be anywhere, if he's still alive.'

'Have you heard of any ransom being demanded for those taken?' said Blackstone.

'None, and if you have wasted time searching for him, then you've done the Prince a disservice. You were expected here long before now.'

'We did as the Prince ordered. We shadowed de Grailly's flank, keeping French forces from attacking him. We took no part in the fighting at Cocherel.'

Chandos could not hide his irritation. 'You continue to test a man's patience. We have work to do here.'

Killbere picked his nose, examined the contents on the end of his finger and flicked it away. 'And while you wet-nurse de Montfort, we stay loyal to men who fought with us. Beyard is a captain, he's valued, and worth a few days of our time. And the fight hasn't started yet, so where's the harm?'

'And we took time to escort villagers to safety away from one of your routier companies,' said Blackstone.

Chandos raised his eyes from the map. 'I allow none of the companies to destroy villages. They are led by Englishmen who gather to help us in the fight against Blois and his Bretons. Hugh Calveley, Hewitt and Latimer brought their routiers to me in the Prince's name.'

'It's not them. The French believe you're harbouring and protecting Ranulph de Hayle, who hides behind the name Ronec le Bête. He and his men raped and killed their way from Alençon.'

Chandos shook his head. 'No! I stopped him. He plays both sides. He'll kill anyone who gets in his way: French, Breton or English. I refused to take his routiers under de Montfort's flag.'

'Then you don't know where he is?' said Killbere.

'No. And I would ask you not to pursue him, if that is your intention, because we have a problem. If we are not careful, our plan to defeat Charles of Blois will fail. Our young friend de Montfort might be a favourite of the King but he's strong-willed.' He poured wine and handed Blackstone and Killbere a beaker each.

'Not unlike another twenty-five-year-old I knew,' said Killbere, glancing at Blackstone over the rim. 'And as belligerent now as then.'

Chandos needed no reminding but if he and Blackstone were to deliver Brittany to the King, then antagonism had to be put aside. 'We have had our differences, Thomas, but although you're the King's Master of War I dare not let you chastise de Montfort. He's too young to be rebuked for being impetuous.' Chandos looked through the pavilion's open flaps to where armed men sharpened blades and readied themselves for a fight. 'He insists that we ride and confront Blois. He's keen for victory.'

'Desire for victory is no bad thing,' said Killbere. 'Once he hears the trumpets and drums, he'll fight like the devil. He needs to earn the right to rule.'

Blackstone raised his eyes from the map; he was familiar with the landscape from when he had fought and raided through the territory. 'The Prince said you were to advise de

Montfort. He wouldn't defy you or the Prince. If it were not for Edward's blessing Charles of Blois would have claimed Brittany years ago.'

'And now those years come to a head. De Montfort has the right to make his own decisions, Thomas. I can only intervene if he makes a decision that will cost him, and our King, the duchy. We need the succession to go his way. We both need to convince him that riding across Brittany in search of a battle serves no purpose other than to risk defeat.'

Blackstone turned back to the map. 'We must choose the place to fight; so what would bring Charles of Blois to us? To a place of our choosing? Auray is held by his ally. It's a strategic town sitting at the mouth of the river.' Blackstone traced his finger down to the sea. 'How far to the coast? Ten miles? To seize the town would inflict a wound in Blois's flank. He needs to bring in supplies. Auray lets him bypass the ports in Aquitaine.' Blackstone looked at the two men.

'Then we let de Montfort lay siege to Auray,' said Chandos. 'Yes. A good plan, Thomas. He has ships down the coast at Le Croisic that can soon blockade the river mouth.'

'A siege will draw in the French and Bretons. Norman troops are already moving towards us,' said Killbere.

'And those who defeated de Grailly at Cocherel, from the east,' said Blackstone. He dragged his finger across the map. 'All those men mean Blois has four thousand men, perhaps more by now. He'll make slow progress. His supply line must keep up with him. Bertrand du Guesclin commands the French vanguard. He's the best leader the French have had in years.' Blackstone studied the land mass on the map and stabbed his finger. 'Their two armies will converge here at Brandivy.'

Chandos scratched his beard. The Breton coast was no place to make a stand. 'We would be trapped with our backs to the sea.'

'That's what they expect, Sir John, but we won't be there. We'll be... here,' he said and touched the area north of the town. 'If they step into our trap then we will win the day.'

Killbere swished the wine around his mouth and swallowed. 'And if they don't, we'll be neck deep in marshland mud and lose.'

CHAPTER FOURTEEN

The castle at Auray guarded the bridge across the river that swept around the town, forming an island on three sides. From its heights defenders could see the town with its hospital and church and the busy narrow streets. Those who patrolled the ramparts felt safe looking across the rooftops to the distant plain. The tidal river dropped so low that body-swallowing mud would suck down any man stupid enough to wade across, and at high tide the town's militia could easily kill men clambering from boats onto the quayside. The castle's looming walls were too high for scaling ladders and the narrow strip of land between river and outer curtain walls made it impossible for siege towers to take up position. The ancient Dukes of Brittany knew how to build an impregnable castle. They could not know that a hundred years and more later an English King's Master of War would study the great citadel and see how to breach its walls.

'It cannot be done,' said John de Montfort, who might be twenty-five years old but looked to have only recently crept into manhood. The contrast his youthful appearance made with the veteran fighting men was emphasized by his thin whiskers and drooping moustache. 'Better that we ignore the town and seek out the enemy.'

When de Montfort turned away, Sir John Chandos glanced at Blackstone with a look that said: *I told you so.*

Blackstone remained silent as the impatient young man paced back and forth until he could no longer tolerate being ignored by his elders. 'I have two thousand men. They have rallied to my cause. We must seize Brittany with honour in battle.' He glared from one man to the other. 'Answer me!'

'My lord, you have not asked a question,' said Blackstone.

'Do not talk to me as if I were a child!' said de Montfort.

'I will not if you listen to those who know better. And if you do not then you will never gain the duchy, because you will be dead, consumed by maggots and forgotten by history.' Blackstone's measured tones struck de Montfort as hard as if he had clubbed him around the ear.

His jaw dropped. He stammered, looking from Blackstone to Chandos, eyes tear-filled as rage took hold. 'Sir John! You bring this insolent knight into my quarters to humiliate me?' He faced Blackstone. 'Get out!'

Blackstone didn't move. De Montfort pointed a trembling finger at him. 'His insolence offends me.'

'And at times it offends the Prince – and many others – but Sir Thomas is honoured and trusted and you would be wise to listen to him,' said Chandos.

De Montfort bleated. 'It is I who command here with you at my side.'

Chandos sighed and settled his backside on the edge of the table. 'And he is the King's Master of War. He will tell you that over the years we have lost our tempers with each other, but despite our differences I listen to him – and I urge you to do the same.'

John de Montfort wiped a hand across his face in case the tears of frustration made him appear less in control than he was. He took a deep breath. 'Very well. Sir John urges me to listen. And so I will.' His hand fluttered at Blackstone as if to hurry him along.

Blackstone spilled wine from a beaker on the scrubbed tabletop and, dipping his finger, drew a curving loop. 'The river bends in a horseshoe around the town. There's one bridge from the castle to the town. At the far side of Auray are defensive ditches and beyond that the open plain and forests. From the heights of the castle they will see your army blocking any escape. They will send a messenger to warn Charles of Blois the moment they sight us. This port is vital to him. He'll come to take it back. First the town must fall.'

'Impossible,' said de Montfort. 'I'll wager those ditches are heavy with traps and sharpened stakes. Crossbowmen would cut us down before we even breached the defences. No boat can navigate close enough to the quayside for the same reason. We would need high tide and that tide would spell death for the men. It would take only a few to kill us as we clambered ashore.' His voice rose with confidence. 'If this is your plan, I fail to see how our beloved King chose you as his Master of War.'

The insult made no impression. 'I will give you Auray and then, if you swallow your pride, you will face Charles of Blois on the battlefield in a place of our choosing and you will defeat him and become Duke of Brittany. To do otherwise opens the door to failure.'

The two veterans watched the King's ambitious favourite writhe with uncertainty. He turned to Chandos. 'I will follow your advice, Sir John,' he said, not bothering to hide his contempt for Blackstone.

Sir John Chandos stood to his full height. 'Then do what Sir Thomas suggests.'

The night watch on the castle ramparts stretched and yawned away the fatigue of their long night's duty. The mist enshrouding the river struggled to rise above the town's rooftops. The sentries watched as a flock of colours fluttering from pennons and banners emerged from the ground-hugging fog on the distant plain. The line of cavalry came without fanfare. The army came on and fanned out around the town's boundary, sealing off the land between the two curves of the river. Auray was now an island and if its citizens did not stand and fight, then they would have to flee across the bridge into the castle's safety.

A church bell broke the silence, clanging its warning. Raised voices of alarm reached those on the high walls. Sentries summoned the guard commander, who ran onto the ramparts. No attack was imminent, but he called the garrison to arms. The castle's commander chose messengers to take separate routes on the near side of the river and warn Lord Charles de Blois. They ordered six riders to go in opposite directions and skirt the river until they were clear of the town. Only one needed to survive. The cries of alarm increased as townspeople gathered what goods they could carry and jostled through the streets to sanctuary in the castle.

The citizen militia grabbed what weapons they had to hand and ran for Auray's boundary, gripped with panic as sergeants from the castle stationed in the town to command them barked their orders. Men made the sign of the cross as they gazed at wraiths revealed in the rising mist: armoured knights and men-at-arms whose horses appeared to loom out of the fog. They waited beyond crossbow range, bridles jangling, horses whinnying, scraping the ground, their blood already up, sensing the urgency of their riders for battle.

Every man between sixteen and sixty had to serve in the town's defences. The experienced soldiers who led them ran to designated defensive lines, pushing aside frightened women and children as they forced their way through the choked streets. They ringed the quayside, staring down into the swirling mist and the running tide. Acrid smoke burned the back of their throats as a heavily laden boat loomed into view through the mist. Smoke belched from its burning cargo – bales of hay – as it bumped and scraped along the quayside wall, causing instant confusion. Men on the castle walls bellowed down to the armed men on the quay to guard against enemy soldiers who might be following the blazing hulk, whose tarred timbers soon succumbed to the ferocious heat adding fuel to the inferno.

Blackstone had convinced John de Montfort and the other renowned lords and men-at-arms to curb their impatience. He had waited until the weather settled and the westerly wind from the Gulf of Morbihan had shifted direction and the rising tide took the swirling river higher. The stolen boat's cargo was soaked with lamp oil and pushed into the tide. By the time it was engulfed, blinding terrified citizens with its smoke and flames, Blackstone and four others were already ashore. They were dressed no differently than the citizens of Auray and easily infiltrated the crowds passing through the castle gates, the sentries ushering in the town's citizens unaware that the men beneath their hooded capes were not townsmen. They had appropriated some abandoned goods: Blackstone was bent double, balancing caged chickens on his back to obscure his height; John Jacob bore a squealing pig across his shoulders.

By the time a hundred citizens of Auray had entered the castle, Blackstone and his men were already pushing open a door leading from the outer ward through the curtain wall. Once inside, the shadows from the castle's keep and the rising sun threw its cloak across them. The morning chill reeked of damp and fear. Garrison troops manning the walls had little interest in the refugees seeking shelter: they feared an attack from the town when it fell, which it inevitably would, and then the enemy would storm the bridge and lay tar-soaked bundles of faggots against the castle gates.

Blackstone signalled John Jacob and Will Longdon to check a closed door that looked as though it led down to the dungeons. It was locked. William Ashford was dressed in such ragged clothing that Blackstone lost sight of him in the crush of people. A strong hand grabbed his arm. Blackstone reached for his hidden knife, the only weapon any of the men carried. He stayed his hand when he saw it was Ashford, who nodded towards a cage door at the base of one of the round towers. Blackstone gave a sharp whistle, raised an arm and then pushed his way through the crowd with Ashford at his shoulder. Longdon and John Jacob heard and saw the signal, so too Kynith the Welsh ventenar. Five men against a hundred or more – but they were not there to seize the castle. Blackstone's determination in convincing de Montfort to lay siege served another purpose other than drawing in the enemy; he wanted to find and rescue Beyard.

Kynith pulled hard against the iron gate. It gave way. The stone steps twisted down in a tight, unlit spiral. 'Guard the gate,' Blackstone told Will Longdon and Kynith. Blackstone descended with John Jacob and William Ashford at his heels. The gloom closed in on them but they could smell the foulness of the place. The stench of excrement and the stringent smell of urine was as trapped in the underground chambers as the prisoners. A flame cast shadows as a jailer peered around a pillar.

'Hey, who're you?' he muttered, still groggy from sleep. No noise penetrated from the turmoil above in the castle's yard. The jailer, pallid from spending his days and nights below ground, coughed and spat, peering through the gloomy light.

'We are here for the prisoners taken at Cocherel,' said Blackstone without breaking stride.

The jailer grimaced as the tall figure loomed towards him. No one had told him the prisoners were to be released and these shadow men wore no insignia. As his dull mind grappled with uncertainty over who they were, their leader grabbed the burning torch from his hand, forcing him to stumble back. 'The prisoners,' Blackstone said again.

The jailer's quivering hand pointed to the pitch-dark passageway. John Jacob leaned past Blackstone and lifted the ring of iron keys from his belt. Blackstone held the flame aloft and as he and John Jacob took a pace back William Ashford struck the jailer once behind the neck. The man dropped without a sound. There was no need to kill him: he would be condemned once the garrison captain discovered the loss of his prisoners.

Blackstone bent low beneath the stone ceiling. There were only a few cells, most of which were empty. John Jacob lifted an unlit torch from its wall bracket and lit it from Blackstone's. The furthest and darkest corner of the dungeon showed several men lying in soiled straw. The reek was overpowering. John Jacob spat the awful taste from his throat and turned the heavy lock. Blackstone stooped inside and turned one of the men over: he was unconscious.

'Beyard? It's me. We've come to rescue you.' No response.

Blackstone laid the man onto his back and saw blood encrusted on his face and beard from a scalp wound. His lips were parched. 'William, find water. Back there. The jailer.'

John Jacob gave Ashford his torch, who returned along the dark passage as Blackstone cradled Beyard. He pulled an eyelid back and the light caused Beyard to flinch and then begin to struggle. His efforts were feeble yet his instinct to fight was still there. Blackstone easily restrained him.

At last Beyard's eyes focused. 'Sir Thomas,' he said, voice rasping.

'Aye, me and John Jacob with a couple of the lads. We must get you out.'

Beyard nodded and tried to stand but his legs gave way. Ashford returned with a wineskin and handed it to Blackstone, who raised it to Beyard's lips. 'Slowly, my friend.'

The Gascon captain gulped eagerly until Blackstone pulled it away from his lips. 'How far can you walk?'

'I'm weak, Sir Thomas. No food or drink for... I don't know...' His voice trailing off, he forced his back against the wall but once again his knees buckled.

'I'll carry you,' said Blackstone. 'We must move.'

Beyard pointed to his nearest companions. 'That one's only a boy; the older man is one of de Grailly's captains.'

John Jacob bent and held the flame over the figures lying in the straw. 'The boy's alive but the other's dead.'

Beyard looked about to faint. 'I kept the boy alive best I could... Said I'd... see him through... The other... three... help them... They fought well.'

Ashford and John Jacob roused the men, all weakened by their privation. The wine and the chance to escape gave them strength. One was able to help support his fellow captive, while Ashford wrapped the third, weaker man's arm around his shoulder and heaved him to his feet.

Beyard's head sank onto his chest. Blackstone lifted him up and pressed him against the wall, bent and let him drop over his shoulder. He glanced at the limp child and felt a momentary stab of pain. The boy stared at Blackstone with a look of fear and helplessness. He had seen his own son, Henry, show the same expression when his mother and sister were slain years before.

'John, take the lad.'

Blackstone's squire lifted the frail boy over his shoulder. 'All right, let's get ourselves out of here.'

Ashford and John Jacob lit the way to where Will Longdon and Kynith waited, squatting a few steps down from the entrance. Ashford threw the torch back into the darkness.

Longdon and Kynith scrambled to their feet. 'We kept out of sight. The yard's so crowded you couldn't fit a goose fletching between those huddling there,' said Will Longdon. 'There's enough panic among them to keep their minds off us.'

'We push our way through,' said Blackstone. 'No one will give us a second thought. They'll think we're carrying injured friends. Will, you and Kynith help these men.' He turned to Ashford. 'Lead the way. There's a postern gate in the outer ward.' He nodded for his archers to open the gate.

William Ashford's strength forged a path through the bustling, chaotic surge of refugees crowding in from the main gate. Ashford glanced back to ensure Blackstone and the others were at his heels. The five men twisted and turned through the fear-driven townsfolk. A single soldier guarded the postern gate. He was gazing through the viewing hatch, eyes searching for any assault attempt from outside, no thought of danger from within. When he turned and saw the men bearing down on him, his shock left him no time to challenge them. Ashford's fist put the man down; he pulled the heavy gate open, checked outside, glanced up at the ramparts and signalled Blackstone and John Jacob through.

Ashford pulled the gate closed behind them and took the lead again as the men scrambled down a dirt path towards the track that encircled the walls between the castle and the river. They saw smoke billowing from the far end of the town and knew that Chandos had directed his archers to set the thatched roofs alight. The bridge was still clogged with townspeople trying to squeeze through the castle's half-open gate. Two skiffs waited at the bend in the river, half obscured from the castle ramparts by trees and bushes.

Killbere raised himself from beneath the canvas covering on the first boat and whistled a signal. Half a dozen men-at-arms threw the cover aside. The second skiff was tied up on the riverbank forty yards beyond and as Blackstone and the others scrambled towards the first boat Jack Halfpenny and a dozen archers showed themselves, bows strung.

Blackstone and the rescued men were twenty yards from Killbere's boat when a dozen garrison soldiers shepherding townspeople across the bridge suddenly turned against their own kind, demanding they turn back because the castle yard was too full. The throng of desperate people pressed hard, their raised voices becoming cries of pain and anger as the soldiers struck out at them. Blackstone handed Beyard's unconscious body into the willing arms of Killbere's men. Will Longdon and Kynith clambered aboard and helped John Jacob and Ashford ease the others down into the well of the boat. Blackstone was about to jump aboard when screams rose from the bridge. The soldiers were no longer using staves to keep the people back, they were thrusting swords into them. A woman shrieked, an animal cry, as the man with her was cut down and the child he was cradling tumbled from his arms into the weir below the bridge. The crowd faltered but the woman threw herself into the water. The swirling current caught her clothing, pulling her below the surface. Soldiers turning to watch her desperate attempt to save her child saw the armed men in the boats, one of whom plunged into the swirling current.

Blackstone surfaced. A father's instinct had made him dive into the fast-flowing river. He heard and saw the men hailing their comrades on the walls. He reached midstream; the child bobbed ten feet away from him, its clothes puffed with air keeping it afloat for those first vital minutes. There was no sign of its mother. Blackstone grabbed the child. It was alive, eyes wide, mouth gasping from the cold water. He cradled it to his chest, kicking hard against the current. He heard Jack Halfpenny cry '*Loose!*' and saw garrison soldiers fall as they ran along the towpath towards them. He kept his eyes on the soldiers and then his head and shoulders slammed into a boat. Killbere had cut loose the mooring lines when Blackstone plunged in and the oarsman had pulled hard into the centre of the stream as Halfpenny's archers kept the enemy at bay. John Jacob and Killbere leaned down and heaved Blackstone half out the water as Will Longdon took the child from him.

Killbere shouted. 'Let the current take us! Jack, release your line!'

The boats spun in the tidal flow. Crossbow bolts splashed into the water and thudded into the hull. Halfpenny's men were too unbalanced to shoot back and bent instead to the oars to pull them further out of range. In Blackstone's boat Kynith grabbed Will Longdon's shoulder and pointed as the woman bobbed to the surface.

'There!'

'I can't swim,' said Longdon. 'Leave her.'

Kynith pulled off his jupon. 'I can reach her.'

Will Longdon went to grab him but the Welsh archer threw himself into the current.

'Kynith is in the water,' Longdon yelled.

Blackstone and Killbere turned and saw him striking out towards the woman, who was floating face up.

'Turn and hold,' Blackstone said.

Men on the one side of the boat lifted their oars as the others pulled hard, turning them broadside to the current. Kynith tugged the woman to him as she spat water. He tried to calm her, but she panicked. Wrapping a strong arm around her, he managed to constrain her long enough for them to reach the boat. Ashford and Killbere hauled her aboard as Blackstone and Longdon reached down to the grinning Welshman.

'Can't have a child without a mother, Sir Thomas.'

'You stupid whoreson. You never knew yours,' said Longdon, reaching for the man's belt to lift him clear.

'Aye, well, you and me both, you English bastard. All the more reason to—' His body bucked as a crossbow bolt tore into his shoulder. Longdon fell back as Blackstone held Kynith. Another quarrel struck the Welshman.

'They've got our range!' Longdon said.

John Jacob lunged for Blackstone and pulled him away from the wounded archer. Had he not the next two quarrels that slammed into the boat would have struck him.

'Pull!' Killbere shouted as Kynith was washed past the boat towards the shore. The current twisted the boat. Oarsmen struggled as another bolt found its mark. One man fell across his oar. Kynith was caught on a fallen tree branch, one arm hooked over it.

'There!' said Ashford, pointing at some soldiers running down the track next to the river. One of them, a bareheaded man-at-arms with a torn scalp, wore a surcoat bearing four upturned daggers against a blue background that looked at first to be French fleurs-de-lys.

'Thomas! That's Ranulph de Hayle,' said Killbere.

Blackstone's boat was swept beyond range of the French bowmen. 'Hold the boat steady!' he said.

Ashford pulled aside the wounded oarsman and took his place. He leaned into the oar and helped stop the rapid drift. The boat held long enough for Blackstone and the others to watch as Kynith was hauled from the shallows. The Welsh archer cried out: 'Sir Thomas!'

Ranulph de Hayle bellowed. 'Blackstone? Thomas Blackstone? You dare to take what is mine? Then I take my revenge.' He dragged a knife across Kynith's throat and kicked his body into the water.

Blackstone's men cursed. Will Longdon spat over the side. 'Put us ashore, Thomas. Let's kill this pig.'

Blackstone set his gaze to the turncoat Englishman and then turned to his men. 'This is not the time, Will. The riverbank ends. Ship the oars. The current will take us. We'll retrieve Kynith's body at the bend of the river.'

'Merciful Christ, Thomas,' said Killbere. 'We cannot let this man live.'

'I've given my word that I would deliver his head, Gilbert.' He turned to the men looking at him as they pulled towards the bend in the river. 'Carry what he did to our friend in your hearts and when we face him and his men offer them no mercy. No matter how they plead for their lives. We will kill this Englishman no matter who protects him. King, Prince or Sir John Chandos. Even God cannot shield him.'

CHAPTER FIFTEEN

They buried Meuric Kynith in the cemetery at the Convent of Saint-Esprit. The town of Auray surrendered when the mayor and council agreed to terms with the assurance from Sir John Chandos that his troops would destroy no more houses and inflict no rape or pillage on its populace. They returned the woman and her child to the town and when they heaped Breton soil over Kynith's grave she pushed through the gathered men to lay a small posy of wildflowers on the dirt. Then, cradling her rescued child, she bent a knee to Blackstone and raised his hand to her lips before disappearing through the throng of mourners without a word.

'The woman's life cost us dear,' said John Jacob.

Killbere tossed a handful of dirt onto the mound. 'Better we still had an archer in our ranks than a widow woman who'll end up starving without her man. That or turn to whoring. Kynith's death was a waste.'

'A man's life is not wasted by an act of courage,' said Blackstone. 'No matter the cause.' He turned away from the grave and the priest who had officiated at the burial, despite his fear of the men of violence. They had spared the convent and his church: praying for a dead archer, no matter if he was a hated enemy, had been a small price to pay.

Will Longdon went among Kynith's Welsh archers and gave the most senior of them the archer's pendant, Arianrhod, the Goddess of the Silver Wheel.

'You'll need to send two men to me so I can choose Kynith's successor to act as your ventenar. Find men who match his strength and belligerence in battle.'

The men looked sceptical. 'He was a hard bastard,' said one of them. 'I doubt there's one among us as unbending. You and him, you were at each other's throats in the beginning and Sir Thomas taught him a lesson or two. Kynith came round, Will Longdon, as well you know, to serve Sir Thomas and you loyally. He died a stupid death.'

'And Sir Thomas will seek out the man who killed him. Stand together and keep his memory alive so that when we face this man, the urge to avenge him will bring us victory.'

Their mumbled grunts were the affirmation Will Longdon needed. It was not unusual for men to desert when their leader died, but the promise that Blackstone would lead them to vengeance on Kynith's killer would cleave them to him.

Sir John Chandos questioned Beyard. If the English mercenary Ranulph de Hayle had fought on the side of the French at Cocherel and taken the Gascon prisoner, then any parole given him by the Prince would be cast aside. Now that he had murdered one of Blackstone's men there was sufficient cause for him to be brought to justice.

'I did not see his blazon at Cocherel,' said Beyard. 'But I saw him. The men with him were skinners. Two hundred and more. Some Germans, Spanish and Gascons but Hungarians as well. He was definitely there. He's the kind of man who would remove his blazon so we would not identify him. He's in the French's pay. When I was taken from the battlefield I and the other prisoners saw how viciously he attacked villagers. There were several of us. Two died from their wounds, another in the cell at the castle. He had sport with the others. He let his men kill them slowly. I was worth more to him because I was Lord de Grailly's captain. The castle is not his. He holds it for Charles of Blois.'

'And if he is behind its walls, then that is where he will stay,' said Chandos. 'He knows we cannot take it by siege. He will wait for Blois to face us and then he'll escape.'

'He's already gone,' said Killbere. 'He knows what to expect and if he's in the pay of the French staying behind those walls serves no purpose.'

'Gilbert's right,' said Blackstone. 'He's fled already. I'll find him and I'll have him drawn and quartered and send each part of him to the villages he destroyed.'

Beyard sighed. 'And I'll be the one wielding the axe, Sir Thomas.' He nodded towards ben Josef. 'Whatever potions he makes we should give to the horses. I can feel my strength returning. I saw Meulon training with his men and Renfred said he'd been wounded but the Jew had healed him.'

'It was a wound bad enough to bring him down,' said Killbere.

'Keep the Spaniard with us, Sir Thomas. He can question the boy who was captured with me. The lad was caught up in the fight but his French is poor so I couldn't understand much of what he was saying. But I think what happened to him is important.'

'He seems to trust you. He has a name?'

'Lázaro.'

'I'll have ben Josef question him when the boy's had some nourishment and is strong enough. Sit with him and reassure him that he's safe.'

Sir John Chandos nudged Blackstone. 'We need to talk.'

He led Blackstone and Killbere towards where the commanders waited at his pavilion. John de Montfort sat in a padded chair, one leg over the other, his impatience plain to see. When Blackstone and Chandos came into view, he jumped up. The English routier commanders waited stoically. Their companies had surrounded Auray and breached the low defences when Chandos ordered the archers to set fire to the roofs. The surrender had come quickly and Chandos had restrained de Montfort's Bretons from sweeping through the town.

'De Montfort insists on being in the front line,' said Chandos. 'Hugh Calveley has the bit between his teeth; he wants to be in the front ranks too but I have him in reserve. All these men want the glory but we must control the fight. And between us we must protect de Montfort. Winning the battle against Charles of Blois is worthless if Montfort is killed in the fray.'

'No man can wet-nurse another in a fight. You know that,' said Killbere.

Chandos nodded. 'What I do know is that if Calveley breaks ranks it might jeopardize the outcome. His brigands want booty. If he ignores his orders, his men will run amok.'

'Then you deal with him and I'll shadow de Montfort,' said Blackstone. 'I'll put my archers on the flanks and my men-at-arms at his shoulder. Have you asked him for money? We can buy more men or bribe others. There are still others like Hugh Calveley who can be commissioned to fight.'

'I asked but he hoards what money he has. I suspect he sleeps with it under his bed. His future, he tells me, depends on having gold to hand for favours that can be bought when he needs them.'

'For pity's sake, he's about to be given the damned duchy. How much more does he want? That money could help us turn the tide of battle.'

Chandos shook his head. 'Leave it be, Thomas. It's a lost argument. We just have to give him the benefit of our experience.' Chandos lowered his voice as they got closer to de Montfort. 'He needs it, I promise you.'

No sooner had they joined the young lord than de Montfort's impatience spilled over. 'Sir John, I ask again why we did not destroy Auray. If a message is to be sent to my enemy, then it should be bold and unhesitating.'

'What we have done serves its purpose,' said Chandos. 'We have blockaded the town and the route upriver. Charles de Blois's castle is under siege. We do not need to slaughter innocents. He will come.' The King's chief negotiator during the peace treaty had soothed many antagonistic lords and de Montfort's youth and inexperience posed little challenge.

'If I am to inherit Brittany, then its people must know that I will not tolerate disloyalty,' de Montfort said.

'They are loyal,' said Blackstone. 'But to Charles of Blois. The dead cannot bend a knee to you. You have granted them their lives today. That will be remembered. You have not set your Bretons among them to rape and murder. That will be remembered. If you had done otherwise that would never be forgotten.'

John de Montfort turned away from Blackstone and faced the routier captains. Hugh Calveley was a brawny man. It was said he ate for two men and fought like six.

'Sir Hugh?' de Montfort said. 'What do you think we should do? You have fought across France. You must have an opinion. Are we to sit here and do nothing?'

Hugh Calveley remained stony-faced. The Cheshire knight was a pragmatic fighter who served the Crown; he had forged his own company of mercenaries, men who were as loyal as Blackstone's were to him. If the whelp was looking for some comforting words he had turned to the wrong man. 'You ask me? I follow Sir John's command and Thomas Blackstone knows this land better than any other. Why don't you listen to them? You run the risk of disharmony, my lord. Stabbing away with a blunt argument does no one any good. The men know when their commanders are in disagreement and it seeps through them, it rankles. In the name of the King and for God's sake, relinquish your desire to lead where you have not led before.'

De Montfort's face coloured.

'And you were afraid I would upset him?' said Blackstone in an aside to Chandos.

Diplomat that he was, Chandos soothed de Montfort's discomfort. 'These men are here to give you victory. They have bled on the fields of France. Their bluntness comes from harsh experience.' He cast a warning glance to Calveley who needed no one to make excuses for him.

'And not one man here doubts your courage,' added Blackstone. 'You will be in the front rank. You will lead the army. Our suggestions are only to ensure that it gives you victory. Nothing less.'

John de Montfort's temper cooled. 'Then I had better see to my men,' he said and saved face by walking over to his waiting captains.

'Good to see you true to form, Hugh,' said Killbere.

'He'll bear a grudge, you know that,' said Blackstone.

'Aye, I dare say. The sooner this business is done with the better, Thomas,' said the Cheshire mercenary. 'My men have business to attend to elsewhere. The King might not openly confess to showing support for the upstart and the French the same for Blois, but we're the ones who have to win the duchy for him. There's little gain for us in this affair.' He cast a glance at the smouldering timbers of the burnt houses. 'And there was nothing worth scavenging here, anyway. Let's get to it and face Charles of Blois and his rabid dog de Hayle. You know he's likely to have run from the castle?'

'We thought the same,' said Chandos.

'He's bad for business,' said Calveley. 'He destroys too much in his path. Leaves nothing for the rest of us. The likes of me that is.' He grinned. 'He needs to be killed. Not just for what he did to your man,' he said to Blackstone.

'Then we need an agreement between us, Hugh. If anyone is going to kill him it will be me.'

PART TWO

HUNTING THE BEAST

CHAPTER SIXTEEN

Will Longdon looked at the twenty-three Welsh archers Kynith had led. They had proffered no one to take his place as ventenar.

'Is there not one among you?' Will Longdon asked the sullen men.

'Kynith ruled with his fist,' an archer said.

'Aye, and his tongue. None of us are so bold,' said another.

'And who'd want to tell his fellow bowmen how to shoot?' one of them asked.

'Would I teach my grandmother how to suck the yolk from an egg?' Longdon said. 'Or my father, if I knew who the bastard was, to hone a knife?'

The men grinned, shoulders shrugging, the ageless sign of men uncertain of themselves but who recognized another's life was no different than their own. 'We're better men if we have a leader,' another acknowledged.

'Aye,' came the chorus.

Will Longdon looked from face to face. Their mood seemed better. The loss of their fellow Welshman would pass. 'When Meuric Kynith led you, you obeyed his orders. There is not a man among us here under Sir Thomas's command who would tell you how to nock, draw and loose, but there has to be a man you respect to lead you so that when the time comes to stand your ground against a cavalry charge, then you will stay at that man's side.'

'We know each other,' said an archer. 'We will fight for the man at our side. There is no cause to doubt us.'

'I don't doubt you, but archers do not command themselves. We have fought with Sir Thomas and died when that whore-bitch Fate touched our shoulder. Who would you have stand between you and death? A man who harnesses his fear and shows others only his courage. A man who, when he gives an order, is obeyed without question. God's tears, I've followed Sir Thomas and Sir Gilbert into the devil's lair and if they had not stood firm we would have been lost. Meuric Kynith was such a man too. Honour him and choose another.'

The Welsh archers huddled like a pack of mangy dogs gnawing at the bone of indecision. Murmurs of agreement seeped above their bowed heads. One pushed another, who shook his head. Others urged him to stand as their spokesman.

Will Longdon's patience was nearing its limits. 'You scab-arsed whoresons will have to stand in front of charging horse and pikemen advancing in line. You cannot turn and run. You will need a leader who will stand his ground and you will stand with him. Who is it to be? I need an answer or by God I will send you to Sir Thomas and he will choose and then you will face him if you fail in your duty.'

The man nudged forward as the archers' spokesman pointed at Will Longdon's feet. 'You wear Kynith's boots. He cared more for them than he did a belly full of food and wine.'

'Kynith and me, we had a pact,' said Longdon. 'If I died first he would take my bow, if he died first I would take his boots.'

'They are a good fit,' said the archer.

'They are. Why else would I want them?'

'If you are in his boots then you can lead us. We will follow you.'

'I am a centenar. I command a hundred men. You need your own leader.'

'It's you or no one. We have decided.'

Stalemate. Longdon would have Kynith's archers at his shoulder while Jack Halfpenny commanded his own bowmen. He glared at the grim-looking men. Odds were they might desert if he did not agree and Blackstone could ill afford to lose them.

'I will brook no disobedience. And I swear by the Silver Wheel Goddess I wear at my throat I will put an arrow in the back of any man who turns and runs in battle. It is understood?'

The men nodded their assent.

'Then you've made a pact with the devil. You will stand with me in the front rank. The French like nothing more than killing Sir Thomas's archers.'

Renfred and his scouts brought news of Charles de Blois and his army drawing closer to relieve Auray. Blackstone hoped that de Hayle had joined him but suspected the killer knew when to run clear of a battle. Killing villagers and securing *patis* from towns was more to his liking.

'They'll be here in two days, Sir Thomas,' said Renfred. 'Bertrand du Guesclin has joined forces with him. I saw de Mauny's flags as well.'

'They were chasing the remnants of Navarre's army.'

'And Beaumanoir's blazon. The Breton lords have rallied to his cause,' said Renfred.

'You and your men get food and rest,' said Blackstone but then stepped closer and held his captain's reins. 'Then come to me. I have another task for you.'

Renfred dipped his head in acknowledgement and joined his men.

Two hours later Chandos looked to the horizon. 'The Breton lords are thinking of making a treaty. An agreement not to fight.'

'The Bretons here?' said Blackstone. 'In this camp?'

Chandos nodded. 'They are losing their stomach for a battle. There's talk that Brittany can be divided and if they convince de Montfort and are prepared to parley then we have already lost. Both sides want an agreement. Charles of Blois is a belligerent, stiff-necked man and although his Breton lords have rallied to his flag there are those among them who think agreement can be reached. I think de Montfort's followers here have been sending messengers.'

'You've spoken to de Montfort?'

'He's wavering. They have his ear.'

'I'll have his damned balls if he backs down now.' Blackstone looked back to de Montfort's pavilion. 'These peacocks puff out their chests and pretend they want to take the field against each other. If they withdraw with an agreement then they'll save face.'

'Thomas, I have no love for any of these Bretons but I will not allow minds to change now. The Prince and the King want Brittany. They shall have it. We will ride either side of de Montfort when the time comes and keep those who whisper in his ear away from him. But there is another matter. We have thieves among us.'

'I'd be surprised if we had not,' said Blackstone. 'Mind you, there's nothing here a man could take and hide if it were of value.'

'It's not a matter to treat lightly. Someone has stolen from de Montfort's pavilion.'

'Not his padded chair, surely?'

'For God's sake, Thomas. Two thousand francs have gone. He's ready to scourge the army to find the culprit. He's accusing our archers or any man who rides with us.'

'But you have stopped him from doing anything because to begin a witch hunt now would sow discord in the ranks and take his attention from the fight at hand.'

'I have. But when this business is done his wrath will fall on our heads.'

'I've had piss pots emptied on my head before now. After a while the stench goes. So too will his anger. Once we win the fight the same thing will happen. Two thousand francs is a spit in a lake compared to what he will gain. We need to keep his mind sharp on the task at hand. Now, let's get ready.'

The river north of Auray offered a ford, shallow enough for men to wade across. Blackstone and Chandos took up position on the rising ground on the opposite bank. The two were on the right flank with their men-at-arms and archers, leaving de Montfort in the centre. When the fighting began Blackstone would reinforce de Montfort, which allowed the younger man to think he was at the head of his army, leading it against his challenger for the duchy. Hugh Calveley was in reserve, sulking despite Blackstone's promise that they would win the day when he swept his men around the centre and cut off their enemy.

Blackstone rode to Will Longdon who had positioned the archers in a sawtooth formation between Killbere and William Ashford's men. A sheaf of arrows was stuck in the ground in front of each archer. 'Will, Jack Halfpenny has your back. What of the Welshmen?'

'They choose to be here, Thomas. I could find no one to command them.'

'Then give them their head when the time comes, do you understand?'

Concern creased Will Longdon's face. 'In what manner?'

'We won't fight on horseback. We're putting the horses to the rear. I want Blois and his men on their feet, encumbered with weight and tired by climbing up to us. They will see what we're doing and know their horses offer too tempting a target for you and your men.'

'We'll not be as effective against armoured men as we would against horses,' said Longdon.

'I know. Bring down those you can. Force them to raise their shields and huddle against your arrows. When you have done as much as you can come in hard and fast on our heels when the bloodletting starts. Sword and knife, Will. Get among them.'

Will Longdon nodded. 'These Welsh are a bloodthirsty lot, Thomas, but I'd fancy our chances more if we could kill as many as we can before we abandon our bows.'

'I have no wish to see you or any of the lads harmed, but the French and Bretons will not expect it. Speak to Jack, let him cover you as close as he can when you attack.'

There was no more to be said. The two men acknowledged each other and Blackstone turned the bastard horse away. Longdon faced the Welsh archers who were the closest in formation. 'I warned you. Today we'll see who can thrash the devil and keep the angels at his back.'

CHAPTER SEVENTEEN

The curse that was men's ambitions emerged a few hours later when over four thousand armoured horsemen came within sight of Auray's walls. A wild meadow of colour emerged as pennons and banners fluttered across the open ground. Sir John Chandos and de Montfort followed Blackstone's plan and placed their dismounted army in three front-line divisions with the archers on the right flank. Blackstone, Killbere, de Montfort and Chandos rode out to meet de Blois and his delegates, who splashed across the ford. Blackstone waited, letting them come to him. When the men drew up they remained silent as their eyes went beyond the riders and took in Blackstone's battle formation.

'We can avoid this conflict,' said one of the Breton lords.

'We cannot,' said Chandos.

John de Montfort glanced at the Prince's trusted adviser. 'Sir John, let us at least hear what they offer.'

Chandos shrugged. 'As you wish. Hurry, my Lord de Beaumanoir, the day is waiting.'

The Breton lord curbed his irritation. 'We wish to save good men from dying here today. We can divide Brittany. My Lord de Blois has considered what we, his advisers, have suggested.'

Blackstone's horse took a dislike to de Beaumanoir's mount and lunged against the reins, yellow teeth bared, intent on causing harm. Blackstone restrained its impulse.

'Your horse is like a pit bull dog,' said Charles de Blois after controlling his own mount. 'I know you, Sir Thomas, and am surprised the Prince sends you.'

'My horse senses fear, my lord. He does not tolerate it. Neither my Prince nor my King has sent me for, as you know, this does not concern them or your King. As for my presence, I heard that those who urged you into this war are now pissing their breeches at the thought of a fight and I wanted to see these wretches for myself.'

'You insult us all,' de Beaumanoir said before de Blois could answer. 'There are no cowards on this field today. Your manner is offensive, Blackstone.'

'His manner is always offensive,' said Killbere. 'I have lived with it for many years. It's something I encourage when addressing those who wish to retreat from battle.'

Killbere's additional insult was as vinegar poured into a wound.

'Are Killbere and Blackstone your mouthpiece, my Lord de Montfort?' said Charles de Blois.

'They are not.'

'Then let us parley before blood is spilt. For twenty-two years there has been civil war here. My French and Breton lords are advising me with Brittany's best interests at heart. Sir John Chandos, most respected Constable of Aquitaine, can offer his voice of reason. I believe you will see the wisdom in my advisers' suggestions.' De Blois nodded for de Beaumanoir to offer the terms.

'We will partition Brittany. Lord de Montfort will have the south and the west including the city of Nantes. My Lord of Blois will hold the north and east. We will submit these claims for the peerage and the title to our respective Kings.'

'These are the same terms you offered the Prince months ago,' said Blackstone. 'They were agreed and then my Lord of Blois reneged because his wife who holds the purse strings refused to abide by it.'

The sour look on de Blois's face confirmed Blackstone's comment. 'And I have relented and she has agreed. It is time for peace.'

'And you, Lord de Beaumanoir, you and the Breton barons agree to this?' said Sir John Chandos.

'We do, and we are certain that when you speak to those who support your claimant that they will see this is the way the matter should conclude.'

Blackstone leaned forward and curled his fist over one of the bastard horse's ears. 'I don't want my horse to hear men of honour grovelling for a corner of this worthless place. His disgust would result in violence. You, Lord de Beaumanoir, I last saw at Bergerac when my Prince came to receive fealty from the lords of Aquitaine and Brittany. You said his wife dressed like a whore. I warned you then to keep a curb on your tongue and I warn you now that if you or any of your snivelling Bretons come to parley again, I will kill you where you stand.'

The Bretons reined their horses.

'You should have died in that sewer in Bergerac,' said de Beaumanoir.

'And miss this fight against you? Why do you think I fought for my life? I knew you and your kind would one day need to be whipped like a village cur. This is the day.'

Charles de Blois heeled his horse.

Blackstone and the others watched them canter away to where their men had formed up, readying themselves for the fight should the talks fail. Shouted commands ordered the armoured knights to dismount. Blackstone yanked de Montfort's reins, startling the younger man; the expression of dread on his face was plain to see.

'You wanted a fight: this is how it begins. They are seething with anger from our insults. It will make them reckless. Look to your front and see the four thousand men who want you dead. Look left and right and see those who will keep you alive. Are you ready?'

'I am,' said John de Montfort in a whisper full of fear.

'Then do as we say and follow our lead and we will give you the Duchy of Brittany this day,' said Blackstone.

De Montfort nodded. Words failed him as he watched the massed troops he needed to defeat.

'There's the priest,' said Chandos. 'No man wants to die unshriven. It's Sunday. Get to mass, my lord, and pray for your soul.'

A cart had pulled up in front of the army. They had brought the priest from Auray to give thanks to God and absolution to the men who were about to kill or die. The priest found his balance and stood in the back of the open wagon before the gathered host with raised hands. Charles de Blois and his knights would adhere to the same ritual on their side of the river. A man's sins needed to be washed away, just as the river would sluice away their blood.

De Montfort spurred his horse. Blackstone and Killbere watched him.

'Well?' said Chandos. 'Will he come through this?'

'We'll make sure he does,' said Blackstone. He and Killbere turned their horses and rode along the flanks to the rear. Meulon was strapping on his broad leather belt. Ben Josef stood next to a wagon where the rescued boy and Beyard still lay. Blackstone saw the crease in Meulon's belt. He had tightened it an extra notch.

'You're not to fight, Meulon. Not in this battle at least.'

'Sir Thomas, I am healed enough. I'll not have my men fight without me.'

Blackstone glanced past him to where ben Josef shook his head.

'You're tightening your belt to aid the wound,' said Blackstone.

'The Jew has starved me. He feeds me little more than goat's milk and crushed grain. I shrink from his ministrations.'

'Goddammit, Meulon, you're twice the size of any man here. An ancient oak does not have the same girth,' said Killbere. 'You fight with that wound and it will tear. We bartered to have ben Josef with us so we may continue the fight when we are able.'

'I have fought with worse injury,' Meulon said.

'I want you here,' said Blackstone. 'You and twenty men are to guard Beyard, ben Josef and the boy. The bastard who killed Kynith is not among the enemy ranks. Beyard was his ransom and I doubt he'll let him escape so easily. I need you and Beyard alive and ready to fight again. The Prince has plans for us that go beyond this fight. Arm yourself, set up a perimeter and let no man approach within fifty paces without warning. You can be sure that if Ranulph de Hayle comes he will present himself as an English captain not as Ronec le Bête. I need you here, my friend.'

Meulon looked from Blackstone to Killbere. 'Very well, Sir Thomas. I'll do as you command.'

'And if he does get close, kill the whoreson,' said Killbere.

CHAPTER EIGHTEEN

Blackstone rode back to the front of the army. Sir John Chandos took up position, as did Killbere. Their horses were taken to the rear by the pages. Blackstone pulled the bastard horse up next to de Montfort.

'My lord, you are shriven?'

De Montfort nodded. 'And you, Sir Thomas?'

'God knows where I am if He needs me.'

De Montfort glanced at the pagan symbol nestling next to a small gold crucifix. 'You give yourself to Christ *and* the Goddess of the Silver Wheel?'

'I give myself to my sword that bears the swordmaster's mark of the running wolf. Beyond that it doesn't matter.' Blackstone looked across the enemy host, whose ranks were so tightly packed it would be hard to put a blade between one man and the next. Every man carried a five-foot-long spear and a short-handled battleaxe at his side as well as his sword and knife. 'They'll aim to come at us in unbroken ranks. It will be like hacking our way through a forest. The archers will slow them but men on foot do not yield as easily as if they were mounted – a screaming horse pierced with broadhead arrows thrashes in its agony and creates confusion. Today we'll have to attack when the men close ranks and cover themselves with shields against arrows raining down. That's when we'll break them.'

De Montfort licked his lips, his nervousness palpable. Blackstone handed him a wineskin. 'Drink,' he told the young knight.

'I am not afraid,' he said.

'Then you're a fool,' said Blackstone. 'They outnumber us. They are led by Bertrand du Guesclin, who is the best commander the French have. They are well armed, seasoned in war. Their sheer weight could crush us.'

De Montfort blinked. His eyes focused on the enemy; his heart thudded with the prospect of his own death. Of course he was scared. Sweat mottled his face beneath his helm.

'My lord, they raised you as ward of my King. He is the greatest warrior king known to any of us. Draw on his courage and steadfastness. And wet your throat. You must ride along the ranks and lift the men's hearts.'

'I... I would not know what to say to them. They are fighting men, Sir Thomas, and I am not yet tested.' De Montfort met Blackstone's eyes. Reality faced him. It was no time for false bravado. 'Ride with me. Let them see you.'

'My lord, this is your army. *You* must show them the way to victory.'

'Then tell me what to say,' de Montfort said, his voice edged with desperation.

Blackstone placed a hand on the young man's trembling arm. 'What you feel is common to us all. I will ride behind you and give you the words – softly – but you must rouse yourself and let every man of our two thousand hear you. Think that you are speaking to the men at the rear ranks. The breeze is at our back and will carry your words. We'll canter across the front rank, turn and then slow the horses so your voice will carry to everyone. Is that agreeable, my lord?'

'It is, and I am in your debt.'

'The only debt is to those men waiting to die for you. Now, give them the courage they need.'

De Montfort took a firm grip on the reins and dug in his heels. His courser lurched forward, eager to run off the bunched tension in its muscles. It was a fine horse, with a steady gait, and made de Montfort look like a man born in the saddle. He raised his arm as he rode past the men, the sense of occasion and Blackstone's encouragement giving him the appearance of a man ready to lead. Blackstone and the bastard horse with its uneven gait followed close behind. It snorted, fighting the bit, already sensing battle. Blackstone cursed; he needed the beast to behave long enough so he could prompt de Montfort, who turned at the end of the line and then calmed his horse and eased it back to a trot. Blackstone fell in on his blind side so the men would not see him guiding de Montfort's words.

'Today is a sacred day when God hears our prayers and blesses us with His grace because we have humbled ourselves before him,' de Montfort repeated what Blackstone told him. 'We fight the French again because they wish to deny our King's rightful claim over Brittany in my name: John de Montfort. We must fight twice our number but we are worth four times... FOUR times the value of every man who faces us. Look at them, how they huddle, shoulder to shoulder, fearful of fighting alone; they step forward with spears because they fear your sword and axe. They are already lost souls. To win this day is to gain great honour.'

De Montfort's voice rose as he warmed to his task and the mention of honour. Blackstone nudged the bastard horse closer so he was at his shoulder. 'Now you tell them there's looting and booty to be had,' he said.

De Montfort scowled. 'Today is about honour,' he insisted.

'No, today is about those men killing enough of your enemy so they can strip silver buckles, rich silks and weapons from the dead while leaving alive any worthy prisoners to be ransomed. Honour is for the knightly class, looting the dead for the others. Repeat what I tell you again and this time draw your sword, rise up in the stirrups and bellow so that even your enemy can hear you. Ready yourself, my lord, for now you must unleash the devil.'

De Montfort did and said everything Blackstone told him. He stood in the stirrups, sword aloft. 'You will find riches on the dead. They are yours for the taking! Fill your belly with fire and your hearts with lust for their silver! Kill them and take your rewards!'

A thunderous roar rose from the men. It swept across the hillside, rolling across the river and striking the French in a mailed fist of defiance and threat that wounded men's souls.

Blackstone pulled his horse away. 'Now we stand and fight,' he said.

CHAPTER NINETEEN

The French came forward so tightly packed the line of men wavered like an uncertain tide disrupted by the undulating ground beneath their feet. Blackstone stood a yard behind John de Montfort so that the divisions behind him saw him as their commander. Charles de Blois led his own men from the front, taking them across the shallow ford. French spears bobbed up and down as men stumbled and fell, the weight of their armour slowing their advance and their feet snagging on rocks and river stones. Men behind trampled them underfoot for the unrelenting march forward could not be stopped. Crossing the river fractured the tightly packed formation and only when they reached the near bank where Blackstone and the English army waited did they re-form. As each rank clambered up the hill those behind struggled to find their footing in the wet grass churned into mud by those ahead. The waiting men could hear their curses.

Blackstone saw de Montfort's impatience. 'Wait, my lord, they are not yet sufficiently tired. They still have to gather themselves. Sweat will blind them and chafe beneath their armour. Let them come.'

De Montfort nodded, still eager for the attack to begin. Blackstone looked away to the right flank where Will Longdon's archers stood ready, interspersed between Chandos's men-at-arms and where Killbere stood with Blackstone's men. The approaching French armour clanked and scraped as they shuffled tighter together. Their shields encumbered them, colourful blazons of beasts of the forest and birds of the air. Pennons bobbed, banners furled, dipped and rose again as their bearers struggled on, trying to keep their footing. Drumbeats drove them on. Steady, steady, another pace, another yard. Bellowing voices rose, commands to wheel centre and face the waiting army above them.

'Now?' said de Montfort.

'No,' said Blackstone.

De Montfort watched as Blackstone slipped Wolf's Sword blood knot over his wrist and settled his shield. It would be soon.

The rhythmic thump of drumbeat and men's footfall shook the ground. Any moment now and the archers would loose. Blackstone counted the seconds. Every stride nearer brought the French closer to death. Memory stirred in him. An extended arm, back bent from the effort of pulling the draw weight of his bow. The picture in his mind of where his arrow should fly. And then the release. Bend, pull another yard-long shaft from the cluster rammed in the ground at your feet. Bend, nock, draw and loose. Over and over as the air whistled and fluttered with thousands of arrows. The thud of impact. Hailstones on armour. Clattering, drowning out pain.

'Now?' de Montfort's voice eager. Jarring. Breaking the memory.

Blackstone felt rather than heard the creak of the yew bows. The intake of breath from the archers as they heaved their cords back. And then Will Longdon's cry. '*Loose!*'

Whoosh. Bird flight. Startled from the ground. Beating rapidly upwards. And again.

The French crouched, shields raised. Hundreds of drumbeats pounding down on them. And again. They bent a knee. Huddled. The storm hammered them. And again.

'Now!' said Blackstone and set off at the run.

De Montfort was taken by surprise and was immediately yards behind Blackstone and John Jacob. He gathered his wits and charged after them. The French were still bent beneath the onslaught of the archers' arrows. The final flight of death from the sky would be moments before Blackstone reached the enemy front division. Will Longdon understood how close his archers could shoot to the attacking men-at-arms. Once they clashed it would be time for the lightly armed archers to lay down their bows and join the fray.

The French raised themselves to meet the onslaught. Their spears wavered, and were then knocked aside by the attackers' impetus. Some caught men's groins or legs. De Montfort's front rank kept on, jumping over men writhing in pain. Blackstone and John Jacob broke through. Shields battering men aside, sword blades slashing and stabbing. Blackstone sensed rather than saw Chandos and Killbere press forward from the flank. The ripple ran across the French front division, a wave turning from striking a cliff face. Blackstone saw de Montfort pushing into the fractured front line three yards from him. The force of the attack had caused the French to falter but they quickly recovered and the weight of men from the rear began to trample over their own who lay wounded. It was as Blackstone planned. Tired men succumbing quickly to the onslaught and then being killed by their own weight of numbers. Their bodies slowing the enemy advance as they tried to clamber over their fallen comrades.

John Chandos and Killbere move forward from the sawtooth deployment, their men-at-arms plunging into the enemy's flank, protecting the archers. They pierced the French front division, forcing aside the shield wall that had been slow to recover from Will Longdon's bowmen's assault. The ferocious attack that had caused the ripple down the line forced Blackstone and de Montfort to hold their ground and stop the surge of desperate Frenchmen whose ranks broke into isolated pockets of men.

Blackstone felt the tide of the attack turn. Chandos was fighting forward towards Bertrand du Guesclin's banner. He was a prize worth having. De Montfort had men at his shoulder who hacked their way forward, clearing fighting space for him. John Jacob covered his one side, Blackstone the other. Stride by stride they slashed, jabbed and barged men down. De Montfort did not comprehend that Blackstone and the men around him had created a space ensuring no one struck him from his blind side.

Further ahead the banner of Charles de Blois remained aloft. Now that the second and third division of men, three thousand strong, had forced themselves up the incline, Blackstone knew that the English might not hold the ground. A barrel of wine once uncorked spills its contents: now he needed men to bleed away from the battle. Blackstone's strength forced back two noblemen. Their blazons bore the same emblem. Father and son? Cousins? Brothers? It made no difference. Blackstone rammed the one, jabbed Wolf Sword above the man's gorget and felt the hardened steel penetrate the visor's slit and find bone. The man's knees buckled. Blackstone yanked free the blade, heard amid the bellowing cacophony of men determined to live and kill a cry of despair from the second knight. '*Mon père!*' Blackstone heaved his shield up, felt it connect beneath the man's chin, his neck held in check by his helm's rim, forcing him to throw his arms wide trying to keep his balance. His arms flailed. Blackstone found the gap beneath his breastplate and lunged. The dead man's son fell, mortally wounded, his weight freeing the blade. A wife and mother would mourn.

As would many others.

And then the attacking impetus faltered. There was an almost imperceptible shiver in the French ranks. Blackstone saw a body of men desert from the Breton division. It was du Guesclin's men. They were abandoning the best fighting commander the French had. Those who saw them desert would ask themselves why.

But whatever the reason – now the tide would turn.

Will Longdon held back the archers. Armed only with buckler, sword and their archer's knives, they needed Sir John Chandos and Killbere to hurt the enemy before they could attack. He watched, bellowing for the Welshmen in his ranks to hold fast and rein back their blood lust and desire for plunder, waiting for the moment to set them loose. As the men-at-arms fought hand to hand the archers would run in fast and hamstring the Frenchmen beneath their own men's blades.

Then: 'Get in and take their legs from them! Seize their axes!' he shouted. The Frenchmen wore short-handled battleaxes on ropes around their neck or attached to their armour.

The lightly armed archers surged forward. French men-at-arms peered through their visor slits, sweat stinging their eyes, their steel helms ringing with the animal cry from more than a hundred foes who swarmed at them. Rabid dogs. Teeth bared. Fearless.

Some Frenchmen faltered but others seized the chance to kill the despised bowmen who had slain so many noblemen during the great battles. Around them, French knights continued to punish the English men-at-arms and some of Chandos's men suffered grievous wounds, but their defiance still held back the French, many of whom felt the searing sting of an archer's knife hamstringing them. When they fell, lame, borne down by the burly weight of an archer, those same razor-sharp blades plunged through visors as they squirmed on the ground. Heels drummed, legs bucked, but they could not escape the savage death inflicted.

Will Longdon cursed. He spat venom. Punched a spearman in the face and kicked him hard between the legs. The man vomited, spewing over Longdon. Behind him Jack Halfpenny had taken his twenty archers and followed John Chandos, whose men were cutting a path towards the French Captain of Normandy, Bertrand du Guesclin. Ransom was booty.

Knights jostled in their tight formation. Where a friend had been now was a bloodied corpse, the gap filled by another. Elbows clashed; swords were often useless. Men wrestled, grappling each other to the ground. Longdon heard Welsh curses and screams. Some of his men had gone too far forward. Defenceless against armour, shield and blade they went down, writhing. Arms severed. Legs hacked. Faces torn. Knights pulled up their visors, gasping for breath and freedom from the iron cage. Then they died under sword or knife.

Longdon caught a glimpse of Blackstone. He had cut a wedge towards Charles de Blois but the Breton's banner stood tall. Yet the French and Breton men-at-arms had made no ground.

Blackstone bent his back, brought his shield closer to his chest and forced his legs to pump harder. Two men fell under his weight, then a third. John Jacob followed at his shoulder and slew those who went down. De Montfort was isolated. He killed an axe-bearing knight but then looked around frantically as others closed in on him. His banner wavered and then fell as the enemy pummelled the bearer's helm. Blood spurted from the man's nose and mouth; dazed, he slipped in gore and entrails. A roar of victory rose above the screaming men. They thought de Montfort finished. They thought Brittany was theirs.

They thought wrong. Blackstone barged de Montfort aside to safety and stepped into the breach. There was no victory cry from those he killed. De Montfort regained his balance and stood shoulder to shoulder with him. The heaving mass swayed. Ragged gaps appeared in the French divisions, rent aside like strong hands tearing an emblazoned surcoat, the material resisting and then yielding.

'Now!' Blackstone yelled to de Montfort but the surrounding clamour drowned out his voice. De Montfort fought with courage. He lifted his visor to suck cool air into his bursting lungs. Blackstone swiped Wolf Sword's blade down, slamming it shut a heartbeat before a Frenchman jabbed his spear where de Montfort's face had been. The thrust put the spearman off balance. Wolf Sword arced and cut a wound into the man's neck so only sinew and skin held his head to his body.

Blackstone turned to John Jacob and made the command that should have been given by de Montfort. 'Now, John!'

John Jacob rammed his sword in the dirt and raised de Montfort's banner. He waved it back and forth as Blackstone protected him. A trumpet sounded, and then another: their notes soaring high above the noise of battle. The flag and the trumpet signal caused de Montfort to turn and look across the soldiers' bobbing heads, dipping and rising beneath bloodied swords and axes. He saw Hugh Calveley spur on his mercenary cavalry to outflank de Blois.

John Jacob thrust the banner into the hands of the nearest man, retrieved his sword and strode the few paces to where Blackstone shielded de Montfort. A French knight struck Blackstone hard with his shield as another rained repeated blows against him. A third man had isolated de Montfort. Blackstone blocked, parried and held his ground but were it not for John Jacob coming in at the side and killing one of the attackers Blackstone would have died. The two men were now a stride ahead of de Montfort, who benefited from their killing prowess. They heard Killbere's voice. He was twenty yards away, fighting through with Chandos. Du Guesclin's banner wavered – and then fell. A victorious cry went up from Chandos's men as they hoisted his flag. They had cut the heart out of the battle. Blackstone realized the most competent of the French commanders had been killed or captured and Killbere was leading the men in a flanking attack with the archers at his back, killing the fallen who had no value.

'Blois!' Blackstone bellowed. 'Where is he?'

Killbere had no time to answer as men-at-arms engulfed him; he disappeared from view under raised shields. Blackstone turned towards him. 'John!'

John Jacob and John de Montfort turned at their name. Neither hesitated but cut their way through the mêlée. As they turned so did the men behind them, determined to follow. The action shifted the weight of men in the battle and swayed the immediate outcome, fragmenting the French ranks. Hugh Calveley's horsemen smashed into their rear.

Blackstone's wheel towards Killbere and Chandos had cut the body of the French attack in two. Killbere was lying on the ground on his back across fallen men, knees raised to protect himself from sword points, shield tight across his body, head tucked in. He cursed every whoreson's mother for dropping them from her belly as they struck at him. Chandos was too far ahead to turn back. Blackstone's savagery carved a path to Killbere, and his attackers fell, mutilated, writhing in agony from vicious wounds. John Jacob and de Montfort despatched them as Blackstone leaned down and hauled Killbere to his feet.

'Gilbert? You're hurt?'

Killbere snapped back his visor. Blood trickled into his beard. He shook his head. Slammed down the visor again and, without another word, fought on. The four men became a phalanx. A broadhead arrow piercing through the French division whose strength had now crumbled. A ring of Chandos's men guarded a stocky bareheaded man with a swarthy complexion, his armour filled from his barrel chest. It was Bertrand du Guesclin, alive, captured by Chandos. He was a prize.

Chandos had veered away with his men as Will Longdon and the Welsh archers scurried across, piercing the visors of the fallen with their archer's knives. Jack Halfpenny had held his position with his archers ready to shoot should a counter-attack come in from their blind side, a flank that spilled away across undulating ground, curving down into a broad meadow valley protected either side by forests. If Charles de Blois had reserves, then they would swarm from concealment and, like a knife wound in a man's side, pierce the body of men. No threat appeared. Crushed and suffocated men sprawled underfoot; wounded raised an arm for mercy but none was given unless their blazon denoted rank and then they were claimed for ransom.

Blackstone and the men splashed across the ford in pursuit of the retreating French. In the distance Charles de Blois's banner wavered and fell. It signalled the end. His army turned and ran.

Blackstone and Killbere let the men behind them chase after the survivors. Killbere pulled free his helm and cowl. A blow had cut his scalp. He snorted snot from his nose and spat, then pulled off a gauntlet and tested the wound. It was nothing. He coughed and spat again, gasping for breath like every man around him. 'Much more of these blows to my head will scar me like animal tracks through a forest.'

'I need a new shield,' Blackstone said, freeing his arm from it. An axe remained embedded in it.

'A woodpecker would make less mess,' said Killbere. A hundred blade strikes scarred the shield.

John de Montfort bent double and vomited. He straightened. Men's cries became more distant. Blood trickled down his hand from an arm wound. Blackstone's open helm showed a blood-flecked face.

'Well, my lord. You have won the day. Time to honour our dead and reward the living,' said Blackstone.

A trumpet sounded ahead. Then another.

'That's Chandos. He summons you,' said Killbere. 'They've captured or killed de Blois.'

'Go, my lord,' said Blackstone. 'Claim your rightful title. You are Duke of Brittany now.'

De Montfort nodded and pressed a hand on Blackstone's arm. 'I will do as you say, Sir Thomas. You saved me and you rescued Brittany. I will not forget what you and these men have done this day.'

John de Montfort followed the clarion call and walked up the hill to where pockets of men gathered in the distance.

Blackstone turned away with Killbere and John Jacob. Will Longdon had retrieved his bow and weaved his way towards them. Dried blood on his hands and arms told their own story. He had a dozen silver inlaid belts over his shoulder.

'Will? How many archers did we lose?' said Blackstone.

'Nine or ten of the Welshmen. Halfpenny's lads are safe.' They splashed across the ford. The dead lay everywhere. A keening buzzard circled. Crows hopped from body to body, shooed away by looters stripping the corpses.

'We killed far more than we lost,' said John Jacob.

'Aye, but I don't know how,' said Blackstone. He raised Arianrhod to his lips. 'Angels at our backs.'

'And the devil in our sword arm,' said Killbere.

The rout continued across the distant ground. Those who had fought with Blackstone were content to let Chandos and de Montfort's men give chase and bear down on the straggling army. The view from where Blackstone and Killbere stood showed bodies scattered across the landscape. Death entwined men in their last desperate urge to live. Blackstone sluiced water over his head as men around him stripped off their armour and splashed themselves; others lay in the shallows and let the bloodied water wash the sweat and heat from them. Pennon bearers rammed the shafts into hedges, their blazons still flying aloft in victory. Men-at-arms lay back, drinking from wineskins, spreading out before them the stripped mail and plate they had scavenged.

'Sir Thomas!' John Jacob pointed to the top of the hill where Meulon and his men guarded the baggage train. Black smoke rose above the treeline.

Blackstone ran.

CHAPTER TWENTY

Meulon had watched the battle begin as the wall of men clambered up the incline. The three divisions looked ready to swamp Blackstone and the first line of defence but the throat-cutter had stood in such ranks in the past and knew Blackstone had planned well. Armoured men would struggle up the hill, and every advantage no matter how slight would aid those who opposed them; Blackstone's men never wore full armour.

Beyard was strong enough to walk unaided but if it came to a fight, he wouldn't last long. Meulon moved him and the boy into a depression behind a cluster of rocks. The boy was trembling from fear and when he tried to speak he stammered so that even the Spaniard ben Josef could make no sense of his words. The boy's comfort lay in being close to Beyard, whom he clearly considered his protector.

'Beyard, put an arm around the lad. He needs assurance that no harm will come to him,' said Meulon. 'He's shivering like an abandoned kitten in a rainstorm.'

'He'll be safe with me. Cover us with a shield and put a sword in my hand. If the bastard de Hayle comes, then we must all be ready.'

Meulon did as the Gascon captain requested. The rules of battle dictated a baggage train and its attendants and the pages who tended the horses should remain unmolested, but routiers paid no heed to the restrictions placed on men of honour. He ushered ben Josef to lie beneath an open cart and threw a blanket over him. Ben Josef clutched his medicine satchel to him as closely as Beyard held the boy.

Meulon used the wagons to set up a defence, placing his men between each one. He ordered the reluctant attendants to use the poles from their master's pavilions to build a barricade. Meulon needed only to glare at anyone who dared question his command for that demand to be carried out. He doused the cooking fires, and took six of his men and concealed them in the treeline. A handful of men coming out of hiding and striking an enemy from the rear if they penetrated the camp could turn the tide. How many of the Beast's men would come? Would de Hayle himself try to snatch Beyard? Was his ransom worth the risk? Meulon put his back against a wagon and helped the men shift it into position. His wound complained. He tested it again. He decided it would hold long enough to defend the camp in a fight.

Once the remaining twenty-five men-at-arms were in position, he waited. The roar from the fighting below meant little could be heard in the camp. Birds had fled, flying deeper into the forest. What warning would there be if de Hayle's mercenaries struck? He could do no more than he had done to defend the camp. And if the battle ebbing and flowing below turned in favour of Lord Charles de Blois, and they defeated de Montfort and Blackstone, then concern about an attack by mercenaries would be swept away by the rushing tide surging towards them. The pageboys and baggage attendants would be spared but they would kill him and his few defenders.

He lost sight of Blackstone. On the flank he could see Killbere fighting alongside Chandos and William Ashford. Behind them Will Longdon had finished shooting. De Montfort's banner showed him Blackstone again. He watched, rapt, the cut and thrust of the battle as men wavered and gaps opened in the battle line.

A buzzard circled high, waiting for the dead. Its piercing screech made Meulon turn and as he did so he saw a wisp of black smoke. A swarm of men was running silently around the edge of the forest that had concealed their approach long enough to be within thirty paces before they raised any alarm. One of them wore a leather apron across his shoulder and neck as protection from the burning, tar-filled rundlet he carried. The tar barrel would burn long and choke those downwind once hurled into the defenders.

'To your front!' he bellowed.

How many? Forty? More? No. Experience told him de Hayle had underestimated the strength of Meulon's defence. The arrogant bastard had sent barely thirty men to attack, expecting to find defenceless servants. They swarmed towards the men defending two of the wagons and the weight of their attack was enough to overpower them. Meulon knew the routiers' intention was to draw men away from the other positions to reinforce their comrades.

'Stand fast!' he shouted at the others, who had begun to desert their posts to aide their comrades just as de Hayle's men expected. 'Six men with me!'

The barrel carrier tossed it into the wagon: the folded tents made an ideal target. Black smoke billowed. The breeze caught it, aiding de Hayle's men as it smothered the camp. Meulon speared two attackers clambering over the low barricade. His six defenders locked shields. It made no difference. The routiers threw themselves over them. As Meulon expected, the attackers at the rear peeled away and sought out weak spots in the depleted defence. Meulon's men retreated, re-formed, and beat the enemy back. The thunderous cries from the battle below blanketed their own voices raised in anger and fear. Pageboys and attendants ran into the trees as de Hayle's men spilled into the camp. There was no sign of le Bête himself but his savage routiers needed no leader to show them how to kill. Three of the boys fleeing in panic fell under sword blows. Meulon's command formed up in a line across the centre of the camp and now the attackers were at a disadvantage. As Meulon's men from the other positions struck at them Meulon saw half a dozen routiers hold back. They peered in the wagons but didn't seem to find what they were looking for.

'Now!' Meulon shouted and his men plunged from the treeline and attacked the searchers. Three of the skinners had made it past Meulon's line when one of them saw the panicked boy try to break free from Beyard. The Gascon raised himself, dropped his sword and snatched at the lad, holding him tight, but was defenceless except for his shield. That saved him from the first attack. Meulon hurled his spear into the routier's back and, as Beyard fell, smothering the boy, reached the second mercenary, who was jabbing at Beyard. Meulon's sword blade rammed beneath the man's shoulder blade, caught in his ribs and had to be kicked free, which gave the third man time to reach down and seize Beyard. The Gascon captain twisted, slamming his shield upward, smashing the man's mouth. The man staggered, spat teeth and blood, and died quickly as Meulon dragged his knife across his throat.

As quickly as it started, the attack faltered when the others saw their victim still lived and his attackers lay dead. Meulon's men had killed seven and suffered three dead from their own ranks. The routiers turned and ran. Meulon looked around him. The camp was safe. He pulled the blanket off ben Josef. The old man flinched.

'It's all right; they've gone. Help the wounded.'

Meulon strode across to where fearful attendants peered from the trees. 'Get yourselves back here! Carry the dead away. Hurry. Move your arses.'

They came out, tentatively at first, and then, as the men-at-arms cursed them, they did Meulon's bidding. They were more frightened of the big bearded man than any chance of the routiers returning.

Meulon helped Beyard to his feet. 'Are you hurt?'

'No, but I'd be dead if it wasn't for you.' He tugged the shivering boy to him.

'We lost three men but we gave a good account of ourselves.' Meulon flashed a grin from behind his thick black beard. 'I didn't know you were worth so much. Being de Grailly's captain must carry a ransom worth risking a fight for.'

The Gascon shook his head. 'Not me. They wanted the boy.'

CHAPTER TWENTY-ONE

They were dragging the bodies away as Blackstone strode into camp. A breathless Killbere was not far behind. It didn't take long for Meulon to recount the fight.

'The boy? Why did they want him?'

'I don't know, Sir Thomas,' said Meulon. 'Beyard? You're sure about this?'

The weakened Gascon leaned his weight against a wagon. 'When they breached the defences they saw the lad. I thought it was me they wanted but when they came at me they reached for the boy. "Come on you little bastard," one of them said. Definitely the boy, Sir Thomas.'

'Where is he now?' said Killbere.

Meulon gestured to where ben Josef tended to the wounded. 'Helping him. Whatever's happened to the lad he's scared for his life and I thought the old man might help soothe him by speaking his own language.'

'All right,' said Blackstone. 'I'll have him watched and talk to ben Josef. I don't want the boy running off. We need to find out more.'

'He won't run,' said Beyard. 'He sticks to me like shit to a blanket. He was in that cell with me long enough to watch the others die. I was the only one who helped him. He'll stay with me and I'll feed him.'

Blackstone looked across the battlefield. 'Ranulph de Hayle took no part in the battle. He must have a reason for snatching him. He's playing both sides and as the boy has nothing to do with us then he must be of value to the French. Beyard, you're stronger?'

'The potions strengthen me every hour.'

'Then you will stay as the boy's guardian until we find out more.'

Blackstone looked to where the baggage attendants were heaping dirt on the burning tar barrel until they extinguished it. 'De Hayle hadn't expected to have a fight on his hands. I thank God you're healing, Meulon.'

Meulon looked at ben Josef again. 'He has a touch and a skill I have not seen before, Sir Thomas. I'm glad of it.'

'We need wine and food. Fighting sucks a man's vitals,' said Killbere. 'Thomas, let's rid ourselves of mail and plate and wash the stench of the fight from us. I'll get the attendants to fetch water.'

Killbere placed a hand on Meulon's arm as he passed. 'Well done, my friend.'

Will Longdon followed. 'This was a quiet camp when we left you in charge. Now we have to share it with the dead. I hope my loot was not in that wagon.'

'I fed the flames with it,' said Meulon.

Longdon grinned. 'I would expect nothing less.'

Blackstone pulled fingers through his wet hair. 'Has Renfred returned?'

Meulon shook his head.

Blackstone winced. 'I sent him into a viper's nest. Post sentries. Let's not give de Hayle a chance to mount a sneak attack when the army is scattered and our guard is down. He tried once; if I were him I would strike again when an enemy thought an attack had failed.'

Meulon grunted, cleared his throat and spat. 'But he's not you, Sir Thomas.'

*

Blackstone regrouped his men-at-arms and archers. While others ate and drank, Blackstone's men cleaned their weapons ready to fight again. Once that was done they gathered together, a company of men bonded over the years by Thomas Blackstone, separate from Chandos and de Montfort's men. Will Longdon had lost seven archers, killed when they ran into the fight; more had light wounds. William Ashford brought his contingent back to camp after chasing the enemy survivors. His weariness was plain to see and as his sergeants organized his men, Blackstone went to greet him. He handed him a wineskin.

'You must have chased them halfway to Paris,' said Blackstone.

Ashford gulped down the wine, uncaring that it spilled over his beard. He dragged the back of his hand across his mouth. 'Merciful Christ, Sir Thomas, the assault swept us along with Chandos. Once Blois's banner fell Lord de Montfort went over those hills like a hound chasing a rabbit. You must have put fire in his belly.'

'He did well; we cannot deny him that. You have prisoners?'

'Me and the sergeants took a few for ransom. Nothing like Chandos, mind – my God, he bagged Bertrand du Guesclin; he'll be worth thousands. More than. No, we got some of the lesser knights; they'll bring in enough. We'll put them with the others so we all share in the spoils. And you, Sir Thomas?'

'Norman lords and their knights. They surrendered quickly enough once we overwhelmed them. I have their parole. We won't have to fight again until next year, thanks to the money from their ransoms. What of Charles of Blois? Any word?'

'We came across him lying dead surrounded by his men. It looked as though he put up a good fight but...' Ashford shrugged. 'Fate abandoned him.'

'Where are de Montfort and Chandos now?'

'Their heralds are going among the dead identifying their blazons. Chandos has pickets out to stop locals robbing the bodies.' The two men watched as men streamed back in ones and twos, small groups of comrades who joked and laughed at their victory and their survival. Tales of exaggerated prowess already being bantered back and forth. All of them carried booty.

'He allows the men to take what they find providing it is not from a high-ranking nobleman,' said Ashford. He drank again and corked the wineskin, handing it back to Blackstone. 'We were outnumbered but it worked in our favour. We moved faster and carved into them.'

'Have they made a count of the French and Breton dead?'

'The heralds think eight hundred or more killed. Hundreds died in the crush when they fell and were trampled from those pressing behind them, and near enough two thousand captured. When they fought their divisions were jammed like debris in a river. We went around them and through them. They ended in chaos but it must be God's blessing that we escaped with so few casualties.'

'The blessing was having strong men determined to fight harder than the enemy with a sword arm that never tired.'

William Ashford smiled. 'That too. I must get to my men.'

'Did you see Renfred anywhere?'

'He's not here?'

'No.'

'You think he fell in the fight?'

'I don't know.'

Ashford went on to his men as Blackstone stood gazing at the devastation on the battlefield. Behind him smoke rose from campfires; men prepared food and quaffed wine. Others stripped and bathed in the river. Servants hastily erected pavilions for the noblemen who would return with de Montfort. The aftermath of battle: the banality of everyday duties.

CHAPTER TWENTY-TWO

Jack Halfpenny and his archers were on the battlefield pulling arrows from the dead so that the shafts might be used again when the victorious John de Montfort returned with Chandos. A sergeant-at-arms and his men escorted a bound prisoner. Men gathered to watch the wretched man manhandled up to de Montfort's pavilion. Halfpenny ran hard and fast uphill to where Blackstone and Killbere sat with John Jacob next to their fire. Killbere was reclining, an arm across his eyes as he dozed. Remnants of de Montfort's army were scattered haphazardly across the fields: fires lit, food cooked, men claimed by exhaustion and relief at being alive and, for many, without serious wounds. It was only Blackstone's men who had regrouped and formed a tight body. If a command were given to rise up and take arms, only they would be ready.

'Jack?' said Blackstone as the distressed archer reached them.

'Sir Thomas, they've got Renfred. He's going to hang.'

No sooner had Halfpenny spoken than Blackstone and Killbere were on their feet.

'Who's going to hang him?' said Killbere.

'Lord de Montfort.'

'Where?' said Blackstone buckling on Wolf Sword.

Jack Halfpenny pointed to the far end of the encampment where de Montfort and Chandos's pavilions were surrounded by their knights and noblemen. Blackstone set off, his stride twice that of the others, who doubled their pace as they picked their way through the disorganized troops resting on the ground. Will Longdon and Meulon, who had been arguing about the merits of fat whores over that of skinny ones, saw Blackstone leading John Jacob, Halfpenny and Killbere. The veteran archer and throat-cutter sensed trouble and went after them. Blackstone's men rose and followed like a ripple of danger lifting a flock of birds from the ground.

At the centre of the camp, servants were bringing seated noblemen food and refreshment. They watched as their men threw a rope over pavilion poles hastily bound to make a gallows. De Montfort, stripped of armour, gambeson and shirt, wore an embroidered robe. He sipped wine from a silver goblet, his hair combed back, still damp from plunging his head into a bucket of fresh water to sluice away the grime. He was flushed with victory and spoke animatedly with his noblemen. His laughter subsided when he saw half a dozen men-at-arms step into Blackstone's path. They were there to stop any unauthorized approach to their lord and were as confident with their success in battle as their master. Their leader raised a hand and called for Blackstone to stop and state his business. It was a mistake. The force from Blackstone's fist threw him against the others. They reached for their swords but Killbere and John Jacob already had theirs drawn. De Montfort's shock caused him to take a step back. The goblet fell from his hand. Beyond Killbere, Blackstone's men ranged themselves, hands resting on weapons, ready to cause violence the moment Blackstone gave the signal.

'You dare?' said de Montfort, gasping at Blackstone's audacity. His knights and noblemen were on their feet, but unprepared. Their weapons were being cleaned by servants.

Blackstone looked to where Renfred knelt, hands bound behind him, a rope around his neck forcing his head back as the two men ready to haul him onto the cart and his death were pushed away by Killbere and Jack Halfpenny.

'Renfred is my man. You have no right to take his life. He is *my* man.' Blackstone signalled to Killbere. 'Cut him free.'

A flustered John de Montfort looked panic-stricken as he searched across the heads of the men drawn to the confrontation but saw no sign of John Chandos. 'Sir John!' he called.

Blackstone was so close he could have reached out and taken him by the throat. 'Don't call for your wet nurse. You will not be suckling off victory's teat after today if you hurt my man. Why have you taken Renfred?'

'You dare...' de Montfort repeated himself, trying vainly to find authority in his voice. '... to challenge me? To question my authority here?'

'Your authority ended when Charles of Blois was found dead on the field of battle. Sir John Chandos and I gave you triumph over your enemy. You may be the Duke of Brittany but you do not seize my men without my permission.'

'He is a thief!' said de Montfort – a proclamation to anyone within earshot.

'He is my captain and he is no thief. I vouch for him.'

Servants ran forward with their master's weapons and now Blackstone stood facing men whose sworn lord had been threatened and insulted. Blackstone's obvious contempt was enough to make one of them stride forward. An arrow thumped into the ground barely a yard in front of him. De Montfort's knights saw Will Longdon and twenty archers with arrows nocked.

'You overstep the mark,' said Blackstone to the chastened knight. 'I have come for Renfred and I will leave with him and then you, my Lord de Montfort, can return to your bragging of how you won the battle.'

The gathered men's mood was turning more belligerent and as word spread of the confrontation soldiers raised themselves from their cooking fires and began to move towards de Montfort's pavilion. The sight of those approaching boosted de Montfort's confidence but before he could preen his feathers Chandos's gruff voice separated the crowd.

'Can't a man have a shit in peace? What is this?'

'Sir Thomas insults and threatens me. I demand he is reprimanded, Sir John. You are the Prince's Constable; you outrank him and his behaviour is intolerable. I will ensure the King and the Prince hear of it.'

John Chandos was renowned for his diplomatic skills. He had negotiated with the French after the Treaty of Brétigny, had mollified the Dauphin, brought French towns under the English flag and in the past few hours had achieved his King's desire and helped deliver the Duchy of Brittany into the hands of de Montfort. Such skills were not enough to restrain him.

'God's blood, you should kiss Sir Thomas's arse. It is he who delivered the day to you. Whatever he says or does is beyond reproach when you have been handed such a prize.'

De Montfort's face flushed with colour. There was a collective gasp from those close enough to hear the rebuke.

'Now what have *you* done to deserve Sir Thomas's displeasure? That is the question, my Lord de Montfort, Duke of Brittany,' Chandos continued.

For a moment de Montfort's jaw did not respond to his swirling thoughts. It opened and closed and then finally he regained his composure.

'I will be treated with respect,' he said.

'Aye, you've earned a modicum of that, I'll grant you, but you should find humility before God and go on bended knee and give thanks for victory and for having Sir Thomas Blackstone at your side. Respect is due to him and his men.

They have scant reward for their efforts – unlike you. I await your answer, de Montfort. What act have you committed that has caused this disagreement?'

'My men caught a thief. It is one of Blackstone's men.'

Chandos looked to where Renfred stood, dried blood on his face, flanked by Killbere and Jack Halfpenny.

'You mean Sir Thomas? Respect, my lord. Remember?'

De Montfort grimaced. Perhaps from the bile that rose into his throat. 'As you wish, but they found his man with some of my gold and silver coin. More than two thousand francs were stolen before the battle.'

Chandos looked at Blackstone.

'Renfred is no thief,' Blackstone told him.

De Montfort pointed a finger, stopping Blackstone from offering any further defence. 'You do not have the evidence. My blazon was on the satchel, stolen from my pavilion.'

Chandos had no choice but to question Blackstone. 'Thomas? What's happened here? I know your captain. Renfred would not steal.'

'Of course he wouldn't,' said Blackstone. 'I stole the money.'

Blackstone might as well have struck de Montfort across the face. He staggered back, dazed by the revelation. Even Chandos could not mask his surprise.

'I asked you for gold and silver, de Montfort, but you cosseted it like a hen sitting on eggs. Money is to be used. The odds against us were too great. No matter how valiantly our men fought, the sheer weight of numbers would have crushed us. Therefore I came into your pavilion and took the coin, and then I sent Renfred with it into the heart of the enemy. The Bretons are greedy: whoever offers them more they will take it. You saw them desert. Why did they leave the battle? Abandon a leader such as du Guesclin? Renfred – risking his life – told them that if they deserted they would be paid. Better to collect gold and silver for certain than risk dying before getting the chance to loot the battlefield, no? It was a gamble, but it worked. Your gold weakened the enemy. It helped give you victory. You must learn who to trust. Decide, young Lord of Brittany. Do you wish to put a rope around my neck? Or even try?'

The dumbfounded silence was all the answer Blackstone needed. He looked at Chandos.

'My men and I will leave at dawn. We've done our part. Let us hope we helped the right man win.'

CHAPTER TWENTY-THREE

A week later Blackstone and the men looked at the twenty or more defenders who had been hanged from Villaines's town walls. Wisps of smoke persisted from smouldering timbers on torched houses. Blackstone kneed the bastard horse towards the gates. The town's captain Godfrey de Claville, who had accepted payment for ben Josef and given safe passage so that Meulon could be treated, hung over the main entrance to the town. His limbs had been severed; his entrails spilled from the open cavity. His mutilated body was an obscene act of violence from the vile creature Ranulph de Hayle who rightly called himself le Bête.

'That son of a whore de Hayle is the culprit. Look there,' confirmed Killbere, pointing to men slain by crossbowmen. 'They wear his colours. The bowmen took some skinners down before they overwhelmed them.'

'I am responsible for what's happened here,' said Blackstone.

Killbere groaned. 'Mother of God, Thomas, you are not.'

'He must have come here after he killed Kynith at the river. He made a run for it and took revenge for losing Beyard,' said John Jacob. 'Why here?'

'It was in his path,' said Killbere. 'It could have been any village or town.'

'And we brought the survivors here for safety from his previous attacks,' said Blackstone.

The men let their gaze settle on the slaughter. Bodies lay where they had fallen. A trail of them led away from the town, cut down as they ran. The killing looked little different from the scattered dead across the fields after the battle at Auray.

'Godfrey de Claville said he did not have enough men to defend the town if de Hayle attacked. I promised to bring him the bastard's head. I failed. Now everyone we saved and these townspeople are dead. The debt mounts up, Gilbert. Their blood is on my hands.'

'If the coward had fought in the battle, you would have kept the promise. You cannot kill someone who does not present himself,' said Killbere.

Meulon nudged his horse forward. 'Sir Thomas, do we take them down from the walls? Bury them?'

Blackstone shook his head. 'The French will come. Leave them to their own.' He tugged the reins to turn the bastard horse and saw Halif ben Josef running from the wagon, robes flapping.

'Ben Josef!' Beyard shouted.

The surgeon skirted the men's horses and ran into the town. Blackstone rode after him as he turned into a side street. Killbere and John Jacob followed. The bastard horse ignored the dead lying in the street and cantered across their torn bodies. Ben Josef knelt before a ruined house. Four bodies lay at the entrance, two of whom were children. The surgeon sat palms upward, muttering to the God he followed.

Blackstone dismounted. 'Master ben Josef. Is this your family?'

The old man stared at the two dead children. Their heads had been caved in from what must have been savage blows from a mace.

'Master ben Josef?' Blackstone said again as he dismounted, the tenderness in his voice drawing the man's attention away from the dead.

The kneeling man wiped a hand across his face. Blackstone gently helped him as he struggled to his feet. Ben Josef nodded his thanks. He sighed, and pointed at the dead. 'I saved these children as surely as I saved your man, Sir Thomas. This family put aside any ill feeling towards me – a Jew, a humbled prisoner whose life could be ended in a heartbeat – and then they welcomed me into their home. Against the wishes of their neighbours. Even against the harsh words of their priest. Their gratitude touched me.'

'There's nothing we can do here.'

'You should give them a Christian burial.'

'No, we must ride on.'

'You are a Christian. Do you abandon their souls?'

'I abandon their bodies. Wherever a soul goes, theirs have already departed. I leave that to the Almighty.'

He eased ben Josef away from the bodies as the old physician murmured, 'May the All-Merciful One shelter them with the cover of His wings forever. I will offer my own prayers for them. I beg you. A few moments.'

Blackstone looked around the devastation. Ranulph de Hayle had done little damage to the town's buildings other than burning a few of them. An eerie silence had settled over the place. The scattered bodies seemed out of place. Men, women and children lying as though a powerful wind had cast them down. Perhaps that was God's hand. Killbere eased his horse forward.

'We should move on, Thomas.'

'Gather the men beyond the town. I'll join you.'

Killbere looked from Blackstone to ben Josef, whose open palms were raised heavenward. His eyes were closed; his lips muttered prayers in a language neither Killbere nor Blackstone understood. Killbere shrugged and turned his horse.

Blackstone stood back from the old man's prayers. Le Bête and his men had killed for the pleasure of it. Was it simple blood-lust or was there a greater reason to inflict this suffering? 'It's time,' said Blackstone. Too many prayers dulled a man's brain.

The old man clutched Blackstone's arm. 'There is something I should have told you. I did not think it was important before, but now... This killer has evaded God and embraced the low creatures from the shadows. He is in league with the Angel of Death. I believe I know why he returned here and did this.'

'I offered you my protection. Have you abused my trust?'

'No, no, Sir Thomas, I pray I have not. But sometimes a man drops a clay dish and it shatters so that we do not find all the pieces. So it is with this killing here. My mind makes the pieces fit.'

'Ben Josef, I don't have time for riddles.'

The old man nodded furiously, eager not to have Blackstone dismiss him, yet his steps were faltering, holding back. 'Before you first came here the killer arrived and paid for prisoners from the battle at Cocherel. He and Godfrey de Claville spoke privately.'

'De Claville let him inside the walls?'

'Yes.'

'But he was afraid of de Hayle. He asked me to kill him. I made him that promise. I failed him and this is the result.'

'I believe you are wrong. De Claville took le Bête's money for the Spanish captives and your money for me. I was worth more because of my skills. Better I was kept under lock and key to treat the sick and wounded. But you brought your friend and de Claville saw your need to keep your man alive. Godfrey de Claville was an opportunist. He let you bargain for me. And he urged you to kill de Hayle. That would have stopped any further threat from him against this place.'

'Old man, you're rambling. I am lost. What does any of this have to do with de Hayle coming back here and killing those that did not escape?'

'The boy! Godfrey de Claville sold the boy. That's whom de Hayle was searching for. It is simple. You see it, don't you?'

For a moment Blackstone did not. Then he did. 'I took his prize. It was not Beyard. And how else could I have known about Beyard, and the boy, being kept in the castle at Auray if the information did not come from here.'

'Yes, yes! And that is why he came back to exact revenge.'

'Then why is this boy so damned important?'

CHAPTER TWENTY-FOUR

The stench of death was downwind by the time they camped in woodland on rising round with a clear view of the surrounding countryside. Blackstone summoned Beyard, who had regained much of his strength.

'This boy is the key. Tell me everything that you know and that he has said since they captured you at Cocherel,' Blackstone said.

Beyard played out his memory. 'I was taken to Auray by one of the French lords. I don't remember much because they beat me senseless. Then one day an Englishman arrived and threw some Navarrese prisoners and the lad in the cell with me. I tried to comfort him but he could barely speak – terror had made him mute. The Englishman was Ranulph de Hayle. I was so weak I could do nothing but lie there and watch as he took prisoners out and tortured them to death. He forced the lad to watch. Now I understand that he was trying to get the boy to talk. About what, I don't know. The more de Hayle killed the more the boy withdrew.'

'He never spoke?'

'You saw that dungeon. It was infested with rats and so cold we had to huddle together to survive. I held the boy close to keep him warm. I learnt his name but that was all. I tried to get him to talk but he was just too frightened.'

'What are we to do?' said Killbere. 'If the boy has something vital to tell, something de Hayle wanted, then it's buried in his silence.'

'He cannot be enticed to reveal it no matter what bribe might be offered,' said Beyard.

'So we make the lad feel safe,' said Blackstone. 'We treat him with kindness. No harsh words. He will help in whatever work can be found for him. Does he speak any French or English?'

'I believe some French. Sometimes when I spoke to the prisoners who knew my Lord de Grailly I could see he understood a bit of what I said.'

Blackstone thought for a moment. 'Until we uncover the boy's secret we must protect him. We don't crowd close to him but keep watch at a distance. We go about our daily work, but every captain will take his turn and stay vigilant. Beyard, you will tell him that I wish to speak to him. Do not bring him to me in case he thinks he is being brought for punishment or interrogation by someone in authority. I'll go to him and I want you there when I do. After we have eaten is best. Make sure he's well fed and warmed by a fire. We'll question him slowly. I think it will take time. And until that time comes we double the pickets at night. De Hayle's men outnumber us and if they are tracking our journey, then I see no reason why they would not try to seize back their prize.'

John Jacob attended to the fire and settled the blackened cooking pot over the flames. 'Why keep a secret if you're among those who rescued you?' said the squire.

'Fear dries more than the mouth, John. It takes hold of the mind, pushes it into a dark place then slams closed the door and throws away the key.'

'Like hunger and my stomach,' said Killbere. 'The secret to unlock my misery is for you to make some oatcakes, John.'

'No, Sir Gilbert, that's a luxury you must wait for. Pea pottage with garlic and sage and a few old breadcrumbs to thicken it.'

'Peas.' Killbere sighed. 'They loosen my bowels. I need something to cling to my ribs.'

Blackstone reached into a hessian sack. 'Will and Jack are hunting. If they get back in time John will cook you a choice cut.' He pulled a piece of horse bread from a sack. 'I had one of the lads make a batch while we waited for Hugh Calveley before the fight at Auray. This'll bind you.' He tossed it to Killbere.

'Thomas, hunger is the enemy of a fighting man. When he becomes a beggar at the door of necessity, he will boil his leather belt if that is all he has to eat.' Killbere sniffed the offering and bit carefully into the baked cake of crushed peas and beans held together with bran. 'It's stale,' he said but kept chewing.

'I thought so,' said Blackstone. 'My horse spat his out.'

When the men had eaten their meagre pottage Blackstone walked through the camp checking the picket lines, stopping here and there to speak to the men. Blackstone never had cause to check up on his captains. They knew their duties, so whatever his reason for inspecting the camp they knew it had nothing to do with them.

'Is the boy looking?' said Blackstone to John Jacob, who accompanied him.

John Jacob saw Beyard out of the corner of his eye. The boy was with him, scraping the pot for the last remnants of food, his gaze following the tall, scar-faced Englishman who led the men and whom his new friend and protector Beyard honoured. John Jacob saw Beyard nod. 'He hasn't taken his eyes off us, Sir Thomas. Beyard has just given a sign that he's ready.'

'All right. We'll walk the perimeter and then make our way around to where they are.'

They moved closer and pretended to confirm that the horses were tied and hobbled securely. Then they made their way back, which brought them past Beyard. The boy cowered, eyes lowered, pushing his shoulder into Beyard, seeking comfort.

John Jacob sidled away, leaving Blackstone alone with the boy and his chosen guardian.

'Beyard, you're well now?' said Blackstone, making light conversation for the sake of the boy.

The Gascon captain nodded. 'I am recovered, Sir Thomas. Strong as ever. Lázaro here has been helping me clean weapons and feed my horse. He's a strong worker. Lázaro, greet Sir Thomas. He is my friend and saved us from the dungeon at Auray.'

The boy raised his eyes to look at Beyard, who nodded his encouragement. Lázaro reached out for Blackstone's hand and kissed it, but remained silent. Blackstone gently held his hand and turned it to look at the palm. The lad flinched.

'It's all right, Lázaro,' said Blackstone, releasing him. 'He has callouses on his hands. He's no kitchen boy. He's used to hard labour yet he's as scrawny as a starved rat. Has he said anything more?'

Beyard shook his head. He placed a hand on the boy's shoulder. 'There is something,' he said. He turned Lázaro, who offered no resistance, and lifted his shirt. There were dull marks on his back: old scars. Someone had whipped him. Beyard settled the shirt and brought the boy back to face Blackstone.

'If you tell Sir Thomas how you got those scars, we will stand in good favour with him.'

Lázaro remained silent.

'Was it your master who did it?' said Blackstone.

There was no answer.

'Was it your mistress?' said Beyard.

The boy's eyes widened at the thought and he shook his head.

His answer gave a clue. He had served a noblewoman at some stage but there was still more to uncover.

Beyard was about to interrogate him further but Blackstone raised a hand, not wishing his captain to press him. 'No more questions, Beyard. We rode hard today. Let's get our sleep. Lázaro, I know you understand enough of what is said. You are safe with us. You're under my protection, but there are men who wish to cause you harm. We have stopped them once but – although we will not press you for answers – it would help if you tell us why you are important to them. When you wake tomorrow, look at the meadow flowers around us. Watch how their petals open to welcome the sunlight. Open your heart to us so you may feel the warmth of our friendship.'

Then, without another word, he bade goodnight to his captain and the boy as he saw Will Longdon and three of his Welsh archers approach the camp. They brought no fresh meat and came at the run. The look on their faces told him they had found trouble.

Longdon drew breath and spat phlegm. 'Horsemen. About six or seven. They looked like a scouting party.'

'Show me where.'

Will Longdon went down on one knee and made a crude model with stones and grass. 'This is us. The forest goes down into the meadows here.' He scraped his knife blade in the ground. 'Tracks through the forest here and here. We saw them ride across the valley floor. I think they're camped in the trees here.'

'How far?'

Will Longdon grimaced. 'No more than two miles over that ridge beyond this forest.'

Blackstone looked at the camp's cooking fires. By now most were deep-bedded embers heating cooking pots. The breeze tugged at the treetops. 'We're downwind from them so they won't catch our woodsmoke or smell our food. Do you have room to shoot where they are?'

Will Longdon saw the distance from one edge of forest to the other in his mind's eye. 'Too far for accuracy.' He stabbed his knife point into the model. 'Here. If I have a couple of bowmen at the very end of the forest and if they make a run for it, we could bring them down. The open ground narrows there.'

'Pick three men, then take us to where you saw their tracks. I'll take three others with me. Any more and there's a risk we'll be heard on our approach. If we flush them out you kill them. The moon will be up. You'll have light.' Blackstone left Will Longdon and strode to Killbere and John Jacob.

'Will's seen riders.'

'De Hayle's men?' said Killbere, getting to his feet.

'Probably – they're close. A couple of miles beyond the ridge. I'll take John and two others. If we can get a prisoner, we might learn more about the boy and why he is so important. Secure the camp. Let the fires burn down. Keep an eye on the breeze; it might veer. They're upwind of us now but if the wind changes they'll soon know we're here.' Blackstone unsheathed Wolf Sword and cast aside the scabbard. 'John, pick two of the men. Make sure they have no wounds that will slow us down or put us at a disadvantage in a fight.'

John Jacob turned on his heel to do Blackstone's bidding.

'Gilbert, have the camp ready for an assault. If the men Will saw are a scouting party then de Hayle's men won't be too far behind and we won't know how close they are until we capture one of them. Saddle the horses and be ready to ride at first light, because that's when they'll come if we're not back by then.'

'We'll defend the place should they come before then,' said Killbere.

'They outnumber us; we still have wounded. Send pickets out on night watch. De Hayle won't come through the forest. That's your way out. He'll come up that hill on horseback hard and fast.'

'And you? Where do we meet up if you're not back by dawn and de Hayle attacks?'

'I'll find you.' Blackstone grinned. 'But I'll be back before dawn.'

'Aye, and if you're not then likely you're dead.' He put a finger against each nostril and cleared the snot from his nose. 'Leaving me the damned job of getting everyone back to the Prince. He'll be pissing blood if the King's Master of War dies in a skirmish. A damned useless fight to get a prisoner.'

'I apologize now should my death cause you any inconvenience.'

'Then make damned sure you don't get yourself killed. Sweet merciful Mother of God, the Prince will never let me hear the end of it. He'll blame me. My life on earth will be hell even if you're sleeping with the angels, though I doubt they'll put up with you as long as I have.'

John Jacob returned with two men-at-arms. Blackstone led the way to where Will Longdon and his archers waited.

Killbere called after him. 'And if they have meat, bring it!' He watched as Blackstone raised a hand in acknowledgement. 'A man shouldn't have to fight on an empty stomach,' he muttered to himself.

CHAPTER TWENTY-FIVE

Will Longdon was as good a hunter as Blackstone and the stocky bowman led the men behind him unerringly through the forest, using narrow, twisting animal tracks. By the time they reached the edge of the forest, dusk was settling across the open ground. Four hundred yards across the undulating grassland, the forest opposite became darker as the light faded. Crows and rooks squabbled before settling to roost for the night. Blackstone and the men squatted beneath their own canopy and let their eyes settle on the distance, watching for any movement in the far trees. Further along the valley, nervous deer ventured out of the woodland to graze on the sweet, dew-covered grass.

'If we make a run across, those deer will bolt, and if de Hayle's men are close by then we've lost any surprise we might have,' said Blackstone. They were still downwind from the trees across the open ground but he kept his voice low. Sound travelled a long way in the stillness.

'Let's wait until dark. Their fires will show up,' said one archer.

'No. We'll get lost in those trees. We need to move before they settle for the night,' murmured Will Longdon.

'We don't know how dense it is in there. We'll get entangled and then we're the ones fighting for our lives,' said Blackstone, his voice still a whisper.

The men remained motionless, patiently waiting for the deer to move on. A belly roar startled the crows from their roost as a stag pushed through the undergrowth and trotted towards his harem. The hinds ran as one and then settled again fifty yards on as the stag went among them, sniffing for those hinds in season.

'Now's a good time to get across,' said one of the men.

John Jacob put a restraining arm out in case the man raised himself. 'Wait. Look there. See him, Sir Thomas?'

One of de Hayle's men stepped into the clearing, sword in hand, looking up and down the open expanse. The crows cawed and fought before settling again. The man studied the treeline, and then watched as the stag mounted a hind. He appeared to be satisfied that the stag and his herd had disturbed the birds rather than any human intruders.

'Now we know where they are,' said Blackstone. 'The moment he's out of sight we run. Will, make your way down to the end of the woodland. Bring down anyone escaping and kill any horses that bolt without a rider or they'll make their way back to de Hayle's camp and he'll know his men are dead. Then he'll send even more to seek us out. Ready?' Blackstone lunged into the open ground with John Jacob and the men-at-arms at his heels. Will Longdon slipped away into the trees to take up his cut-off position with the archers.

Blackstone outpaced the others. He plunged into the undergrowth, eyes searching for an enemy who might have pickets beyond their camp. The forest became darker the deeper he looked through the trees. No challenge was made; no sudden movement of panic came from an outlying sentry. John Jacob and the others crouched and slowed their breathing, listening hard for any sound. The men needed no instruction from Blackstone; they were all experienced fighters used to closing with an enemy. They crept forward, following Blackstone's lead, careful where they trod, choosing leaf mould wherever they could to cushion the sound of their approach. Fingers of light still filtered in from the edge of the trees.

Blackstone moved slowly now. It made no sense to be overeager in hunting the man. Blackstone's killer instincts bore all the hallmarks of a predator. His senses were alert, and he was rewarded by hearing a sound that was out of place in the forest. It was the low murmur of men's voices. Like a stalking wolf, he smelt the air. There was no scent of food or woodsmoke, which meant these men were prepared to sleep rough and eat cold food. The dull light meant he had no chance of seeing them. He raised a hand to stop the men behind him and turned his face into the breeze. The soft scent of leaf mould and forest plants wafted over him, as did the pungent smell of horses. The enemy was close. He pictured them in his mind's eye. If he were leading a scouting party, he would have each man lie under his blanket apart from the others in a perimeter, so that if one man was set upon the others could quickly react. These men he stalked had already proved they were experienced. They would lay less than twenty feet from the edge of the forest so that if there was a surprise attack, they had a quick escape route.

Blackstone crouched, gesturing the men to move closer.

'I can smell their sweat. They're close,' he whispered, showing the direction. 'No more than thirty paces. If they're seasoned fighters they'll be spread out. If we push forward we'll stumble on one or two of them. We need to move around them. If they escape they'll go for open ground and then it's up to Will and his men.' He pointed to each man and showed where he wanted them. 'If for any reason they're alerted I'll draw them and you attack.'

The men nodded their understanding and slipped away. Blackstone waited, letting his men creep as silently as they could to encircle de Hayle's skinners. Instinct was everything.

When to move. When to melt into the forest. And instinct warned him he would have to move sooner than he wanted. He felt the breeze on his neck. It had veered. If the routiers were not alert enough to sense it then the horses would be. He felt the comfort of Wolf Sword's hilt in his grip and his archer's killing knife in the other. He was already moving forward before his thoughts considered the options. Better to be closer to the horses that would soon raise the alarm than wait, hoping forest smells might obscure his men's scent.

Ten, fifteen strides and he was at the horses, their chestnut colour blending them into the trees. They swivelled their heads and whinnied, tugging at their tied reins. Blackstone was lucky. Had he hesitated any longer the mercenary who was already on his feet would have landed a fast blow from his sword. There was no need for the man to raise his voice in alarm; his companions were already free of their blankets. Blackstone's lunge into the camp and the nervous horses had alerted the men. They had been where he thought they would be, lying around the perimeter. Six men turned on him. John Jacob and the others would attack now the alarm had been raised but vital seconds would pass before then. Six fighters came at him hard and fast. Blackstone parried the nearest man's strike. The second man came in on his flank. Two more closing: yards away, snarling faces, swords raised, legs pumping hard to reach him. The fifth man was no threat. Not yet. He had further to travel. The sixth man stumbled in his desire to reach his comrades, slowing his own advance. Six men. Blackstone killed the first, and pivoted onto the second, who thought he had the advantage until the knife in Blackstone's other hand came out of nowhere and rammed into his throat. Six men. Instinct tormented him. Something was wrong. And then he knew. There were seven horses.

John Jacob and the others burst out of the trees, their yells turning Blackstone's attackers away from their target. As Blackstone's men fought the routiers Blackstone's sixth sense made him drop down. A blade whispered through the air where, a heartbeat before, his head had been. The seventh man struck from the blind side. Out of sight of the others, on the far edge of the perimeter. Blackstone pivoted, arcing Wolf Sword's blade to take away the man's legs, but he danced away, an experienced fighter who lunged down, his sword tip biting dirt seconds too late. Blackstone rolled, kicked out his legs and caught the man, who stumbled, buying Blackstone time to get to his feet. Out of the corner of his eye he saw one of his men go down, bettered by de Hayle's mercenary. John Jacob was too late to save him but thrust his blade beneath the man's armpit. Two of the routiers ran, leaving John Jacob and his remaining fighter to battle against the survivor's stubborn resistance. There was chaos as the two riders crashed their mounts through the camp. Low branches snapped back. Blackstone's man was barged aside and the skinners broke free.

It all flashed past as Blackstone felt his opponent's strength. The fury of his attack meant Blackstone had little choice other than to parry. He sidestepped but the flurry of blows was unabated. The man's strength matched Blackstone's; his skill did not. Blackstone eased his grip, letting the man's blade feel the give. Seducing him. Feeding his confidence. It was a lesson Blackstone had learnt when he'd fought a Teutonic knight. The mercenary stepped in for the killing blow but Blackstone had feinted. Wolf Sword dropped low as the man's weight forced down the blade. Blackstone was already turning his shoulder. The archer's knife struck beneath the man's chin with such force it was wrenched from Blackstone's grip when the routier fell.

Blackstone bent, yanked the knife free, ignoring the man's wide-eyed gaze as he writhed, choked on blood, and then slumped into death. The camp was silent except for men's heavy breathing as they gulped air from their exertions. John Jacob and Blackstone's other man had clubbed the last routier to the ground. He continued to fight but Blackstone's squire hit him again. Between them they hauled the unconscious body to the remaining tethered horses as Blackstone pushed through the undergrowth to the open grassland. Four hundred yards away, where the strip of land narrowed, two horses and their riders lay dead. Blackstone raised his arm to signal the all clear. Will Longdon and his bowmen stepped out of the woodland and returned the gesture and then went forward to check the dead and retrieve what arrows might be used again. John Jacob handed Blackstone a horse's reins. The unconscious routier and Blackstone's dead man-at-arms were tied over another. When they reached Will Longdon, the rest of the men doubled up on the routiers' mounts.

As darkness fell the dead lay gazing at the heavenly moon whose silver cloak bathed the dew-laden grassland in a field of glittering jewels.

CHAPTER TWENTY-SIX

Darkness protected Blackstone's camp. No enemy would attempt an uphill attack at night and when Blackstone returned Killbere ordered the fires to be rekindled and torches lit. The long shadows of the returning men with their prisoner stretched across the hillside, looming giants stalking the fearful boy. Beyard saw his dread and put him to work building the fire. The primal comfort of watching flames lick the darkness, sparks rising to the heavens, offered warmth and banished menace.

They laid the dead man-at-arms, bound in linen, on the back of the wagon away from any opportunistic wild animals. They tied the prisoner, hands behind his back, the rope looped around his throat. John Jacob lowered a flaming torch close to his belligerent face.

'Be done with it, you bastards,' he said, throat hoarse from the tightness of the rope. Men needed courage to face death as often as they did during violent times and his contempt for his captors was evidence that he understood his fate.

'Save yourself,' said Blackstone. 'If you tell me what I want to know I'll set you free without weapons or horse but you will find food and sanctuary within a day's walk.'

'And without a flint or fire the night beasts will take me if I don't find sanctuary before darkness.'

'Then you'll have to walk quickly,' said Killbere.

'What is your name?' said Blackstone.

'What difference does that make?'

'You're an Englishman riding with a murderer for profit. I don't like killing Englishmen but if I have to it's good to know who they are. Humour me.'

'Fuck you.'

Killbere delivered a swift kick to the man's ribs.

'And fuck you too,' he said to Killbere.

John Jacob slapped him hard enough to split his lip. 'It's a simple question, scum. An answer spares you more pain.'

He spat blood. 'Geoffrey of Dover.'

'So, Geoffrey of Dover, where is Ranulph de Hayle?' said Blackstone.

'What good will it do to tell you even if I knew?'

'It will make your death quick.'

'Death is death.'

'Not when I roast you on a spit over that fire,' said Blackstone, pointing to a blazing campfire.

That caught the man's attention: being burned alive was a terrifying prospect; but then he challenged the scar-faced man looking down at him. 'I know your reputation, Thomas Blackstone. You kill as much as any other man but you do not torture. Hang me and get it over with.'

'We have Navarrese soldiers among us. They survived Cocherel and de Hayle's stinking dungeon. They saw their comrades taken out each day and butchered by the man who calls himself the Beast. They do not share the same reservations that I have about torture. Where is le Bête?'

The threat was enough for the doomed man to try to save himself. 'I cannot be certain. We were to ride until we found your tracks and then return towards La Fontaine. De Hayle does not stay in one place. He would find us. I swear he could be anywhere by now.'

It was a convincing enough answer. 'You were searching for me because you knew we had the boy.'

Geoffrey of Dover flinched. So, this was no straightforward interrogation. Its purpose was to find the truth about their interest in the fugitive child. 'Aye, he wants the lad. But I don't know why.'

'Who pays de Hayle?' said Blackstone.

'Whoever needs his services the most.'

'And who is it that wants the boy?'

Geoffrey shook his head. 'I do not know, that I swear. We rode from Spain. Someone in power wants the boy dead. I am not privy to who pays de Hayle.'

'Then why keep the lad alive in the prison?'

'Le Bête sent word to Paris. He said the French King might pay more for him than the Spanish.'

'Why would King Charles of France have any interest in a Spanish urchin?'

'I don't know.'

'Who in Spain shares that interest?'

The man shrugged. 'If I knew I would save myself by telling you but I don't.'

Blackstone studied the man a while longer, then, satisfied, he nodded his acceptance. 'Then tonight you remain tied and at dawn I'll set you free.'

A shadow fell across him. Halif ben Josef stared down at the wretched man. 'That charm you wear around your neck belonged to the wife and mother of a family who showed compassion to a stranger. A man who, like you, was once a prisoner.'

Geoffrey looked from one to the other. 'Who's this? I won it in a tavern years ago.'

'No, you took it from a woman raped and murdered in Villaines. I know because I gave it to her after she treated me with kindness. You looted it when you slew her family. And what of her daughter? She was no older than twelve. Did you rape her too, before attacking her mother? And why did you steal it? It is a worthless stone. A trinket for a woman who had nothing but calloused hands and barely enough food to feed her family.'

Blackstone tugged free the leather cord that bore a small, dulled and scratched brown-red stone. He handed it to ben Josef, who looked at it and nodded.

'I fight, I get paid,' said Geoffrey. 'We take what is there to be taken. What difference is there between us, Sir Thomas?'

'You ask what difference there is between us?' said Blackstone. 'I hang rapists and murderers.'

They broke camp soon after first light. They buried their comrade and shared his clothes and arms among those closest to him. They abandoned the wagon because Blackstone needed to travel fast. Halif ben Josef rode with a pack horse to carry his satchel of medicines while Lázaro rode at Beyard's side. The boy showed no sign of recognizing the prisoner and remained as silent as the day they had rescued him, yet Beyard sensed there was a change coming over him. He trembled less and he didn't seem so sullen when he attended to his duties; nor did he show any sign of trepidation when Blackstone spoke to the men around him. Beyard watched Lázaro as they rode past the hanged man. The boy displayed no emotion but when he turned his gaze away from the corpse Beyard noticed the tell-tale sign of a smile.

Hours later Blackstone beckoned Renfred to bring the routier's horse to the front of the column. La Fontaine was less than ten miles from where they stopped. It raised its head and sniffed the breeze.

'Let it go,' said Blackstone.

Renfred slapped the horse's rump. It trotted across the open grassland, veering after a few hundred yards to follow its instincts and the scent on the wind that would take it back to de Hayle's horses.

'There's no saying where de Hayle is hiding,' said Killbere. 'Do we follow or wait until he sends out another scouting party?'

Blackstone beckoned the captains to him. 'Renfred and a scouting party will follow the horse. We'll go in two groups. I'll lead; Sir Gilbert will follow. If we ride into an ambush, he can cover us. Will, the boy and ben Josef stay back with your archers. You're our rearguard. If we sight them and are forced back you'll cover our withdrawal and then you kill as many as you can before we turn and make our stand. Questions?'

There were none. It was a simple plan. Find and kill the enemy or draw them back to Will Longdon's archers. They returned to their men.

'Gilbert?' said Blackstone. 'Is there a better way?'

'It's exactly what I would do,' said Killbere. 'Except...'

Blackstone waited.

'I would eat first.'

Beyard armed himself, allowing Lázaro to help him tug on his mail and then strap on his sword belt. Tears welled in the boy's eyes but he held them back. When a dog has spent a life being beaten any act of kindness is rewarded with an undying loyalty and it seemed no different with the boy. He was frail for his age, his spirit broken. Now the signs of his recovery looked to be threatened again.

'I must fight for Sir Thomas. You understand that, don't you? Just like he fought for us when we were rescued?'

Lázaro nodded.

'Then you know that there is no choice and we must find our courage.'

The lad stammered, his words blockaded by fear. 'I... do not... want you... hurt, my lord.'

'I have good men with me. We have fought together for many years. We are like brothers. You'll be safe here. Master Will Longdon and Master Halfpenny are the best of comrades. They are men of strength and bravery. You must find such things within yourself. Halif ben Josef will be your companion when I am gone. I will ask him to tell you tales of cities and places that you have never been.'

Lázaro nodded but did not relax his grip on Beyard's arm. 'Come back... my... lord. Will you... p-p-promise?'

Beyard placed his hand over the boy's white knuckles. 'It is God and my destiny that decide such things. Just as we were saved together and rescued from torture and death. Shall we make a pact?'

Tears overcame the boy's resolve and cut lines through the grime in his face. 'A pact?'

'Yes. An agreement that we pledge to each other. If I return you will tell me and Sir Thomas everything.' He saw uncertainty on the boy's face. 'It is time for us to know the truth, Lázaro. Shall that be our pact?'

The boy released his grip and smeared away the tears. 'I... will... tell you.'

CHAPTER TWENTY-SEVEN

Renfred and his half-dozen men followed the riderless horse at a distance. It became confused at times and stopped, losing its sense of direction. It grazed and then trotted off again when the breeze shifted, led on when its instincts returned. Renfred waited patiently and followed downwind in case the horse caught their scent and turned back, seeking companionship and safety with their mounts.

It was late afternoon when they crested a hill and saw the horse standing, ears pricked forward. They heard screams from a small town a mile ahead, likely to have no more than two hundred burghers. Wails of misery carried on the breeze, tormented, ghostly sounds that sent shivers down men's spines. Men other than Blackstone's. This was no haunted graveyard possessed by devils; Ranulph de Hayle's men were the demons. It was a defenceless place without walls or gates, an ancient town that had once been no more than a village. It was likely that in the war those who lived there would have sought refuge in a bigger town under the protection of a manorial lord. But now there was no war. Heralds had travelled the land announcing the treaty between the English and the French. Even the civil war would not have touched them because there was no benefit for the warring sides in seizing the small enclave. The casual violence had fallen on them from routiers as if God and Satan had rolled the dice.

The lone horse shuddered, stepped forward and then skittishly danced away from what it knew to be danger.

'Fetch it,' said Renfred to one of his men. 'It's served its purpose. We know where de Hayle is now. If it went into the town, it would warn the bastard. We'll keep the odds on our side now.'

The hobelar urged his horse forward at a slow trot, making sure the lone horse saw it. He held back, letting the horse come to him, eager as it was for the company of another. Renfred's man lifted the trailing rein and led it back to where the others waited. Then, with a final glance at the doomed town, they rode back to meet Blackstone. There would be no need for Killbere or the archers to hold back; the German captain knew what Blackstone would do. Attack and kill.

The autumnal night wind blew spectral clouds across the starlit sky. Shadows danced as the moon held court over the fleeting images of men running across the open plain. They dropped into a shallow ditch eighty yards from the beleaguered town, hidden from sight, cloaked by the next tranche of darkness.

'We don't know this place,' said Killbere, wheezing from the effort of the dash. 'It could be as deadly as a bear pit.'

'We don't need to know it, Gilbert. The streets are narrow, the houses small. De Hayle's men have had their sport and they'll be sleeping it off. There are no high walls for crossbows to shoot down on us.' Blackstone stared through the scattered light. Now that they were closer he saw the bank around the town more clearly; it was spoil from a defensive ditch dug so many years ago it was now nothing more than a grassy mound thick with weeds and meadow flowers. The narrow wooden bridge across the ditch was sturdy enough for a cart and horse. Blackstone looked along the line of men awaiting his command. Beyard's men would race around to the rear of the town as Meulon's clambered over the bank left of the main assault, with Renfred's on the right flank. All eyes were on Blackstone. They were ready.

Blackstone signalled Beyard, who peeled away into the night. They would wait long enough for him to get into position. Blackstone looked back across the dappled fields. On the ridge, two woodlands faced each other across a gap: Will Longdon was hidden in one edge of the forest with Jack Halfpenny in the trees opposite. If anyone escaped Blackstone's attack and rode for safety away from Beyard's cut-off group, then that was where they would die.

Blackstone waited for the moon to go behind the clouds. He stood and the line of men rose with him. He strode forward, walking not running. Meulon and Renfred's men peeled away, a slow and silent approach. Blackstone's boots thudded across the planked bridge. Ten more yards and they were past the first buildings. Shadows slipped over the ditch wall, steel blades catching what light there was – barely any showed from the houses. Dark shapes lying in the dirt streets revealed themselves as corpses of the slain townspeople.

Laughter suddenly pierced the silence. It came from deeper within the town. Blackstone gestured his men to fan out as they crept from corner to corner, stepping over the dead. A door creaked; a drunken routier staggered outside the house to relieve himself. He leaned an arm against the wall, gazing down at the stream of piss; then he yawned and farted. He finished and turned. John Jacob's arm wrapped around his throat as Killbere's knife plunged into his heart. John Jacob stepped back as Blackstone entered the small room. A candle flickered. A man was stretched out on the floor, dead; a naked woman, her face bruised from an assault, lay shivering on a palliasse, knees drawn up to her chest. Her mouth opened to scream but Blackstone raised a finger to his lips and the unusual gesture from such a fearsome man caught her by surprise.

'I am here to help you,' Blackstone said, keeping his distance, palm outstretched to calm her. 'Where are the routiers?'

She shook her head, eyes fixed on the giant who loomed even larger from the shadow thrown from the candle glow. 'Where are they?' he asked again.

She licked her cracked lips and pointed vaguely. 'Everywhere,' she whispered.

'Did they take over the houses?'

She nodded.

'Where are the majority of them? Is there a town square?'

She nodded again. 'They hanged our mayor and his officials. The square. Yes. The square. They took some of the women there.'

Blackstone glanced down at the dead man. 'Your husband?'

She nodded again, too exhausted and hurt for more tears. There was evidence enough on her stained face that she had wept until she could weep no more. She licked her lips again. 'They are everywhere. They will kill you. You will die here like the others. There are so many of them.'

Blackstone reached for a blanket and draped it over her. 'Stay here. The man who hurt you is dead. I will come back when it's finished and we will help you bury your husband.' He turned at the door. 'Don't be alarmed when you hear screams, they'll be from the routiers when we kill them.'

Blackstone's men ran silently through the alleyways. Voices rose from the darkness. Killbere laid a restraining hand on Blackstone's arm. 'Over there.'

They crouched as thirty or more drunken men tumbled out of the tavern and across the town square. One taunted another;

a fight broke out. Those sober enough to stand encircled the two men, who slashed at each other with knives. The onlookers cheered their favourites until one fell dead. Someone kicked the body to make sure the knife wound was fatal and then those who could still walk staggered back inside the tavern. Blackstone signalled for a dozen men to follow him. They dashed from shadow to shadow until they reached the tavern's window. Men sprawled on the floor; even more slumped across the crude wooden tables and benches. If thirty men had spilled into the night there would be another twenty too drunk to join them. Two women were tied to an upright post, their clothing torn, their hair soaked from the routiers pouring wine over them. One was not young, a matron of childbearing age, the other likely her daughter: mother and child licensed to run the tavern. These men were followers of le Bête, and beasts begat beasts. No woman or child of any age was safe from their violence.

Blackstone scrunched down. 'Fifty men crammed into one room. Kill them and we reduce our odds.'

John Jacob pointed to a blacksmith's shop. 'Let's burn them out. There'll be a coal bed there.'

Blackstone looked around the scattered houses; his men all edged closer to the square. He beckoned Meulon and Renfred. 'We'll burn down the tavern. Send ten more men to me and then position yourselves in the alleyways. When it catches fire, de Hayle's men in the houses will arm themselves. Kill as many as you can. If others escape, Will and his archers will finish them.'

'We found their horses,' said Renfred. 'They're split up. We don't have enough time to cut them all loose.'

'Ignore them. The flames will frighten them and they'll break free without any help from us. Bring bundles of faggots and any lamp oil you can find.'

The two captains ran back to their men. Blackstone pointed to three of those with him and gestured them to kill those that had been too senseless with drink to return to the tavern. A dozen fast strides later they were dead.

'There are two women in there,' said Blackstone. 'There's a front and a back door. Pile anything that will burn around the place. John, fire up the coals, light torches.'

'You'll let those women die?' said Killbere. 'I'll get them.'

'You think I'd leave them there? When the flames bite I'll go in the back door. You come with me. Use your axe and cut them free. We'll drag them out.'

Killbere grunted. 'At least let's slit a couple of throats in there while we're about it.'

'There'll be no time.'

'Cutting a throat takes no time at all,' said Killbere.

Men scurried back and forth as they raided winter log stores and brought sheaves of dry kindling, then stacked them against the wattle-and-clay-built tavern. As each man settled his bundle another spilled lamp oil on them. Blackstone saw John Jacob's face glow as he pumped the blacksmith's bellows. Torches flared. Blackstone beckoned the men to him. 'Surround the tavern. Kill everyone who gets out. When it's alight, Sir Gilbert and I are going in the back door to bring out two women.'

Blackstone's men waited, torch flames exposing grim features, eyes stark in the light, teeth grinning through their beards: eager to kill a foul enemy. He looked to where Meulon and Renfred slipped out of sight into the passages between the houses. They stayed out of the moon's glow so when de Hayle's men emerged they would not know the buildings' shadows concealed those intent to kill them.

'Burn it,' said Blackstone.

Flames leapt as oil and dry kindling ignited. Within moments the tongues of flame reached hungrily for the roof. The heavy thatch, matted with moss and age, smouldered with brown, choking smoke. Blackstone and Killbere joined the men at the rear as billowing smoke obscured the moon, sparks swirling upwards as the thatch beneath caught and then leapt through the support timbers. Blackstone nodded to John Jacob, who wrenched open the door. Blackstone and Killbere lunged inside. The smoke was lower than the ceiling. Drunken men blinked in confusion. The two Englishmen pushed past the first tables and reached the bound women, wide-eyed with terror. Killbere's axe cut into the rope and wooden beam as Blackstone shoved them to the door into the arms of the waiting men. They were pushed swiftly away.

Blackstone and Killbere came out, an arm across mouth and nose, eyes streaming from the smoke. The night air soon cleared their stinging eyes. Two of Blackstone's men stood on each side of the door. De Hayle's men fought each other to escape, jamming the door frame. Axes fell; their bodies tumbled. Men shocked sober by the fire gathered their wits and kept pushing through, the weight of their numbers forcing the men ahead over the threshold. Those who escaped the axe fell onto the raised shields and soul-stealing blades of Blackstone's men.

Chaos swept the town. Doors slammed open as half-dressed routiers ran into the night. Meulon and Renfred's men blocked the streets. Some of the mercenaries tried to fight their way through but they were unready and died in agony. Those that turned to escape ran into the square where hell's jaw gaped, ready to devour them. Heat sucked air from men's lungs and seared their skin. They faced armed men and were killed as efficiently as those trying to escape the tavern. The roof collapsed; a whoosh of air and debris flared into the night sky, hurtling the condemned remains into the devil's embrace. Timbers crackled; clay walls burned red. Killers more disciplined than the mercenaries pressed down the narrow streets, driving the desperate before them into the square. The encircled men, those who survived, threw down their arms. They knelt in surrender and heard a voice call out from somewhere in the night's torment that they be spared. The man who issued the command strode out of the night's conflagration. One of the mercenaries cursed, recognizing the scar-faced knight who stood before them as Thomas Blackstone and calling him a son of a whore. The veteran knight at Blackstone's side rammed his sword point into the man's throat.

No one else damned Thomas Blackstone that night.

CHAPTER TWENTY-EIGHT

The stench of burnt flesh and old thatch lingered. First light revealed men smudged with soot and sweat, eyes red-rimmed from the acrid smoke. The townspeople emerged, fear still etched on their faces as they stared at the battle-hardened men who had come in the night and killed those who had inflicted violence on them. Meulon and Renfred told them to drag the dead routiers from the streets and alleys into the square. One by one the bodies were laid out alongside those Blackstone had spared and who sat with hands bound. Blackstone's men guarding the prisoners made no attempt to stop the women from spitting at the routiers.

Killbere and Blackstone stood at one of the town's wells. Killbere plunged his head into a bucket and shook free the sweat and fatigue.

'How many dead?' Blackstone asked Meulon.

'We lost three men, but we killed forty-seven. It was like trapping rats in a sewer. They were full of ale and wine; most were half asleep when we killed them. We finished off their wounded.'

'Forty-seven in the streets and another twenty-eight from the tavern,' said Killbere. 'A good night's work. And I'll wager there were another ten or more in that tavern who never got out.'

'Has Ranulph de Hayle's body been found?' said Blackstone.

'Not so far,' said Renfred.

Blackstone looked at the huddled prisoners. He pointed to one of the older men. 'He looks like a veteran. He should have served de Hayle long enough. Pull him out and take him among the dead, see if he can identify him.'

'Shall we call in Will and Jack from the forest?' said Meulon.

'Not yet. We killed near enough ninety of de Hayle's men but where are the others? If they're out there, then we still need the archers in place. Send a runner, tell them we won't stay here much longer but for them to stay vigilant.'

The crowd gathered more confidently when they realized that Blackstone's men posed no threat. One man stepped forward.

'Sir knight, what are we to do with these bodies?'

'Strip them of any clothing, boots and weapons, then bury them,' said Blackstone.

'The nearest monastery is two days away. We have no place for burial here.'

'You have a defensive bank around the town. Drag them into the ditch and pull down the dirt onto them. Then close the gap with a wooden palisade. When skinners come you must stand together and show some resistance. Better to die fighting for what you cherish than to lie down and let them tear you apart.'

The man looked uncomfortable. 'We are farmers; we have no skills with weapons. We don't know how to fight.'

'You have a manorial lord?'

'We never see him. He's a week's journey from here.'

'You pay your taxes?'

'Aye, my lord.'

'Send word and tell him what happened here. Ask him to give you instruction. If the town falls again, he will get no taxes; if that happens he cannot pay the King; and if the King does not get the money he needs, then your lord will forfeit his land to another. Do you understand how it works?'

The spokesman grinned. 'I do now, lord.'

'Good.'

'How do we repay you for saving us?'

'Find me lengths of rope so I can tie these men together, and when you send the men to your master, tell him that Sir Thomas Blackstone, the English King's Master of War, who serves the Prince of Wales and Aquitaine, saved this town. Can you remember all of that?'

Blackstone saw the man chiselling the information into his memory. He finally nodded.

'And don't forget the rope,' said Blackstone.

Lázaro watched as Blackstone's men began walking back from the town across the hillside's meadow in small groups led by their captains. They were weary but seemed no less determined than when they left. They were in good spirits. Blackstone and Killbere were among them. Will Longdon and Jack Halfpenny had remained vigilant as Blackstone had ordered. Outlying scouts had reported no sign of routiers but the archers stood at their posts guarding Blackstone's return.

Lázaro looked at the men. His pounding heart squeezed the breath from his throat. There was no sign of Beyard. He counted eighteen prisoners roped together, shuffling in line towards their fate. The men moved past him. Further along the line they carried three bodies on makeshift stretchers. Trembling, the boy took a few faltering steps forward. Blackstone and Killbere broke off their conversation when they saw him. The look on his face told Blackstone all he needed to know.

'Lázaro, come here.'

The boy shook his head. It could only be the worst of news. It rooted him to the spot.

Blackstone took pity on him and strode towards him. Lázaro gazed up at the looming figure. 'You fear for your friend Beyard.' He took the boy's shoulder and turned him slightly so he could see Meulon's huge frame bearing his shield that blocked out one man behind him. 'There he is. Unharmed.'

The Gascon captain came into view, saw Blackstone standing with the boy and raised a hand. Lázaro broke free of Blackstone and ran downhill to Beyard, who opened his shield arm and held the lad to him. It reminded Blackstone of an eagle protecting its young beneath a wing.

And then another thought. Of his own son, Henry, far away, without his father's protection or a mother's love. Blackstone caught John Jacob's eye. His squire nodded. He knew and he understood.

Men's voices called out, captains shouted orders, and the moment passed.

Blackstone moved his men several miles away from the town. Despite their fatigue they rode alert for any counter-attack but none came. Then a warning arrived from Renfred's scouts. A large body of men appeared on the distant hilltop. Blackstone drew up the men and placed the prisoners in front so they would be the first to die in any attack.

The riders advanced in extended line and then slowed, one man riding ahead of the others. Blackstone kneed the bastard horse forward. 'It's Hugh Calveley,' he told Killbere. 'Keep the men ready. He fights for the highest bidder.'

Blackstone reached the centre ground. The Cheshire knight grinned. 'Thomas, you find trouble even on your return to the Prince. Those are de Hayle's men you have.'

'Some of them. He's elsewhere.'

'And their fate?'

'Hanging. I'll execute them on the road so that every traveller from Paris and Rouen going towards Poitiers will know that I kill routiers who commit atrocities. Do you ride to Bordeaux with us?'

'No, I have a contract with the new French King. He pays well now his father is dead, and he has what's left of the ransom money they collected to pay Edward for his release. We ride south. I thought you might join us. The fighting's done with up here; we've played our part, now we need to earn money. What do you say?'

'I cannot, I'm sworn.'

'Aye, well, a man's word might be his honour but facing a pauper's future should make him reconsider.' He grinned. 'I had thought of seizing Charles of Blois's body when they took it for burial at the Franciscan monastery at Guingcamp. His widow is wealthy enough.'

'But you decided against it because if there was a delay in payment you'd have a rotting corpse on your hands,' said Blackstone.

Calveley laughed. 'That's the measure of it, Thomas. Come with us. There's even more money to be made than the ransoms you took at Auray and what the King pays you.'

'My men and I are paid fairly and we have money banked in Florence. We take booty from fights like Auray, and there'll be others.'

Hugh Calveley admitted defeat. 'I thought you'd turn me down, but it was worth asking because I can use you. I'm short of a hundred men or more and I need bowmen, and you've some of the best. Can I not tempt you? I'll make it more than worth your while.'

'I'm wanted back in Bordeaux by the Prince. He'll be vexed enough as it is given my slow return.'

Calveley gathered the reins. 'Fair enough, but if he gets so damned vexed that he disowns you again then you come and find me. I sell my sword, Thomas, you know that. I hope we do not find ourselves on opposite sides.'

'That is my wish as well.'

'So be it. And unlike those unfortunate wretches I'd not let you hang any of my men.'

'Then let us hope they do not commit rape and murder of women and children.'

'Not while I lead them.'

Blackstone gripped Calveley's extended hand. 'God go with you, Hugh.'

'Aye and you, Thomas.'

He turned his horse and cantered back to the waiting men. Blackstone watched Calveley's men fall in behind him and make their way across the hills until they were out of sight. A part of him rode with them, free to roam where they wished and choose their own cause. It was a fleeting vision. He had earned his honour from the King of England, his men were honed and he had made a vow years before to keep the Prince of Wales safe. That was enough ambition for any man.

When the sun rose higher in the sky behind the veil of clouds, he turned the men deep into a forest and found an open glade where a narrow tributary spilled across a shallow bed. They made camp as men took it in turn to bathe and wash blood and grime from their bodies, shirts and braies, while those who waited kept watch and organized a meal and a place to sleep.

Lázaro worked diligently, helping Beyard, eager to please the fighting men and their captain. He carried water and prepared food for the Gascon. Men came and went, alternating in their duties until most were washed and fed. Blackstone had gone among the men, checked that Halif ben Josef was allowed to treat any wounds needing attention and the prisoners were secure. Ariz and Saustin, two of the Navarrese fighters rescued from the prison, had fought well. Their companion, Tibalt, had suffered a grievous wound. Halif ben Josef confirmed the young man's shattered arm needed to be amputated. Blackstone looked at the wound.

'If you want to live, it has to come off,' he told the Spaniard. 'I've seen lesser wounds turn black. You'll be dead in a week if we don't cut it off.'

The young man swore vehemently as his friends held him down. It made no difference that Blackstone did not understand. A curse sounded the same in any language.

'Get a blade heated. The wound will need searing. Master Josef, I leave you with the wounded.' Blackstone left the stricken man and continued walking through the camp. His clothes stuck to him and he yearned for the cool embrace of the river to wash away the stench and dirt.

Halif ben Josef placed a hand on the man's forehead. 'I have herbs to put in wine that will make you sleep. The cut will take less time than it takes a man to mount a horse. It is quick. Accept life, my friend.'

The wounded man shook his head vehemently. His comrade, Ariz, put a knee in his chest. 'Choose. Live or die. It's not even your sword arm. We have fought together many times, Tibalt, but I will cut your throat now if it is death you want because we have all seen men die, blackened with poison and in agony. See the cut as a blessing in disguise. The whores of Saragossa will take pity and charge you half-price.'

'Fuck you, Ariz,' he said without malice. He stared at ben Josef. 'Jew, do it quickly or I swear I will shave your beard and whip you all the way to Navarre.'

Ben Josef sighed. 'My friend, if I were lying where you are and you were in my place, I would speak more sweetly to the man with the knife in his hand. That way he would administer the potions that would take away my pain.'

Saustin leaned over the man's sweating face. 'Tibalt, you arse, you should be grateful. The Jew is no barber-surgeon. I have heard how he helped Blackstone's men. You should not abuse him.'

Tibalt glared at ben Josef. 'Save my arm and I will reward you.'

'You would not live long enough to do that, my young friend. It is time to choose.'

The Spaniard sucked in a lungful of air and breathed out, releasing his fear. He nodded.

'Very well,' said ben Josef. He gestured Saustin to pass the small bottle from his satchel. 'You will sleep and I will quickly cut, and then I will cauterize the wound. I will wrap it in linen and I will change that dressing every day until we reach Spain.'

Blackstone and Killbere stripped off mail and gambeson and walked to the sandy bank to bathe and wash their shirts.

'Do you think Beyard will take him as a servant?' said Killbere. 'With training he could be a page.'

Blackstone shook his head. 'Beyard is a Gascon. The day will come when he'll return to Lord Jean de Grailly and they have enough men serving them. He'll protect the boy until he's strong enough to go off on his own. And before then the lad will tell us why he's being hunted.'

Clouds broke free and sent spear shafts of light onto the water. Blackstone and Killbere stripped naked and lay in the cold water, heads back lazily watching the contest between sun and clouds.

'I would prefer a copper tub of hot water scented with a whore's cheap perfume, but given the past few hours I will let that thought settle until we come across the next decent-sized town.'

Blackstone rubbed the dirt free from his hair. 'When my father taught me to hunt, we sat in a glade like this once. We watched a fox carry a stick in its jaws and paddle out into the water until we could only see its head. It turned his back to the current so the water lifted its fur. We saw a swarm of fleas smother his head as they tried to escape drowning; then they went onto his muzzle and then onto the stick. The fox let the stick go, came out of the river, shook himself and went back into the forest.'

Killbere knelt on the sandy riverbed and vigorously rubbed his crotch. 'In truth, Thomas, nature teaches us all. I have an idea to rid myself of these damned lice. I'll lie facing the current and clench a stick between the cheeks of my arse. When my arse itches like a demon's fingernail from scurrying lice I'll fart and blow them all downriver.'

Blackstone stood and scraped fingers through his hair, squeezing out the wet. 'I'll remember never to take drinking water downstream from you.'

John Jacob came towards him from the trees, carrying Blackstone's spare linen shirt. 'Sir Thomas, Beyard says the boy is able to speak more easily now. And he has a story to tell.'

Blackstone and Beyard settled Lázaro by the fire. At first he only muttered beneath his breath. Beyard urged him to find his courage and tell Blackstone his story, as he had promised. He gave him wine and pressed his arm to reassure him. There was no one close by, and no one would interrupt: John Jacob would see to that.

The boy's nervous stammer eased and his voice grew stronger but he kept his eyes lowered. He had been a five-year-old orphaned urchin on the streets of Pamplona when officials of the Castilian royal household, making their way south through Navarre to Castile, found him. They had been scouring the slums for children to work in the stables and kitchens. Garderobe buckets needed emptying, floors swept and pampered dogs' excrement cleaned from reed floors: the urchin learnt fast and soon began to anticipate the needs of those who wielded power before they made their demands. Two years of back-breaking work ended when the young Queen of Castile turned down a wrong corridor in the labyrinthine castle at Burgos. The boy's willingness to please and angelic looks touched her heart. Who would deny the lonely Queen a child that had engaged her affections? The boy was gifted to the isolated bride, and he faithfully served the mistress who elevated him from his lowly position.

The memory halted Lázaro's telling. He raised his eyes to Beyard and Blackstone, confirming to himself that it was at last safe to recount what he had witnessed.

CHAPTER TWENTY-NINE

Medina Sidonia, Southern Spain
Three years ago

It was a death foretold.

Terror stalked the castle's corridors. The woman's screams echoed as the relentless killer followed her retreat. There was no need for the assassin to hurry. The prey had nowhere to run. No escape. No doors could be bolted. No lock held a key.

The young Queen had been confined in various fortresses since her marriage eight years before so that the King could live with his mistress. In recent months she had been sent to the castle at Medina Sidonia. The child bride was Blanche de Bourbon, niece of King Jean II of France, cousin to the Dauphin, married for political convenience when she was fourteen years old to King Pedro of Castile and abandoned by him once treaties were signed. Eight years of near solitude except for attendant women and in latter years a boy taken under her wing. There were to be no witnesses to the murder: the killer had strangled her servant women.

The boy scurried after his mistress until she could go no further. He slammed closed the door and dragged a heavy bench across it. Blanche reached the open window and stared down at the rocks a hundred feet below. To jump or face the assassin?

'Hide!' she told the boy.

The nine-year-old flung himself into her arms. He felt her heartbeat. Rapid, thudding against the brocade dress. She calmed him. 'God bless you, child. Now, Lázaro, you must hide. It is over,' she said, and then lifted her crucifix over his head. 'Do not be afraid,' she said. 'Pray to God for my soul and live according to His will.' She pulled a thin, plain ring of gold and pearl from her finger and pressed it into his hand. 'Find a money changer and this will buy you life.' She bustled him into the garderobe and pulled closed the curtain.

The boy held his breath and smeared tears from his face as the pursuer pushed aside the heavy bench. Peeping through the curtain he saw the burly assailant stride into the room. The young Queen found her courage and faced him. He forced her onto a stool, embracing her from behind in a vice-like grip. Then a second man, hooded, stepped inside and stood for a moment staring at the helpless woman. *This* was the assassin. A nod to the burly man and he forced the Queen's mouth open. Her killer took a step forward and spilled the contents of a small phial into her mouth. Blanche struggled. She coughed and choked as the poison sent her body into a spasm. The man holding her stood back as she fell to the floor.

Her lips turned blue. Blanche de Bourbon, twenty-two years old, Queen of Castile, wife of Pedro the Cruel, stared lifeless towards the boy trembling behind the curtain.

When the killers left, panic seized him; he ran, careering down the spiral stairs, pressing his back against the rough stone walls as voices echoed upward: the killers as their horses galloped away. Part of him yearned to return to his dead mistress, to cradle her, hope rising that she was not dead. But he brushed it aside. He was so close to her when she fell that he'd seen her life slip away from her eyes. Pulling his shirt and jerkin higher to obscure the rosary, he waited at the stairwell. There was a small gate nearby; he would use that for his escape – but where to go? When the assassins realized that one of the Queen's servants had survived they would look for him. There were no sentries. The castle seemed deserted. The main gates remained open. Venturing into the courtyard he ran for the gate, but horsemen thundered on the approach road from the town. He recognized Iñigo Ortiz de Estúñiga, the captain who had devotedly guarded the queen. The boy ran but was easily caught. He struggled, but the soldiers held him with ease.

'Lázaro,' said de Estúñiga, 'Look at me.' He grabbed Lázaro's shoulders, forcing him to cease struggling. 'We could not stop it but I refused to be a part of it. I defied the King.'

Tears of anger and grief choked the boy.

'They will find out they left you alive. I will help you escape. You must run and never stop running and you must tell no one what you know.' He rubbed a thumb across the boy's face to clear away the tears. 'Did you see who did the killing?'

Survival instincts tightened every sinew in Lázaro's body. He shook his head. His fist curled around the Queen's ring.

For a moment it seemed the young nobleman doubted the boy's answer. 'Good. We will get you to the coast and then... then we will face our destiny. I will pray the Virgin Mary protects you.'

Years of servitude had conditioned Lázaro to answer respectfully. 'And I will pray for you, my lord.'

Iñigo Ortiz de Estúñiga smiled. 'Bless you, child. I am protected by my family's standing and will return to their estates but you must understand, Lázaro, you in comparison are nothing more than a fly to be squashed by the King. Better to cut out your tongue than ever speak of this. I save you only because the Queen held you in as much affection as I did her.'

'It's time, my lord,' called one of his men. 'They'll soon be here under the pretext of finding her.'

The Queen's guardian climbed into the saddle, extended his hand and pulled the servant boy up behind him; then he spurred his horse down into the dry grasslands towards the coast and Cadiz. Lázaro turned his head to look for the last time at the castle of Medina Sidonia sitting high on the hillside. It was the one place he had found happiness. Now all that lay ahead was the promise of being hunted and, one day, when he failed to watch the shadows, being killed.

PART THREE

BETRAYAL

CHAPTER THIRTY

The battle at Cocherel was won the day before the twenty-six-year-old Dauphin was anointed King of France in the cathedral at Rheims. The elaborate ceremony masked how diminished a country France had become. The English had humiliated his late father. The country was torn apart by routiers' claws. So little remained of what had been the greatest nation in Christendom, beaten to its knees and humiliated: the Dauphin Charles was determined to seize it back and destroy the English hold on his beloved France.

He was radiant. The rays of sunlight embraced him. His coronation robes glowed as if the Almighty had touched him. As if God himself had beatified him. It was the rebirth of France. The newly crowned King, the pious Charles V, was a man of culture who loved art and literature and who schemed with the instinct of a foraging sewer rat.

Weeks later, when the joyous celebrations had waned, Simon Bucy, the late King's senior adviser, a man who had once led the French Parlement, stood waiting to be acknowledged. The young King seemed not even to see that he was in the same chamber, but that was little different from when Charles was Regent, ever distracted by teeming thoughts clamouring for his attention. Bucy knew that over the years the young Charles's mind had squirmed with intrigue. He was a thinker. Not like his father, who reacted emotionally to events. No,

Bucy thought, Charles would always look as far as the horizon and see what road they should take to reach it.

Bucy had given his undivided loyalty to the Dauphin, as he was then, as he tried to rule France during his father's imprisonment in England. However, the elder statesman never revealed his feelings. Inscrutability was the key to holding onto whatever influence he had. He had wavered in his loyalty to the old King when Jean had weakened and the Dauphin had shown that he had a mind like a mantrap. Bucy had chosen well. Like the astute lawyer that he was, he saw the strengths and weaknesses of those around him. And now the calculating lawyer in him warned him to tread carefully. Charles, the sickly youth, had grown into an equally illness-ravaged, twenty-six-year-old man. He was no soldier. He could not even ride a horse. But despite his weakened body he had a general's strategic mind. It was rumoured that the loss of his hair and fingernails was due to him being poisoned as a boy by the King of Navarre. Victory at Cocherel had finally rid the nation of any threat from the odious Navarre and his attempt to claim the crown. But bad news always followed good.

'Sire?' said Bucy.

King Charles V gazed at the elder statesman with a tolerance that bordered on affection. Bucy had made his choice to support him when he was Dauphin rather than the King who had not wanted war, a man burdened by the English treaties, a monarch who suffered personal humiliation eight years before when he was captured by the Prince of Wales at Poitiers. Edward of Woodstock now held the duchy of an enlarged territory in Aquitaine and resided in Bordeaux, one of the great cities of France. His very presence taunted the nation. Bucy, the man before him, reflected the past as clearly as a mirror.

'Sire,' Bucy repeated. 'Heralds came from Brittany with news of Charles of Blois.'

'What?' said the King, his reverie broken by Bucy's comment.

'Brittany, sire. Charles of Blois.'

'Yes?' Irritability already looming. 'You intend to keep us in suspense?'

'I regret to tell you, highness, that Lord Charles is dead. He has lost Brittany.'

Bucy waited for an outburst. There was none. Only the King's eyes betrayed his sense of loss.

'Where did he fight?'

'Auray, sire.'

The King frowned. 'Auray?'

'A small town on the Brittany coast, sire,' Bucy added quickly. 'It was under siege by John de Montfort, a vital port for the duchy.'

Charles nodded. 'We understood Blois's forces outnumbered those of John de Montfort.'

'So they inform us.'

'And yet he lost.'

'Sir John Chandos took command, sire. Had it been otherwise de Montfort would have failed – I am sure of it.'

'Chandos. Yes. We can see how he had the skill. A pity. De Montfort? Did he survive the battle?'

'Yes.'

The King fussed with his cloak. The courtiers who gathered behind Bucy waited for their new King to express his intent. Scribes sat at small knee desks at the back of the room, quills already scratching across parchment.

'Then, Simon, he is cradled in the arms of the English and we will deal with him in a generous manner. We will draw him to us through kindness. He has won the right to be called the Duke of Brittany so we will welcome him as such. He is a young man with little experience in politics or diplomacy. We will lure him away from the manipulative Prince of Wales and the King of England.'

'An excellent strategy, sire.'

'Simon, do not flatter us. There is no need. We know our strengths and how to employ them. There is more, is there not? We can tell when you have news that will grieve us. We have had your company over the years and know discomfort when we see it.'

'Quite so, sire. You know me too well. There is another matter. The chamberlain has an Englishman who seeks an audience.'

'An Englishman. Here? Do we know him?'

'We do not, highness. He arrived at the city gates with sixty or more men. They are English and Breton routiers. He came in the wake of the news from Auray.'

'What purpose?'

'A private matter. I have questioned him.'

'And you think we should grant him an audience?'

'I regret to usher such a vile man into your presence but I feel it is important.'

The King nodded, sniffed into his perfume-laced handkerchief and waited as the chamber's great doors were opened on Bucy's signal.

Simon Bucy turned to meet the man-at-arms, who bent his knee, head down until Bucy told him to stand.

'You came from Auray?' said the King.

'I did, your grace.'

'You have further news of Sir John's victory over Lord Charles de Blois?'

'Chandos, sire? No, it was not John Chandos who led the battle. It was Thomas Blackstone,' said Ranulph de Hayle.

CHAPTER THIRTY-ONE

The news brought by de Hayle – that Blackstone had led the attack against the French favourite in Brittany – inflamed an already aggrieved heart. That, and the story the mercenary recounted about the boy who'd witnessed the death of Charles's cousin Blanche de Bourbon three years before, shook Charles, but his keen mind saw an opportunity. He did not act rashly but spent the following weeks with his advisers. He listened as some outlined an act of war against Don Pedro of Spain, others insisting it better to blockade his ports – a foolish notion given that the Castilian galleys outnumbered those of the French. It was similarly poor advice that had weakened his father but it was not yet time to sweep the court clean of the men whose aim was only to please him. He dismissed them all except for Simon Bucy.

'Simon, you have remained silent these past weeks.'

'Your grace, I had affairs of state needing attention. Better that I do what I can while these circumstances demand your time.'

The King looked pensive. He stared across the Paris rooftops and the hive of activity on the city streets and barges on the River Seine. 'Our France is becoming prosperous again. We have lost much but we will regain it all, of that we are convinced. God will look kindly on our Christian endeavours.'

Bucy had heard the same words being uttered for years but no action had followed to make them a reality. And a council advising war had not yet convinced the young King. No warrior spirit lurked beneath his ermine-lined robes.

'Sire,' said the old lawyer: the only word he could muster.

'Duties aside, you are not usually shy in giving your comments, yet not a word from you, Simon.' Charles was gracious enough to smile at the old man. 'The evidence about the death of our cousin Blanche sounds believable to us. Despite Don Pedro's protestations to the contrary, she was murdered and now we find there is a witness.'

'Is the ring proof enough, highness?'

Charles nodded, turning the ring in his fingers. 'I know it. It is plain. A gift that is not ostentatious. It reflects the innocent child she was. She had no craving for precious stones and jewellery. I believe it was that humility which led to her death, so her husband could fornicate with his lewd mistress without further criticism.'

Bucy gave an unconscious shrug and regretted it when he saw the King take notice.

'You doubt it?' said Charles.

Bucy did his usual trick of pausing long enough to make the King believe he was giving the matter much thought. How was he to tell the King that the truth was more likely to be the lack of the dowry promised by the old King to Don Pedro when he offered the child bride to cement their alliance? The non-payment from a French King broken by English demands had prompted Don Pedro to abandon Blanche de Bourbon for his lover. 'Your grace, the ring is evidence enough that it was given, or... taken by someone. Ranulph de Hayle's story sounds believable. He tells us Don Pedro commissioned him to find the boy. How Don Pedro knew there was a witness has not been explained. It might be that he wishes to lay blame on the King and that it was one of his couriers who commissioned him. The man seeks recompense. He sells his story to you and returns the ring to the royal family. Now he will ride back to Spain and tell Don Pedro, or the King's agent, that Blackstone holds the boy witness. He will be paid again.' He shrugged to emphasize that there was some doubt in what the routier had told them. 'But...' He sighed. 'Blackstone. His presence yet again that none could anticipate.'

'When he was not seen at Cocherel you and every other counsellor thought he had turned from our border back to Gascony. And yet now he has defeated our favoured claimant to Brittany and holds the witness to our cousin's murder. You're right. How does he appear yet again in our life? We have a nation to rebuild and yet Blackstone turns up time and again like the pestilence.

'However,' Charles continued, 'if Fate smiles kindly on us and Ranulph de Hayle does as we expect and returns to Don Pedro, then he will advise him that the last time he knew of the boy's presence it was with Thomas Blackstone. How will the treaty between Castile and the English Prince fare, knowing his Master of War holds the boy?'

'It is a complication to be welcomed,' said Bucy. 'It makes Don Pedro suspicious of any help extended by the Prince.'

'Exactly. A welcome outcome that is in our control. We must create the circumstances that will drive Don Pedro from his throne.'

'Forgive me, highness, but whatever animosity you harbour towards Don Pedro, I urge you not to go to war. Do not be drawn into conflict or hope to entrap Blackstone. If he is involved in this matter, we have no way of knowing how, or where he will be in the future.'

Charles dabbed his nose. 'He will go to Spain.'

Bucy could not hide his disbelief.

'Did you think we would declare war?' The King laughed and settled himself in a chair. A servant darted forward and poured wine into a silver goblet. 'It is a game of chess between us and the Prince of Wales.'

Bucy shook his head. Was he becoming so feeble-minded that he could not keep up with the young King's rapid thoughts? 'I... I fail to understand the connection.'

'We made our decision weeks ago when de Hayle was paid for his story. We sent de Bagneaux south to negotiate with the King of Aragon's chamberlain.'

Bucy's mind raced. Sending his confidential secretary Gontier de Bagneaux to open negotiations with Castile's enemy, Aragon, had required such secrecy that they'd kept even him in the dark. But to what end?

'Your dismay is plain to see,' said the King. 'Have no qualms. We wanted you here close to us. You were correct in thinking affairs of state needed attention when our efforts were needed elsewhere. We had to be seen to be doing something, which is why the counsellors were engaged. No one knew.'

'How do the Prince of Wales and Blackstone fit into this, highness?'

Charles watched servants stack more wood onto the fire. The flames leapt. He huddled in his cloak. He was cold all the time. His frailty was a concern to the likes of Bucy, but where the body faltered the mind's projection was as sharp and true as a well-aimed arrow. 'We have the Englishman Hugh Calveley and his men waiting in Languedoc with our brother Louis.'

'Was he not contracted to fight other routiers in the south?'

The King nodded. His thin lips showed yellowed teeth. Bucy saw the sewer rat's cunning. His voice fell to barely more than a whisper that seethed with energy. 'I have made plans over these past weeks, Simon. Hugh Calveley will not ride against the routiers, he will lead them.'

Bucy broke protocol and stepped rapidly towards the King, drawn by his explanation that suddenly filled the old man's heart with hope. The future opened before him. This bold, calculated act was the beginning of France's resurgence. 'And... and the Prince of Wales will do what?' he asked himself and then answered his own question. 'It is already too late to form an army, but he will need to protect Don Pedro. He will send his Master of War, Thomas Blackstone.'

'And if good fortune smiles on us, Simon, we rid ourselves of him at last.'

CHAPTER THIRTY-TWO

Bordeaux, capital of the mighty principality of Aquitaine, offered red wine fit for a king. A man ought to savour its sun-blessed richness on his tongue, though most quaffed it with a determination suggesting it might be their last mouthful. Brothels were plentiful but controlled by the city fathers; bathhouses kept its citizens and itinerant soldiers cleansed of lice. It was a city alive with merchants and travellers and a new hope bred by the Prince's presence. Blackstone's men had yet to enjoy what the city offered. There were no street entertainers or dancing bears where they were confined. Narrow alleys stank of piss and excrement. Pigs ran freely, snuffling household waste, and men's voices echoed through the labyrinthine passages as they caroused or fought.

Blackstone and Killbere sat huddled in the corner of a tavern. Weeks had passed since their arrival in Bordeaux. They had expected a warm welcome from a grateful Prince; instead their men were kept on the far reaches of the city, encamped beyond its walls. Merchants and stallholders feared the fighting men's presence within the city walls and had petitioned the Prince's chamberlain, who had granted their wish. Blackstone had refused to allow the city officials to separate Halif ben Josef from them and went with him to Mont Judaïque, the hilltop Jewish quarter. They found a room for him at Arrua Judega and, after ensuring his comfort and safety among his own people they camped a short distance away close to one of the gates to the city at Port Judaea. Their horses were stabled and fed but the men were allowed only to the taverns where whores plied their trade. There had still been no sign of the Prince, nor any summons to the palace.

'Whores, Jews and fighting men: we are all outcast one way or another,' said John Jacob as he put three large clay jars filled with wine on the table.

'Is he in bed with his Lady Joan, do you think, Thomas? He has the sexual appetite of a goat despite his Christian piety,' said Killbere.

'I don't know why we cannot gain an audience with him. If Chandos is right and he's ill then we need to know. A weak Prince leaves Aquitaine exposed and if I am to protect him and the duchy, then I should be told,' said Blackstone.

John Jacob settled down on the bench and nodded towards two men-at-arms who shared a table with their women. 'I was speaking to those two—'

'The whores?' interrupted Killbere. 'I thought you were choosy about that kind of thing, John.'

'The men with them, Sir Gilbert: they were saying the Prince had a great tournament here. Hundreds took part. There were thousands of horses and he paid for it out of his own purse.'

Killbere scowled. 'And they treat us like lepers.'

'He took part, but he fell when he was dismounted. Rumours were a piece of a lance had pierced him. But word is that he didn't seem to be hurt.'

'There'll be a reason,' said Blackstone. 'But it won't be a fall from a horse. He's fought in tourneys before and the lances would have been crowned. No, it's something else that keeps us from him.'

'As long as he doesn't think we pissed in his wine barrels. Thomas, the wait is too long. We'll have trouble with the men, mark my words. Keeping us confined here is too frustrating. There's a city waiting to be enjoyed.'

'I know. It worries me as well. And there are no walls to build to keep the men busy and no forays into the hills looking for brigands.' Blackstone's own frustration was obvious.

'Perhaps if we had brought some of those you ransomed at Auray, Sir Thomas, they'd have let us further into the city,' said John Jacob. 'There's a thriving business in Bordeaux of selling and exchanging prisoners and armour. The Prince has no issue with it; in fact from what I've heard he encourages it.'

'He's a soldier's soldier; he likes the world we live in. He let Navarre cross through Gascony without hindrance and he has little love for him – I think it was partly because his heart went with him to fight the French. He'll rejoice in our victory when the feasting starts again. Our success is his glory. Where's Lázaro?'

'With Beyard. He's teaching him how to serve a man-at-arms. He bought the lad new clothes and boots today. He found a Jewish stallholder who brought clothes back to the quarter.'

'Well, we're wasting time. Gilbert, you and John have the captains check on the men. I want no trouble here. If there are arguments over women, then pay them. I'll not give the arse-clenching officials any excuse.' He swallowed the last of the wine and pushed the heavy table away from him.

'Where are you going?' said Killbere, saving his wine from spilling.

'To insist on seeing the Prince.'

Killbere groaned. 'Thomas, in God's name say nothing untoward.'

'I want a commission, Gilbert. We're not garrison soldiers. If I don't get these men into a fight soon, then half of them will end up with ropes around their necks. And if it came to that my own would be in a noose.'

Killbere nodded. 'Like I said, Thomas, watch what you say. He's as hot-tempered as you. We might all be hearing the creak of the rope's song.'

Sir Nigel Loring, the Prince's chamberlain, stood ramrod straight in the great hall of the Prince's palace at Bordeaux. His sallow features reflected many hours trapped in dimly lit rooms poring over documents of state. Loring was a man of influence but it was an unhealthy price to pay for such power, Blackstone thought as he waited for the Prince to enter. They had kept him waiting for far too long since his return from Brittany. A sure sign that something Blackstone had done displeased the Prince. Blackstone's stomach growled. He had been standing for two hours. No food had passed his lips since yesterday and now that the wine had cleared from his head, insisting on an audience with the Prince had begun to feel like a bad idea.

'He will not be pleased at your demand,' said the chamberlain.

'I'm not too pleased myself. My stomach thinks my throat has been cut, my head is thumping from Gascon red and the coating on my tongue is rough enough to tan a cow's hide. I am at my Prince's convenience but I am not a beggar at the door. Getting past your petty officials and gown-clad clerks who are more familiar with their quills than their cocks is worse than fighting through French lines. He knows I'm here?'

'Your manner is unbecoming,' said Loring.

'I am holding my manner on a tight rein and observing the protocol of this place, my lord chamberlain, but beyond these walls and this city, there is a world of misery and my men have endured it.'

'You should come back at another time.'

'I will wait here until I can stand no longer and that is a length of time in which you will grow old and die.'

The Prince entered through the far door, a gaggle of gowned advisers in his wake. He moved slower than usual and lacked the burnished look of a man used to riding and hunting and enjoying tourneys. Perhaps, Blackstone thought, John Chandos had been correct when telling Blackstone that there were days the Prince suffered from a mystery illness.

Blackstone followed the chamberlain's example and bowed. Edward of Woodstock, Prince of Wales and Aquitaine, settled himself in the upholstered chair. He fussed with the sleeves on his robe without raising his eyes to Blackstone.

'We offer our congratulations for the victory at Auray. You and Sir John Chandos gave our father the desired result. John de Montfort will be an ally in the north-west. It is as hoped.'

'Thank you, highness,' said Blackstone. The Prince's tone of voice held little enthusiasm in making the compliment.

When the Prince's eyes met Blackstone's his face hardened. 'They tell us you hanged fifteen prisoners. This causes us distress. The King's Master of War who is seen to fight for this duchy is expected to honour the rules of war. Those who surrender are spared and ransomed.'

'Your information is incorrect, highness,' said Blackstone.

The Prince looked at Sir Nigel Loring, who blanched. It was his responsibility to ensure that information he passed to the Prince was accurate. 'Sire, I have it on good authority from merchants who travelled under escort from Poitiers that they saw fifteen men hanged on a makeshift gallows at the crossroads.'

'Not so. You should get your facts straight, Sir Nigel. Our Prince depends on it.'

Loring smirked. 'A piece of cloth was pinned to one of them declaring that Sir Thomas Blackstone was responsible.'

'I hanged eighteen,' said Blackstone.

The confession was enough to get the Prince's full attention and a look of triumph from his chamberlain. 'Condemned by your own admission,' he said.

'Thomas?' said the Prince.

'They were routiers. They were not prisoners of war. They rode with Ranulph de Hayle, an Essex knight pardoned by the King to fight during the war. A foul creature who calls himself Ronec le Bête. His men raped and murdered their way across Brittany. We saw the towns and villages they destroyed. Sir John banished him from fighting on our side against Charles of Blois. I rescued my Gascon captain, Beyard, and other prisoners from the castle at Auray, held by de Hayle. *Those* are the facts.'

The Prince smiled. 'You see, Loring, Blackstone is correct: we would have condemned him unjustly.'

The chamberlain was about to offer up a defence but the Prince dismissed him with a wave of his hand. 'Leave us. And everyone else,' he said.

Sir Nigel extended his arms like a farm girl herding geese and ushered the courtiers away. When the door closed, the Prince smiled. 'Thomas, you cause upset with little effort.'

'Highness, it took some effort to save villagers from de Hayle's men. I am sorry if my actions kept me from your presence.'

'We kept you waiting so long, Thomas, because we were unwell.'

'I'm grieved to hear of it. Did you take part in the tourney? I heard they unhorsed you.'

'And what do you believe?'

'I doubt it. I couldn't unhorse you at the Windsor tourney all those years ago.'

'You were inexperienced at jousting, Thomas, but you came the closest. It took weeks for our bruises to heal after you near battered your Prince to his knees. No, it wasn't the tournament here. We spend our time travelling to every town to give constant reassurance to the Gascon lords. We are impatient, Thomas. Protocol and diplomacy are better suited to others. But we have our duty. The constant journeying aggravates the malaise. It is nothing.'

'One of my captains was wounded fighting de Hayle's men and that led me to another town where I paid ransom for a Jewish physician. Halif ben Josef served your friend and ally the Captal de Buch. The man has great skills. Will you allow him to attend you?'

The Prince dismissed his malaise with a brush of his hand. 'No need. We suspect it results from too much rich food on too many occasions with too many members of the Gascon aristocracy trying to impress with the weight of food on their table.' He paused as if considering the offer. 'We are pleased your men accepted a Jew among them; our father granted the Jews safe residence here these twenty years past.' He allowed a smile of regret. 'It was to annoy the French more than anything but their payment of eight pounds of pepper every year to the Archbishop is a price worth paying for them to escape persecution.' He shook his head. 'Thomas, I am a prince of the realm and it would be unseemly for me to have anyone other than a Christian physician in attendance.'

'Even privately?' said Blackstone.

'Even then,' said the Prince with a look of regret. 'Now, what of this other matter you have waited patiently to bring to us?'

Blackstone recounted how he had rescued Beyard and Lázaro and then the boy's story of what he had witnessed.

'After they murdered the Queen, the lad escaped to the coast. The captain of the guard who played no part in the killing was a man from a noble family who abhorred what they had done. The boy worked on galleys for three years and then came ashore. He went inland with the supplies destined for Charles of Blois and was caught up in the fighting at Cocherel and captured. From there he was sold to Ranulph de Hayle. I questioned one of de Hayle's men and he told me they had been in Castile. It seems a stroke of ill fortune for the boy and the opposite for de Hayle but I think the lad was being hunted and had been for the past three years. I believe the boy's survival confirms King Pedro's complicity in his wife's murder.'

'But why was the boy held captive by de Hayle and not slain?' said the Prince.

'Because Ranulph de Hayle was going to sell him to the French.'

Realization dawned on the Prince. 'Of course! She was King Jean's niece and the boy's evidence would give the new King added impetus to his desire to attack Castile in support of Pedro's half-brother.'

'And that will draw us into war because of our treaty with Don Pedro,' said Blackstone. He took a small pouch from his belt and emptied out a beautiful crucifix, too exquisite to belong to a servant. 'The Queen gave the boy this to protect him moments before they murdered her.'

The Prince fingered the delicate gold filigree. 'She wore this moments before she died?'

'Aye, lord. She had only a few breaths left in this life after she gave it to him. Once he had made his escape, he stitched it into the seam of his hose.'

The Prince made the sign of the cross. 'The boy's story can be challenged, Thomas. These past years King Pedro of Castile has denied any involvement in Blanche de Bourbon's death. The Pope brushed aside the notion that such a devout woman would take her own life. Pedro laid the blame on others.'

'But the lad is a witness. We have coached him to give a false name if he is questioned by strangers but his life remains in jeopardy.'

The Prince nodded. 'And in your care until we can find a means of using his testimony.' He handed the crucifix back to Blackstone. 'Return it to the boy. It was gifted with affection by a grateful queen. We pray it gives the lad comfort.'

'There is one problem we cannot solve, highness. She gave the boy a ring. The Queen told him to sell it to a moneylender, but where was a cabin boy going to find one of those outside a city? Besides, he was terrified he would be accused of theft – something the Queen would never have anticipated. What would a queen know of a servant's life? De Hayle took it from him when he was captured. The last I heard he was riding for Paris. And if the ring is recognized and the story of the witness is believed, then we are drawn into a war in Spain because the French King will strike at Pedro in revenge.'

The Prince stood, his height matching Blackstone's, the spark of the fighting man reignited. 'Years ago when you were still recovering from your wounds after Crécy and then gaining your fighting skills our sister Joan travelled to fulfil her betrothal to Don Pedro. He was to be our brother-in-law. Our father needed Castile at his back even then. When she died in the plague he lost his alliance – until this recent treaty. History binds us, as it does you and me, Thomas.' He paused in thought and then realized that everything Blackstone had told him now fell neatly into place. 'The French King has already betrayed his hand. The Pope sent emissaries to me. He proposed a crusade.'

'Against the Turks?'

'No, against the Kingdom of Granada. The French have always wished to rid themselves of the brigands that flood the Rhône Valley and Charles has sided with the King of

Aragon. They have raised two hundred thousand gold florins to pay them. The Pope has committed a hundred thousand more from the Church's purse. They intend to rid Spain of the Moors. The Pope thought we would take the cross and join a crusade against them. Perhaps he did not look beyond the desire to seize a Muslim kingdom. The Pope has unwittingly showed us Charles's plan.'

'Then Ranulph de Hayle reached Paris. They know about the boy,' said Blackstone, immediately seeing the French King's plan. 'Charles will use the thousands of routiers and rid France of their threat in one fell swoop. They will not attack Granada, they'll ignore the Muslims in the south and seize Castile to avenge the Lady Blanche. Not only revenge, my lord, but he'll put Don Pedro's bastard half-brother on the throne. Then you will have our enemy at your back.'

'Exactly, Thomas. And the new French King has paid the ransom for Bertrand du Guesclin. He will command the army. You and your men must reach Castile and the King before them.' The Prince paused, his voice no longer tinged with a sense of urgency, but more of concern. 'We ask of you what I would ask of no other, Thomas. If the routiers are well organized, and I suspect they are, then you and your few men would be heavily outnumbered. You could not survive a fight against them.' He hesitated again. 'We would not wish to lose you, Thomas. A legend can die as easily as the next man.'

'Legends are nothing more than tavern gossip. As long as men drink themselves senseless such exaggerations will go on – forever. Until the wine barrels run dry.'

CHAPTER THIRTY-THREE

Blackstone made his way through the bustling streets. Pilgrims jostled with stallholders; robed judges accompanied by their clerks cut through the throng with a provost leading the way. Blackstone tagged on behind them past the courts into the narrower streets where tradesmen plied their craft. Blacksmiths and metalworkers, glowing iron, plumes of smoke, grinding stones casting sparks from blades being sharpened. The blacksmith raised his eyes and bowed his head to the Englishman who had paid him well to have his farrier shoe the men's horses. All except one. Only the scar-faced man and six others who had roped the bastard horse securely could manage the savage beast. Sweet Mother of God, it bit and fought as if it were being sent back to its maker: Satan.

The acrid smell of smelting iron gave way to the tang of spice merchants on the next street as Blackstone strode briskly to the city walls and stables where Killbere and the men were quartered. Bathed, rested and fed, the men were restless. Meulon had already stepped in between two of his men whose argument had escalated via insults to a full-blown fight. Petty differences arise when soldiers are kept too long away from fighting an enemy.

'Some of the lads are spending what's left of their money in the brothels,' said Will Longdon when Blackstone brought his captains together.

'Then get them out, Will. The Prince has work for us and we leave immediately.'

Blackstone recounted the conversation with the Prince and the threat now posed by the French and the Aragonese King.

'What threat can they offer?' said Renfred. 'Bertrand du Guesclin is their most capable general but they ransomed him to John Chandos. They have no one to lead an army.'

Blackstone took the food offered by John Jacob and began to wolf down the smoked meat and bread. He picked out a piece of gristle and threw it into the fire and then spoke, his mouth still full. 'The new French King paid his ransom. As Dauphin he always longed to seize back France and ignore the treaties we made. Now as King he puts his longing into action.'

'He has an army?' said Will Longdon.

'Paid for with the money his father had gathered in taxes for his own ransom to our King. When he died, the debt died with him. Events are turning decisively against the Prince.'

'The French wouldn't attack Aquitaine,' William Ashford said. 'They would bring down Edward's wrath. They would be slaughtered in greater number than at Crécy and Poitiers.'

Blackstone drank from his leather flask, rinsing the meat from his teeth. 'William, how best to separate a man from his strength? You cut off his right hand and then plunge a knife into his back. King Charles uses the pretext of crusade. The Pope has swollen his coffers.'

Killbere snorted. 'A damned crusade? What poor bastards does he crusade against?'

Blackstone let the question hang and Killbere quickly saw the truth that lay behind it as Blackstone had done with the Prince. 'I'll be damned. The Muslim Kingdom of Granada lies on Castile's southern border.'

John Jacob retrieved the tin plate from Blackstone and scrubbed it clean with a handful of coarse dirt before plunging it into a pail of water. 'So he uses the pretence of striking down through Castile – and who is it that stands in the way? King Don Pedro himself,' he said. 'Sir Thomas, who else seeks to dethrone him?'

'His bastard half-brother, who has sanctuary in Aragon. They favoured him from the start. As did a younger brother, but Don Pedro had him killed.'

'He likes to turn the odds in his favour,' said Meulon. 'And is willing to kill anyone who stands in his way.'

'Like his wife,' Beyard said. 'Lázaro saw the killer, Sir Thomas. If it was not Don Pedro himself then who?'

'That we've yet to discover, but who would wager against him being the paymaster behind the assassin? Ranulph de Hayle was last known to be riding to Paris. He has the Queen's ring he took from Lázaro. That, and the knowledge that there is still a witness alive, might be sufficient proof for the French to seek revenge,' said Killbere.

Blackstone swept crumbs from his jupon. 'There is no doubt in the Prince's mind that they and the Aragonese will attack Castile. After Cocherel and Auray there are even more men joining bands of routiers. The Pope is worried they will attack Avignon. King Charles has convinced him he will turn the skinners away from the papal city and strike against Granada. The Pope has paid for a crusade, and the French pay the routiers with the Pope's money.'

'This new King is a shrewd businessman. He gets the Pope to fund much of his campaign in Spain,' Killbere said.

Blackstone plunged his greasy hands into a bucket of water. 'If they seize Castile our Prince will have an enemy at his back. And if we believe the boy, we now have to help a murderer,' he told them, wiping his hands dry on the cloth offered by John Jacob. 'We are obliged to be Don Pedro's ally. It sickens the Prince but the treaty between us is binding.'

'Not for the first time we're surrounded by foul men,' said Jack Halfpenny. 'De Hayle murders Kynith and rapes and murders helpless villagers for sport and gain, and the King of Castile does it to satisfy his desire for power.'

'You're right, Jack. Our Prince loathes Don Pedro for his foul treatment of those who fall prey to his blood-lust. It's a burden on him so he's sending Sir Nigel Loring to England to seek guidance from the King.'

'Then until the King decides there is nothing we need to do,' said Will Longdon.

'Not so. The French support Pedro's half-brother. They want him on Pedro's throne. If they do that they control Castile and Aragon. They've moved quickly.'

Beyard saw the reality. 'We're not ready. There's no time to raise an army.'

'The Prince has no choice. If any of Pedro's enemies threaten him, then we must go to his aide. The Prince cannot allow a bastard to rule Castile, a bastard who is a French and Aragonese puppet.'

'The Pope could stop this war if he knew the truth of the matter,' Ashford said.

Blackstone shook his head. 'William, we are caught in a trap. Pedro is already excommunicated. The Pope instructed him to break all association and alliance with the Muslim Emirate of Granada. He has not. He favours their women as mistresses. He has Moors as his bodyguard. He defies the Christian Church. The Pope would welcome him being removed. Do you see how this man stands for everything the Prince hates?'

Killbere poked the fire. 'What would the Prince have us do?'

'Routiers in their thousands are gathering ready to enter Spain. Until our King sanctions war we will not commit an army, but we cannot let Pedro be taken and killed. We're charged with keeping the boy witness safe and then taking our men to Castile and helping Pedro escape to safety.'

He stood and looked across the encampment. 'Gather the men; check our supplies. We leave for Navarre and then Castile as soon as we are ready.'

CHAPTER THIRTY-FOUR

Halif ben Josef packed his satchel and stepped gingerly down the narrow staircase from his attic room, careful the satchel's weight did not cause him to lose his footing. Fear was never far from the old physician. His service to a Gascon lord had taken him to war and close to death, but even away from a battlefield he was at risk from those who hated his kind and might express their loathing in an act of violence at any time. The Jewish quarter was usually safe but even in his own community there were thieves and murderers: men who would steal for gain and kill for profit, and his medicines were of great value. He hugged the weight of the square satchel to his chest.

The chatter of voices from the occupied rooms, the clang of a cooking pot and slamming of a door from the breeze or by human hand initially obscured the sound of another coming up the stairs, but now he heard footsteps pounding towards him. He looked back up the winding staircase. Too late now to retreat. He stared into the gloomy stairwells and saw the shadow flit across the turn in the stair. Whoever it was they were determined to reach his attic room. Thoughts raced through his mind. He would surrender the satchel without a fight. Then decided he could not. The satchel was his life. Without it he might as well be dead. A lifetime of knowledge and learning was held in small bottles that skilled apothecaries had helped him create. The thud of boots came closer. He saw the figure emerge from the unlit staircase.

'Lázaro! You frightened me,' he gasped.

'Maestro Halif, I beg your forgiveness. Maestro Beyard sent me to help you. The men are waiting. Let me take that for you.'

Ben Josef was happy to be relieved of its weight. The youth was strong despite his frail appearance. He tucked the bulky satchel under one arm and extended the other to let the old Spaniard lean on it. 'You are travelling home to Navarre, Maestro Halif. Your family will welcome you.'

'I am an old man with no wife or children, Lázaro. You and I, we are alone in the world except for the watchful gaze of God.'

The boy's voice had become stronger since telling Blackstone his story. 'He did not help my Queen. There are places in Castile where even He does not venture. I have seen a raven land on a cow's back and curdle its milk.'

'The mind conjures fear, my boy. It takes pleasure in fooling you into seeing something that is not there. I know, I have been afraid for most of my life and at times I feared dark forces had seized my mind.' They reached the lower stairs. 'But the benevolent warmth of the Almighty, no matter what name we call Him, that sunlight penetrates the darkness and lifts a man's spirits.'

Lázaro helped him down the final steps into the passageway. 'There is evil in Castile and I wish Sir Thomas would leave me here. I don't want to go back.'

Halif ben Josef followed the boy towards the beckoning daylight at the end of the passage. 'Here? What safety is there among the French? The English Prince rules but cannot protect you here. He has hundreds in his court so even if he gave you shelter, you would still not be safe. Anyone can be bribed. And if not in the palace where else? There are street urchins who will slit your throat for those clothes Beyard purchased for you. My advice is stay with your protector. Captain Beyard is your shield and Sir Thomas is your sword.'

They stepped into the day's glare. Blackstone and his men were waiting. The bastard horse swung its head and glared at him. Ben Josef felt its displeasure.

'We thought you had fallen asleep,' said Killbere.

'I lost track of time,' said the old man.

'You can manage a horse? There's no wagon. We ride at a pace.'

One of the men strapped the satchel securely to the horse as Lázaro cupped his hands as a stirrup for ben Josef.

'Once I am wedged in the saddle, Sir Gilbert, I am as unmoving as Moses when he held aloft his staff and parted the Red Sea.'

Killbere gathered his reins. 'Aye, well, if you have any such influence you can part the tide of our enemies who wait ahead.'

They rode south towards Navarre, the narrow pocket of land lying between the coast and the eastern border of Aragon. Blackstone had to travel through the kingdom north of Castile to reach the beleaguered Don Pedro across the Pyrenees. When they crossed the River Ardour at Bayonne the broken peaks appeared closer than they were, a trick of the light making their passage onward seem more daunting. They reached Saint-Jean-Pied-de-Port and turned their backs to the ocean. The steady climb through the wooded foothills and defile through the pass at Roncevalles was where they made the most time once the road widened and Blackstone could urge the bastard horse forward at the trot and canter. The defensive mountain peaks allowed few safe passages through the high-sided passes and as they climbed higher the fall to the gorges and rivers below became more precipitous.

'What do we do with the boy when we get to Pamplona?' said Killbere. 'Leave him with the old man?'

'I don't know, Gilbert. It might be the safest place for him. No one knows his true identity or what he witnessed but you know how slippery Navarre is. He might root out the truth and sell the boy to gain favour with Don Pedro or even Aragon. The boy's testimony has value to them all. I'll decide when we get there.'

'Navarre holds the key to Castile. We have to get through those passes before early snowfall. Bad enough now with rockfalls. Thomas, I fear the Prince sends us on an unwelcome mission. We are risking ourselves for a half-crazed Spanish king.'

'Navarre or Don Pedro?'

'Both.' Killbere spat dust from his throat. 'Goddamn peacocks, the lot of them. Remember when we fought the Jacquerie and Navarre was there with his knights? It looked like a damned coronation with all that pomp.'

Blackstone indulged him. 'You're right. They're both tyrants. But I think you will like Spain.'

'I will?'

'It's like Italy without the Visconti. Don Pedro is a lesser tyrant.'

'Oh, that's comforting. I can see why I would warm to the place.'

'Their women are as beautiful, their wine is as rich and the weather is agreeable.'

'Unless we are caught on the mountain passes in winter.'

'That aside.'

'So we will rescue King Don Pedro of Castile with our few men against thousands of routiers paid for by the Pope and the King of France, keep the boy Lázaro with us if Navarre is inhospitable, ignore the fact that Pedro has Moors riding for him, that he has been excommunicated, murdered his wife, executed his closest advisers and is rumoured to be in league with the devil... but all of this is agreeable because the women are beautiful and their wine is good.'

'It could be worse.'

'I don't see how.'

'The wine might have soured in the barrel or the women less attractive.'

'A woman lying at your side needs no beauty, Thomas, she needs enthusiasm. The wine, though, that is a concern.'

CHAPTER THIRTY-FIVE

There were days when the black-capped peaks hurled wind and rain at the huddled riders but the hardened men bore the stinging assault without complaint. Killbere taunted Blackstone with his false promise of fine weather. When the mountain gods saw their efforts did not turn back the determined strangers riding into the high peaks, they relented, allowing sunshine to bathe them as they descended into the fertile valleys.

They reached the Navarrese capital before nightfall on the fifth day after the Prince gave Blackstone his sealed letter for the King of Navarre. Blackstone held up his men a mile from the city gates. Pamplona lay in a wide valley against a backdrop of the mountains. The fortified walls had been built on an escarpment whose cliffs dropped to a broad meandering river, the opposite bank lined with tall poplars, meagre in height compared to the distant mountain spires.

'Shall we camp in or out?' said Killbere. 'I think I would rather have the open valley than the confining walls.'

'We're guests, not beggars. They can feed us for a night and a day. Skulking outside Navarre's walls demeans the Prince.' He spurred the bastard horse forward. Before he had come within four hundred yards, the parapets began to bustle with soldiers. Blackstone pulled up in front of the main gate.

'State your business,' a sentry called.

'Tell him we're here to pillage the city, seize their women and burn it to the ground,' Killbere muttered. 'Stupid bastards. They can see our blazon.'

'Perhaps that's why they ask,' said Blackstone. He raised his voice to the men on the walls. 'I am Sir Thomas Blackstone, sent by Prince Edward of Wales and Aquitaine, seeking permission to bring my men into the city. I have a letter for the King.'

'Wait!' called the sentry.

'Wait?' Killbere groaned. 'Does the man think we intend to lay siege out here? Merciful God, we should be rulers of the world you and I, Thomas. Think how much better we would manage events.'

'You would spend the taxes on women and wine.'

'Better than squandering it on war.' He raised himself in his stirrups and shouted at the men on top of the walls. 'There's respect to be paid to the King of England's Master of War! Sir Thomas Blackstone does not like to be kept waiting!' He turned to Blackstone. 'You don't, do you?'

'Not when you ride with me, Gilbert.'

The gates creaked open.

'There, you see, Thomas. A firm word is all that's needed.'

The King of Navarre paced back and forth across the room, the majestic Pyrenees framed in the large opening to a balcony. The austere King had no hanging tapestries or carpets to soften his echoing footsteps in the sparsely furnished stone hall. His palpable agitation was echoed in the nervousness of the midday church bells ringing out across the city, each a heartbeat behind the other, their clangings a procession of hesitant disharmony.

Prince Edward's letter lay unfolded on the room's only table. He stopped prowling, picked up the letter again as if to ensure he had understood the Prince's request. There was little to understand. Give the King's Master of War unhindered and safe passage into Castile.

'You are familiar to me,' said the King, the letter fluttering from his hand onto the table.

'We met briefly, highness, when we fought the Jacquerie those years ago,' said Blackstone.

'Ah,' said the King, not remembering. He glanced at the letter. 'It would appear that your Prince sees me as a vassal of Aquitaine. Be under no illusion: I am not.'

'There has been no such suggestion,' Blackstone said, eager to soothe ruffled peacock feathers.

The defeated usurper ignored his assurance. Keen to impress King Edward's trusted knight, he went on: 'I am the rightful heir to the throne of France. My mother was King Louis X's daughter and yet I am spurned and now defeated and condemned to live my life here. Had your beloved Prince aided me in my fight at Cocherel I would be more inclined to agree to his request. I am not in so generous a mood. You can find your own way. I care not. Feed and rest your men and horses for a day and be gone.'

It was a dismissal. Blackstone ignored it. 'With respect, my lord. Prince Edward gave your army free passage through Aquitaine when Jean de Grailly led your troops against the French at Cocherel. I took their flank and kept the French from attacking their march. My Prince expects a similar courtesy.'

'Expects? His request feels like a demand,' said Navarre as he fingered the letter again. 'I will give it my consideration.'

It was another dismissal. Blackstone ignored that as well. 'Sire, I rescued three Navarrese soldiers and a Jewish physician who accompanied Lord Jean de Grailly. I have returned them to their home here in Pamplona. One lost his arm but would have lost his life if it weren't for the Jew. I can't use a man with such an injury but will keep the other two with me if you have no objection.'

'It is of no concern to me. Pay them if they wish to stay with you.' He barely kept the self-pity from his voice. 'I have no need of soldiers now. The French have released de Grailly from imprisonment at Meaux so that he can attend to their terms of surrender on my behalf. What your Prince desires with Don Pedro has nothing to do with me.'

'But you are allied to Castile, my lord.'

'I need no reminder of my responsibilities, Sir Thomas!' He paused and reconsidered. 'Rest your men. Take the pilgrim's route south-west to where Don Pedro hides in his fortress at Burgos. I will give you a guide. That is all I am prepared to do.'

The King turned his back and strode from the room. Blackstone and the King's courtiers bowed. Navarre blew hot and cold. If he was discussing terms of surrender and renunciation of his claim to the French Crown Blackstone's presence might be a problem. Giving the English King's Master of War safe passage might leave the duplicitous King no means to protect himself from the French and their desire to see Don Pedro's half-brother on the throne of Castile.

Guards opened the door behind Blackstone. He glanced at the Pyrenees. If a guide deliberately took them on a dangerous route through the mountains and tragedy befell them the Prince could not blame Navarre, but the French might reward him.

★

The sun's glare reflected from the cluttered buildings. Blackstone stepped through the palace's porticos into the square where John Jacob and William Ashford waited. He had ordered his men to stay close to their quarters and when purchasing supplies to go through the streets in groups of no less than three. No man was to venture out alone and all taverns were banned. Blackstone did not trust Navarre; it would take only a small incident to escalate. A spark soon became a fire if the tinder was dry, and Blackstone's presence might be seen as fuel. The King of Navarre had been wounded by his defeat even though he had never left his castle when he sent Jean de Grailly and his men to fight at Cocherel. He would lay blame for his defeat on others but that festering wound would take more than time to heal. Bending the knee to France was inevitable now. The English Prince and King were close to losing an ally.

'Sir Gilbert has quartered the men,' said Ashford.

'And we've bought enough smoked meat to last a week,' said John Jacob.

'I want the horses attended to before the men sleep tonight,' Blackstone told them. 'We're leaving tomorrow. The King doesn't want us here and I have no desire to outstay his meagre welcome.'

The three men made their way across a square confined by tightly packed houses before turning into a suffocating alley. As they shouldered their way through the jostling crowd, the unmistakable figure of Meulon appeared ahead of them, head and shoulders above the rest. He was unaccompanied; his size alone would make any disgruntled Navarrese hesitate before acting aggressively towards the black-bearded fighter.

'Sir Thomas. Halif ben Josef asked me to fetch you.'

'Is there trouble?'

'No, I don't think so. He's waiting for you in a safe place. Safe enough for now, that is.'

'William, John, return to the men. Tell Sir Gilbert I'm going with Meulon. And make sure we keep the boy with Beyard and out of sight. There's unease in the city and if the lad lets slip where's he's from then it opens the door for questions to be asked.'

CHAPTER THIRTY-SIX

Meulon led Blackstone into the Jewish Quarter. There was little difference from the other streets of Pamplona. The size and strength of the two men meant the shoppers and street hawkers quickly parted.

'In here,' said Meulon, opening an inconspicuous door in the house's sun-bleached wall, as pockmarked and crumbling as those around it. Blackstone stepped into a cool, dim corridor. Meulon's frame blocked out the light at the far end. They reached a small courtyard where a lemon tree grew in the centre of the tiled floor. There was a wicker chair with a brightly striped cushion beneath its shade-giving branches. Meulon did not stop but entered another passage that soon broadened into a large room with honey-coloured bricks arching across the entrance. A single high window beamed a shaft of dust-speckled sunlight into the gloomy interior. It was only when Blackstone stepped further into the room and turned that he saw light flooding walls as tall as any town's church.

'I have never seen such a place before now,' said Meulon.

The unexpected volume of what appeared to be a hidden building within the city was as much a surprise to Blackstone's stonemason's eye as it was to Meulon. Below the vaulted wooden ceiling, colonnettes supported arches around the wall with intricate patterns of leaves, flowers and tendrils, above which were letters that Blackstone did not recognize.

'What writing is that?' Blackstone said aloud to himself, not expecting to be answered.

'They are quotes in Hebrew from my faith and also from the Bible and Qur'an,' said Halif ben Josef.

Blackstone turned to where rows of cushions and mats lined the end wall on which hung large silk tapestries. The Jewish physician sat with two other men. By the look of their fine clothing Blackstone guessed they were merchants. Ben Josef beckoned him.

'Sir Thomas, come and meet two friends of mine who have important news that you need to hear.'

'I'll guard the entrance,' said Meulon and turned back towards the courtyard.

The three men stood when Blackstone reached them. Halif ben Josef introduced his companions. 'Sir Thomas, these are good and trusted friends, Elias Navarette and Salamon Bonisac. I have told them how you rescued me.'

Blackstone nodded to the two distinguished-looking men. 'Master ben Josef saved my friend's life. It pleased me and my men that he chose to ride with us.'

Ben Josef gestured for the men to sit so Blackstone could face them. 'Elias is a silversmith, Salamon a weaver. They travel far and wide, including in Italy, France and the Holy Roman Empire, to secure the materials they need. Both have returned these past few days. Elias across the eastern borders, Salamon further south.' He nodded to the older of the two men. 'Salamon, tell Sir Thomas what you told me.'

The weaver unconsciously ran a smoothing hand across the silk sash holding his robes. 'A large army approaches. Men of war, paid to fight. They have broached the south-eastern border of Castile and laid waste to town and village. They are led by English and French captains. They were riding south for Granada but they have turned north towards Santa Elena and Cordoba. Seville will be threatened.'

Blackstone saw the importance of the attack. As did Halif ben Josef. 'They are blockading Granada, denying Don Pedro any reinforcements and any chance of escape to a friendly country. Yes?'

'Yes,' said Blackstone.

'There is more. Elias, tell my friend what you saw in the east.'

'I came close to being attacked by mercenaries. Fortunately, we knew the route and evaded them. They seized two of our Navarrese escorts. They butchered one; the other escaped and rejoined us. He learnt they were riding towards Burgos where Don Pedro has what few men he commands.'

Halif ben Josef scissored two fingers open and closed. 'They cut him off.'

'Yes,' Blackstone agreed, feeling time closing in on him.

Ben Josef turned to the silversmith. 'What name did you hear spoken?'

'Le Bête.'

Blackstone looked from one to the other. Ben Josef nodded. 'Could there be any mistake, Elias?'

'No. They spoke it in fear.'

'I am grateful for the information,' said Blackstone. The elderly physician got to his feet; Blackstone followed his lead. Ben Josef extended his hand to the silversmith and the weaver as they took their leave. Blackstone did the same. 'Thank you again. Do you know who le Bête rode with? Was it the Englishmen Hugh Calveley or Latimer?'

'I do not know,' said Elias Navarette.

Each merchant respectfully dipped his head. 'We are happy to see our friend again and if what we have told him is of use, then we are pleased to be of service. Ben Josef is a prince among men. There are five hundred Jews in Pamplona and all know him for his skill. We will be sorry to lose him again.'

Blackstone waited until they were out of earshot as they left the synagogue. 'It was good of you to bring your friends to meet me,' he said. 'Their information might help save my men's lives. So Ranulph de Hayle is part of the invasion.'

'I did not think your English friend would entertain his presence.'

'Calveley? No, he wouldn't. But if de Hayle has learnt of me being here and he thinks I still have Lázaro with me, he might return to the man who paid him to find the lad three years ago.'

'Don Pedro?'

'Yes.'

'And by coincidence you ride to help him.' Ben Josef placed a hand on Blackstone's arm. 'Coincidence is another name for Fate, Sir Thomas. Nothing happens that is not predetermined. If de Hayle has learnt of your presence in Spain, then he will know it possible you might leave the child here for safekeeping. Either way, be on your guard. If he is near, then he will scurry ever closer like a rat in the night. The only solution I can think of is to leave the boy with me. The Queen's murder took place at Medina Sidonia in the far south and it might be that the assassin is still there. We are a long way from the place and in Navarre rather than Castile. I will educate the child and let him work with me. It might save him.'

'But your friends said you're leaving.'

Ben Josef shrugged. 'Not far. There are other younger physicians here. They don't really need me any more.' He looked down the corridor where the two merchants had disappeared. 'Their generous comments are born of a long friendship. I have a vineyard on the other side of the river, a few miles away at Estella in the valley below the mountains.

It is a town where Jews have lived for two hundred years and more. It is twenty miles or so from here. I will ride with you that far. Everything I need to live comfortably is there. The King taxes wine brought into the city but does not tax grapes. It's a good arrangement. I drink my own wine and sell what grapes I don't need. The boy might be safer with me there than with you. You ride into the heart of violence and evil.'

Blackstone considered the offer. The Spanish boy would have a roof over his head and food in his belly. Would his presence arouse suspicion? A Christian child working in the service of a Jew? Eventually someone would ask questions in the marketplace. One wrong word or a moment of hesitation from Lázaro about his background could prove fatal.

'I can think of no finer man to leave him with, but the risk is too great for both of you. If I keep him close then he has a better chance and brings no threat to your door. He is a witness to murder and the assassin might be close to the King. Lázaro might identify him.'

'I understand. Know that if you ever have need of my help you only have to send word.' The physician raised an arm towards the darkest corner of the synagogue. A young Spaniard, in his teens perhaps, stepped into the light.

'This is Andrés. His family have farmed in the mountains for generations. He is a Christian of good faith and I have helped his family in the past. I trust him. I have asked him to take you through the safest places to avoid ambush or injury. He is a shepherd and knows the country as I know my own hand. He should ride with us and see what route the King's guide suggests. If it is safe, Andrés will return home. If it is not, then he will take you to Burgos. I will translate whatever needs to be said between you.'

Blackstone acknowledged the boy's presence and then faced the elderly physician. 'You know that sooner or later

Navarre will make a deal with the French and the routiers. He will betray you to them if he is so inclined. The victor determines the conditions of surrender. If there is a pawn to be offered up to help him make a suitable truce it might be the Jews here who suffer.'

Ben Josef smiled. 'When the English and French expelled us it was Navarre and Castile who took us in. We are grateful to the Spanish Kings for accepting us along with our Muslim and Christian brothers. Navarre and Castile defy the Pope's orders for us to wear an identifying mark on our clothes. So we are wary of speaking out against either of these Kings. We do not wish to abuse the freedom to live, trade and worship that has been granted to us. Beyond that we know that we live a precarious existence. Like you.'

CHAPTER THIRTY-SEVEN

The following day Blackstone's men gathered, ready to leave Pamplona. Blackstone had no desire to stay confined in the city. They had granted him a guide and two of the Navarrese fighters rescued from de Hayle's prison had requested they stay with the men. Their Spanish would be helpful and he kept them under the command of Beyard, who understood their language. The one-armed Tibalt had not been seen since they entered the city.

'Sir Thomas, this man has been sent as our guide,' said William Ashford, presenting one of Navarre's men. He wore a grease-streaked jerkin beneath his cloak. There was no visible sign of the King's blazon.

'My lord,' the man said, swept off his cap and bowed. 'I am Santos.'

He was in his fifth decade, hair gone except for fringes straggling over his ears and with a beard that might have been raided by mice for nest material while he slept. He bore no visible scars but his knuckles were flattened from years of punching others. A tavern brawler. He was as bereft of teeth as he was hair. He stank.

'Stand downwind of me,' said Blackstone. 'You reek of a soiled rat's nest.'

'I sleep in the King's stables, lord. I tend his horses, I trap fresh food, I am allowed one bucket of water a day for the animals.' He bared his gums. 'I am given what you would call pottage and what I would call slop. The horses eat better than me.'

'And you know the route to Burgos?'

'With my eyes shut, lord. I have hunted in the mountains and forests since I was a boy and have slipped under the noses of the pagan bastards whose faces are as black as the inside of a cat's arse.' The man saw Blackstone did not understand. 'The Moors, lord. They serve Don Pedro. They are as black as—'

'I understand,' Blackstone interrupted. 'I intend to ride south-west and go through Estella. I have a companion who wishes to return there.'

The man nodded. 'A good route. There are three rivers to cross, lord. I will guide you south of the mountains. That will keep open ground on this side,' he said, waving his left arm. 'If there are those who wish to cause us harm, then we will see them in good time. I know where the fords and bridges are and then once we reach Estella I will advise you of the route to Burgos.'

'Why not tell me now?'

'Because, lord, the weather changes quickly in these mountains.'

'Is there snow on the passes?'

'No, lord, and if it comes we will travel below the snowline.'

'You'll have no wine until I give it to you.'

'Lord?'

'You reek enough and I want your head clear.'

'I see the way more clearly with a belly full of wine, lord.'

'Then I will find someone else and you can lose the King's goodwill and payment.'

The old man cleared his throat. His hand trembled as he scratched his mangy beard. 'A drink to start the day, another when the sun is above our heads and some to help me sleep. I would be grateful, lord.'

Blackstone nodded and Ashford tugged the man away to where the horses were tethered. Blackstone beckoned the young man who stood next to ben Josef. The lad tipped his head respectfully.

'You heard the old man?'

Ben Josef translated the boy's answer as if Andrés was speaking himself.

'Yes, Sir Thomas. He is correct. I too would have taken you by that route. I know the fords across the river. It is what he decides once we have reached Estella that will tell us if he is being a true guide.'

Blackstone dismissed him and thanked ben Josef.

'I pray the wind is at our backs, Thomas,' said Killbere. 'I've smelled a sweeter stench from a tanner's yard.'

The twenty-nine miles from Pamplona passed without incident. Renfred and his forward scouts reported no threat but there were sightings of riders, barely visible on far mountain tracks behind them. They posed no threat and soon disappeared from view, but Blackstone kept the German captain and his men wide of the column and when night fell ordered them to camp without fires and protect their flank. As the evening sky began to darken their guide led the men through fields of olive groves and then crossed the southern loop of the River Arga. Lanterns began to twinkle in the distant Estella households built on the river's northern slope along a narrow corridor between the river and the mountains.

'We'll camp here and ride on at first light,' Blackstone said. 'Unless you are anxious to return home?' he said to ben Josef.

'I have been away for some time, Sir Thomas, another night in good company will be no hardship. I have no family waiting for me, only my books.'

'My son, Henry, he is a lover of books. He got it from his mother. Not me.'

'Your wife is waiting for you somewhere?'

'Not in this world, Master Josef.'

The physician nodded. 'I too await my reunion.' He paused and let his gaze meander across the landscape. 'Encourage your son. We are blessed with knowledge from Greeks and Arabs, and we Jews shared in that knowledge. We stand across a divide that is not always easy to bridge but medicine builds trust and understanding. We forget so much that should be remembered and honoured. We are all men of learning and what greater gift is there than knowledge to share among our fellow men?'

'My son fights me. I don't understand him. He craves knowledge but wishes to serve with me. I wish I had the words to explain to him what worlds of mystery must lie in books.'

'Tell him that learning and practice derived from study bring a greater understanding between us all. Let me give you an example – perhaps listening to an old Jew might allow you to impress him. Hundreds of years ago Hunain bin Ishaq al-Ibadi translated Hippocrates and Galen into Arabic. The original texts were lost so these were the only sources of medical literature in the Islamic period. Such a gift to us all is a blessing. Hunain was a heretical Nestorian Christian; I am a Jew. You hear those bells ringing for prayer in the town? Why do they ring at certain times of the day? Because the Christian Church followed the Jewish tradition of praying at the third, sixth and ninth hour and after midnight. The Christian prayer of that time comprised much the same elements as the Jewish: recital or chanting of psalms, reading of the Old Testament, and then the Christians added readings of the Gospels and epistles. The past holds us together and yet serves to tear us apart.' Halif ben Josef rested a hand on Blackstone's arm. 'Let him learn about us all. I hope I might be privileged to meet him one day.'

'I would be honoured. You have no children?'

'Lost in childbirth, and then my wife herself was taken. And so I reach out to these young people.' He looked to where the young Spaniard, Andrés, was attending to ben Josef's horse and setting up a place for the elderly physician to rest for the night.

Blackstone's eyes followed ben Josef's. 'The boy, does he live nearby?' he asked.

'The mountains, over there, but they are known to us here. He and his family live a harsh existence but they are good people, like the other peasants who bring their food to our market.'

Blackstone studied the terrain before darkness shrouded the mountains. The fertile valley was vulnerable from the surrounding peaks, most of which looked to be no more than two thousand feet high. 'You're safe here?'

'As safe as anyone in these dangerous times. There are a hundred and eighty Jewish families over there among fifteen hundred Christians,' said ben Josef. 'The King protects us.' He shrugged. 'Thirty years ago the Christians in the town rose up and massacred many of us. The town was fined heavily and made to pay reparations and those who led the uprising were executed. A royal decree makes us his property, so he is responsible for us. For some years now we have lived in harmony with our Christian neighbours.'

'And the castle?' said Blackstone pointing to a rocky outcrop and imposing fortress in the distance.

'Zalatambor. A defence against Castile from the old wars. It serves to protect pilgrims going to Santiago de Compostela. The King stays there when he visits.' Ben Josef smiled. 'Especially when he wants to borrow money from us.' He nodded towards gentle sloping land in the distance. 'My vineyard is this side of the river. It is away from town and faces south so my vines do not fall under the mountain's shadow. If your guide is an honest one then I'll keep Andrés with me for a few days. He's strong and willing.' He gestured to where the young Spaniard and Lázaro were helping each other carry pails of water from a stream. 'Young boys need the company of those their own age. Andrés is the older but it looks as though they might form a friendship. Hard work and freedom are medicine I can recommend.'

'I'm tempted to leave him with you: his safety is my responsibility. My son endured violence and is now studying under his mother's name because of who he is. Lázaro has a similar cross to bear.'

'And your Lord Jesus bore his to his death.'

Blackstone placed a hand on the old man's shoulder. 'But I will take its weight for the lad.'

'My Lord Thomas?'

Blackstone turned on hearing his name called. Santos the guide approached him, cap in hand, shoulders bent in supplication. 'I beg leave to ride forward before darkness falls. There were heavy rains a week ago, up there.' He twisted a shoulder by way of pointing to the mountains that lay beyond. 'Roads were washed away and there's a danger it has damaged an ancient bridge. If that is the case then I must find a shallow ford.'

'How many days to Burgos?'

'At this pace, three, my lord.'

Blackstone looked for confirmation to ben Josef, who nodded.

'Wait until morning,' Blackstone told him.

The tavern brawler winced. 'My lord, if I do that and the rains have indeed washed away the road, then we will lose valuable time.'

Ben Josef nodded his agreement. 'Sir Thomas, if time is not a constraint you can find another route if the bridges are down.'

Blackstone thought for a moment. 'I want the most direct route if the road is open. I'll send someone with you.'

'The boy could go,' said ben Josef.

'No, if the way is clear then he stays with you.' Blackstone said. He stood. 'I'll send one of the men with you,' he told Santos.

The guide grimaced. 'Not the Navarrese, lord. They despise me.'

'Then they are the perfect escort.' Blackstone raised an arm and beckoned Halfpenny. 'Jack, send Ariz and Saustin to me.'

Halfpenny strode through the camp calling the men's names. Blackstone watched as the ventenar pointed the two men towards where he waited.

'You'll ride in darkness?' he asked Santos.

'The sky is clear tonight, lord: we can see enough. And the river shines at night. It won't be a hardship. I will be back before dawn.'

The two Navarrese edged around the guide's stench.

'He wants to check the route, but he feels threatened by you. You bear a grudge towards this man?'

'Only that he is what he is, Sir Thomas, a thieving poacher who beats his women and is a stranger to bathing,' said Ariz.

'Yet he's the man sent by the King's bailiff to guide us to Burgos, so you'll escort him. I want him back safely. Put your ill feelings aside. Don't beat him and keep him from your wineskins.'

The three men nodded their understanding. Blackstone watched them walk towards the horses, the two Navarrese fighters keeping upwind of the guide. 'When they report back I'll speak to Andrés so I know we are not being led into trouble. My thanks for your knowledge. I shall try to impress my son with what little learning I have gained from you. Now, excuse me, Master Josef, I must attend to my men.'

He left the physician and walked through the camp. Pickets had been posted and food prepared. He found Beyard with his men. 'I've sent Ariz and Saustin with the guide, who wants to check our route for the morning. I don't trust him enough to let him ride into the night alone.' Blackstone scanned the foothills. 'It would be easy enough for the French and routiers to be getting closer to Burgos, and if they have swept up from the south-east then they might be closer than we think. If we come under attack on this journey, keep Lázaro close to you. Have your men defend him as you did before.'

'I will. Don't worry, Sir Thomas, the men have taken to him. He fetches and carries without being asked. He's changed since he told us what happened. The secret he carried weighed too heavily on him. It closed his heart and paralysed his tongue. His speech is clearer now but sometimes I see the old fear creep into his face and then he struggles with his words. This journey to Castile is frightening him. I try to reassure him, and he doesn't know about Ranulph de Hayle going to Paris with the Queen's ring, but it's easy to understand how terror must gnaw at his belly.'

'Keep him as a servant so he appears to have no importance. He has one thing on his side: the assassins who killed the Queen and all her servants – I'll wager they wouldn't recognize the boy even though they have learnt of his existence.'

'The captain of the guard who saved him knows what he looks like,' said Beyard.

'But even if he is at Burgos instead of further south, he might not recognize someone after three years. And let's say he does, then he has already risked his life by helping him escape. It's the brute de Hayle who poses the threat.'

CHAPTER THIRTY-EIGHT

Santos led the Navarrese fighters along a winding track that followed the contours of the rising hills, and beyond them the mountains. White cowls nestled on the high peaks, christened by the moonlight.

Ariz and Saustin stared beyond the rolling haunches of Santos's horse. The silver-lit river in the valley below meandered into darkness as it curved around the opposite mountain range. There was no threat of ambush as the grassland wavered in the night breeze.

'Old man, how far?' said Saustin.

Santos did not turn in the saddle to answer. 'As long as it takes.'

The riders had heard the distant clang of the midnight bell from Estella's church. The moon's arc across the sky told them they must have been riding for three hours or more.

'That's no answer, sewer rat.'

'It's the only one you'll get,' came the reply.

Saustin sighed with frustration. He turned to his companion. 'Ariz, we should let the wretch go on without us. We can bed down here and wait for his return then go back to Blackstone.'

Ariz looked up at the shifting clouds. 'We have to, Saustin. We'll soon lose the moonlight and then it'll be only his stench to guide us. Let's go on a while longer.'

'I see no sign of damage from the rains on this track. Do you?'

'It depends where there was flooding. Be patient. We'll turn back soon enough.'

'And that's too long to wait,' Saustin insisted and spurred his horse forward to draw up alongside the guide. 'Santos, you're leading us nowhere. If this is the route you've chosen then I see no reason to continue.'

'We follow the track down and then I can check the bridge.'

'Bridge?' His eye followed the line of the river. In the distance was the unmistakable block of darkness across the glittering water. 'That bridge? I can see it from here. There's no need to ride any further.'

Santos shrugged. 'Do what you want; I need to check for myself.'

Saustin snatched at the belligerent man's reins. 'The way is clear, I say!'

'Piss on what you say. Go back if you want. Tell the Englishman you know better than a guide sent to him by the King.'

Saustin tossed the reins back. 'As far as that break in the hillside. Another mile, no more.'

Santos heeled his nag, urging it into a shuffling trot far enough clear of the Navarrese fighter. Ariz caught up with his companion. 'You always were impatient. You should let it go. Everything will be sorted out sooner or later. It can't be far now because he promised Blackstone we would be back by dawn.'

'Then we should wait here when he reports to him and save ourselves the arse ache of riding back this way again.'

Santos disappeared from view around a rocky outcrop. The two men followed moments later and reined in abruptly when they saw another horseman in the shadows talking to him.

Saustin's sword was half drawn when Ariz laid a hand on his arm. 'No need. Can't you see who it is?'

A cloud shifted from the face of the moon exposing the rider's features.

'Tibalt!' Saustin said. 'My God. What are you doing here?'

Saustin dismounted as the one-armed Tibalt stepped down from the saddle. The two friends embraced. 'What are you doing out here?' said Saustin and cast a quick glance around. 'Are you alone?'

'There's no one else.'

Saustin stepped back. 'I don't understand. Why here? And how did you know we would travel this road?'

'I paid the wine soak before he left the city. And he played his cards right.'

Saustin shook his head. 'What? You're talking in riddles.'

Tibalt laid his good arm onto his friend's shoulder. 'He told Blackstone that you and Ariz despised him. That made you both the perfect escort.'

Tibalt unslung his wineskin and handed it to Saustin. 'Let's drink before he gets his filthy mouth on it and I'll explain.' He took a mouthful and handed it to Saustin, who hesitated.

'Something's not right.'

Tibalt laughed. 'Drink! When have you ever refused good wine?'

Saustin handed back the wineskin. 'Not until you tell me what's going on.'

Tibalt sighed and tossed the wineskin to Santos. 'The boy. We seek the boy.'

'We?'

'I sought out Ranulph de Hayle. He's paid good money to tell him where Blackstone rides with the boy.'

Uncertainty clouded Saustin's mind. 'This makes no sense. The bastard held us captive. He tortured and killed our comrades.'

'And I lost my arm to the Jew butcher. Saustin, I sold him the boy, or his whereabouts at least. De Hayle is ten miles away. He'll ambush Blackstone and seize the lad once Santos here guides him.'

Saustin staggered back. 'You'd betray the man who saved us!'

'For money. Yes. A lot of money. We won't have to fight for pay any more.' He turned to the saddle. 'I have yours here.'

Saustin drew his sword. 'I'll have no part of this and you and your whoreson friend will—'

The horses shied as a mace-wielding Ariz clubbed him down from behind.

Tibalt and Ariz stood over their friend's body. 'I knew he wouldn't go along with it,' said Ariz. 'You have the money?'

Tibalt reached into his saddlebags and pulled out two leather drawstring purses. He tossed one to Ariz, the other to Santos. The purses' weight was enough to tell them they had been well paid.

'Is he dead?' said Santos before raising the wineskin again to his lips.

Tibalt grabbed it from him. 'No more! You stay sober. You need your wits to convince Blackstone about the route.' He looked at Ariz. 'Is he?'

Ariz grabbed a dirt-encrusted rock and smashed it down onto the mace wound. 'He is now.'

CHAPTER THIRTY-NINE

Santos and Ariz rode back in at dawn. Blackstone and the men had struck camp; the horses were saddled. Saustin's body was draped across his horse.

Blackstone and the captains gathered around them.

'His horse stumbled and he fell,' said Ariz. 'Caught his head on a boulder. It was treacherous out there no matter what this foul-smelling drunk told you.'

Meulon held the horse's reins as Will Longdon looked at the back of the dead man's head. 'Caked with blood and dirt.' He looked at Blackstone. 'Must have been a hell of a fall.'

Blackstone examined the wound. There was no evidence to contradict the story. 'We'll bury him and then ride on.'

'*Sí*, my lord,' said Ariz and heeled the horse away, followed by Santos.

Blackstone grabbed the startled guide's reins. 'The route?'

'Clear, lord.'

'How do you know?'

'Lord?'

'When Saustin fell did you stop and turn back or did you go on to check the bridge?'

Santos licked his lips. 'I saw the bridge in the moonlight. It was bright enough for me to see it. Like daylight. All is well.'

'Did he fall before you saw the bridge or after?'

Santos's face creased with uncertainty. 'We reached a turn in the track, we saw the bridge, as I said, and then his horse stumbled and he fell. So we did not need to ride on further, which is why we turned back. With your man.'

'Then how did his horse stumble? Were you riding hard?'

'No, lord. I... I do not understand the question.' Santos looked from one face to the other as Blackstone and his captains stared at him.

'Bright moonlight, the horses at the walk, an open track, it's hard to see how a horseman like Saustin could fall.'

Blackstone saw the panic in Santos's eyes. 'There must have been a rockfall. There were boulders and stones in our path.'

Blackstone nodded, a look that said he accepted the version of events. Santos relaxed, convinced he had said all the right things to the scar-faced knight whose expression still frightened him.

'Then you will take us back along the same route where the rockfall caused his horse to stumble?'

Santos clamped his jaw tightly in case Blackstone noticed his trembling lip. He nodded a bit too energetically.

Blackstone smiled at him and patted the horse's neck. 'Thank you, Santos, you've done well. Get some food and we'll ride on.'

The look of relief on Santos's face was clear to the men. He urged the horse away.

Blackstone looked at the men. Their doubt was as obvious as his own.

'The wretch is lying,' said Killbere.

'And unless his horse stumbled with a slope on one side, then I don't see Saustin falling,' said Beyard. 'He rode with me long enough – he was a good horseman.'

Meulon's voice could boom like a war drum but he spoke softly. 'There was no dirt on his shoulder. His beard was caked with it. It looks as though he fell face down.'

Will Longdon nodded his agreement. 'When a man falls from a horse he reaches out with his arm or he strikes the ground with the back of his shoulder first.'

Beyard saw where the conversation was going. 'Sir Thomas, those men shared a cell with me. Ariz and Saustin fought side by side at Cocherel. They helped each other stay alive in that stinking pit. It makes no sense thinking Ariz and Santos killed him.'

'No, it doesn't,' said Blackstone. 'Santos would sell his own children for a drink, but why would Ariz be involved? Unless we are wrong, then someone paid them.'

Beyard shook his head. 'I don't believe it. They were like brothers, those two.'

Killbere placed a comforting hand on Beyard's shoulder. 'My friend, I've seen family squabbles cause wars. Killing a brother is nothing.'

'We say nothing,' said Blackstone. 'Let their story stand for now. We'll find out the truth.'

Killbere's gaze followed Ariz and Santos's journey through the camp. 'Santos would break with a knife at his throat.'

'And if we're wrong about them? Accidents happen. Horses are dumb beasts; they shy at a rock's shadow. A sudden lurch and a man falls. It's happened before. We've all seen it,' said Blackstone.

'We'll see for ourselves when we get to the spot where it happened,' said William Ashford.

'You believe them, Sir Thomas?' said Renfred. 'I'll ride with my men along the same route and see where this rockfall is.'

Blackstone thought on it but shook his head. 'Ready the men. If there's trouble waiting for us on that road then we'll be prepared. I have a plan in mind. Captains, stay with your men. I'll tell John Jacob and he will tell Meulon, and he the next captain. It is to be done quietly and Ariz and Santos must not learn of it.'

Halif ben Josef and Andrés were ready to leave for the physician's vineyard. Blackstone clasped ben Josef's hand. 'I wish you happy days growing your grapes, Master Josef.'

'And I wish you a long life, Sir Thomas.' He glanced past Blackstone's shoulder. 'One of the Navarrese is dead?'

'Yes. A fall from his horse.'

Ben Josef's eyebrows raised.

'My thoughts as well,' said Blackstone. 'He was too good a rider. Master Josef, translate for me so the boy understands.' He turned his attention to the goatherd. 'Santos said there were rockfalls on the road.' Ben Josef's gentle voice lilted and rose with the Navarrese dialect's cadence.

The boy nodded. 'Perhaps. It happens, but on that road, I am not so sure. The rain came from the west but where he was taking you was the dry side of the hills.'

'Can you give me another route to Burgos if I go the way Santos suggests?'

The boy nodded. 'There are two or three ways. Follow the river in the valley and that will take you there.'

'Routiers are driving up from the south-east into Castile. If there is trouble, then we have the river at our back. Is there a northern route?' Blackstone asked.

The boy listened as ben Josef explained Blackstone's need for a safe route.

Andrés nodded; ben Josef listened and translated. 'If you come down from where the man fell from his horse, you cross the valley and the river, and then go through the lower mountain passes; no one will attack there. It's a road wide enough only for two or three horsemen. It will put another two days, perhaps three on your journey.'

'Then that's the route we take. Villages? Towns?'

The boy shrugged. 'A few but when you climb through a mountain pass, look for stones, high stones.' He opened his hand wide and pointed to his outstretched fingers. 'Sharp like wolf's fangs.'

'They are the Sierra del Cordel,' explained ben Josef.

Andrés recognized ben Josef's words. He nodded again. 'That is what they are called. And then below you is a narrow valley and on the other side more hills and mountains, but not as high, yes? Keep following the sun as it goes down and the plain ahead and then the river, the big river.'

'He means the Ebro,' added ben Josef.

Andrés smiled when he heard the name of the river. 'Yes, that is the river. Follow the sun west and you will find a bridge or a ford. I have not been that far for a long time. My father took me when I was a boy, but I do not remember it clearly. Perhaps when I see it again. Shall I take you?'

'Not that far but I want something more from you. On the road where my man was killed: where is there a place for men to hide?'

Andrés thought and then squatted and drew a twisting line in the dirt; he pointed to the rising ground meaning the track that curved around it, then he drew an elongated shape. 'El Talo.'

'It is called the flatbread. It is open ground between two mountains,' ben Josef said.

'Then that is where Andrés must go.' Blackstone spilled Spanish maravedis from his purse and pressed them into the boy's hand.

'Sir Thomas,' ben Josef said in gentle admonishment, 'that is too generous. It is a lot of money for someone like him.'

Andrés looked disbelievingly at the coins in his hand.

'It's a small price to pay for safe passage,' said Blackstone.

'I will offer prayers for your safekeeping, my lord,' the boy answered.

Blackstone placed a hand on the boy's shoulder. 'And I for yours.'

After they buried Saustin, Blackstone told Killbere and John Jacob his plan and as they went to the captains, he beckoned Santos to him and explained that he had changed his mind about the route to Burgos.

'North?' said Santos. 'That is a long way around. If we climb through the mountains it will take days longer.'

'Once we pass where Saustin died then I cannot risk a column of men being caught in the open ground. We will ride for the Sierra del Cordel. You know them?'

Santos was confounded. His lips moved but uttered no words until he had collected his senses. 'I know them, yes.'

'Good,' said Blackstone. 'You will lead the way.'

'Lord, there is also another chain of mountains that runs from the north all the way to the Mediterranean. Are we to travel across all the peaks once we clear the Sierra del Cordel?'

'No, we will go down into the valley and then ride west across the Ebro straight to Burgos. If the nights are clear we ride until I call a halt. Understand?'

Santos nodded. 'My lord, it would be safe enough on my route. It would not slow us down. Ask Ariz, he will tell you the same thing.'

'I did. He said you had a wine flask hidden and took them on the wrong track. I cannot trust you.'

Santos looked panicked. 'I did not drink, I swear it. Yes, when the accident happened, I took a mouthful from Ariz's wineskin. Why would he say that? He's lying. I am not in the wrong, Sir Thomas.'

Despite the morning chill Santos's florid face speckled with sweat.

'As you said: he dislikes you. Perhaps it was not your fault. Did Ariz and Saustin make you ride downwind of them? Is that what happened?'

Santos's mind juggled with the excuse being offered. Blackstone could almost hear the wind whistling through ear to ear as a thought tried to find purchase.

'Because if they were ahead of you on the track then you could not have known there was danger coming,' said Blackstone. 'You could not have warned them. And if Ariz does not wish to take any blame for the accident, then perhaps he threatened you to remain silent.'

Blackstone saw the escape he was offering finally drop in Santos's mind like a stone into a deep well. The wine-soaked guide bit his lip and cunningly held back from making such a confession.

'I would rather not say, lord.'

It was enough to shift blame without directly accusing Ariz.

'I understand,' said Blackstone. 'Now, you must regain my trust and lead us on the best road you know through the mountains. Only half my men will travel at a time. Once we are through, then you will return and bring the rest of my men. Can I trust you to do that?'

'You can, lord. I will do it.'

'Then I will permit you a drink before we leave. Don't let it cloud your judgement.'

'Bless you, lord. I will not fail you.'

Blackstone turned away to where Killbere waited.

'Sow the seeds of distrust between two men and watch the poison take hold,' said the veteran knight.

'That and as much wine as he wants. Dissent between those who share a secret will spew out the truth better than a knife at the throat. They'll show their hand soon enough.'

CHAPTER FORTY

One by one the captains listened to Blackstone's plan. It was an unhurried conversation, seemingly innocent to anyone who walked past the men being briefed. Ariz watched Santos press between the tethered horses. As one of Beyard's men helped him on with his mail, Ariz kept an eye on the king's guide. Santos was dipping his hand into his saddle satchel. Ariz pulled on his surcoat and buckled his sword belt, watching as Santos pulled free his hand, bent low and skulked into the bushes.

Ariz checked he wasn't being watched himself, and then rolled his blanket and food sack and walked without haste to his own horse. He secured the blanket roll, keeping an eye out for any of the captains approaching. They were busy. Some were speaking to Killbere, others to John Jacob. Meulon bent a knee and spoke to the Gascon, Beyard. No one was looking in his direction. He ducked below the tethering reins and pushed aside the bushes. A movement caught his eye. He pressed forward to where Santos squatted on his haunches drinking from a leather flask. The moment the tavern brawler saw the Navarrese fighter, he rolled to one side and crouched, knife in hand.

Ariz looked quickly behind him, ensuring none of the men were any closer. 'What are you doing?' he hissed.

'Keep your distance, you whoreson. I'll gut you and leave you to rot here. It'll be self-defence, and the Englishman will believe me. He trusts me now. Not you. You scum.' Spittle rained from his toothless gums.

'Keep your voice down. What's happened, you old fool?'

'Fool, is it? Blackstone told me what you said about me.'

'Put down the knife and we'll talk,' Ariz told him, stepping closer, hand outstretched.

'No! Stay where you are. You told him I was drunk, but he's no fool. He thinks you took the lead on the path. I am not to blame. Not me.'

Ariz sighed; his arm lowered, he took another step. 'You are an old fool,' he said without malice. 'Blackstone is playing with you. He was trying to find out if we lied.'

'I kept my mouth shut! I said nothing! You blamed me.'

Ariz's innocent gesture of opening his palms to appeal to the old man brought him another step closer. 'There is no blame. Don't you understand? He is testing you. Us. I have not spoken to him. He has not asked me anything.'

A cloud of doubt shrouded Santos's eyes and in that moment Ariz lunged, seized his wrist and clubbed him with his fist on the side of the head. The drunkard's legs folded. Ariz held the older man with little effort, knee pressed into his chest, the old man's knife seized and held at his throat. Santos, the wind knocked out of him, wheezed and spluttered from Ariz's weight. Once he saw the older man was incapable, Ariz raised his weight from his chest. 'Tell me everything Blackstone said to you.'

Santos propped himself against a tree and related Blackstone's instructions.

'Then he hasn't changed the route?' said Ariz.

Santos shook his head and coughed the phlegm from his wheezing chest. 'Not until we clear the track, then we go across to the mountains.'

'Then we're safe. All Blackstone did was to put the fear of God into you in case you had been drinking. He used words I never said to provoke you. He's a sly bastard, the Englishman. See it for what it is: he was searching for lies and never found any.'

'But if anything goes wrong I die first. I am the one who's leading them into the ambush.'

'You'll be safe enough. You know the place: you stop and tell them you need to check the road ahead. Now that Blackstone is halving his force we will be safer. Tibalt and de Hayle's men will overwhelm them.' Ariz stood and tossed the knife down next to Santos. 'Hold your nerve and we live to spend our money.'

'Just kill the boy,' said Santos as he got to his feet. 'Kill him and then ride hard for Tibalt.'

'And what proof could I offer? You think they would take our word for it? Besides, I'd have a dozen arrows in my back if I made a run for it. Just do what you've been paid to do. By tonight the boy will be in de Hayle's hands, Blackstone might even be captured and if he isn't then there'll be a reward for taking his head to the French.' He picked up the fallen flask and poured its contents into the dirt. 'You can drink yourself to death when it's done.'

He threw the empty flask at Santos and went back towards the camp.

Blackstone randomly picked men to be in the first group to follow him. He plucked Ariz from Beyard's command and told him to act as translator in case Santos spoke to anyone on their route and to ensure what they said was accurate. The Navarrese was already suspicious of Blackstone's intentions but had no choice but to obey. When Blackstone rode out of sight Killbere signalled the remaining captains. Andrés reined in his horse next to Beyard, who spoke Spanish.

'It will be a hard ride, lord. Will the boy keep up?' he said, glancing at Lázaro.

'He's under my protection and when we are in position, you will stay with him and the horses.'

The boy nodded and heeled the horse.

'What did he say?' said Killbere.

'A hard and fast ride, Sir Gilbert,' Beyard answered.

Killbere grunted. He glanced at the fearful boy whose life was in their hands. William Ashford and his men were waiting. 'Keep Lázaro close.'

Will Longdon and Jack Halfpenny's archers rode behind the lead troops with Beyard's men protecting their rear. Andrés waited and when Renfred signalled him to go his horse lurched forward.

Halif ben Josef was halfway down the hill on the way to his vineyard. He turned and saw the men spur their horses. His heart beat a little faster. He had ridden with Jean de Grailly and been captured at Cocherel. Then sold and held prisoner until Thomas Blackstone strode into his life and gave him his freedom. He was glad not to be caught up in the fighting and death that would surely come now that Blackstone was using himself and his men as bait. If Ranulph de Hayle was waiting in ambush on the plateau known as El Talo then Blackstone would be caught with a narrow track behind him, a cliff on his right flank and the rising broken ground on his left. The old physician watched a blade of sunlight cut through the low clouds and settle on his rows of vines. It was a good omen. He was happy to be home.

Ranulph de Hayle and his men were silent. A hundred and seventy-eight men squatted next to their hobbled horses, pressed back into the trees on the edge of the El Talo, the broad plateau. A quick tug to free the leather rein securing the horse's fetlocks gave them a fast mount and attack. The moment Thomas Blackstone and his men entered the open ground they would be on the defensive and would force those that survived the initial assault over the cliff edge. The craggy hillside rising to the right offered no escape: its steep broken ground would stop any horseman. It was a good plan that had taken days to put into place once Ranulph de Hayle had accepted Tibalt's betrayal. The one-armed man had promised Blackstone's guide could be bought. One of de Hayle's Navarrese men had met secretly with Tibalt in Pamplona. It did not take long to establish that the boy was still under Blackstone's protection. It came as a shock, though, because he'd thought they might have left the lad in Bordeaux with the Prince.

De Hayle chewed on a piece of dried meat and picked his teeth with a grubby fingernail. He looked at the men down the line. French money paid their wages, but it would be Castilian gold that would make de Hayle a wealthy man once the boy was delivered. He didn't know why the lad was so valuable to those who wanted him. It made no difference. The pursuit of the boy had come full circle, and the prize was about to be handed to him. And when he took Blackstone's head back to the French King, then he would be showered with even greater rewards.

'There,' said a man at his shoulder.

De Hayle looked to where the man pointed. A hawk, its grey-striped underside blurring as it sped across the sky; it spiralled upward, circling on a thermal, and gazed down on the men. Its sudden urgent cry drew the men's attention.

'Bad luck,' said the man and crossed himself.

Ranulph de Hayle spat out the sour taste of old meat. 'It's an omen,' he said. 'A good one. It's telling us they are close by.'

The man did not look convinced and, shaking his head, returned his attention to the narrow gap where the track entered the open ground.

De Hayle licked his lips. Whether or not it was an omen, it would feed on the dead by nightfall.

'Did you see that?' said John Jacob as they edged around the bend of the track. 'The last time I saw one of those it heralded Perinne's death at Brignais.'

'A French sword heralded his death as he saved my life. Ignore the superstitions, John. If we've seen the hawk, then so have de Hayle's men. Let them think it presages their deaths.'

Blackstone raised an arm and the column halted. Santos rode on oblivious that the men were no longer following. Blackstone glanced at Ariz, who looked uncertain. 'Let him ride ahead alone for a while,' he said. 'Just in case.'

Ariz nodded. There was nothing he could do. He eased one hand from the reins as the stationary horse shifted its weight. He patted its neck by way of a distraction and then returned his hand to his belt, letting his hand curl around the knife there. If Blackstone suspected an ambush, then Ariz would slash and run. Blackstone watched the hawk a moment longer. He thought he glimpsed its yellow eyes glaring at him. It was a trick of the light, he decided. The hawk was too high but such a bird liked to hunt in forests and if there was woodland around the bend in the track on the other side of the plateau, then that's where de Hayle's men would be.

Santos finally realized that Blackstone was no longer following him. He turned in the saddle and the waiting men saw the look of alarm on his face. Confused, he hesitated. As Santos looked back and forth, Blackstone knew his instincts were correct. He lifted his shield onto his left arm, and his men followed his lead, all except Ariz, who knew their plan had been foiled.

'Did you expect me to follow you and Santos to my death?' said Blackstone.

Ariz swept the knife towards Blackstone's face. Meulon, a yard behind him, struck him with his mace. Ariz slumped across his horse's withers; the horse shied, tumbling him to the ground. Panicked, Santos spurred his horse away.

'Drag him off the path,' shouted Meulon, turning in his saddle towards two of the men.

'Let's flush them out!' Blackstone said and spurred the bastard horse. There was a heave of saddle leather and jangle of horse bridle in a gathering surge of energy as horses' hooves clattered on the stony path. Blackstone pulled Wolf Sword free, raised it high, ready to strike the moment they swept around the corner and charged into the men waiting to kill them.

CHAPTER FORTY-ONE

Ranulph de Hayle saw the panicked Santos pound around the corner. He knew at once what had happened.

'Mount!' he bellowed. Caught unaware, they had only moments to untie their horses and ride into the clearing. Barely half the men were in the saddle when Blackstone and his men charged into sight. There was near enough five hundred yards for Blackstone to cover. Men cursed as their horses fought the rein when they tried to mount, startled by the sudden appearance of the other riders. As Blackstone's men spilled into the open ground, de Hayle saw how few they were. He spurred his horse forward. Santos was halfway across the clearing when he saw the horsemen appear from the trees; he yanked the reins too hard and his horse stumbled. He pitched forward, landing heavily on the unyielding ground. He lay still.

Le Bête's men broke free of the trees in extended line. Blackstone would soon reach the centre of the plateau. De Hayle's swarm of men would dictate the fight. The mercenary grunted with satisfaction. Blackstone must intend to strike hard at de Hayle's centre. It would suck them into the fray and then his men would encircle the foolhardy Blackstone and crush him.

'We have them!' he bellowed, waving his sword to signal the encircling command.

No sooner had de Hayle's men broken left and right than Blackstone's men halted, heeling their horses into defensive ranks, shields raised. If de Hayle's men punched through from any flank, front or side, Blackstone's men could isolate and kill them. It was too late for de Hayle to halt his own manoeuvre; his men were peeling away, now as uncertain as himself. Blackstone's sudden change of tactic made de Hayle pull up; the men who rode with him were now scattered across the plateau, wheeling horses away from the attack.

A screeching call reached them. De Hayle looked up. The raptor flicked a tasselled wing tip and swept away as the sky darkened. A whispering breeze broke the still air as arrow shafts arced and fell, followed by another deadly swarm. Blackstone had not moved but de Hayle's men were exposed. Most had not seen the sky darken. The sudden impact of arrows an inch thick, tipped with three-inch-long bodkin points, ripped into them. A third flight of arrows inflicted more heavy casualties. Man and horse screamed in pain. Riders fell, pierced through their backs; others had thighs pinned to their saddles. Horses fell too, crushing wounded riders, causing panic, forcing others to veer and stumble. Unseated men staggered in disarray. The relentless thud of iron-tipped shafts sowed a death crop across the field. Where once le Bête had had an overwhelming advantage, he now had a third of his men down. At least. Bodies lay everywhere: skulls pierced, some with more than one arrow in their backs, others crushed by dying horses that still whinnied in agony. De Hayle looked to the direction of attack and saw as many men as Blackstone had on horseback clambering down the broken ground on foot. The first ranks were already forming up to deliver the killing attack that would surely be coming.

He heard the flutter of goose-feather fletchings and ducked instinctively. An arrow struck his horse's neck, the force of it punching through the thick muscle. His horse bellowed and fell. De Hayle rolled clear. He hit the ground hard. Winded, he clambered to his knees and saw Blackstone's men spur their horses forward. The fight would be over before it had started. The mercenary snatched at a loose horse's reins and hauled himself into the saddle. Any dream of taking Blackstone's head from his shoulders vanished with the bitter taste of defeat and dust on his tongue.

As the clash of steel reverberated above men's curses, he wheeled the horse away from the fight.

Killbere, Beyard, Renfred and their men held their line at the foot of the hill. While de Hayle's men turned this way and that to escape the assault, Sir Gilbert and his companions hacked horse's legs from beneath them, struck limbs from their riders and, when a man fell, plunged blades into face, chest and stomach. Savagery was the fighting man's most important weapon. Will Longdon's archers were coming downhill, halving the distance from where they had shot from their vantage point. There was no need for them to shoot again. De Hayle's men were dead and dying. Some had broken free from the slaughter, followed de Hayle into the forest and escaped. Most could not.

Blackstone's men struck at the pockets of men who came together to strike their leader down. Men who fled on foot were pursued and killed. Meulon's men fighting with Blackstone wheeled and blocked horsemen trying to escape down the ongoing track, entrapping them between himself and Blackstone. Those who raised arms in surrender barely drew their last breath before being slain. There was no mercy given for the likes of these men.

Killbere and the others advanced on foot. Every flank was closed off to the survivors. Blackstone carved a path through the gaggles of men desperately trying to fight their way clear.

The battle shifted as men fell back, others advanced and the flanks closed in. They had yet to be counted, but it looked as though eighty of de Hayle's men had died, sixty had escaped through the forest and down the mountainside with de Hayle, and the remaining thirty-four survivors were surrounded. The fighting ceased as the encircled men turned this way and that trying to find a weakness in Blackstone's men. There was none. Blackstone edged forward.

'You men fought well, but I cannot let you live. Ranulph de Hayle paid you to inflict terror. I will offer you the rope or you die where you are.'

One of de Hayle's captains glared at Blackstone, then looked at the surviving men around him.

'A slow strangling death kicking our life away? Pissing our breeches? No rope! We're fighting men. We'll die but we'll take enough of you with us.'

Blackstone turned and nodded to the men. They parted, exposing Will Longdon and Jack Halfpenny's archers, arrows nocked, ready to kill without further injury to Blackstone's men. Will Longdon bent his war bow; his archers followed as one.

They loosed.

Blackstone's boot turned one of the dead. The man's face was contorted in agony. Beyard and his men clambered back up the hill to retrieve the horses and Lázaro then followed Andrés down a goat path to the killing ground.

Killbere cleaned the blood from his sword blade. 'De Hayle escaped, Thomas. Him and fifty or more of his men with him.'

'No matter, Gilbert. We finished him this day.' He looked up at the sky.

'The hawk's cousins are here now,' said Killbere.

Vultures circled.

'Saves us burying them,' said Blackstone. 'Meulon?'

The hulking man was striding towards them. 'Seven of our own dead. Others wounded. Mostly nothing we cannot attend to but two of my men have lost a great deal of blood and their wounds are deep.'

'We could ride back and fetch ben Josef,' Killbere suggested.

Blackstone shook his head. 'Six hours there and back? Even if we took the badly wounded with us, they would not survive even half that time.'

Meulon understood. 'I'll get Will to stitch them. He has herbs and potions from the Jew.'

Blackstone called as the throat-cutter turned away. 'Meulon, only for those who have a chance. What we have is precious. It's not to be wasted. Give them wine and theriac for the pain. If the wounds are bad, they won't last the night.'

'And our dead?' said John Jacob.

'Find soft ground, John. Cover their graves with rocks. We'll stop and rest the men and horses a few miles further on. A night's sleep and rest will serve us for the long day ahead.'

The archers went among the dead pulling free arrows as Renfred's men slit the throats of the enemy's injured horses. The circling vultures dared to settle closer.

'Lázaro! Andrés!' Beyard called the boys from where they attended to the horses. 'Keep them away until we are done here.' He pointed at the hillside and the bobbing scavengers. The two boys gathered stones and hurled them, scattering the vultures, who immediately settled a few feet from where they had been. Keeping the birds at bay would distract the boys from the carnage.

William Ashford dragged Ariz, hands bound behind his back, ankles tied with a length of rope long enough for him to shuffle, over to Blackstone and threw the murderer at his feet.

'Some of the horses caught him when they rode past him. He has some broken ribs.' Ariz clambered to his knees. A cut on his scalp had dribbled blood into his beard.

Ashford handed Blackstone Ariz's purse. 'In his saddlebags. Santos had one as well.'

'You sided with my enemy,' said Blackstone. 'You and him.' He turned to face Santos, now tied to a tree. 'I saved your life and you betrayed me.'

Ariz winced from the pain in his ribs. 'Money, Sir Thomas. Le Bête wanted the boy and Tibalt knew you had him. He was bitter about losing his arm. How else could he earn a living? You would not take him because he could no longer fight. He sold Lázaro for good money. Enough to let us buy a bed in a tavern and drink and whore ourselves to death.'

'Where is Tibalt now?'

'I don't know. I swear.'

'Who killed Saustin? It was no accident.'

'I wish you had not sent him with us that night. I knew he wouldn't betray you. He was my comrade but I wanted money more than friendship. I killed him.'

'Where is de Hayle going now? Where has he run to?'

Ariz shook his head. 'I had no dealings with him. Only with Tibalt.' He looked up at the scar-faced man towering over him. 'A quick death, Sir Thomas. I beg you.'

Blackstone beckoned Renfred to release Santos and then walked to the edge of the road and looked across to the distant valley where they would find their route to Burgos. The drop from the track was sheer. It had been a well-chosen ambush site. It was easy to see how he and his men could have been forced over the edge with an overwhelming charge. He signalled Renfred and Ashford to bring the men to him. They resisted, heels digging in. Their escorts hit them hard, forcing them on.

'What information do you have about Lázaro?'

Both men shook their heads.

'What did Tibalt tell you?'

'Nothing, lord,' said Santos, spittle dribbling into the curls of his beard. 'Nothing. I swear. De Hayle paid good money. All he wanted was the boy.'

Blackstone looked at Ariz, who searched in vain for anything that might grant him a quicker death than being flung over the edge onto the rocks far below. 'I swear by Our Lord's tears on the cross he told us nothing.'

'Santos?' The drunkard shook his head. Tears filled his eyes.

Blackstone nodded to Renfred, who grabbed Santos by the collar with one hand and by his belt with the other and hurled the screaming guide over the edge. Rocks smashed him into silence.

Ashford hauled Ariz to his feet. He was no match for the man who had served King and Prince as captain of their bodyguard. 'No! No! One thing! He told me one thing!'

Blackstone stepped closer to the terrified man.

'I did not believe him – Tibalt. I thought he had drunk too much wine. But he feared what lay at Burgos. With the King.' Ariz spat out the words, desperate to save himself from the crushing fall. 'Evil, Sir Thomas. A force so powerful it can kill men, fling birds to their death from the sky, turn wine sour and curdle milk. Enough malevolence to destroy a kingdom. Ranulph de Hayle knew. Even he was scared. Tibalt said he saw de Hayle tremble with fear when he mentioned it. There is a witch there. She serves the king. That is what he told me. That is all he told me.' Ariz sobbed, sucking air into his chest, forcing himself to blurt out the last words he would ever utter. 'She has... the power... all men fear.'

'Her name?'

'I don't know.'

Blackstone nodded, accepting the man had told him all he could. His hand swept across Ariz's throat. Blood spurted. Ariz's eyes widened at the speed of Blackstone's blade. He convulsed. Ashford let him fall. Blood spilled below his fallen body, soaking into his beard. His eyes glazed. Ashford kicked the dead man over the edge.

'So now you take us into a witch's coven,' said Killbere. The others crossed themselves.

'Superstition, Gilbert. There's no such thing.'

Blackstone turned away and strode across to where the men went about their work, yet as he did so he raised Arianrhod to his lips and asked the pagan Goddess of the Silver Wheel for her protection.

PART FOUR

THE DEVIL'S MISTRESS

CHAPTER FORTY-TWO

The devil fell in love with Velasquita Alcón de Lugo when she was fourteen years old. The girl was everything he desired. Her heart was imbued with the love of God, her knees raw from prayer, her soul pure, her life one of devotion. She served pilgrims who stayed at her father's inn on their way to find redemption at Santiago de Compostela where the apostle St James was buried. Ten years ago, when the devil, disguised as a pilgrim, pushed open the door of the inn, the girl's radiance smote him. The innkeeper spoke proudly of his only child's spirituality. It was common knowledge in the town that she was so blessed God whispered to her during her prayers.

That night the innocent girl, unable to resist the pull of the devil's desire, took her bedside candle and made her way to the hayloft where he seduced her. When she awoke she was alone: her virginity stolen, his seed planted, her soul led into temptation, her pure heart smothered by the dark veil of passion. There was no longer the need for candlelight. Darkness became her friend. It held no fears. She breathed its blackness deeply into her.

The devout parents witnessed the change. Her mother saw it in her eyes. They flickered with fire. Her father whipped the girl and spent good money on salt, sprinkling it on the coarse wooden floor, forcing her to kneel and pray for ever longer periods. But no prayer came from her lips. When the truth of the union showed itself, the innkeeper once again spilled hard-earned coins from his purse, this time into the hand of an old crone who knew how to rid the body of an unwanted child. They purged the girl and the devil's offspring was flushed from her body.

The girl lay ill for days, tormented with something more than fever. The priest refused to enter her room. The stench of evil was more pungent than that of her stale sweat and soiled bedding. Her parents begged and paid the last of their money for him to rid her of whatever foulness had entered her soul. Fearful but emboldened by the weight of the purse at his belt, the priest knelt at the door and offered prayers of redemption. After five days her torment eased. By the seventh day, she was calm and the priest found his courage and knelt at the child's bedside. She slept free of fever. It was a miracle that showed the power of prayer and the grace of the Almighty. The priest's work was done. The parents embraced their smiling child, bathed and fed her and retired for the night, humbled by the power of good over evil.

Before the cock crowed the fourteen-year-old Velasquita Alcón stepped lightly up the scuffed wooden steps to her parents' bedchamber and cut their throats. Villagers found the priest slaughtered like a sacrificial lamb on his own altar.

Over the years the child seduced by the devil journeyed to village and town. Like attracted like and she found those who knew the world of shadows, who cast spells, who turned men blind with a curse and who merged into darkness to witness events that had not yet occurred. At every step of the way along the dusty roads her pilgrimage gathered pace, drawn to those who with poison and necromancy hid their skills from the prying eyes of the Church. She killed or betrayed many of those who guided her so that her own secret was kept safe. When she reached the court of Don Pedro of Castile and

León, she was a gift to a King who relied on astrology and the predictions of a favoured heretic priest. Don Pedro was tall and muscular, blue-eyed with fair hair, and occasionally spoke with a sibilant lisp. He was a dangerous man, prone to fits of violence followed by an eerily calm lucidity. A King who bathed in his own greed and licentiousness.

How easy it was to let the King taste the pleasures she offered. He accepted her potions on his tongue: droplets that swayed his mind. He succumbed to sexual promises, his desire stretched as taut as a bow's cord until near breaking, teased over time until his lust was rewarded. Her enticements for him to act against his enemies were more seductive than those of the heretic priest Garindo. She knew how to manipulate the King's erratic behaviour; the man's skilled hunter's instincts were easily inflamed so that he saw those who stood in his way, or who in any way challenged him, as prey. Velasquita Alcón sowed doubt in his mind about the commander of his royal bodyguard, Gutier de Toledo. There was no more loyal soldier than de Toledo. He had fought the King of Aragon for years, keeping at bay Don Pedro's bastard half-brother and any threat of invasion. He knew how dangerous her influence was on the King and had vowed to expose the depth of her evil. It was child's play to undermine him. She had others lay false claims and evidence against him, showing that he colluded with the enemy, that he supported the half-brother's claim to the throne and intended to help the Aragonese seize the crown of Castile for him. The innocent man was beheaded with great fanfare.

The shadow witch continued her master's work. The young Queen had been an easy victim and Velasquita laid the blame for her death on two Jews. One by one those close to Don Pedro fell: threat or not, their demise weakened him. Her purpose was not to help any one man succeed to the throne but to cause dissent and disruption. The King's beloved mistress, María de Padilla, mother to four of his children, died within months of the Queen. The plague was blamed and her death caused Don Pedro great suffering; his grief allowed her to manipulate his weakness still further. Now the time had come to remove the heretic priest so she and she alone controlled the mind and emotions of the King of Castile.

She stood naked in the morning glow in her chamber high in the palace tower: an eyrie for the woman feared by everyone in the court. The sunlight was pushing its warmth across the mountains into her chamber and she let it bathe her like a jealous lover teasing aside the veil of darkness. The devil's inheritance was a mysterious gift. Never questioned. Never doubted. Her mind's eye soared across the peaks. The light blinded her and then opened a portal. She saw the men's approach. Still days away, yet fighting their way towards the king.

The images faded and, letting the knowledge of the men's approach comfort her, she dressed, as ever, without the help of servants. Amid the dozen or more aristocratic women who graced the palace she might have been invisible, apart from fleeting glimpses caught of her around the corridors and stairways of the King's various palaces. Wherever the King travelled she accompanied him and his courtiers, yet still was not seen. The rumour, barely whispered among the fearful, was that she took the form of a bird. How else did she appear so unexpectedly in different parts of the palace? Obviously she flew through windows and soared above the turrets. Others said not just a bird. A raptor.

Garindo, the heretic priest, stood with Don Pedro in the King's private chambers. A celestial chart of the planets and stars lay spread out across a table. Don Pedro chewed his fingernails.

'Sire, you can see that it is not a propitious time to attack Aragon. I urge you to wait for at least a month when the planets align more favourably.'

'There must be retribution for the cross-border raids. Our wounds will never heal unless Aragon burns,' said the King, his voice clear with barely a sign of his lisp.

'But, highness,' said the priest, 'will you not follow my advice? I have spent hours of daylight and darkness studying the charts and I bring you details of the heavens. I have devoted myself to your endeavours but your decision can only lead to...' He pulled himself up. To issue dire warnings was one thing, to predict defeat another. Garindo bowed his head. 'My lord, may I implore you to consult with your closest advisers? The Pope will direct all his power against you.'

Don Pedro looked past the heretic priest to the devil's child.

'You are already excommunicated,' she said. 'Strike fear into your enemy, my lord.'

Garindo faced her and summoned his courage. 'Your dark soul blights the radiance of my Lord Don Pedro. It would be better if a malignant creature like you plunged to earth with an arrow through her.'

She grinned. 'You believe palace rumours?'

'I believe in the God I have always believed in. I stand at the border between heaven and heresy because I have a skill that alarms the Church. You have nothing but venom for all mankind. I know who you are and what you are capable of.'

'That I have the powers of flight?' Suddenly she stepped towards him, making him retreat a pace. 'Is that why your heart squirms with fear?'

'Enough,' said Don Pedro. 'I will think how best to act.'

She turned her back to the priest. 'Send your Moors and tell them to kill every living creature. Strike fear into your enemy and your own men. Let them bring the heads of the slain on pain of forfeiting their own. It is through displaying might that you command respect,' she said.

Garindo saw the King's chin tilt, head raised, her words firming his resolve.

'Sire,' the astrologer said, desperation in his voice. 'Your enemies will come tenfold if you commit such an atrocity.'

Velasquita tore the chart in two. 'Your prophecy is weak.' She faced Don Pedro once more. His eyes widened with the expectation of a lover about to see the object of his desire naked before him. Her black eyes held his.

'Do what you must,' she whispered. 'And do it quickly. A man of death rides towards us.'

CHAPTER FORTY-THREE

Garindo shuffled along the winding corridors, his way lit by cresset lamps. He pulled his cloak around him, head down, deep in thought yet watching where he trod on the uneven stone floor. Footfalls had scuffed the passageway over hundreds of years. Common men and holy priests had skulked and connived their way through history down these corridors of power, bending the will of kings, influencing their weaknesses and embellishing their strengths. Garindo had spent too many years in unheated rooms: his body ached. His sixty-three years were as sixty-three crosses to bear. At least now his rooms were furnished with carpets and a canopied bed to keep the chill from him at night. The feather mattress and bolsters were a luxurious gift intended to ease the fatigue of his old age. All in all he had done well for himself ever since Don Pedro had learnt to trust his astrologer's prophecies and had elevated him to a position as adviser at court.

Garindo knew that cleaving himself to the Castilian King meant there was little chance of the Pope absolving him of the charge of heresy, even though the pontiff had not excommunicated him as he had Don Pedro. He saw the future unfold in conflict. Everything the old astrologer saw in his charts for the year ahead indicated the kingdom would soon be lost. He had tried to dissuade the King from further acts of aggression but had failed to inform him of the impending defeat. There were times it was better to let Fate's decrees unfold in her own time.

He pushed open the iron-studded door into his room and saw the lit candle on his table flicker from the draught. Every night kitchen servants laid out his food with a jug of wine and lit the stout candle so that he could retire for the evening with minimum effort. The room was pleasantly warm; the fire replenished by servants. He took a bottle of wine from his cloak's pocket and tipped the contents of the jug on the table into his chamber pot. The easiest way to drug a man was by poisoning his wine, for that masked the taste of anything untoward. Every evening he would make his way through the kitchens, ignoring the boys turning the spits of meat and bowing at his presence, and then go down into the wine cellar. He would select a dust-encrusted bottle far away from where the kitchen staff would choose wine, close to the kitchen door. It took rare skills to mask the taste of poison in food, so now he sniffed the cold cuts on his plate and placed a small portion of each meat on his tongue. Satisfied that no one had tampered with his food and the crust of freshly baked bread, he uncorked the bottle and poured himself a generous measure.

When he finished eating, he added seasoned logs to the fire for a slow burn through the night and then closed the internal shutters on the window. His room was too high in the tower for an enemy to scale the walls, but spirits condemned to the dark world knew no such barrier. The shutters bore the sign of the cross to ward off such creatures. Such caution had kept him alive so far. Plucking bits of meat from his teeth, he refilled his wine glass and spread out the original of the chart that his clerks had copied for the King – the copy Velasquita had torn in half. He looked again at his prophecy as dictated by the planets. Satisfied that his advice to the King had been correct, he disrobed and climbed naked beneath the sheets and blanket. Tiredness crept over him. He dozed for a while and then stirred himself to blow out the bedside candle. The dull, comforting glow from the fire with its dancing shadows lulled him to sleep. He slipped away into dreams of his youth in the monastery and then the priesthood: fractured images of a life that had been harsh but relieved by a deep sense of wonderment as the buried knowledge slowly surfaced within him. The weight of the blankets embraced him with their warmth.

Something slithered against his leg. It was not unpleasant, yet his sleep-fogged mind told him it was a snake and panic interrupted a dream about those first summers and the heat of Castile. He tried to roll away from whatever now pressed against his side but his body would not obey. His eyelids remained heavy, the dreamlike state holding him captive. He imagined he saw the firelight dance across the ceiling. And then he felt the joy of sexual arousal as warmth crept into his groin and massaged his cock. He gasped. How many years had it been since he had enjoyed the charms of a novitiate nun? Or an alehouse whore pleasuring him in exchange for absolution? He reached for his cock, but his arm would not move. It lay as if pressed beneath the weight of a stone slab. But still the blood pulsed through his groin. He was nowhere near release but the heightened pleasure became almost too much to bear. The years fled by. He saw the alehouse whore lift her skirts and pull free her breasts as he plunged into her. *Merciful Christ.* The joy. The tang of lust on his tongue. He thrust his hips but again was held by an unknown force. A breeze brushed his ear. It carried the scent of a woman. The soft cool air urged him to open his eyes. He tried, God how he tried, but they were held fast by the dream that imprisoned him. Then, slowly, as if released by a spell, they lifted and he saw the aroused brown-encircled nipples that swayed close to his face. He tried to raise his head to suckle but the force held him fast. His eyes focused as the woman leaned back. She straddled him, her face in shadow. His pleasure was beyond everything he remembered from before – more than twenty years had passed since work and age had robbed his body of any sexual desire. His heart thudded. Although he did not, could not, move, the gift of sexual union excited him beyond measure. And then the dream broke. He saw her face. Heard her whisper.

'The poison will only work when your heart is forced to beat faster and faster.'

'No,' he gasped. 'I am dreaming. There can be no poison... there... cannot.'

She kept moving, rocking gently, rising slowly and then pressing down again, raising the pitch of his excitement at every thrust of her pelvis.

'Old fool. Who else would brush dust from bottles of wine as they made their choice? It was easy to pierce a cork as you pierce me now.' She smiled and leaned forward, placing a hand on his chest, fingers wide, as if she could pull his heart from within. 'You are paralysed and I am here to see you die.'

He gasped for breath, his mind tormented by the witch's hold over him. The King had sworn he would protect him. That no harm would come to him.

'Is this pleasure worth dying for?' she whispered, leaning down against him.

A tear trickled down his face. He begged God to forgive him. His thudding heartbeat deafened him. His throat pulsated. A fragment of his mind, a mind ever devious, taunted him that at least he would be given release. His face felt on fire. Blood surged. A pain began in his chest. Deep. A wound as sharp as a knife blade. It travelled into his neck and down his arm, an arm that still couldn't be raised.

'Please,' he begged. He saw her eyebrows rise. 'Please... let me...'

She knew what he wanted. His flushed face, his gasping mouth, spittle clinging, eyes bulging in desperation. 'No,' she said. 'You will not have the pleasure of release.' She raised herself from him and stood back, watching his final strangled convulsion.

The fire's shadows flickered over her naked body.

The devil's imps dancing for joy.

CHAPTER FORTY-FOUR

The morning brought cries of alarm resounding through the corridors when servants found Garindo's body. The bailiff dragged a half-naked girl found cowering in the priest's room to the *Mayordomo mayor*, the High Steward, and he reported the circumstances of the death to the King.

'A girl?' said Don Pedro. 'How old?'

'No more than fourteen years, your grace.'

'How did she get into the palace and – more importantly – into Garindo's quarters? If he was fornicating, then it must have happened more than once. Who is she? Does she serve my daughters? There are no women servants here except in their chambers.'

'Sire, she is from the town. She is a gatekeeper's daughter. She claims the priest seduced her some weeks ago.'

'Garindo? The old man could barely take a piss, let alone bed a girl.'

'Sire, it appears she had the desired effect of arousal. Your physician says his heart gave way.'

The distressed King slammed a fist onto the table. A glass of wine fell and spilled across a map of Castile Don Pedro had been studying. A servant darted forward.

'Leave it!' He pushed back his chair. 'Let it stain,' he fumed. 'It soaks into parchment as blood seeps into my kingdom.' He turned his back on his steward and the clutter of courtiers who hovered in the background. A confused sea of thoughts fought one against the other inside his mind. Invasion and defeat stared back at him as he looked across the sweeping landscape. His half-brother, the bastard Henry of Trastámara, was gathering his forces on the border, supported by the Pope, backed by the French and driven by the King of Aragon to dethrone him. He faced the anxiety-ridden men. 'He didn't predict this, did he? He did not say to me, "Sire, I will die fornicating the gatekeeper's daughter"!'

No one answered. Don Pedro glared. 'Say something! You are my advisers! Advise me!'

The High Steward stepped forward nervously. 'My lord, news has reached us that the English are close.'

'An army? Edward sends troops?'

'No... no, sire. He sends his Master of War.'

Don Pedro's eyebrows rose. 'Oh,' he said with flagrant mockery. 'One man? Is that all he can spare? Then our concerns of being overwhelmed are banished.'

'And... er... men with him. We are uncertain how many but... but at least... eighty. Probably a hundred. Or even more. We have no news except that they are close,' he repeated lamely.

Don Pedro glared. Blood seeped up his neck, veins throbbing, face flushed. He squeezed closed his eyes to lock in his rage. And failed. 'Get out! All of you!'

Spittle sprayed the steward. Tears of frustration welled in the King's eyes. He wiped them away and leaned on the wine-soaked table. Castile lay before him. Its borders too wide to defend. He had written to the Portuguese on his western border in case he needed to run for his life and seek sanctuary; Portugal was his mother's country of birth, which allied them to him, but they had not yet replied. He needed a plan and none was forthcoming. He had vowed to put on his armour and lead his troops against the invaders. Except he had few troops to lead. He depended on the Moors. It was not enough.

'I told you he could not predict events,' said Velasquita, who had appeared unnoticed through the curtained door in the room's corner.

Don Pedro looked at her with a mixture of desire and fear. 'Did you kill him?'

'No. I knew you wished no harm to come to him. So I did not,' she lied effortlessly. She looked out of the window down into the courtyard as the girl she had paid handsomely to be in the priest's room – and threatened with eternal damnation if she confessed to the subterfuge – was escorted to the main gate. 'But I warned you, my lord. You should strike hard against those who harbour your enemies. Garindo advised you against such an action. He knew I was right. He did not have my ability to see events.'

He calmed. She hadn't moved, staying exactly where she entered the room, making no approach to entice him with her body – an intimacy he found increasingly difficult to resist when turmoil surged around him. He nodded. 'I considered everything you told me and I did as you suggested. The Moors ride to the border. They will kill without mercy.' He poured a fresh glass of blood-red wine then stared into its opaqueness for a moment. 'You said a man of death was coming.'

'He's close.'

'To cause me harm?'

'No.' She paused. 'He will die in Spain. He will sacrifice his life to save you.'

Blackstone and his men had followed the Río Arlanzón and saw the city of Burgos as they rounded the low hills rising from the valley. The walled city nestled on the lower slopes of the hills that rose to where the pale stone of the castle's rounded turrets caught the light. The same light bathed the horsemen along the skyline who had been shadowing them since sunrise.

'Here for trouble, do you think?' said Meulon.

'Doubtful. They're Moors. More likely to be seeing who we are. They have been there for hours but now that they are closer it is easier to identify them.'

The riders wore flowing robes of various hues, belted with sword and knife; each carried a steel-tipped spear that glittered in a wave of light and a double ellipse shield across their backs. Their horses were small compared to those Blackstone's men rode.

'Light cavalry,' said Killbere. 'No use in a major battle. They're used for skirmishing raids.'

'Those shields won't help them against English arrows if they ever tried,' said Will Longdon.

'North African shields,' said Beyard. 'They're called adargas.'

'I don't care what they call them: they'd be useless in a real fight,' said Longdon.

'You should hope you don't face such men,' said Meulon. 'They look as though they can ride like the wind and you couldn't hit a baggage train wagon at three hundred paces if it was moving as slow as a legless leper.'

'At three hundred paces I and any of my men could trim your damned nose hairs.'

'Which is a useless skill. We don't need archer barbers.'

Killbere twisted in the saddle. 'What we need is for the two of you bickering washerwomen to look more closely at men who could be our enemy before nightfall.'

Meulon spat one side, Will Longdon the other. 'Thomas,' said Longdon. 'Remember when we first landed in France and you were as green as young oak? I teased you into pulling your father's war bow and you killed a crow high in a tree.'

'I remember,' said Blackstone. 'And I felt Sir Gilbert's slap around the back of my head for wasting an arrow. My ears still ring.'

'And Will Longdon will feel my boot up his arse if he thinks I'll put up with archers wasting shafts.'

'I see no harm in bringing down that hawk to show them what an English archer could do.'

The men looked up but there was no sign of the raptor.

'It was there. I swear it,' said Longdon.

'Now you are blind as well as stupid,' said Meulon.

Will Longdon searched the sky. If the hawk had been there, it had clearly flown from view, but how it had done that so quickly he did not know.

The men fell silent as the Moors spurred their horses forward off the sloping hill, riding into the valley a half-mile ahead of Blackstone.

'They might test us sooner than we think,' said Ashford.

'They ride fast. Did you see how quickly those horses stretched out? I would like a horse like that, one that moves as fast as a snake strike,' said Meulon.

'You need a carthorse with the size of your arse,' Longdon said.

Killbere's voice was calm enough to be heard by the men behind him. 'Be prepared, Will. Ride left and dismount on command. Captains, we ride in phalanx.'

As Blackstone maintained the pace of their approach, watching as the Moors effortlessly formed up across their route, his captains eased their men either side of Blackstone, John Jacob and Killbere, who now formed the point of an arrowhead formation. If the Moors attacked, they would suffer heavy casualties from the archers long before their horsemen reached Blackstone. When they were four hundred paces from the Moors, Blackstone called a halt. The two sides faced each other. Suddenly the Moors yelled a blood-curdling challenge and spurred their horses. In no time at all the small Arabian horses were at full gallop.

'Damn,' said Killbere. 'Ready yourselves. Will, stay where you are. They're too fast for you to get into position.'

'No one move!' said Blackstone.

'Thomas, they'll be on us soon!' said Killbere.

Blackstone turned in the saddle. 'Sheath your swords. Hold your nerve.'

'What?' Killbere said.

'They haven't lowered their spears, they have no swords in their hand and they have not brought their shields to bear. Hold fast!' he called again.

At eighty yards the Moors reined in hard. By the time the fleet-of-foot horses pulled up they were at fifty. Blackstone's men saw dark faces break into wide grins, spears raised, the warriors ululating. Their ranks parted, allowing Blackstone's men to ride through the fierce Moorish cavalry.

'My balls tightened so much they're at the back of my throat,' said Will Longdon.

'Which is where I always thought them to be,' said Meulon.

The Moors fanned out as escort at a respectful distance either side of Blackstone's men. The approach to the city took them past farm buildings where peasants pulled free their cowls and bowed. Sheep grazed, grain barns were full and men gathered firewood, watching the procession of horses trotting on the road to the city. Thousands of men waging war needed feeding and the rich heartland of Castile offered enough food to support them. If the bastard usurper was not careful, the routiers would strip his new-found kingdom.

The closer Blackstone came to the city walls the fewer the buildings. Burgos was a strong defensive city, and it was plain to see why Castilian kings had favoured it as their main fortress palace.

'Lay siege to this place and you could live off the land and starve them out,' said Killbere.

'Which is why we have to convince him to abandon the city,' Blackstone said.

'A man protected by such walls and castle will not believe he can be defeated if he stays where he is,' said John Jacob.

'Convincing him is not the only problem, Sir Thomas,' Beyard told him. 'Castilian kings rule with the favour of a council.'

'When they know how close Hugh Calveley is with the French routiers, then he will see how fragile those walls are. Without men to fight there is no battle to be won.'

They rode uphill to the fortress-like city gates of Arco de Santa María. The double iron-studded doors swung open. As they trotted into the paved streets, crowds of citizens pressed themselves against the walls, watching the strangers' arrival in sullen silence. Houses were boarded up; merchants' stalls abandoned. The horses' clattering hooves echoed up the high walls and along the narrow streets. An unmistakable death knell for the city.

'Welcome to Burgos,' said Blackstone.

CHAPTER FORTY-FIVE

Once Blackstone and his men had taken the mountain path, Halif ben Josef returned to his beloved home and farm. The scent from his lemon orchards was a seductive reminder that he had abandoned the second love of his life. His wife had died in Pamplona years before and had never enjoyed living on a remote hillside while her husband cultivated his vines, caring more for them, she would claim, than he did for her. An untruth not worth contesting. Ben Josef's country house was a modest affair: stone and timber walls with a reed roof cut from the riverbank. The isolation was not absolute. There were three smaller houses, two for the six servants, another for the overseer. The wells were deep, the water plentiful. On his return the servants prepared food and drink, and a cauldron was lit so their master could bathe once he had toured the farm and assessed what needed to be done before the season deepened.

Ben Josef's servants had done their best to keep his vineyard in good order under the watchful eye of his overseer – the grapes in the drying sheds had not been lost and the lifeblood of the vineyard, the Arabic waterwheel, was in good order – but the physician saw to his dismay that the work he had instructed be done while away on campaign with Jean de Grailly had fallen behind. Wages for the farmworkers had not been forthcoming as promised by the King of Navarre, a condition of service that had placed the skilled physician with

289

the Gascon lord. Consequently, many of the labourers had left and sought employment elsewhere.

'I could not help it, Master ben Josef,' the loyal overseer told him. 'I have worked without payment these past months so that the servants had enough to buy food.'

'I am grateful.' He handed over the purse Blackstone had insisted on pressing into his hand before riding to meet whatever fate awaited him on the road to Burgos. 'See that everyone is paid and recruit more labour,' said ben Josef.

Andrés returned a day after the battle and told him of the slaughter. The boy, flushed with success and reward for his part in taking the veteran knight, Killbere, behind Ranulph de Hayle's lines, had been gifted the horse. That, together with money Blackstone had generously given him, meant his family would not face hardship that year or the next. 'I will stay and help, Master Josef. I will return to my family in a few days,' the boy insisted, eager to share what he'd seen of the battle and how the English knight had defeated the greater odds.

Ben Josef readily agreed. Andrés would share the overseer's room and eat with the servants and, when ben Josef had finished his evening meal, then the boy could tell him everything that had happened since he'd returned to the vineyard.

It was a homecoming to be celebrated.

Screams and the flickering light through the muslin coverings on his bedroom window woke Halif ben Josef. Gripped with fear, he grabbed his robe and pushed open the front door. The drying shed was ablaze, but the screams came from the burning waterwheel. Two men, one of them his overseer, were strapped to the wheel being burnt alive. Bodies lay in the yard and striding towards him, silhouetted against the flames, was Ranulph de Hayle and a one-armed man.

'Tibalt! Why do this? Why?'

Three others followed the Navarrese fighter, and ben Josef saw half a dozen more ripping the meagre furnishing from the servants' quarters. The sudden onslaught sharpened his senses. The bodies lying in their blood were of the women and men who served him. There was no sign of Andrés.

Tibalt pushed the elderly man back into the house.

'You have something of value,' said de Hayle forcing ben Josef into a chair.

'No, there is nothing here. Whatever money I had I gave to my servants. They had not been paid.'

Tibalt slapped him hard, whipping his head aside. His lip split, trickling blood into his grey beard. De Hayle's routiers ignored him and began tearing apart the house.

'You're a Jew. You have money. And something else I want.'

'Take whatever you find, but spare my servants.'

'Too late for that, old man. The women were crones, so they evaded rape, and only two of your men tried to fight.' He glanced outside. The screams fell silent. 'The wheel burned quicker than I thought.'

Ben Josef looked past the mercenary leader and appealed to Tibalt. 'I saved your life. I tended to you.'

'And took my arm.'

The routiers ripped apart the floorboards and chopped holes into clay-lined walls.

The noise of his home being destroyed about him tore into ben Josef's heart. 'Had I not you would have died a lingering death.'

De Hayle beckoned to one of the men. 'Tie him up.'

The routier went into the bedroom and returned with a sheet. He ripped it into strips and bound the old man to the chair. Tibalt stretched out ben Josef's arms so they could be secured to the armrests. De Hayle tried tugging off the physician's two rings, but was unable to get them past his knuckles, so he cut off the two fingers. Ignoring ben Josef's screams, he pulled the rings free over the bloody stumps.

'There's nothing!' one of the destroyers said. He strode to ben Josef, snatched at his beard and shouted: 'Where's the gold? Jews hoard gold.'

Tears spilled into his beard. He could barely mumble through his pain. 'I have no coin, no gold, no silver. Out there... the grapes... that is my wealth.'

'Keep looking,' said de Hayle. He grabbed ben Josef's slumped head. 'Where is the boy?'

Ben Josef looked uncertain. 'Boy?'

'I caught up with Tibalt after they ambushed us. He said that when he met Santos on the road with Aziz and Saustin, Santos said he'd heard you talking to Blackstone about the boy. That he would come here to be with you. He's worth money. Where's Lázaro? Where's he hiding?'

'He's not here. I swear it. You're mistaken.'

'Santos heard you!'

'Yes, yes, but the fool misunderstood. Lázaro is with Blackstone. It was another lad who was to return here. A peasant boy. He acted as a guide for Blackstone.'

De Hayle jerked upright as if someone had slapped him.

One of the routiers saw the mercenary leader's reaction. 'What?' said the skinner. 'What did he say?'

De Hayle recovered and smiled. 'The stupid old drunkard got it wrong. The boy's not here.'

'We did all this for no reason?' said the routier, lifting a rundlet from the floor and forcing the small barrel's lid free with his knife.

Ben Josef shook his head. 'Sir Ranulph, Tibalt, all you will find here are sweet peppers and meat in brine. Stored for winter months. Smoked river fish in the smoking shed and salted goat in the barn. We have nothing else. Nothing. Take the food, I beg you, and do no more harm. The people in Estella will see the flames. The militia will come.'

The routier plunged his arm into the brine and came out with peppers. He abandoned the barrel and went into the bedroom, tipped over the bed and began tearing up more floorboards.

De Hayle looked around the ruined house. The two rings he clasped in his fist were a poor recompense for tracking down the old physician, and an equally poor substitute for Lázaro, a prize worth delivering whether alive or not.

Ben Josef trembled from shock. Blood dripped from his severed fingers.

'There must be more, old man,' said Tibalt. He pulled a fighting axe from his belt and in frustration smashed its honed blade into a spindle chair. 'The King paid you to go with the Captal de Buch. What treasure did he give you? What precious stones?'

'The only thing precious to me are the rings you cut from my hand. They were my wife's,' ben Josef gasped through his pain.

One man strode in from the night's conflagration. He gripped a terrified Andrés.

'Is this the boy we seek?' said the routier.

Tibalt snatched at the lad's hair and pulled back his head. How well did he remember Lázaro? He had been delirious in the cell with Beyard and the others and by the time they reached Pamplona he had already deserted Blackstone.

'It must be him,' he said, though there was doubt in his mind.

Andrés fell to his knees begging. 'I am nobody, lord. Nobody.'

'He's not Lázaro,' said de Hayle.

'That's right. He's a peasant boy I brought to Blackstone. Remember your time at Blackstone's camp. You must have seen the boy there.'

'This is not Lázaro?'

'No. He came here to help me on his way home. His name is Andrés. He is not the lad you seek. Sir Ranulph knows it.'

The routier holding Andrés grinned and hefted a money purse. 'He had this. It's enough for drink and whores in the next town.'

De Hayle looked down at the terrified boy, and then glanced at the routier. 'The three years since the boy ran from the court would blur anyone's memory.'

'Leave him, I beg you,' said ben Josef.

The mercenaries looked at each other, Tibalt and de Hayle letting their thoughts follow the same route.

'Providing he didn't blab his true identity,' said Tibalt.

De Hayle nodded. 'We'll deliver his head and see if it's convincing enough.' He gestured towards the oak table. Andrés screamed. Ben Josef cried out. The boy struggled; the routier hit him with his fist and then dragged him across the width of the table, pressing his weight onto the boy's back as Tibalt snatched at Andrés's hair, tugged hard and then struck down with the axe.

The head severed, the boy's body convulsed. Blood poured onto the floor. Ben Josef wept aloud, cries to God, cries of animal pain. He moaned and sobbed, chin pressed hard into his chest, eyes squeezed tightly closed to avoid looking at Tibalt ramming the boy's head into the rundlet's brine.

The routier grinned and tossed aside the corpse. 'Let's get out of here. The old man's right. The militia will come up from the town.' He thumped the rundlet's lid closed and hefted the barrel.

De Hayle called to one of the others. 'Burn it. We ride for Burgos.' He went back into the night as the man smashed an oil lamp and sprinkled it across the bedding and furniture. He kicked free the burning logs from the fire and spread them onto the oil. After a few moments the oil caught, tongues licking across the floor, catching the muslin window covers.

Ben Josef's anguish turned to anger. 'I saved you! I saved your life!'

Tibalt looked at the stricken man. 'You took my arm. That's what saved me. Perhaps it will do the same for you.'

He swung hard and fast and severed ben Josef's arm at the elbow.

The elderly man gasped and vomited. He slumped unconscious. Flames raced across the floor and caught his gown.

'The debt's repaid, old man. You saved me from the pain of a slow death. I do the same for you.'

CHAPTER FORTY-SIX

Velasquita stood high in the castle, looking out of her window. The sound of horses' hooves drifted up the steep streets. Satisfaction glowed within her. Her heartbeat raced. She had seen a vision of the future and now the final journey would take place. The King would flee, his enemies would be victorious and she would use the killers she had drawn to her to wreak more havoc. The missing witness was her only concern. Where was the boy Lázaro? Had de Hayle found him? The fool had gone against her wishes and sought out the man sent by the English Prince. She had warned him. She had seen the unfolding slaughter. But de Hayle had survived. She knew it as surely as if she had been at the battle and witnessed it. However, not everything was clear. At times, as in a misted mirror, she could not see what lay behind the veil. The boy. He eluded her. He was too well hidden. Perhaps already dead.

The men rode into sight. The resolute figure of their leader projected his strength ahead of him. *Look,* her thoughts commanded. *Up here.* I am waiting for you. I have already felt your sweat on my body. I already know when and where it will end. *Look, here.*

Blackstone raised his face to the high turret.

King Pedro I of Castile received Blackstone and Killbere in a sumptuously decorated hall where banners and tapestries vied for attention. It was a room to impress, to show the

English King's Master of War, sent by a Prince of Wales known to be as extravagant as his father, that the Spanish knew a thing or two about luxury and flamboyance. Twenty or more courtiers crowded together at the rear of the hall, Spanish *ballesteros*, wearing cuirass and mail, armed with sword and spear, reinforced the gaggle of peacock courtiers. There was one Moor present, a tall, robed man who bore the look of a commander. None of his men were in the room despite the Moors being Pedro's main force. It seemed to Blackstone that the few Castilian guards were more for show than fighting. There was one burly Spaniard, dressed as a fighting man. His studded black gambeson had seen better days, as had his face. The High Steward waited, tall and dignified, layered dark-hued robes sweeping the floor, a staff of office gripped as tightly as any pikeman's weapon, unyielding in gaze and stance. To one side half a dozen young women stood, modestly dressed, cleavage covered, unlike the Prince of Wales's wife, Joan, who set the opposite trend in fashion. There was only one among those present the Princess would have admired for challenging courtly modesty. The woman in question revealed the enticing cleft of her breasts covered only by a black lace veil. It was the dark-eyed woman Blackstone had seen at the window.

The King sat, resplendent in layered silk gowns beneath brocade and pearl-encrusted robes. The High Steward stepped forward, bowed and bent to speak to the King. The two men engaged in muted but earnest conversation. Blackstone and Killbere were at the far end of the hall waiting until summoned. They were far enough away that anything said between the King and his steward would not be heard.

'Thomas, all we do, it seems, is to be brought before princes and kings. I cannot bow any lower, and my knees creak like Will Longdon's war bow. Does any more royalty await us on this journey?' said Killbere quietly, without turning to face Blackstone.

'No, God willing. The burden of keeping my tongue in check is like having the bastard horse's bit between my teeth.'

Killbere sighed. 'Is he taking our measure or wary of us approaching because we stink?'

'He's being a king.'

'I need a piss.'

'Then hold it. You cannot puddle a royal carpet. Take your mind off it.'

'I try but when a man reaches a certain age, the bladder takes on a life of its own. What about those women? His concubines, you think?'

'By the look of their dress they're his daughters. I'm supposing the others are their ladies-in-waiting.'

'Ah. Perhaps. Do you notice how their noses are snub, like a pig's snout? And their skin is bad. Pock-marked and pimpled. If those are their faces imagine what their arses must be like. You promised me beautiful women.'

'The one in black has a certain beauty,' said Blackstone, glancing towards Velasquita.

Killbere studied her a moment. 'I've seen women like that before. She's a man-eater.'

'Perhaps she has not yet found the right man to tame her.'

'And I suppose you have desires in that direction.'

'Come forward!' the High Steward called before Blackstone could answer.

'Merciful Christ, if he loses the crown in the coming fight we might all be saved from wet-nursing him back to the Prince,' said Killbere through gritted teeth, disguised as a smile.

They bowed.

'Your highness,' said Blackstone. 'My noble lord, Edward, Prince of Wales and Aquitaine, sends his warmest regards and prays each day for you to retain your rightful place.'

'Yet he sends you and a handful of men,' said Don Pedro.

'Men who have fought in every great campaign, and who stopped a mercenary force only days ago. Men who will fight for you and your family and escort you to safety in Bordeaux.'

Don Pedro's head jerked back. 'Leave Spain?' He laughed. 'They've sent you on a fool's errand. I am ready to face my bastard half-brother on the field. It is why I am here in Burgos. Henry of Trastámara will attack from Saragossa in the east. We are blessed with God's own defences, the Sierra de la Demanda stretches from the north to Valencia on the Mediterranean in the south-east. The terrain and the snow already sweeping down into the passes will make invasion near impossible. I am ready.'

There was a murmur of support for the young King from the gathered courtiers. He was playing to the gallery. They might as well have been minstrels eager to garner favour and play any tune the King demanded.

'No sire, that is not true,' Blackstone said.

'I will not be contradicted. I have spies. I have troops on my border. I have that information. Navarre has closed his borders. My enemies cannot strike from the north.'

Blackstone looked past the King. Those men had the standing to advise and insist on a course of action. If their own lives were at risk, and their private wealth threatened, they would soon clamour to escape. He raised his voice so those at the back and the sides of the hall would hear. 'Navarre has closed his borders so you might not escape through the Pyrenees and into Gascony. It was your shortest route to safety.'

He heard a murmur of concern.

'Ten thousand and more routiers are coming under the command of Sir Hugh Calveley, Bertrand du Guesclin, Matthew Gourney – these names are known to you, your grace. The Count of la Marche, le Bègue de Villaines, Arnoul d'Audrehem – I could name a dozen others. Men of France, Spain and England, destroying everything in their path because they seek your death and are being well paid for it. They want your gold, silver and treasure. This man who stands with me is Sir Gilbert Killbere. He has fought at our King and Prince's side and he is a veteran knight who knows what these men plan. I prize his experience beyond all measure, as do our King and Prince,' Blackstone said, boosting Killbere's status in one easy breath. 'If you will not believe me then let him speak.'

Don Pedro did not notice the slight flexing of Killbere's shoulders as Blackstone laid on him the burden of persuading the King. The monarch looked as though he needed no more convincing but he nodded, the misery of the looming truth already creasing his features.

'Sire,' Killbere bowed again. 'One group has already cut off Granada and turns north towards you. Hugh Calveley will not try to come through the mountain passes: he travels the same route we did, through the valley of the Ebro. We crossed the river at Miranda de Ebro. Thousands of men are less than one hundred miles away. If they ride slowly to save their horses, they will be here in four days or less. Once he reaches here, he will join up with those from the south. They will encircle you.'

Killbere's information had the effect Blackstone desired. The King sprang to his feet. The collective groan from the courtiers and the shocked look on the women's faces meant they finally understood the imminent threat to their lives. Blackstone watched Velasquita. She showed no sign of surprise or panic. She glanced quickly at him, catching him by surprise as if she knew he had been watching her. She smiled. Blackstone felt the visceral chill plunge from his chest to his gut. Ice cold. The chill felt moments before battle.

And then the warmth of arousal.

Blood pounding, welcoming the fight ahead.

CHAPTER FORTY-SEVEN

They summoned Blackstone to attend the King in the solar. He instructed Killbere to organize the men in their quarters and then followed the clerk who led the way to the upper room above the great hall, which was smaller and less ostentatious, although there were still significant signs of wealth with the bejewelled gold and silver reliquaries, candlesticks and various ornaments on display. Don Pedro had shed his finery and now wore a padded gambeson, quilted and silk-embroidered with the lions and castles blazon, the royal crest of Castile and León. A broad leather belt held an ornate dagger. Blackstone thought the man was likely to be capable in a fight and guessed he was no coward in battle. His weakness was his temper and cruel streak that undercut the affability a ruler needed to employ in convincing others to do his bidding when they doubted the wisdom of a proposal. Don Pedro's manner was like a flanged mace rather than an Italian stiletto.

The only woman present was the one whose smile had sent a shiver into his belly. Her black dress was adorned with a tear-shaped enamelled pendant that nestled in the delicate hollow of her throat. She stood against the wall as the High Steward and the Spaniard Blackstone took to be the King's commander flanked their monarch, who leaned against a broad table gazing down at a wine-stained map of the Iberian Peninsula. The tall Moor kept a respectful distance behind the King.

'Come closer,' said Don Pedro to Blackstone.

Blackstone obeyed and stood on the other side of the table. The King traced a finger over the stained map. 'We will abandon Burgos and go to Seville. There we are closer to our allies in Granada. If what you say is true, then we can hold there long enough to regroup and then take sanctuary in Portugal. My daughter Beatriz is betrothed to the King's son. We will be welcome there.'

Blackstone glanced at the Spanish commander, who remained silent. The High Steward made no comment either and the woman who stood behind them appeared to have no authority. The King looked at Blackstone. 'You will escort us while my army and my allies from Granada hold back the approaching mercenary forces.'

The two advisers remained silent. It was obvious neither man was prepared to contradict him.

'That's a risk too far,' said Blackstone. 'You will be slow-moving. You will be riding directly into the enemy approaching from the south. If you wish to sign your death warrant, sire, that is the quickest way to do it.'

Don Pedro bristled. For a moment he held back his obvious anger at the small size of the English force sent to rescue him, but self-pity soon got the better of him. His finger tapped the map with increasing irritation. 'You are a stranger here. You come uninvited and now you challenge me. If the Prince had sent an army instead of a handful of contemptuous men to aid the true King of Castile, I would not be obliged to retreat!'

Blackstone ignored the insult. 'The contempt comes from your enemies, your grace. I offer an escort to the Prince in Bordeaux where he can best serve the treaty between you. Once the French army joins the routiers then they have broken the treaty. Until now the French King and the Pope have only been employing brigands and men contracted to war. We need to get to Santiago and then the coast. Going south would be dangerous.'

'You fear conflict? The King's Master of War?'

'I fear being unable to serve my Prince. His command was to escort you to safety.'

Don Pedro stared down Blackstone, who returned his gaze without blinking. 'You challenge me.'

'I disagree with your decision.'

'But you will do as I command.'

'I will but with reservation and a suggestion.'

'You are insolent.'

'I am a soldier who knows a bad decision when I see one. I have a duty to serve you and take you to safety. If I did not voice my disagreement I would be doing you and my Prince a disservice.'

Don Pedro turned to the commander. 'Well?'

The Spaniard eyed Blackstone. 'Our men are stretched across our border, sire. Those who remain to protect you are few in number. Let this man draw the enemy away from your journey to Seville. Then we can reassess what we can achieve from there. It will take ten days to reach the city but we know the route and the river crossings; our enemy does not.'

Don Pedro waited for Blackstone to answer.

'Highness, you need as many of my men alive as possible so we can take you to France. We know the routes into Gascony that bypass Navarre's men. If you squander my men, you will lose valuable support from my Prince. We are his best men, proven time and again.'

'Your men are of no concern. If the enemy is four days away, then we have two days to prepare before evacuating Burgos. Sir Thomas, you will escort us halfway and then seek them out and engage them. You will buy me time. When I reach Portugal, there is no need for me to run to the Prince.

I will regroup my army and seize back Castile. Discuss this and be ready.'

The King tapped the table, a small gesture concluding business. He turned and left the room followed by the High Steward and Velasquita. The Moor followed. The Spaniard watched them leave and then offered his hand. Blackstone gripped the man's fist: it was as hard and unyielding as his own. 'I am Álvaraz and would rather sacrifice your men than what few I have. You understand?'

'Of course. But you must convince him to keep half my force with you.'

'I will. I need all the men I can get but I also had to convince him you and your men served him better by riding free of the column. I would not ask you to engage an overwhelming enemy but you might draw them away. We're weak. Our troops are scattered. And I assure you we cannot hold Seville any more than here. Less so. I'll show you the route and give you men to guide to you when the time comes.'

'More trustworthy than Navarrese, I hope. I've already been betrayed by them.'

'I'll give you a handful of Moors. They're savage bastards. The man who stood behind the King is Sayyid al-Hakam; he's their commander. The King sent most of them to the border to kill man, woman and child. He wants to inflict terror.'

'And that will give his half-brother the moral right to claim the throne.'

'I'm a soldier. I do what I'm told. If I don't, it will be my head on a pole.'

Blackstone made no argument; his eyes followed the King, the High Steward and Velasquita as they walked along the colonnade, high above the open inner courtyard.

Álvaraz noticed what drew his attention. 'Do not even think about approaching the woman. She's dangerous.'

'His concubine?'

'No one knows for certain. She has power and authority. Some say she's a witch. He keeps her close in case his food is ever poisoned. That amulet she wears is supposed to hold the antidote to whatever poison assassins use.'

'Then I'll steer clear of her.'

'A sound policy if you value your life. That way it will not be forfeit to the King's wrath or her bewitching.' He bent over the map. 'Now, let me show you the route we will take.'

Blackstone looked across him to where Velasquita had disappeared from view along one of the many other corridors. Was it his imagination or had she turned at the last moment to glance in his direction?

CHAPTER FORTY-EIGHT

The stables were built along the outer curtain wall with enough stalls to stable more than twice those needed by Blackstone. Killbere had billeted the men in the extra space so that man and horse remained close. The yard outside provided an area large enough for the men to bathe and cook and ready themselves for the coming journey and fight.

'The grain stores are full. There's oats and barley and fodder. The horses are better fed than the men,' said Killbere.

'They need their strength; we must fill our grain sacks, Gilbert, and have the captains draw supplies from the King's stewards. We have the right. They won't be denied. There are hard days ahead.'

Killbere pointed to where the captains had organized their own men.

'Meulon and Renfred's men guard each end; Will and Jack with the archers are in the middle. William Ashford will rotate the men through the night. These are strong walls, Thomas, but there is violence in our midst and I'm not so sure this King would weep into his wine if some of our throats were cut in the night.'

Blackstone looked along the length of the stables. Men rested in the stalls opposite their mounts. Beyard was cleaning his weapons as Lázaro bent and lifted his horse's hoof to clean out the accumulated mud. Blackstone caught Beyard's eye and beckoned him. A glance towards Lázaro was the only question that needed to be answered.

'Now we are in Castile and close to the King, he's frightened,' said Beyard. 'I've talked to him and settled his fear as much as I can. He's never been in this castle so no one serving here would ever recognize him.'

'And may not wherever we go,' said Blackstone. 'Henry grew so much over the same length of time that I barely recognized him and he's my son. And Seville?'

'Never been there either. The only place he knows is Medina Sidonia and we're nowhere near the place.'

Killbere scuffed the straw-covered cobbles. 'Do we concern ourselves too much? The assassins killed everyone there. They probably didn't even know what he looked like back then let alone now.'

'That's a good point, Sir Thomas,' said Beyard. 'He could easily just be a page like any other.'

'Except we have no other page riding with us and if Ranulph de Hayle believes Lázaro is still protected by us then the danger remains.' Blackstone looked around at the stables. Every thirty paces gaps in the walls gave access to the outside yard. If there was trouble it was unlikely they could catch his men unawares. 'We do not know if de Hayle still serves this King. What we do know is that, before he captured Lázaro after Cocherel, he had previously been here and then he sought the boy. The only witness to that murder is Lázaro.'

Killbere lowered his voice. 'And if Don Pedro seeks the Prince's help then he cannot afford to have a witness speak out. If the killer is identified and confesses that the Queen's death was ordered by this King, then the Prince would no longer support him. Rumours are one thing, the truth another. The boy stands between him and the treaty being fulfilled should the French invade.'

'We should have left the boy in Bordeaux or Pamplona where he could be a servant unnoticed by anyone,' said Beyard.

'A Navarrese boy in the wrong place,' said Blackstone. 'How easy would it be to unearth the truth under threat or investigation? There was no choice. Beyard, you cannot have eyes everywhere. Always keep at least two men with you and the boy at all times. When we ride keep him in the midst of your men.'

'And when do we leave this place?' said Killbere.

'Two days, no more. Calveley and others will be at our heels. I'll speak to the captains later.'

Beyard returned to Lázaro.

'Thomas, let's look around,' said Killbere. 'I like to know whose company I keep when I'm sleeping with my horse in a stable surrounded by walls guarded by men. If the cruel bastard decides he doesn't need us after all we could be caught like rats in a trap.'

Blackstone nodded. Don Pedro was not a king to be trusted. 'Have Ashford and Renfred go one way, you and Meulon the other. I'll take Will with me.'

A mile away from the city the bell of the monastery Santa María la Real de las Huegas clanged dully across the hills. Peasants in the field would halt their day's labour and make their way home, merchants and burghers in the city would cross themselves, put aside the counting of the day's profit and attend vespers as the murderous King knelt piously in his private chapel.

The castle's servants, denied the comfort of evening prayer, criss-crossed the yard diligently attending to their labours. Will Longdon had left his war bow in Halfpenny's care. He carried his archer's knife and sword. Blackstone took his time. 'Will, we need to see who is where and whether we need concern ourselves about being trapped in these yards if trouble flares.'

'Be damned rare if it didn't. We draw violence to us like a moth to a flame.' Will nodded towards the upper colonnades that skirted the main rooms of the castle. 'Palace guards.'

Blackstone watched two Moors standing at a double door of thick planks studded with ironwork and heavy hinges. 'I think the King uses them as his personal bodyguard. This way.' He turned into a doorway at yard level and immediately stepped into half-darkness. It was a storage area. The passage followed the length of the outer walls, broken by archways and bays built to accommodate materials. A waft of cold air brushed their faces.

'Smell that?' said Longdon. 'Damp air. There must be a stairwell leading down.' Blackstone's centenar lifted the nearest oil lamp down from the wall and held it in front of him. He handed Blackstone a tarred reed torch, tipped the lantern and let the flame catch. Lantern and torch illuminated the way ahead. As they drew closer to the fresh air, the flames flickered. They saw a spiral staircase cut into the rock that would have passed unnoticed without light. Its narrow entrance was barely wide enough for a man's shoulders. It was most likely used by child servants who could bend and twist their bodies up and down the steep spiral steps. Will Longdon tested the width. 'I don't think you'll fit, Thomas. It's too narrow. I would have to go down sideways.'

'Use this,' Blackstone said, offering the burning torch, exchanging it for the lamp. 'Can you see anything?'

Longdon raised the lamp. 'No.'

'Let's try it.'

Longdon followed Blackstone's example and unbuckled his sword, which would have wedged against the walls if remained belted to his waist. It was a torturous descent, slowly moving sideways to accommodate the width of their shoulders, pressing the side of each foot into the risers. No light penetrated the funnel and the exertion soon had them sweating. They emerged into a small square room. The remains of dead birds littered the floor.

'There has to be another way into here,' said Longdon.

Blackstone barely fitted through the final turn. 'Will,' he called, extending Wolf Sword's wrapped scabbard. The archer took it, allowing Blackstone to use both hands to pull and push himself free of the stair's coils.

'Here's the passage, Thomas.'

Longdon bent low under an arch, torch extended, and then straightened to his full height. His voice echoed. 'Big enough for you as well.'

Blackstone crept underneath and then stood upright. The limestone walls reflected more light and the hewn tunnel bore the scars of men's efforts with pick and chisel. They felt the breath of cold air more keenly. Longdon led the way. Blackstone tried to gauge which direction the passage was taking them but after two hundred yards the floor dropped by several feet in a gentle slope and came to a dead end. Ahead was the rock face. They moved closer and then saw a gaping black pit to one side, unnoticeable at first because of a stone half-wall. They peered into the abyss.

'It's a well,' said Blackstone.

The cool air stroked their faces as they leaned over. There was no glimmer of water at the bottom. The well looked to be as wide as a war bow was long. 'Six feet wide but no telling how deep. How did they ever dig this deep through this bedrock?' said the archer.

Blackstone raised the lantern and studied the egg-shaped tunnels. 'If it's as old as the castle then it was dug a hundred years or more ago. Our forefathers were tougher men than us, Will. Drop the torch.'

The flame plumed into the darkness. It showed the cut, stone-clad walls, bounced and ricocheted; sparks flew but still the burning torch did not reach the bottom. Will Longdon shook his head. 'Thomas, perhaps we've found the entrance to the devil's lair?'

The dim glow grew fainter and then finally disappeared. Blackstone raised the lantern. The well's curved wall had another turn on the far side, as if they had built a second well alongside. 'Will, look there.'

The two men edged around the half-wall.

'God's tears, Thomas, were these miners goblins?'

Blackstone stepped down onto the spiral staircase. 'We'll see where it leads.'

Will Longdon groaned. 'That means we have to come all the way back up.'

The deep spiral stairs followed the curve of the well, wide enough for both men to cautiously edge down. Blackstone held the lantern with one hand and used his other to feel the way. His stonemason's eye marvelled at the precision of the ashlar stone that had been so meticulously laid. It took highly skilled masons to cut dressing stone. Every so often a window slit was cut into the well's wall, allowing light to penetrate the darkness. Blackstone mentally calculated their descent and after thirty feet the spiral staircase became a corridor that curved around to the other side of the well to meet the next staircase that wound down in the opposite direction, no longer right to left.

'They must have changed the way down because the goblins got dizzy digging this,' said Longdon. 'Have you ever seen anything like it?'

'Nothing,' said Blackstone and carried on his descent. The same change of direction occurred every thirty feet as stairs became a corridor around the well and then reversed direction again.

'The muscles in my legs feel as though they are being torn from the bone,' said the stocky archer as they turned again at the next level.

'Can't be much further, Will. This is the fourth change so we are about a hundred and twenty feet deep.'

The lower they descended the clearer they heard the soft echo of flowing water. Blackstone halted. Will Longdon nearly bumped into him, his mind numb from the tedious descent.

'What?'

'You hear that?' said Blackstone.

'The water?'

'Listen.'

They half cocked their heads as the stairs funnelled the sound from below. At first there was only the whisper of splashing water. Then, another sound was caught between the splash of water against rock. A sharper sound. Indistinct. Voices.

CHAPTER FORTY-NINE

The shallow river flowed beneath the rock's curved roof and led out through a low opening to an area beyond the castle walls. The breeze had strengthened, sweeping the smell of the damp earth and the voices of those in the tunnel's entrance. Ranulph de Hayle stood with Velasquita, her cloak wrapped tightly against the wind's bite.

'We have found the boy you seek,' said de Hayle after explaining how they had been caught in Blackstone's trap. It had been his voice that Blackstone had heard; its strength had carried into the tunnels, but not the words.

Velasquita showed no sign of relief or surprise that the witness to the Queen's murder had been found. Her cold demeanour offered the mercenary no room to ingratiate himself. 'I do not see him among your men,' she said, glancing at the several men on horseback, obscured from being seen from high above by the rock face.

De Hayle wiped a hand on his greasy jerkin. He was nervous of this woman. 'He died trying to escape. We had no choice.'

'You killed him?'

De Hayle winced. The woman's dark eyes bored into him. He had faced men in battle, he knew the grip of fear when facing a vicious enemy, but she made his heart squeeze tight in his chest. 'I brought his head.'

He beckoned one of the men, who offered the rundlet, prised open the lid and reached into the brine. He hauled out Andrés's head. The setting sun's rays bled across the boy's sallow features. Velasquita stared at the face, the gaping mouth exposing the discoloured tongue. Was this the boy? She had seen him once when they banished the queen to Medina Sidonia. A glance only. Years before. She remembered the room into which the Queen had been ushered by the *ballesteros*. The frightened women who served her and who would later go under the knife. A boy, a peasant child, serving her loyally, skulking in a corner, head down as the High Steward instructed the guard commander how she was to be treated, how she could not leave the grounds, how she was to be kept under surveillance. There had been too many people in the room for her to remember one nine-year-old boy.

De Hayle grimaced when she reached out. Her fingers lifted the dead boy's eyelids. The glazed opaque eyes stared sightlessly at her. After a moment she sighed.

'This is not him.'

'My lady. It's the boy who sought refuge before Blackstone attacked us. Who else could it be?' he bluffed.

'You have failed.' Her calm words were as deadly as a judge's sentence of death.

'Then I'll continue to search for him,' he said hurriedly, desperate to appease her. 'If Blackstone has left him for safekeeping in a convent or with others then I will find him. You have Blackstone behind the walls of Burgos. Search among his men, my lady. If there is a boy there, then he might be the one you're looking for.'

'If I must search myself, then I have no need of you.'

De Hayle swallowed hard. 'What I meant was that the lad might be in plain sight.'

'Then it's a pity you did not see that for yourself.'

De Hayle struggled to control his nervousness. 'I will do everything to find him. If this is not the boy, then he will be close.'

'If you believe he is with the Englishman, then you know the way into the castle.'

'My lady, that can entrap me. If there is a boy with him might you not recognize him?'

'And if I did not? Would you have me kill him?'

De Hayle looked uncertain.

'No, of course not,' she said. 'I must keep my distance to avert suspicion. Once the boy is found he must be seized and questioned, then you kill him. Unless you would rather I end our contract?'

'I beg you to give me another chance. I have lost most of my men. I have only these here and twenty more nearby.'

She considered the mercenary's plea. He still had his uses. She saw two rings dangling from a leather thong around his neck. She held out her hand. De Hayle saw what she wanted and tugged the cord free.

'I took them from a man whose hands were as small as a woman's. They belonged to his wife.' He hesitated, hoping to buy himself favour. 'A Jew's wife. They're valuable.'

She turned them over in her palm. Jewellery a rich merchant or lord's wife might wear. For once de Hayle spoke the truth. 'A small recompense for your failure,' she said and put them into the purse on her belt. 'Keep searching for the boy. We leave the day after tomorrow for Seville.'

'And if we cannot find the boy here, what would you have us do?'

'Shadow our journey to Seville and beyond. The King's fate is determined. He will desert his prized city. You should find your courage. Fear of death can kill a man before the blade enters his heart. The time is coming when you will fight the Englishman and he will die.'

De Hayle blinked. 'How?'

'It will happen. I have seen it.'

'But I have not,' he insisted. His uncertainty mingled with hope of gaining victory over Blackstone. 'My lady, only God can determine our fate.'

'God determines everything but the devil provides the means. Fate is inescapable. I do not determine it, I foresee it. The moment will present itself; Blackstone will be weakened. You will seize the moment. Trust me, you will *know* when that time comes.'

She turned away and walked towards the opening in the rock. De Hayle breathed a sigh of relief and wiped the back of his hand across his dry mouth. He looked at the man still holding the boy's head. 'Get rid of it. Put a rock in the barrel and throw it in the river. It mustn't be found.' De Hayle knew that if Blackstone discovered the boy's head he would know they had murdered the old Jew and his rage would be unleashed on him. He watched the woman's dark cloak merge into the darkness. There was no doubt she had the second sight. She saw the future and she saw into men's souls. And she had no reason to lie. The fear eased from him. There was comfort to be had in that. He did not know when or where, but he would defeat and kill Thomas Blackstone.

Blackstone and Will Longdon reached the base of the well on the final turn of stair.

'Two hundred feet down, Thomas, I reckon.'

'Not far from it. I don't hear the voices now.'

'No. But whoever it was needed to be down here.'

Blackstone watched the lantern flame waver and turned his face to the incoming air. 'Or out there.' He walked along the flat rocks bordering the river until he reached the cavern's opening. There was no sign of anyone. He stepped out.

'The overhang would obscure anyone.' He looked around. 'Back there,' he said, seeing the sloping pathway beyond where they had reached the base of the well and the river slid away out of sight underground. They found another passage and clambered up the worn incline. Blackstone led the way as the limestone walls twisted left and right, and as they climbed higher they saw steps cut into the rock.

'What is this? It's beyond the well,' said Longdon.

Blackstone looked back at where they had started and then up at the hewn roof and walls. 'It's a siege tunnel. At some time in the past an enemy dug their way beneath the castle walls.' The steps ahead were less curved than those built in a spiral around the well. Eight steps, a turn, a dozen more, a passage, then more climbing higher. Every cut in the stone showed either that the defenders had built a staircase to stop an enemy tunnelling or that those who laid siege had breached the castle's defences.

They had climbed forty feet by the time they saw a dull glow at the end of the inclined passage. They looked up. Ten steps led to an opening. Blackstone took them two at a time and pushed against a stout wooden lid above their head. Blackstone cautiously lifted the trapdoor. It gave way with little resistance. They hauled themselves up. The tunnel led beneath the curtain wall and had brought them into the outer yard. They stood at the far end of the castle from where they had started and had come out beneath a stone canopy with wicker gates where barrels and sacks of grain were stored. It was clear someone had dragged a sack clear from the cover. Whoever had gone down had left it open, expecting others to follow. Blackstone strode out from under the canopy, turned and looked up. Sentries patrolled the battlements, their backs to the yard where torches and lanterns had been lit now that the sun was down. A hundred yards ahead a stout wooden canopied stairway led to a lower colonnade, and that ascended to one higher. These were the royal apartments. A door slammed closed at the end of the lower colonnade.

Blackstone passed the lantern. 'Will, get back to the men. Keep everyone in the stables now the sun's down. Stay cautious. If there's a threat here it might come from outside the walls.'

'Where are you going?'

'Up there,' he said, looking to where a shadow glided across the face of a cresset lamp on the floor above.

CHAPTER FIFTY

Blackstone followed the same route as the shadowed figure to the upper tier of the castle's colonnade. Cresset lamps lit the way every thirty paces. A figure moved at the far end of the passage: a sentry walking his route along the cross passage. Blackstone froze. Movement was the enemy. The Moor was a member of Pedro's bodyguard. He moved out of sight. Blackstone knew that the far end of the passage was the approach to the King's private chambers. A door closed somewhere ahead. He edged along the passage and saw a side corridor. It was darker than where he stood. There were no doors in sight so he followed the unlit corridor until a heavy door barred his way. He gripped the turning handle and raised the latch. Five paces beyond the door a dozen steps rose, twisting narrowly as they climbed higher into the castle's tower. He followed them.

Embrasures opened in the castle walls, allowing cold air to sweep into the corridor. The evening sky turned a deep blue as the first stars forced their way through the darkening heavens. Moonglow threw its light across the landscape, shaping hills and mountains before gliding behind a sliver of cloud. The moon's shift swallowed what light there was in the corridor. Blackstone stopped. Whomever he was pursuing could have gone into the labyrinth of passages and to continue was likely to be a waste of time. He was about to turn back when he heard a crow's guttural cawing somewhere further on. There was sufficient light from the darkening sky to feel his way forward. More steps. Another turn. A longer passage. Narrow openings in the walls forcing the breeze to whistle softly. Its sound took him back to childhood and the memory of blowing through a split piece of grass to impress his younger brother. A brother whose destiny took him to the battlefield at Crécy where he was hacked to death.

'Sir Thomas?'

He spun around. The darkened opening was a deep doorwell where a door had silently opened and Velasquita now stood. The fine dress she'd worn in the great hall had been replaced by a modest, plain gown buttoned down the front with loose hanging sleeves that brushed her neck as she raised a hand to tuck back a strand of black hair. Blackstone wondered if she had been in a hurry and only just arrived in her room. In that moment he realized he had reached the room in the turret where he had first caught sight of her. He looked beyond the open door. The room was simple but warm with coloured throws over the bed. There was no sign of witchcraft or symbols of evil. It appeared to be nothing more than a woman's bedchamber. Except for the raven on the windowsill that glared back, bobbed its head and then took off.

'I heard what I thought was a crow and that it might have been trapped,' he said. It was a lame excuse, and he regretted saying it.

'It is unlike a soldier to care about a crow's welfare,' she said.

'It is.'

'And yet.'

'And yet I was drawn to it.'

'Only the crow?'

Blackstone recognized an invitation when it was blatantly offered. 'I stumbled my way here as I was searching.'

Velasquita made no overt sign of enticement. She didn't have to. Blackstone already desired her.

'There are many crows and ravens here. They settle in the high towers. They demand attention by their insistent calling. And...' She studied him, holding his gaze, unwilling to yield from it. 'And they are portents of a man's character and fate. An Arab astrologer once made a prophecy about our King. He compared him to a crow: one who steals from his subjects and lusts for shiny objects. Our King covets gold. He seizes what he wants with impunity. Such actions show his place in the hierarchy of creatures, yet a life of such misdeeds can only end in a painful death. Who would think a King would be compared to a crow?'

'I prefer hawks, falcons and eagles. They fly high and strike fast.'

'Which are you, Sir Thomas? Falcons kill with their beaks and hawks and eagles snatch with their talons.'

He stepped closer. 'How much longer are we going to spend talking about birds of prey?'

She smiled. 'My knowledge is already exhausted,' she said and closed the door in his face.

Lanterns burned low in the stables. Men bedded down as comfortably as their horses. Pedro's wealth extended to his stabling and the deep straw and thick walls offered a sense of security to men who spent their lives sleeping rough with a hand clasped on sword hilt or knife. All the men snored and turned in their blankets except the captains on guard and Killbere, whose shoulders were propped against his saddle as he drank from a leather-clad flask. His boots stood next to the remains of his meal.

'You missed your food,' said Killbere as Blackstone approached. 'The kitchens here are generous. We'd all look like pregnant sows if we stayed much longer.'

'Then thank God we move soon.' Blackstone's blanket had been laid out, his saddle ready as a pillow. He settled down next to Killbere and scraped a finger around the bowl, lifting what remained of the grease to his lips.

'Will told me what you found.'

'A damned army could get beneath these walls.'

'Or a king could escape.'

'And if we delay beyond another day Calveley might be the one forcing him to use it.'

Killbere offered the flask. 'Spanish brandy. Sharp on the tongue but fire in the belly.'

Blackstone shook his head. 'I want an eye half open tonight, Gilbert. There were men at the bottom of that tunnel. And who in these parts is it likely to be? Who could have returned?'

'Ranulph de Hayle.'

John Jacob appeared with a pewter plate covered in a cloth. 'I saved your meal, Sir Thomas. Cold mutton and bread with cheese.'

Blackstone took it. 'I'm starving. Thank you.'

The squire smiled as Killbere glared at him. 'John, I told you he would not be eating tonight. That he was chasing shadows and would end up in the spectre's bed.'

'A man needs his strength, Sir Gilbert, no matter what challenge he faces,' said John Jacob and returned to the comfort of his stall.

'You think I was chasing a woman?' said Blackstone with his mouth full. 'I did not follow a woman.'

'And yet I smell her scent on you.'

Blackstone shrugged. 'I bumped into the man-eater.'

Killbere nearly choked. His glare was more damning than words.

'By accident,' Blackstone added.

'No such thing with a woman whose beauty could turn a man to stone. You propositioned her? Or she you?'

'We talked about birds.'

Killbere corked the flask. 'Any more of this and I'll think I heard you say you talked about birds.'

'It's a long story,' said Blackstone and went back to eating.

Blackstone walked along the stables to where Beyard and Lázaro shared a stall. Beyard's men were bedded down in side stalls as protection. Beyard and the boy were awake; the boy jumped to his feet.

'Sit down, Lázaro, eat your food.'

'Sir Thomas, is there trouble? I heard about the men below,' said Beyard.

'We'll stay vigilant. I want to talk to the boy because I have to decide how we travel onward with him.'

'You think we should leave him at that monastery outside the city?'

'Whatever chance he has, he has a better one with us. But we travel with the King and a handful of his courtiers and the Moors. I don't want him to get separated from us if we're attacked. But now that we are in the King's court he might identify the assassin without the killer knowing he's here. We cannot risk the lad taking fright and running, but if those who killed the Queen are part of the court, then best we are forewarned.'

'What about the captain who helped him escape?'

'The nobleman? I have had no word or sight of him. He has either left the court or was discovered and killed.'

'You know the lad has no English. French is best. If he doesn't understand I'll explain to him in Spanish.'

Blackstone laid a reassuring hand on the boy's arm. 'Lázaro, it is time we talked more of what happened that day they killed your Queen.'

Lázaro's reaction was less fearful than previously. He shuddered but nodded obediently. 'Is my lady's killer here, do you think, lord?

'I don't know. They killed her a long way from here, but we will keep you with us surrounded by Beyard and his men.' He let his words sink in. The boy nodded, willing to help. 'Tell us again what happened and what you saw.'

Lázaro spoke slowly; his effort not to stutter was noticeable as he recalled the terror of that day in Medina Sidonia. He faltered once or twice but then found his voice and whispered his account of the events. The final moments of the Queen's death when the man held her and the assassin poisoned her brought him to a halt. His eyes widened. He realized something he had not known all these years.

'I did not see his face.'

Blackstone and Beyard exchanged glances.

Lázaro shook his head. 'The assassin wore a cloak and hood. The man who held my lady, I saw him. He was a *ballestero*. Perhaps I closed my eyes at the moment the assassin killed her. It happened quickly. And then she fell and I ran.'

'You cannot describe the assassin?' said Blackstone.

'The man who killed her was small, which is why the soldier held my Queen and he killed all the servants. He cut their throats. My lady and I ran from him. I saw his face, but the man who poisoned her. Him I did not see.'

Beyard patted the boy's shoulder.

'Have I caused trouble because I did not see his face?' said Lázaro, looking from one to the other.

'No. You have made your life safer,' said Blackstone. And then spoke in English. 'It makes it more difficult now. If he can't identify the killer and give us warning then every shadow might conceal the assassin. He might not have seen who did it, but the man who did doesn't know that. And if he ever recognizes the *ballestero* he saw, then through him, we'll find the killer.'

'Sir Thomas, years ago Pedro slaughtered his younger brother and then ate dinner while his body lay torn and bleeding on the floor. A man that cruel and mad might kill the Queen himself. Is the King as tall a man as you or shorter?' he said.

'Shorter, by some way.'

Beyard nodded. 'Then let us tread carefully, Sir Thomas.'

Blackstone got to his feet. 'Nothing has changed, Beyard. They might still come for him.'

CHAPTER FIFTY-ONE

Ranulph de Hayle faced his survivors of the battle against Blackstone. Some had deserted but men still fed by greed had stayed. Tibalt swigged from a wineskin as he pushed the toe of his boot into the fire. The woman in the castle was their paymistress. If they wanted gold, they had to obey her. Trouble was, who would dare to go into the castle and search for the boy among Blackstone's men? No one volunteered.

De Hayle cursed them. 'Listen, you snivelling bastards, I have led you these past years and put gold and silver in your purses. I say we must discover if the boy is in there.'

'And do what?' said Tibalt. 'We cannot seize him; we cannot kill him. Why doesn't the bitch in black go among Blackstone's men and see for herself?'

'A woman of the court does not go among scum, that's why. And if she did, it would alert Blackstone. We seized the boy after Cocherel; we held him at Auray so we can do it again. We deliver him – we get paid. If he's here, then we can take him on the road to Seville.'

'Your plan is stupid,' said one man. 'Why did we kill the boy we found with the Jew? For what purpose? You risk our lives for a fool's errand. I have enough money in my purse. I'll not go into the castle.'

Ranulph de Hayle took a threatening step towards the tough-looking mercenary. 'I pay you well. You don't get to choose.'

'Someone else can go under the walls. I'll take my chances and fight Blackstone in the open. Whoever goes in there and gets caught will be dragged in front of the mad bastard King. I won't face him. He'd gut a man and hang him from the battlements while he still lives. No. Not me. And if you don't like it then I'll ride and sell my sword to Hugh Calveley.'

De Hayle stood his ground but his voice softened. 'You're right, we're being held to ransom by the woman but our reward will be a sack of gold and then we need never sell our swords again. So now there will be more for the rest of us.' His hand swept up, driving his knife under the man's chin and into his brain. He dropped. De Hayle turned on his heel, bloodied knife threatening the startled men. He stooped, plucked the dead man's purse and then threw it in among the men. Hands grabbed for it.

'You fight when I tell you to fight and you will crawl on your bellies through shit if that is what's needed. Now, whoever goes inside and sees if the lad is with Blackstone I will pay three times what I have in my purse.'

The sour-faced men, knowing the risk, shuffled uncertainly. Tibalt watched them. 'If I could go I would, but a one-armed man does not clamber easily through passages.'

Three of the men stepped forward. 'Pay us now,' said the one.

'If we are to die, then we die richer than we lived,' said another.

De Hayle bargained: 'Half now. Half on your return with news.'

They considered the offer and then agreed. They would sneak beneath the castle walls and locate the boy. They would do nothing more than identify him and then return for payment.

Blackstone's men slept. The stench of horses relieving themselves offered comfort rather than disquiet. Men and horses spent their lives together. Worn leather, horsehair and sweat mingled in a man's clothing and never left his nostrils. The men grunted, farted and coughed in their sleep. The cresset lamps flickered and died, their oil exhausted, the pungent smell of burnt wicks blanketing the stables. The castle's night watch went about their duty, moving across the yards, maintaining lanterns, changing guard with those on the walls. The moonlight had fled behind the clouds, the castle sucking what light remained into its massive walls. The darkened landscape concealed any movement beyond the cliff's overhang.

Three men ran for the old siege tunnel entrance. Once inside, the damp air hampered their flints from lighting the reed torches. None of the men liked the dark tomb and they cursed at the reluctant sparks – and then cursed with pleasure when the torches flared. The torchbearer led the way up the steps that took them behind the curtain wall and into the yard. One man peered out of the trapdoor into the darkness. A group of four men, one of them holding aloft a lantern, strode across the far side of the yard and disappeared through a turret door.

'Night watch moving around,' said the man. 'We stick together and if anyone challenges us then that's who we are. We make no sound; we need no damned conversation as to what's what. It's a simple job. Look among the sleeping men and identify the boy.'

His companions nodded their understanding. The torchbearer stepped past the man at the door and led the way. 'Stables run the length of the wall,' he said. The men stooped as they hugged the dark wall, unconsciously seeking invisibility. They reached the stable opening, raised the torch, checked no one was in the yard and stepped inside. The arched roof bounced the flames several yards into the stables. Horses on one side, sleeping men on the other. They crept along the walkway with one hand on their sword hilts, stopping only to check if it was a youth who lay sleeping rather than a bearded man. If the boy was here, his lack of whiskers would betray him. They reached halfway. A brute of a horse, its mottled hide looking like burnt cinders, was roped alone, a clear space either side of it. The stalls opposite held one man, asleep. They stepped behind the horse; a hind leg lashed out, narrowly missing the second man. He stumbled as he avoided the strike but was grabbed by his companion behind him, who saved him from falling onto the sleeping man. They were sweating. How long before a man woke to relieve himself or heard a startled horse? They quickened their pace, dipping the torchlight over the sleeping men. They reached the end of the stable and turned back into the night. They needed no words as they quickened their stride towards the entrance to the siege tunnel.

The men in the stable waited and then threw back their blankets, swords already in hand. Blackstone had warned them to make no move. That whoever had parlayed below ground would come in the night. Meulon and Ashford gathered their men and followed Killbere into the yard. The remainder guarded the stable entrances. Three figures ran across the yard from the wood store on the opposite side: Blackstone and Beyard shepherding Lázaro between them.

'We let them pass through,' said Killbere. 'Your bastard horse nearly gave the game away. One of the men damned near fell on top of me.'

Blackstone checked the twenty gathered men. Any more than these would be difficult to move quickly down the siege tunnel with any haste. 'Lázaro, go back to the stables with Beyard. The danger has passed now.'

Beyard pressed a hand onto the boy's shoulder and guided him back to safety.

'We must hurry. We depend on their torchlight,' said Blackstone, taking his shield from John Jacob. He led the way, hugging the outer stable walls towards the narrow entrance where a man the size of Meulon would struggle to squeeze through. When Blackstone had briefed the men, he'd told the throat-cutter he should stay, but Meulon had refused. Blackstone came up to his shoulder and if Blackstone could squeeze through, then so could he.

The river cushioned the sound of their footfalls and the occasional scrape of shield against rock face. The biting wind moaned through the underground chambers like trapped souls in hell. It had increased in strength, blowing across the hills from the distant high mountains, heightening the sound of the gushing water.

De Hayle's men doused their torches and quickened their pace. They were two hundred yards beyond the castle walls when Blackstone and his men emerged into the night. Their eyes scanned the half-darkness ahead, looking for the men. Had they lost them? Meulon ran forward, clambered onto a boulder and looked beyond the broken ground. The veil of clouds flattened the moonlight, showing the three shadows running. Meulon signalled and Blackstone's twenty men gave chase.

An hour later they skirted a ravine that obscured a narrow valley, well hidden from those travelling the road to Burgos.

At first it appeared to be a dry riverbed but the churned ground told Blackstone it was a herder's route. At the far side a campfire tucked between the boulders sparked as someone pushed more wood into the embers.

'We have them,' said Killbere, catching his breath. Sweat dribbled down the men's backs. Their mail and shields had made the fast-paced pursuit hard going.

'Down there,' said John Jacob, pointing out an animal track in the hillside. 'The rocks will hide us until we reach the bottom.'

'And then it's a fast run across open space,' said Meulon. 'Let's hope they have no crossbowmen.'

William Ashford glanced at the sky. 'There's a storm coming – fast.'

Killbere's flask spilled wine down his chin. 'He's right, Thomas. That ground will suck up rain like a child at a mother's teat. It'll be a damned quagmire. Let's get this done.'

Blackstone looked at the men behind him. They had exerted themselves. It was a good thing they had. Their blood was up.

'Sir Thomas,' John Jacob said. 'It's de Hayle. I saw his blazon.'

Blackstone looked to where his squire pointed. De Hayle's men were breaking camp.

'They didn't find what they came for so now they'll look elsewhere,' said Killbere. 'God have mercy on any poor soul who gets in their way.'

'God sleeps tonight, Gilbert. There's no mercy to be had,' said Blackstone.

He drew Wolf Sword and ran down towards the valley floor to kill Ranulph de Hayle.

CHAPTER FIFTY-TWO

Ranulph de Hayle had cursed his three men when they returned from the castle. He demanded twice over that they repeat everything they saw. They were adamant. No boy slept among Blackstone's men. If Lázaro rode with him, then he was elsewhere in the castle. That wasn't likely, de Hayle retorted. No boy would have better quarters than the men and their horses and Blackstone would not risk letting him be seen inside the walls. The three insisted they were right, and demanded their payment. De Hayle had no choice. He was reaching into his saddlebags when the storm broke. The horses panicked: mounts broke loose and careered into the scrubland and forest.

Thunder rumbled across the mountains. Swirling clouds overcame the peaks, surging past the sentinels, seeking an easier passage. Blackstone's men's lungs heaved as they ran hard across stubborn ground, turning their shields half across their chests as they fought the increasing wind, letting the buffeting glide across the shield's face.

The gods of war, desiring to see the men's efforts, threw spears of lightning across the storm clouds. The flashes of light allowed Ranulph de Hayle's men to see the night fighters racing towards them. De Hayle realized they had followed his men. He shouted over the storm to alert his followers. Those who hadn't time to find or fight over a horse ran towards Blackstone's fast-approaching men.

'They've seen us,' said Meulon, his great strides already pushing him ahead of the others.

'Meulon! With me!' Blackstone shouted.

The big man slowed to run next to Blackstone, ready for the two of them to act as a battering ram as they charged towards the disorganized routiers.

Killbere fell back into the main body of men, spat the excess phlegm from his mouth and sucked more air into burning lungs. Two more men went past his shoulder. God's tears, he was getting too old to run into battle; he needed to be there already waiting for an attack not lumbering like a three-legged hare. He ran on, pacing himself, knowing he needed to conserve enough strength to wield his sword. He silently cursed Blackstone for going at such speed and then himself for thinking he could still run as hard and fast as he had years before. He comforted himself that the enemy had turned to face them and were sprinting towards them. There would be a shorter distance to go now.

John Jacob was at Blackstone's shoulder. 'There are many more than us. We're outnumbered,' he said, glancing at Blackstone, who turned his head.

'Whenever are we not? Stay close, John. William! Go left! Gilbert?'

Killbere snarled from his exertions. He was close enough to hear Blackstone and knew how he would strike. 'I'm here damn you! I'll go right!'

Seeing how few of Blackstone's men there were, De Hayle's men set themselves into a defensive position, shields at the ready to take the shock wave about to strike them.

They didn't know the power of men the size of Meulon and Blackstone.

The impact rattled men's teeth. The attackers struck the routiers' shields with such force that a half-dozen men fell back into their comrades. It was a wound opened in their ranks and the ferocity of the two men who led the assault scythed into them. Blackstone's men flanked left and right, suffocating de Hayle's, hemming them in so they could not break free. Rats in a trap with no escape. The bellowing cries of violence forced strength into men's sword arms. Killbere's right flank held fast, striking against men determined not to die. Kill and stride forward. Kill and move again, trampling over the fallen, pressing boots into necks and torn wounds, ramming sword points down to still the squirming men.

Cold, hard rain hurtled down from the mountains, flaying men's faces, blinding the attackers, who ignored the discomfort. Swords raised and fell. Shields slammed into men's faces, bones broke, teeth and blood were spat free of mouths gulping for air. Blackstone and Meulon's strength had forced more men aside. They turned back to back, covering each other. Meulon and Blackstone slashed through de Hayle's men while John Jacob stooped low, shield high, jabbing below men's raised arms or sweeping his sword across hamstrings. Blackstone's men executed a cruel but efficient slaughter. Men cried out, wallowing in the churned mud, weeping in pain; someone in the mêlée's midst cried out: 'De Hayle! Help us! Where are you?'

Blackstone looked through the lashing rain. Blood trickled into his eye from a cut above his eye. Rain washed it clear, stinging the small gash. They were caught amidst the heaving men, their legs entangled in the dying. They saw horses rear as lightning streaked down into mountaintops, booming thunder slapping the air with immortal power. The gods of war's drumbeats urging on the butchery.

Blackstone couldn't see de Hayle. If he was among the horseman attempting to escape, he was out of sight. The wind shifted. It swirled the stench of blood towards the riders, who already struggled to keep their mounts from bolting at the overhead thunderclaps. Once they smelled the blood-letting, they would panic still further.

'On me!' Blackstone yelled. The half-dozen men nearest to him kicked and slashed their way clear. If Blackstone could reach the panic-stricken horses, he could kill de Hayle.

The one-armed Tibalt strove to mount and control his panicked horse at the same time. His strength failed him in the wet. He tumbled below its thrashing hooves, tried to roll clear but de Hayle had not yet calmed his own rearing horse. Tibalt screamed, his one arm raised to ward off the lethal iron-shod hooves. De Hayle paid him no heed and yanked the reins, the bit cutting his mount's tongue and mouth as Tibalt's head was crushed. De Hayle bellowed for his men to form up. Blackstone was fighting on foot and had so few men that horsemen could trample them to death. De Hayle's twenty riders and those that were still fighting would, this time, overpower the arrogant Blackstone who must think himself invincible.

So what was it in those vital moments that stopped him from attacking? The lightning slashed across the sky. Boulders exploded on the distant hills. Burgos Castle loomed high on the escarpment, its turrets unyielding against the storm's force. Velasquita's words struck him again. He would *know* when the moment came. When Blackstone was so weakened, he could slay him. De Hayle saw Blackstone raise his head, shake free the blood and rain, bellowing over the howling wind, his words swept away but his intent as lethal as sheet lightning. De Hayle *knew* this was not the time.

He yanked the reins and galloped into the night followed by those who could. Leaving those who could not to their fate.

★

Velasquita stood at the open window in the high tower. Buttresses shielded her from the wind shear sweeping around the walls. A wailing banshee that was her friend. The rain soaked her linen shift; the wind moulded it to her body. She raised her face to the storm. She had seen the shadowed men in the distance once they had cleared the castle walls, soon to disappear into the night. So few of them. She let her mind ride the tempest. It showed her blood and death but little else. This was not the night Blackstone died. There was still work to do. They had not yet found the boy. The cold gave her gooseflesh. A shiver across her skin. No, not just the cold. Anticipation. The final killings had not taken place. She had yet to take him to her bed.

CHAPTER FIFTY-THREE

The men were drenched and weary from the fight and the biting cold, but Blackstone had not lost a man. What wounds they sustained were not fatal and by the time they returned to the stables the enemy dead were food for wolves. The storm broke by dawn. The clear skies revealed the night's snowfall on the high peaks blurred in part by the specks of mountain vultures circling over the place of death.

Blackstone and those who'd taken part in the fight looked as though they had been in a tavern brawl. Cuts, bruises and a closed eye for William Ashford bore testimony to the hand-to-hand violence. Blackstone's men sat outside the stables sharpening weapons as they watched the castle bustle into activity. Moorish cavalry rode out to investigate the dead as the High Steward's officials prepared the King's departure to Seville. A delegation of city merchants swept across the yard.

'These people have money,' said John Jacob. 'Their clothes alone are testament to that.'

'And they'll want the King to stay. If he doesn't, their fate is uncertain,' said Will Longdon, sitting with Jack Halfpenny and their archers as they checked the fletchings on their sheaves of arrows.

'This place could withstand a siege for a year,' Killbere said, carefully running his finger along his blade's edge. 'In fact, he might have a better chance staying here.'

'And that's not what the Prince wants. If Don Pedro's half-brother camps outside for two years the result is the same. Don

Pedro will be dead and the French have their man in place and that leaves the Prince vulnerable. Henry of Trastámara will be crowned King of Castile no matter what we do. We have to get Pedro out of Spain and back to Bordeaux even if he plans to do otherwise because then the Prince will raise an army and we'll be coming back.'

John Jacob looked at Killbere, who shrugged.

'You don't like it, John, I know,' said Blackstone.

'An excommunicated King who abandons Christianity, Sir Thomas. A murderer. A man who would slay young Lázaro if he were ever discovered.'

'And us for shielding him,' said Killbere. 'Thomas, John's not wrong. We give aid to a vile man. When he came to power, he murdered his father's mistress; he's slain his Queen and his young brother. And there are men and women and children being slaughtered in villages as we sit here and plan to help him escape.' He spat into the dirt. 'We have no business being here.'

Blackstone watched the scurrying burghers go into the palace. 'We do the Prince's bidding. That is where our loyalty lies. John, tell Beyard to bring Lázaro here.'

John Jacob knew better than to question Blackstone, even as Killbere raised an eyebrow at the boy being brought into the open. Blackstone hauled bales of straw to where they sat by the grinding wheels. Men's clothes and blankets were already strung out to dry. The scene was no different from where any fighting men rested. The area was of no importance to the King, courtiers or officials. Only castle and palace servants who might mix with the fighting men came there, and then only to barter food for coin. A servant's life was worse than any soldier's.

Beyard ushered out an apprehensive Lázaro. Blackstone placed a reassuring hand on the boy's shoulder as his eyes darted back and forth to the preparations going on in the yard. 'Lázaro, sit here.' He guided him onto one of the straw bales. 'Can you stitch clothes?'

'Lord?'

'Mend clothes. Did your Queen's ladies ever show you how?'

The boy nodded.

'Good, I want you to sit here and stitch my shirt. There is no hurry. No one in the yard is interested in a servant sewing a shirt. Understand? No one will be looking over here.'

'I must just sit here? And sew your shirt?'

'You sew and you watch. You look at the people who go in and out of the palace doors. They come down the steps and go about their business.'

The boy looked from Blackstone to his protector.

'Watch for anyone who was at Medina Sidonia,' said Beyard. 'Do you understand?'

'Yes, I will look and see if there is anyone who caused my Queen harm.'

'And Beyard and others are around you. See? Men sharpening their weapons, attending to saddles and bridles. We're all sitting out here in the sun's warmth and no one is interested in us. You're safe.'

Lázaro smiled. It was true. These harsh-looking men had become his friends and he felt secure among them. 'I will sew the shirt and I will watch,' he said.

Blackstone followed the merchants of the city into the palace. If unrest were to flare up then the King's life would be in danger. His bodyguards were few and most of the Moorish cavalry were engaged on border raids. Blackstone and his men might be the only line of defence if the city rose up. He passed the guards and strode down the corridor to where a dozen armed men had secured the corridor. Raised voices echoed under the vaulted roof. Álvaraz stood with his men.

'Sir Thomas, I heard men were killed outside the walls last night,' he said, looking at the cut above Blackstone's eye and the bruising on his cheekbone.

'So I'm told,' he answered.

'You know anything about it?' he asked, pointing to the same place on his face as Blackstone's wound.

Blackstone smiled. 'I walked into a stable door when I was drunk.'

Álvaraz didn't believe a word of it. 'I don't know who those men were but I'm guessing they're routiers.' He paused, letting Blackstone's unlikely explanation go. 'Probably fell out with another band of brigands.'

'Most likely,' said Blackstone.

Álvaraz was no fool, nor inclined to play the game. He stepped closer. 'There is a sentry at the tunnel entrance.'

Blackstone knew there was little point in continuing the charade. 'Not last night.'

Álvaraz blinked twice. 'Someone with authority removed them.'

'And you will never know who because the guard would be well paid or dead.'

'Then they were routiers?'

'They were. Three came into the castle, most likely to reconnoitre its defences,' said Blackstone, obscuring the truth. 'I and some of my men followed them back.'

'Then there is a traitor.'

'It could be anyone. Someone who serves the High Steward or even a merchant willing to buy their safety,' said Blackstone and glanced at the door. 'Like they're doing now. I need to be in that room.'

'You have no authority to be in there, Sir Thomas. The council and the merchants are discussing the city's fate with the King.'

'Álvaraz, if there's an insurgency here you and I will be all that stands between the mob and the King. I need to know. And so do you.'

The Spanish commander looked uncertain but then nodded. He turned and opened the door wide enough for Blackstone to squeeze through without his entrance being obvious to those in the hall.

Blackstone stayed on the other side of the thick door. His presence went unnoticed as the inflamed passions of the city fathers bore down on the seated Don Pedro. Sayyid al-Hakam stood behind the chair, two Moorish soldiers with him. There was little doubt in Blackstone's mind that if the emotions became any more heated the temperamental King need only nod at the Moor for these merchants to be massacred. One man raised his arms and called for the others to settle down. His voice became more strident and the men finally quietened. From what Blackstone could see by the men's dress they were a mixed group of Muslims, Jews and Christians. Their businesses and wealth a common faith.

The High Steward nodded, giving permission for the man to speak.

'Most gracious lord,' the spokesman said, bowing low, arms extended. A Muslim trader wearing silk robes beneath his woollen cloak. 'Your ships carry our goods from the river at Seville and the ports of Castile to and from the Islamic world and Christian Europe. We trade from Cairo to Cordoba. As we speak, lord, I have a cargo waiting in Cordoba to load on my galley on the River Guadalquivir. I have news the vessel has been seized on your command. Friends here: men who have camel trains loaded with silks and spices from the

East dare not bring them to Seville or any other city for fear of what approaches. We are, merciful lord, in your hands. We beg you, do not abandon the city. There is money enough here to pay an army. We sell Sudanese gold to merchants travelling to Tunisia and Sicily and beyond: it can pay men like those who are already in the city. The Englishman can find more men like himself. Why would Castile abandon its riches? And its people?'

Another man pushed forward. 'Sire. You know me. Pérez of Burgos. You asked for a contribution to the cathedral. I and the other Christian merchants gave without question.' He made the sign of the cross. 'God bless our beloved and merciful saviour who died for us. Let others die for us now. If you abandon us, we all know Henry of Trastámara will not protect our fellow citizens, the Muslims and the Jews. They live here under your protection. And neither will being Christian mean anything to these hordes that will sweep across our city like a plague. We will die if you leave the city.'

Another merchant tried to speak, but the King raised his hand and silenced him. 'The galley was seized because the royal coin and plate from Almodóvar is being taken by my treasurer. He will sail for the Atlantic and join me in Portugal. I cannot stay here. Your homes and lives are in your own hands now. Welcome the mercenaries and the bastard they serve and buy your lives with your wealth.'

The merchants' wails rose higher. The High Steward slammed down his staff of office but it did not quieten the men's fury. Blackstone felt the door give at his back. Álvaraz had heard the commotion. 'Guard the entrance and stairs. The King has just thrown a fox in the henhouse,' Blackstone told him.

Don Pedro got up and left the room. For one moment it looked as though the merchants would surge forward. Sayyid al-Hakam half drew his sword. His two men did the same. The threat was enough. The disgruntled merchants turned to leave.

The door was already open. Blackstone had slipped away. He needed an audience with the King.

Sayyid al-Hakam and the King went up the stairs to his quarters, followed by the two Moors. The High Steward turned away, heading for a different part of the palace. Blackstone followed the King, waiting until his escort turned a corner before moving closer. They walked down a long passageway turning left and right and Blackstone realized he was getting closer to where he had followed the unidentified figure from the underground tunnel. He turned another corner and the two Moors faced him, swords drawn. Beyond them the King was ushered away without a backward glance.

Blackstone kept his hands away from Wolf Sword.

'You speak English?' he said, 'Or French?'

One of the burly Arabs said something in a harsh voice and put the point of his sword onto Blackstone's chest as a warning. Blackstone's instincts were sharper than the blade. No sooner had its point touched him than he pivoted, swept aside the sword and slammed the Moor into the second man. They fell heavily but despite their size quickly recovered; however, before they clambered to their feet Blackstone had Wolf Sword at the first man's throat. No words were needed. He took a step back and sheathed the blade. Point made. The Moors gathered their weapons and remained uncertain what to do next. A door opened somewhere behind them before they could decide and Velasquita stepped into the corridor from a side passage. She was barefoot and wore a linen shift. She said something to them that Blackstone did not understand. They obeyed without question and retreated to where the King and Sayyid al-Hakam had gone.

'You fight the King's bodyguard?' she said.

'I was challenged. I answered.'

'You're bleeding,' she said and turned back to her room.

Blackstone's hand touched the skin above his eye. The fracas had opened the cut despite Will Longdon packing the wound with astringent witch hazel. He followed her. Her door was open. More welcoming than their last encounter. He stepped inside. She was busy preparing something in a pestle and mortar. She didn't look up when he entered and closed the door behind him. A hawk stood on the windowsill, tearing apart a small rodent. Blackstone was superstitious enough to wonder if it was the same hawk that warned them of de Hayle's ambush on their way to Burgos.

'You draw birds to you?' he said, watching her grind whatever it was into paste. She added drops from a small green bottle.

'I feed them. They come,' she said and then turned to face him. 'I live in the high tower. I see the world below. I understand them.' The light behind her showed the shape of her body through the linen. 'Sit,' she told him.

Blackstone looked but other than a stool on the other side of the room saw only the bed. He squatted awkwardly on its edge, his scabbard making it impossible to do anything but half sit. He loosened his belt and laid aside the sword. She watched him for a moment, waiting until he was ready, then stepped closer and dabbed a piece of clean linen on the wound. He could not place the alluring scent of her perfume.

'It's sandalwood and rose,' she told him as if reading his mind. His chin lifted in surprise at the immediate answer to his thought.

'Keep still,' she said. 'Have you been to al-Andalus?'

'No.'

'Arabs bring sandalwood oil from North Africa. Don Pedro embraces their culture. You will see, he fashions the Alcázar in Seville after the Moors' palaces. This will sting.'

She pressed the paste into the wound. Blackstone didn't flinch.

'Men were slain outside the walls last night.'

'So I'm told.'

'You look as though you could have been in a battle.'

'If I left the city, I would have been reported by the guard commander at the gate.'

'Perhaps you did not go through the gate.'

'Perhaps I did not go at all.'

'Perhaps.'

She smoothed the paste. He felt the skin harden as it rapidly dried and formed a hard covering. She wiped her fingers clean on the cloth. But she did not move away. The swell of her breasts pushed against the linen. The enamelled pendant at the base of her throat caught the light. He stared directly at her. Neither spoke but the beat of the pulse in her neck quickened. He placed two fingers on the beating hollow, and then let the palm of his hand flatten against her breast, feeling the seductive beat of her heart. She raised her arms to lift free the shift and the action pushed her breast more firmly against his hand. Blackstone clasped her waist, pressing his lips to her breasts. She pushed down onto him, her mouth hungrily seeking his own.

A moment before her hair fell forward to smother his face, he caught a final glimpse of the hawk ripping apart its victim.

Held in talons and devoured.

CHAPTER FIFTY-FOUR

Twenty pack horses fitted with linen nosebags filled with fodder were loaded with the King's possessions: jewellery and fine silks strapped in bundles or baskets and secured on the hardy beasts of burden. Álvaraz's men saddled their horses on the far side of the yard as Blackstone returned to the men.

'The morning has gone. Do not tell me you have been discussing strategy with the King, or troop deployment with Álvaraz. He came over here looking for you.'

'I was waylaid,' said Blackstone.

'Thomas, you reek worse than a wet horse blanket. Was it the woman?'

'It was.'

'After all the warnings from de Hayle's men about her being a witch?'

'Álvaraz warned me as well.'

'And still you risk lying with her?'

'There wasn't much lying, Gilbert. Getting close to someone who might pose a threat is how we discover their intentions.' Blackstone smiled but Killbere wasn't amused.

'And you think she is not doing the same to you? For God's sake, Thomas, she already draws you into her web. One venomous sting and you are no longer a threat to her.'

'And what threat am I now? We're here to get the King to safety.'

Killbere spat in disgust. 'We are preparing to flee the city and you're fornicating with a whore witch. You're a damned fool.'

'As you so often remind me, old friend. What would I do without your admonishment?'

'Live longer.' Killbere picked up his weapons and turned for the stables.

Blackstone felt his friend's genuine anger. Perhaps the encounter with the woman had been foolhardy, but it had been satisfying. He glanced at Beyard, who was sitting with the boy. 'Has Lázaro recognized anyone?'

'He's been as attentive to those coming and going as he has sewing this,' said Beyard, handing Blackstone the shirt as the High Steward came down the steps on the far side of the yard and approached Álvaraz. Moments later Velasquita followed him, her cloak's hood on her shoulders revealing her face. Neither looked across to where Blackstone's men sprawled along the stable wall.

Blackstone saw Lázaro look intently at her. His heart thudded. Had the boy seen the assassin? 'Lázaro?' he said. 'Do you recognize anyone?'

Lázaro nodded. 'The woman and the man.'

'The soldier?' said Blackstone.

'No, the older man.'

'He's the High Steward. Where have you seen them before?' Blackstone said, suppressing hope of anyone who had been with the assassin being identified. And if it was Velasquita? He did not answer his own question. What was it he hoped for? Her guilt or her innocence in the murder?

Lázaro slunk down onto the floor to hide behind the draped clothing drying in the winter sun. 'When I went with the Queen to serve her at Medina, the man and the woman came into my lady's room. She was there with her servants.

The man told my Queen that she was never to leave the palace grounds.'

'And the woman?'

Lázaro shook his head. 'She stood back. It was the man who instructed her. It was the King's order, he said.'

'And later, when the Queen was killed, did you see them again? Were they in the room?'

'No, lord. The killer had his back to me and his hood pulled high. The *ballestero* who held her – I never saw him again. And I have not seen him here among the men.'

Blackstone looked across the yard to where the High Steward and Velasquita stood with Álvaraz. If they were not involved in the murder then the unidentified assassin was still on the loose and might still, if he recognized the boy, strike without warning. Blackstone took pity on the boy's fear and nodded to Beyard.

The Gascon placed a protective arm around the boy's shoulder 'Lázaro, come, let's attend to my horse. We have a long journey ahead of us tomorrow.'

Blackstone watched as Álvaraz appeared to argue with Velasquita and the High Steward; then, as the other two turned away, Álvaraz looked across to where Blackstone stood. He waited while Velasquita and the steward walked towards the palace entrance and then strode across the yard to Blackstone.

'We are to seize goods from the merchants,' said Álvaraz. 'A distasteful task, given their support for the King.'

'And one which will throw them into the arms of his half-brother. Is this not enough for him?' said Blackstone, gesturing to the laden horses. 'Is he mad? If we're attacked, they'll seize everything.'

The Spanish commander glared. 'No, Sir Thomas, I and my men are being sacrificed. We are to draw away any enemy attack while you and his Moors ride hard for Seville. If it comes to a fight, then we are to try to buy our way out with what we seize from the merchants. He loses nothing. The merchants and my men risk everything.' He looked to where the High Steward and Velasquita had re-entered the palace and then turned back to Blackstone. 'You must have friends close to the King. You were supposed to cause the diversion and draw away the routiers. My men are loyal, as am I, but now we are asked to throw away our lives.' He studied Blackstone. 'How did you take my place at the King's side? Did you bed the witch?'

Álvaraz turned on his heel. Blackstone knew that it was Velasquita who had changed the King's mind. 'Álvaraz!'

The Spaniard turned.

'I'll not let you be sacrificed. If the routiers come, I'll be at your side.'

The noble gesture was not lost on the seasoned fighter. He bowed his head and returned to his men.

Blackstone returned to the stables where he found Killbere rubbing goose fat into his saddle.

'Gilbert, the woman favours us. We ride with the King.'

Killbere wiped his hand across his jerkin, adding to its sheen. 'Your whoring serves us well. I believe she means to keep you close so when the time is right she can cause you harm.'

'I see no reason for her to do that.'

'Thomas, there's a malevolence about her beauty. It's as strong as the scent she wears and which rubs off your skin. We all lust for women but she... she curdles a Christian's heart.' He studied his friend. 'We will ride to our deaths if we ride with her and the malicious King. I feel it, Thomas. Do you not? Our Prince has cast us down into the serpents' pit.'

Blackstone did not make light of his friend's discomfort. He had felt the tingling mix of lust and what might have passed for fear – an uncertainty when he pressed his flesh to hers. The moment had startled him, for the woman's fragrance had lulled him as if it drugged him, and he had slipped into an almost dreamlike state. It unsettled him, despite the shared pleasure. He had been careless – he should be so no longer. 'I'll take heed of what you say about the woman, Gilbert, but our Prince chose us for a reason. If our orders are to take the King to him, then that's what we will do.'

Killbere uncorked his wine flask. 'And the Queen's assassin?'

'We protect Lázaro. Nothing more than that. Whoever killed her is not here.'

'He hasn't seen the King yet.'

'He will.'

Horses clattered into the yard. Blackstone and Killbere stepped out as the Moors returned from their patrol. Sayyid al-Hakam strode to meet them. He listened to what his patrol leader told him, raised his head and stared directly at Blackstone.

'He knows,' said Killbere.

'He can't prove it,' said Blackstone.

'He has a torn surcoat in his fist,' said Killbere, hiding his words behind the wine flask he raised to his lips.

Sayyid al-Hakam walked to where the two men stood. 'Dead Englishmen lie beyond the walls. They are Ranulph de Hayle's men.'

'How do you know that?' said Killbere.

The Moor's face creased. He touched his chest where a hobelar's blazon would be. 'His mark.'

'And how would Sayyid al-Hakam, master of Don Pedro's cavalry, know the blazon of an English routier?'

The Moor had been prepared to challenge Blackstone. He faltered but held his nerve. 'I have seen him.'

'Here?' said Blackstone.

Once again al-Hakam hesitated. 'No. Outside the walls. We gave chase once when he raided a village.' He tossed the torn surcoat bearing Blackstone's blazon on the floor. 'You killed those men. How did you get past my guards? Or Álvaraz's men? I must report to the King.'

Killbere picked up the bloodstained surcoat. 'This means nothing. We fought de Hayle's men days before we got here. Some of our men died; those of de Hayle who escaped could have taken this as a trophy. Last night we slept in the stables. Who would go out into a storm and try to find routiers?'

Sayyid al-Hakam looked from one to the other. 'You dry your clothes.'

'The roof in the stables leaks and some of the men are washing their shirts to keep the lice at bay,' Killbere answered without missing a beat.

The Moor studied them a moment longer and then turned his back and returned to his men.

'Do you believe him?' said Killbere. 'About how he knew they were de Hayle's men?'

'No. He is the King's man and we know de Hayle was here before setting out to search for Lázaro. That's how al-Hakam knows de Hayle's blazon. He and Pedro are conspiring to kill the only witness.'

Killbere swilled some wine and corked the flask. 'My God, Thomas, life was simpler when all we had to do was kill the French.'

CHAPTER FIFTY-FIVE

When the gates of Burgos opened, its citizens cried out at being abandoned. Don Pedro rode at the head of the column with his flag bearer at his side. His daughters and their servants followed. Five paces behind the small royal entourage Velasquita rode alone, flanked by al-Hakam and his Moors. It was hard to determine whether it was she who commanded the Moors or whether protocol demanded they ride further to the rear of the royal party. Even so, it made Velasquita look regal.

Álvaraz followed with his contingent as Blackstone and his men rode to one side, skirting the half-dozen boys who ran alongside every fourth pack horse bearing the King's treasures, their scrawny hands, tough and sinewy, grasping the horse's cheek strap. One boy rode the front horse, tethered by rope to those that followed. There were only six pack animals bearing the merchants' cloth and spices, easily controlled by their rope halters, and led by a single mounted soldier from Álvaraz's contingent.

Some citizens ran half a mile beyond the gates, still begging for the King and the men to return. There was no sign of the merchants.

'A common man has nothing to barter with when the enemy walks into the city,' said John Jacob.

'Their cries will soon turn to cheers when they welcome the man who'll become their King,' said Killbere. 'The merchants will try bribery with what they have left but I'll wager Hugh

Calveley's men and the other routiers will take no heed of what they say. If they haven't got their most valuable goods cached, they'll be ripped from their homes.'

Blackstone had waited with Beyard and Lázaro as the King's entourage filed through the city gates. Blackstone wanted to see if Lázaro recognized the King as being in the castle when the killer put his Queen to death. Once again the boy shook his head. The Queen's assassin remained a mystery.

'Perhaps the lad was so terrified his mind has erased those responsible,' offered Killbere.

'He remembers the *ballestero* who held the Queen while the assassin poisoned her,' said Blackstone.

'And who do we know in the court who knows about poisons? For God's sake, Thomas, she wears a potion at her neck to save the King.'

'And Lázaro didn't recognize her as being with the killer,' countered Blackstone.

'Then perhaps she gave the poison to a hireling.'

'Gilbert, in our time we've come across many who understand poisons. Physicians and barber-surgeons ply us with their pain-killing potions each time we're wounded. For all we know, the court physician killed her.'

Killbere remained silent; then he glanced back at Lázaro who rode with Beyard. 'We should let the boy find a home. He's too young to be riding with us, Thomas. If he has identified no one from the court, and by now he's seen all of Don Pedro's people, then surely there's no longer any threat against him.'

'You're forgetting Ranulph de Hayle. He still seeks the boy, and that means he is being paid by someone to do so.'

Killbere cleared his throat and spat. 'Thomas, we ride with a murderous, excommunicated King who employs pagan Moors, robs his citizens and keeps a demon witch at his side and likely in his bed. If this adventure does not drag us down into the bowels of hell then I will forsake women for a month by way of thanks.'

'Gilbert, such an act is against nature and would unleash unknown forces.' He spurred his horse. 'Better we fight in hell.'

The servants were hard pressed to keep up the pace but on that first day it was important to put as much distance as possible between Burgos and the enemy approaching the abandoned city. It was already dark when torchbearers, riding ahead under a leaden sky, bereft of moonlight, reached a small town. Servants prepared the King's quarters in the church and secured a farmer's barn for Velasquita. Everyone else pitched tents, lit fires and posted sentries. Blackstone walked through the camp, seeing that his captains and men had the food promised by the High Steward. As he circled the camp, looking out into the darkness where an enemy might approach, he sensed rather than saw a movement in the depth of shadows beneath a cliff's overhang. Wolf Sword was in his hand when he challenged the unseen figure.

The sky's dull glow was sufficient for Blackstone to make out the features of Sayyid al-Hakam as he stepped forward into the night.

'*As-salāmu alaykum,*' said the Moor, keeping distance between him and Blackstone should the Englishman lunge forward with his blade.

'I don't speak your language,' said Blackstone.

'I greet you in peace, Sir Thomas.'

The Moor had made no attempt to draw a weapon and Blackstone's instincts told him the man was alone. He sheathed Wolf Sword. 'You lurk in shadows like your mistress.'

'I serve the King.'

'You do as you are bid by those who do the bidding.'

The Moor's teeth flashed white in the darkness. 'And you serve your own desires, Sir Thomas. The King would not take kindly knowing you sleep with the woman who also offers him comfort.'

'If it were true then you should tell him,' said Blackstone. 'And see what comfort that brings you.'

Al-Hakam dipped his head. 'I see you know that Don Pedro does not like to hear bad news.'

'And I see you desire to keep your head on your shoulders.'

Sayyid al-Hakam took a step closer. 'What would it achieve to have both our heads on a pole? Who would protect the King then?'

'What do you want?'

'As you say, I do the bidding of those who send me.'

'The lady sends for me?'

'Why would she do that if you say you do not lie with her?' Once again the Moor smiled. 'It is the King who summons you.'

Al-Hakam led Blackstone through the torchlit church to where Moorish sentries stood guard outside a curtain of silk screens, three paces behind which hung another layer: soft barriers to be pulled aside before reaching the King. Don Pedro's quarters looked little different from the finery at the palace. Servants had turned a corner of the barren church into a warm enclave of opulence. Don Pedro sat eating from a silver plate. The High Steward stood to the rear, eyes focused on Blackstone. The King had not raised his eyes from his food or the map that lay spread before him.

'Closer,' said the King.

Blackstone stepped forward. The King flicked the map away from him. It landed at Blackstone's feet. Blackstone looked at the High Steward, who barely hid the smirk on his face. Obviously, Blackstone was expected to stoop and pick it up. An act as subservient as the bending of a knee. The King had not yet raised his eyes. He, like the steward, was waiting.

Blackstone did not try to pick up the discarded document. He looked down and saw the contour lines, realized that the marked cross was where they had stopped for the night and saw that it matched the approximate distance he reckoned they had travelled from Burgos.

'A fine map, highness,' said Blackstone.

Don Pedro glared at him. 'There are reports of enemy activity to the south and east.'

'As I told you, they are closing the door on help from Granada. And by now those from the north-east will be at the gates of Burgos.'

A servant offered a small bowl and cloth for the King to rinse his fingers. 'We must hasten for Seville.'

'Why?' said Blackstone.

The High Steward's gasp at Blackstone's impertinence was loud enough for the King to raise a hand to stop his trusted servant from berating Blackstone.

'It is my preferred city. I have Moors there. The city is strong. I can regroup.'

'You won't get there in time,' said Blackstone. 'If Burgos falls then Hugh Calveley will bask in the glory offered by your bastard brother. A day, perhaps two. Your army stretched across the eastern border will have been defeated. Toledo will have fallen. Next will be Seville. Riders to the east will be the French. They are closing in on you. You should slow them. They won't know your route. Send a diversionary force. Even a day will make a difference. Spur your horses and ride longer hours. If the moon blesses you, then ride through the night.' Blackstone cast a critical look around the comfortable quarters. 'Setting up accommodation fit for a king takes time. Valuable time lost.'

Don Pedro's temper flared. He kicked a stool; the plates and a goblet of wine crashed onto the floor. Servants ran forward to clear up the mess. The King stepped closer to Blackstone, who stood as unmovable as a rock.

'Your reputation for insolence precedes you.'

'My reputation for winning battles is what you should care about, my lord. I am not here to let you be blinded by those who seek your favour or fear your displeasure. I am here to save you. Break camp before first light. Let the boys ride the pack horses instead of running next to them. Give everyone who serves a chance to live.'

Don Pedro stood his ground. His eyes gleamed with anger. Blackstone knew a dangerous moment when he saw it and realized that if he was going to persuade the violent King to follow advice that would lead him to the Prince's safety in Bordeaux, then he needed to restrain his own insistence. He bent and picked up the map. 'This tells its own story, sire. You go one way and send a diversion another.' Blackstone did not need to look at the map. 'South and east around the hills and escarpment. If du Guesclin is closing in, then they will burn villages and towns. Your people will run from them. They won't be able to run fast enough. They'll be butchered on the road. A group of men between them and the French will buy them and you time.'

Blackstone's words appeared to calm the King. After a moment he nodded. 'I am sending Álvaraz and twenty men at first light.'

The King raised his eyes to look at Blackstone, as if wanting agreement.

'I will split my force and accompany him. Sir Gilbert and the rest of the men, with most of my archers, will take Álvaraz's place and ride with you.'

Don Pedro had calmed his temper and in cold contrast he stared at Blackstone. 'If reports are accurate of the number of French-led routiers, then you are likely to die on the road.' He shrugged. 'Álvaraz is expendable. If you die, then the Prince will be unhappy I let you go.'

'Then what is your preference? Let Álvaraz die outnumbered and alone or risk upsetting my Prince?'

Don Pedro examined and then savoured a piece of fruit. 'Since when does a King concern himself with what a Prince thinks?'

Blackstone went back into the night. Firelight from the scattered campfires cast shadows of huddled men and horses. On the horizon a sliver of sky showed itself. The cold wind was picking up. Tomorrow it would be at their backs, sweeping down from the high snow-covered mountains. Blackstone smelled the earth and the fragrance of the brush and pine-scented forests carried on the wind. And something else. Sandalwood.

He turned into the darkness, letting his senses find the direction. Fifty paces beyond the church and the firelight the night became blacker still. At first glance he saw what looked like a rock outcrop, but Blackstone knew it was the small barn. As he came closer a soft light flickered and then disappeared and then appeared again. He realized it was candlelight behind a cloth over an opening and the wind was lifting the material exposing the flame. Without haste he eased the covering aside. The inside lacked the luxury of the King's quarters; here candles and incense burned and it was their sandalwood aroma he smelled. There was no sign of

Velasquita. He stepped further into the barn. A brazier heated the chilled expanse. An unrolled mattress lay on the ground, covered with richly woven blankets, their deep dyed colours adding to the sensuousness and comfort of the sleeping quarter. Food and wine stood untouched.

A fluttering in the beams drew his attention. A bird found a hole in the clay tile roof and flew free, showering down a sprinkling of dust. It had diverted his attention from the room but instinct made Blackstone lurch aside as a cloaked figure appeared at his shoulder. His rapid reaction and the speed at which a knife appeared in his hand meant Velasquita had no time to avoid the sweep of his hand. Blackstone took a step back, letting the knife strike die in the air between them. She hugged the cloak tightly and then lifted her chin and smiled. She seemed fearless. Or was it she embraced fear and that inflamed her passions?

'You could have killed me.'

'You shouldn't sneak up on me.'

She shrugged, smiled again and, stepping to where the food lay on a linen-covered tray, nonchalantly teased away a segment of orange and sucked its juice, some of which trickled down her chin. 'If I did not sneak up on you, then I couldn't surprise you.'

'And risk death,' he said, staying where he was, resisting the urge to untie the cord at her neck and let her cloak fall because he knew, he did not know how, that she was naked beneath the mantle.

'I will die long after you, my English knight. Death does not frighten me.' She paused and watched him.

Once again Blackstone felt that slithering chill which ran from gut to groin. He desired her. The heat in the room mixed with the heady fragrances of candles and incense.

'Does death frighten you?' she asked.

Neither she nor Blackstone had moved. Her attention was on the orange segments, the conversation about death seemingly incidental.

'No. I will die in battle. That is the way of my world.'

She faced him. 'No. You will not.'

'You cannot know my destiny.'

'But I do,' she said matter-of-factly. 'I see men's lives. It is a gift. And a curse. Lives are an embroidered tapestry. I will be there and I will hold you in your dying moments. You will drown and your body will be swept away.'

Blackstone felt a moment of uncertainty. When the Welshman Gruffydd ap Madoc made the assassination attempt on the Prince at Bergerac, Blackstone had chased him into the city's underground river chambers. Wounded, Blackstone had plunged into the current and had come close to drowning. The story of him saving the Prince's life and coming close to his own death was well known. Travellers spread tales. Perhaps it had even reached Spain.

'What you think you see is the past, not the future,' he told her.

She threw the discarded peel into the brazier. It flared. Blue flames crackled. She watched them settle and then turned to face him. 'No. You will die in my arms. It is foretold.'

Blackstone took three strides to her, undid the cloak's tie and let it fall. Her nakedness was no surprise, only a delight. He lifted her onto the mattress.

'Then let's find out if it's tonight.'

PART FIVE

THE PROPHECY: DEATH OF A LEGEND

CHAPTER FIFTY-SIX

In the hour before dawn Blackstone strapped on Wolf Sword and readied himself to brief his men before accompanying Álvaraz to draw away the approaching enemy. Velasquita lay beneath the covers watching him. He looked at her. 'I live to fight another day,' he said.

She stretched and half turned, pressing her face into the pillow. The brazier had gone out in the night and the cold air made her tug the covers up to her neck. She was barely awake. 'Take care, the King will betray you,' she murmured drowsily.

Blackstone barely caught the whisper. Was it a genuine slip from the woman close to the King? If so, it had value for him and the safety of his men. 'How?' he said, matching Velasquita's low tone of voice. He stepped closer to her. Two empty bottles and spilled wine from overturned beakers were testament to the night's drinking and intimacy. There was no answer, her breathing slowing. 'How will he betray us?' he asked again.

'Seville,' she said, hardly audible. Blackstone lowered his face to hers. 'He abandons you... in Seville.'

Blackstone waited a moment longer, listening to her slow regular breathing. He went to the entrance and pulled aside the cloth covering the entrance. When he stepped outside, he remained there watching Velasquita through a chink between cloth and wall. If her warning was a ploy, she would have feigned sleep and then raised herself to check he had gone. She did not move. He waited a moment longer and then returned to the men.

As the door cover whispered back across the opening, she opened her eyes. Telling Blackstone of the King's plan in Seville benefited her. It was necessary if the vision she had seen of Blackstone dying in her arms was to be fulfilled.

Killbere and the captains squatted around Blackstone, ignoring the cold of the morning. Their horses were saddled, bedrolls tied and fires doused.

Blackstone repeated what the King had told him.

'He needs to move faster if the skinners are closing in,' said Killbere.

'That's what I told him,' said Blackstone. 'But while he rides harder there's a need to create a diversion to the east.'

'You mean a sacrifice,' Killbere said.

'And I'll wager we're it,' said Will Longdon.

'Don Pedro is sending Álvaraz and his twenty men.'

'And you promised Álvaraz to ride with him,' Killbere said.

Blackstone nodded. 'It's more than helping Álvaraz. There are villagers being burnt out of their homes and they're on the road north thinking they can get refuge and protection with the King.'

'Then we go to give them safe passage?' said Meulon. 'That's worth more than protecting this King.'

'We can't escort them, you fool,' said Longdon. 'Didn't you hear? They're going north, we're going south and east. We would need the wisdom of Solomon to divide ourselves to do everything.'

'I know the direction of the sun and the moon but if we get between them and the skinners then it gives them a chance. That's what I was saying,' Meulon answered.

Blackstone raised a hand. 'You're not going, Meulon, nor you, Gilbert.'

Killbere grimaced, wary of arguing with Blackstone in front of the men. 'You wish us to coddle the King? He has his Moors to do that.'

'Gilbert, I'm taking Renfred and John and Will Longdon. We halve the men. You and Meulon, with Ashford, Halfpenny and Beyard protect the King's flank. His safety is the task set us by the Prince.'

'And if we're attacked?' said Beyard. 'What do I do about Lázaro?'

'He stays with the baggage train and the other servants. He's no different from them to anyone else's eyes. We keep the boy alive and safe as long as we can. If when we finally deliver the King to the Prince he still hasn't identified the killer then it's likely he no longer poses a threat. We know it is not the King, the Lady Velasquita or anyone else at court who murdered the Queen. If it was hired killers then they will be long dead on the orders of those who arranged the Lady Blanche's assassination. We will have done our duty by the boy.'

'Aye, but the question is, who did the ordering?' said Killbere.

'We needed to identify the killer so we could extract a confession of who commissioned it. But we will have done all that can be done,' Blackstone said.

'If routiers are in Álvaraz's path then how will you slow them sufficiently to give the King extra time?' said William Ashford.

'You and the King must ride longer into the night and put distance between us,' Blackstone said.

'Then convince him to sleep rough and sleep little.'

'That's your task.'

'While you have the pleasure of killing French lords and their skinner friends. You leave us with the short straw, Thomas.'

'Of course,' said Blackstone.

The captains wished each other good fortune and went to organize their men. Killbere scratched an armpit. 'I swear Spanish lice bite harder than French,' he said as Blackstone tugged the bastard horse's rein to stop it twisting and snapping at him as he mounted. 'The witch wasn't trying to keep you safe with the King instead of riding with Álvaraz, she wanted you in camp so you were available for rutting.'

Blackstone looked down at him. 'Gilbert, do you think I am selfish enough to take my pleasure whenever I please, without good reason?'

'Reason, Thomas? You should keep that blade of yours sheathed when you are around a temptress.'

'I do it for the good of the men,' said Blackstone, but had the grace to smile.

'And I believe you as much as I believe that virgins inhabit hell.'

'If you reach Seville before me, stay alert. The King intends to betray us there.'

'She told you that?'

'Yes. As I said, I sacrifice my sleep for the good of the men.' He spurred the bastard horse before Killbere could answer. But he heard the veteran knight curse and then laugh.

They had left Killbere and the King's main group half a day's ride back. Blackstone and John Jacob rode with their men behind Álvaraz's column, letting them gain distance as they trailed the pack horses bearing the merchants' goods. As they left the camp a detachment of ten Moors drew their lithe horses alongside. Seeing their approach, Álvaraz reined back and rode to Blackstone, who faced the fierce-looking horsemen. Their lances bore the King's pennon.

'The King and Sayyid al-Hakam send us,' said their leader.

'What is your name?' said Blackstone.

'There is no need for you to know it.'

Blackstone and Álvaraz glanced at each other. The cavalryman's aggressive tone suggested they were not there to support the English and Spanish. Blackstone shrugged. 'They have not equipped you to fight a battle. You're skirmishers. If we meet the routiers in force, you'll be the first to die. Are you to be sacrificed for any particular reason?'

'We are not here to fight; we ride with you to make sure you and the Spaniard do not steal the merchants' wealth. It is the King's wealth now and must be protected.'

Álvaraz cursed, but Blackstone raised a hand to stop him reacting violently. 'If it tempted us to steal we would have done so already,' Blackstone said.

'Get back to that savage bastard al-Hakam and tell him we will not be insulted,' said Álvaraz.

'You have no say in the matter,' said the Moor.

Álvaraz's hand went to his sword but Blackstone reached out an arm and restrained him. 'Let them ride with us. An insult is not worth fighting over.'

'They dishonour us,' Álvaraz said.

'They are men following orders. The King commands al-Hakam: he instructs them. If we are to argue it will be with the King.' Blackstone eased the bastard horse between the two antagonists. 'And I don't have the time.'

Álvaraz had scouts riding ahead and Blackstone had sent Renfred and his men in a wide looping search for routiers. The land opened before them as they descended from the contours of the foothills onto the valley's plain.

'A long day in the open,' said John Jacob.

'We'd be better on the higher ground,' said Blackstone, 'but the tracks twist and turn too much for all these pack horses.'

'Look there,' said John Jacob, pointing to the shadow in the sky. A hawk rode a thermal, tail fanned out, and then a dip of a wing let it drop lower over the woodland. Its keening call carried across the sky. Blackstone saw the look of concern on his squire's face.

'Remember when we fought de Hayle? A hawk warned us. It's a good omen, John.' But Blackstone also felt the unease. The memory of the hawk on the windowsill of Velasquita's room was as firmly etched as the woman's nakedness. Some images lodged as deeply as a bodkin-tipped arrow shaft.

The forest's edge blurred. People swarmed out and along the ridge that ran high above the valley. They were villeins bearing what few possessions they had on their backs. Blackstone saw Álvaraz spur his horse towards them. By the time the column had travelled a half-mile the Spanish captain galloped back.

'Roving bands of mercenaries burned their homes. What few possessions they have they carry. Their numbers have increased during the day. They hid in the forest when they saw us approach but once they saw Don Pedro's flag they knew they were in no danger from us.'

Blackstone watched as the slow procession of villagers edged their way along the narrow track.

'Let's give them food. A few sacks of flour at least.'

'Yes, the poor wretches have nothing,' said Álvaraz.

Blackstone turned to Will Longdon behind him. 'Will, have your lads take some bags of flour to them. See what else we can spare.'

'We could ask them Moors if they have anything. Don't see why they can't contribute.'

'You'll have a spear in your arse for your trouble,' said Blackstone. 'And Meulon isn't here to pull it free for you.'

Will Longdon's grin was as wide as Blackstone's. 'He'd probably hurl me like an apple from a knife point. At least we know he has some use.' He tugged his horse's reins and rode back to his archers.

The wind on the hilltop was more bitter than below in the valley. The fighting men tugged their cloaks higher as the wind veered down from the heights onto their backs, sending cold waves of snow-chilled air from the distant high peaks.

'I don't envy those villagers' chances, Sir Thomas, and if they're running from routiers ahead, then I'm not so certain about ours either. We could spill out the merchants' wealth and leave a trail for any skinners. Like seed to a bird trap,' said John Jacob. 'Rather than be caught in the open like this, I'd prefer to choose where we fight.'

Blackstone pointed to the distance and the horsemen galloping towards them. 'That decision might be made for us, John.'

Renfred reined in. 'No more than two hours away. Three or four hundred. It's the French.'

'And we have a hundred,' said Álvaraz. He looked at Blackstone. 'Very well. We will die with honour. We will attack them and show how a Spaniard dies.'

'It would be better to show how a Spaniard lives,' said Blackstone. He knew they were trapped. No escape to their rear and no means of defeating the heavy odds soon to arrive in force. 'Renfred, ride out again. Let them see you. We must make certain they do not stumble on Sir Gilbert and the King.'

Renfred patted his mount's neck; then wheeled the horse and set off, followed by his men.

Blackstone looked at the villagers making their way along the contour track on the hill behind them. 'They'll be massacred. Álvaraz, we must defend this place.'

'Stop here?' the Spaniard said, looking around the open ground. 'The hills at our back and open ground on all sides? They will outflank us whenever they wish. No, Sir Thomas. At least we should die with glory. We strike them and if any of us survive they ride hard for the King.'

Blackstone grabbed his arm before Álvaraz could issue the command. 'We can buy time for these people.'

The Spaniard yanked free. 'With so few men? How?'

'With those villagers' help. We make the skinners think we are stronger and that if they attack, we can overcome them.'

Álvaraz squinted in the biting wind. 'Did the witch drug you? Have you lost your mind?'

'Listen to me. Let me explain.'

'No, Sir Thomas, there is no time. There's nothing we can do. Those peasants are on the run. They will die just as we will die if we stay here. Let them return to the forest where they might have a chance.'

Blackstone let him walk away and then called after him. 'You're a man of courage who serves his King. These people look to the King for protection and so they look to you. It's your name that will be reviled throughout Castile if you abandon them and praised if you stay. Not his.'

Álvaraz glared at the Englishman, but the words made him pause. Blackstone had had no reason to accompany him. He had relinquished his place riding with Don Pedro. He had given his word that the Spaniards would not fight alone. He looked up at the wretched creatures fleeing the approaching horde of routiers. There would be no mercy given to anyone who stood in their way.

'Very well. Tell me what it is you wish us to do.'

CHAPTER FIFTY-SEVEN

Blackstone spurred the bastard horse uphill with Álvaraz at his side. The village men pushed back their women as the sturdy war horses loomed over the contour track. Some turned and ran in fear but Álvaraz called to them. Once they saw that the two men and those with them posed no threat they stood obediently, vassals of a King they dared not to disobey.

'Tell them this,' said Blackstone and recounted that hundreds of routiers would soon attack but if they stayed together and did as the Spanish captain told them then they would live through the day and find sanctuary in a town further west. The men listened to the plan and Álvaraz tried to quell their fears and persuade them they could run and die, scattered across the hills, or stay and have a chance to make the enemy turn away.

The villagers looked down to where John Jacob and Will Longdon were helping the archers empty the pack horses' loads, stripping away yards of different coloured cloth and silk.

'You cannot do this!' said the Moor.

'I do it to save lives,' said Blackstone.

'By destroying the King's treasures?'

'We take cloth and silk. There's no coin or plate here. If you wish to return alive to al-Hakam then help the Spanish at the forest or my men cut silk.'

Álvaraz's men were already hacking down saplings in the forest the fleeing villeins had used for concealment during their escape. The Moor scowled and said something neither Blackstone or Álvaraz understood, but took to be a curse. He turned his mount away. Blackstone and Álvaraz watched as the Moor shouted unintelligible commands to his men. There was an argument of sorts but the men dismounted and started slashing the valuable cloth.

'I wish their wits were as sharp as their swords,' said Álvaraz. He grinned. 'Who would sacrifice their life for a bolt of cloth, no matter whose it is?'

Blackstone gestured to the villagers. 'Tell them again what it is I ask of them.'

Doubt still creased the villagers' faces; some voiced dismay at what was being proposed. Blackstone raised himself in the stirrups so they could all hear the strength of his voice and then Álvaraz's echoing translation became an appeal and not a command. Slowly, as their leaders quelled contradictory voices, agreement took hold. Those with influence over the villeins took knives and axes and ran into the forest to assist the soldiers in cutting down as many tall saplings as they could before the killers arrived.

'And now, Sir Thomas?' said Álvaraz.

'We ready ourselves. What does the lie of the land dictate if we are to have a chance of success?'

Álvaraz knew Blackstone already had the answer, but replied anyway. 'I would put your archers a hundred feet behind an extended line of our men. The height and the wind behind them will give their arrows longer flight.'

'My thoughts exactly. Unfurl every banner and pennon. Have your commanders prepare your men and I will attend to the bowmen.'

They urged their horses down the incline. Time was short and if Blackstone's gamble didn't pay off, they would all be dead before nightfall.

Renfred and his scouts returned from their reconnaissance, galloping back to where Blackstone and Álvaraz defended the valley. The French and the routiers were minutes away. They saw their comrades waiting in extended line and, a hundred paces behind them, Will Longdon's archers spread out on the slopes, split into three groups: an archer in the gap behind each horseman. Twenty angled on the left, twenty on the right and Will Longdon with the remaining ten in the centre. It was a tried and tested formation that created a withering flight of arrows into any advancing troops attacking into the killing zone. Behind them, on the crest of the hill, hundreds of men stood, indistinct at a distance, but everyone held aloft a flag, the fluttering cloth whipped forward by the wind at their backs. It looked to be a formidable array of men waiting in a strong defensive position.

Renfred drew up his horse. 'They're right behind us, Sir Thomas.'

'How do we look to the enemy from a distance?'

Renfred smiled. 'With the cold wind in their faces and the low sun in their eyes, they'll be uncertain about the banner men on the hillside. As we were at first.'

'Good, then let's hope it dissuades them from attacking.'

Renfred heeled his horse and took his place in the line with his men as the Moor cantered from the flank. 'You will fight?'

'Go back to your men and do nothing stupid.'

'I will take the pack horses.'

'You will keep your arse in your saddle and your mouth shut. If you move, I will have my bowmen cut you down. Go back and do not move. Sayyidd al-Hakam chose you for a reason. Perhaps you are a man who has a brain and can see how things are. They outnumber us.'

The Moor fought the temperamental horse. He was eager to argue but the size of the man he confronted and the look from his archers told him all he needed to know. He dug his heels into his horse's flanks and returned to his men.

'It would be easier to kill them before we start on the French,' said Will Longdon.

'It would have been easier for the Prince not to have sent us in the first place,' said Blackstone.

They waited amid the cracking of cloth as the wind whipped the flags and pennons.

Blackstone turned in the saddle. 'Will? What distance can you give me?'

'Three hundred and fifty yards, and with help from the wind another thirty.'

'When they draw up, send up one shaft, just one, and shoot it as close to them as you can. Then they'll know where they will die.' Blackstone heard his centenar send the order down the line to his bowmen as he urged the bastard horse twenty paces forward with John Jacob at his side bearing his unfurled banner. Thirty yards away Álvaraz did the same with his flag bearer. To all intents and purposes they looked like a disciplined army of men led by captains of renown, backed by archers and supported by hundreds more on the hill. If luck favoured them, then the approaching men would not identify the varied colours of the silk and dyed cloth banners that flapped tautly towards them.

The routiers spilled over the far hills, a breaking wave of ill-disciplined men intent on slaughter. The only visible banner was that of Bertrand du Guesclin, whose ransom had been paid by the French King so the Breton captain could lead the routiers into Spain. A lone trumpet sounded from the centre of the swarm where the banner tugged hard against its staff. At first the front riders did not hear the clarion call, but when it was blown again they slowed and halted. The banner carrier nudged his horse aside, which revealed that the man riding next to him was du Guesclin. Five hundred routiers stopped several hundred yards away and then edged their horses slowly forward. When they reached 430 paces in front of Blackstone Will Longdon bent his back, hauled on his bowstring and loosed a yard of ash high in the air. It reached its zenith, was carried and then flattened by the following wind and struck fifty-five yards to the front of the approaching men. The warning was clear.

The routiers' horses' blood was up from their strenuous journey, making their riders hold them on a tight rein, no one wanting a bolting horse to take them into the lethal storm that awaited. The nervous beasts fought their riders but kept their distance. Du Guesclin rode his horse forward another ten yards and then stopped. He squinted against the low sun; then he raised an arm in a peaceful gesture. Blackstone rode to him.

'Sir Thomas, we met on the field at Auray.'

'And you have gained your freedom.'

'A generous king has made Sir John Chandos a wealthy man.'

'The French monarch is playing a deceitful game. He sends you and others to dethrone Don Pedro when in truth he seeks to put a French army at my Prince's back.'

Bertrand du Guesclin was a swarthy, short man, well muscled with a pugnacious face. His smile did not soften the features. 'What do we know of politics?'

'You know about tactics. Your reputation is well earned.'

'And yours.'

The Breton eyed the skyline again. He was still a good distance away, which made him less certain as to the men half obscured by the crackling banners.

'A hundred of Don Pedro's lords sent men,' said Blackstone. He paused. 'There are more.'

Du Guesclin scrutinized Blackstone. 'Behind the hill? Waiting to surprise me if I break through – which I surely will?'

'Where would you place hidden men?'

'You're bluffing.'

Blackstone shrugged. 'My archers are few but they'll bring down enough of your men and horses to cause chaos. Then you have to get past me and the Spaniards. Then fight uphill to those who hold the high ground. And then... then you will know if I am bluffing.'

Du Guesclin grimaced. 'You tempt me, Sir Thomas. By God, I believe you are anxious to engage with me, as few as you are.'

The bastard horse swung its misshapen head and bared its teeth at the Breton's horse. Du Guesclin fought the rein. 'Your beast takes exception.'

'He's a belligerent curse on my enemies. He suits me. Is Ranulph de Hayle among you?'

'Le Bête? No. I saw him and a few men ride south.' The routiers' commander looked quickly at the men waiting to kill his own. 'Hugh Calveley waits for me at Burgos. Another time, Sir Thomas.'

He wheeled the horse and spurred it back to the waiting men. Blackstone watched as the Breton raised his arm and gave the signal to turn away, but one group of men, twenty or so, ignored the command. Perhaps they believed that if they broke ranks, others would follow. Their horses lunged forward under pressure from raked spurs. Bertrand du Guesclin bellowed a command to stop them but was ignored. Blackstone raised a hand restraining Álvaraz from riding forward. Moments later the unmistakable sound of Will Longdon's archers drawing back and loosing their arrows ripped through the air. The cross hatch of falling shafts felled most of the men. Horses whinnied in their agony and crashed to the ground as the two survivors careered towards Blackstone, unable to stop their terrified beasts. Behind them du Guesclin and his captains screamed at their men to hold.

Blackstone did not need to dig his heels into the bastard horse. Ears up, it fought the bit, gathered its strength in its haunches and reared forward. Blackstone cursed but had half expected the temperamental beast to take the fight forward. It barged the first horse, forcing its rider to sway in the saddle. The man's guard lowered. Blackstone swung Wolf Sword and cut deeply into the man's neck. Before he tumbled from the saddle Blackstone was already past him to face a more determined mercenary, who controlled his mount, swung hard into Blackstone, hammering down with a spiked mace towards the bastard horse's head, intent on blinding or maiming the great war horse. Blackstone pressed his leg into its side. It responded instantly and changed direction. The blow missed. The attacker's arm swung low between the two horses; with his body protected by his shield the man immediately curved the lethal mace upwards, intent on catching Blackstone's exposed side. He put too much effort into it, mistiming the wild strike. His arm was now level with his shoulder. Blackstone rammed Wolf Sword's hardened steel into his ribs. The mercenary roared with pain, tried to stay in the saddle but lost control. He slumped; his mount swayed uncertainly as it faced the line of horses. John Jacob rode forward to meet the wayward horse and swung his battleaxe into the mercenary's face guard. The blow spilled the man from his saddle, his horse galloping clear.

The mêlée was short but Blackstone saw the madness had stirred others from du Guesclin's company to surge towards the lightly armed Moors on their flank.

'Will!' Blackstone shouted.

Longdon and the men nearest to him pivoted, bent their backs and shot. A dozen arrows sped across Álvaraz's front ranks. So accurate was the volley that the attackers died only yards from the Moors, who fought to hold their horses still at the sudden enemy onslaught. The brief attack was over.

Bertrand du Guesclin called out to Blackstone. 'I will find you again and next time I will choose the ground.'

'You'll need more men,' Blackstone answered.

'Then I will have them.' He yanked the reins and the horsemen rode off, abandoning their dead and wounded.

The Moors' leader urged his mount towards Blackstone. 'You send your arrows so close you nearly kill my men!'

'Your men were safer with my archers than the Frenchmen. Either get back to your position or run home to al-Hakam and tell him how fearful you were when English and Welsh bowmen shaved your beards. Decide!' There was a short silence as the Moor fought to control his fury. Blackstone continued: 'Stop your damned bleating – you sound like a goat being dragged to slaughter. Or next time I will leave you to the wolves.'

Álvaraz nudged his horse towards Blackstone as his men went among the fallen to kill any badly wounded men and horses. 'They will not be fooled again, Sir Thomas.'

'They don't have to be. If we're lucky, the King's route ahead is safe now.'

'Then we ride back to the King. What of the villagers?'

'Let them keep the silk and cloth,' said Blackstone. 'It's a small payment for their courage. If they head west, they have a better chance. Du Guesclin rides for Burgos to join Hugh Calveley. The routiers are behind us. They won't stay at Burgos long. They'll soon be on our heels and at the gates of Seville. Don Pedro lives another day but by nightfall he will have lost the crown. They will declare Henry of Trastámara king in the cathedral.'

Álvaraz looked miserable. 'I would be in your debt if you told him. If I deliver the news they will leave my body hanging at the next crossroads.'

CHAPTER FIFTY-EIGHT

They caught up with Don Pedro and Killbere two days later as they camped for the night before entering Seville the following day.

'The King rides with the Moors and ignores us,' said Killbere.

Blackstone handed the bastard horse's reins to John Jacob and then plunged his hands into the bucket of water that Lázaro had carried to him when he saw the men return. Blackstone sluiced the grime from his face, running fingers through his hair. 'The damned French are giving chase.'

'Du Guesclin?' said Killbere.

'And five hundred men.' He glanced to where Álvaraz waited before going to the King's tent. 'There was a skirmish but I'll tell you later. We need to push harder, Gilbert, and I need to tell the King.'

'He did listen to you – he rides late into the day and breaks camp early.'

'Then he needs to listen more.' Blackstone beckoned Álvaraz and strode across the camp to where the King's tent stood apart from the men. Killbere watched them go.

'Will?'

Will Longdon turned from where he was addressing his archers. 'Sir Gilbert?'

'How close was it?'

The centenar walked over and shook his head. 'They would have trampled us to death in the first charge.' He told Killbere how Blackstone had used the retreating villagers to fool du Guesclin. 'Mark my words,' said Longdon, 'we looked into the face of death as certain as I am facing you.'

Killbere nodded. Will Longdon's creased grimace said it all. 'And there was another bloody hawk. My guts churned. I thought it heralded bad tidings, but Thomas said different, didn't he? Said it was there to help. And by God no sooner had the damned thing screeched like a castrated cat than the villagers swarmed out of the forest. Truth is without them we would have been crow bait. That and a few bolts of silk.' He hawked and spat. And then he grinned. 'Balls of iron and a few well-aimed arrows saved the day.'

Moors guarded the King's tent. They raised a hand to stop Blackstone from entering and called out for the High Steward. When his voice from inside gave Blackstone permission to enter, the sentries stepped aside.

Don Pedro was studying a map; the High Steward stood to one side. Al-Hakam was pointing out a route to the King when the two men stepped beneath the tent flaps.

'Sir Thomas?' said the King, without looking up. Only the High Steward and al-Hakam gave the two men their attention.

'My lord,' answered Blackstone. He was not prepared to deliver what news he had until Don Pedro was obliged to raise his eyes. Blackstone's silence did the trick.

'Well,' Don Pedro said. 'You have returned, which means something happened, or you saw the enemy. Which is it?'

'There were hundreds of villagers retreating from the routiers—'

'I have no interest in them,' the King interrupted. 'What of du Guesclin? Did you see him?'

'Saw him and was ready to engage, highness,' said Álvaraz.

'Ah, but you are alive, Álvaraz, so you did not engage. That makes me think you betrayed me.'

'No one betrayed you,' said Blackstone. 'We avoided a fight.'

'The great Master of War refusing to fight?' Don Pedro smirked.

'We fooled them into thinking our numbers were greater than they were,' said Álvaraz. 'Were it not for Sir Thomas they would have massacred our small force and slain the villagers.'

Don Pedro settled into a chair the High Steward positioned in place. A brazier burned nearby. The King stretched out a hand to its warmth. 'Your orders were to draw the routiers away from here.'

'There was no need,' Blackstone said. 'If du Guesclin had fought us, it would have slowed them down by only a few hours.'

'And those hours are vital to me,' said the King.

'You would have lost Álvaraz and his men as well as mine and you will need every man who will rally to your cause. They were riding for Burgos. Calveley is already there.' Blackstone paused. 'So too your half-brother.' He let the news sink in. 'By morning you will no longer be King of Castile. They will crown Henry of Trastámara.'

Whatever demons lurked in Don Pedro's heart, they ate into him slowly. He swallowed the news like a man chewing maggot-riddled meat. And then he retched, spewing whatever food and wine he had consumed across the tent floor. He wiped a hand across his mouth, got to his feet and flung the chair across the breadth of the tent. The High Steward stepped nimbly aside. Perhaps, Blackstone thought, he was well versed in dodging things thrown by his master.

'We must make haste,' said Blackstone. 'Du Guesclin and Calveley will join forces at Burgos and turn south. Du

Guesclin knows you must head for Seville. Where else would you go on this route? They'll attack in force.'

Don Pedro leaned on the table and beat his fist several times. 'I am hunted. Wolves chase me down.' He straightened. 'I have six hundred Moors in Seville and Portugal will give me sanctuary and a thousand men to escort us to safety. Once there, I will plan my counter-attack.'

No one in the tent spoke. A drowning man slipping beneath the waves draws a final deep breath and then succumbs. Don Pedro, King of Castile for a few more hours, looked to be such a man. Blackstone decided it was not worth arguing that the King was a spent force and instinct told him there would be no help from Portugal. If the offer to send a thousand men had been genuine the advance party would already be riding across the hills to offer the King the reassurance he needed. There had been no sighting of such a troop.

Don Pedro ignored them and bent down over the map again. Blackstone and Álvaraz bowed and left the tent. Once outside, Álvaraz lifted a lantern and turned to the Englishman. 'You stand between me and Don Pedro. I offer my gratitude. You spare me grief at his hands.'

'Álvaraz, we will soon have a battle on our hands. I think we'll reach Seville in time, but you said we cannot defend it.'

'We cannot. If they catch us there, we will soon be dead.'

'They'll come in force. Three, perhaps four days if we are lucky. Most of my men need fresh horses.'

'The King's are the finest in Spain. There is a place outside the city where they are bred. He will not part with them. They are his wealth and his pride.'

'Then I won't ask,' said Blackstone. 'I'll take. You'll show me where?'

Álvaraz grinned. 'With pleasure, Sir Thomas.'

'Good. Then we'll do as he asks and run for the Portuguese border and strike south for an Atlantic port. We must convince him to return to Aquitaine. The sooner I see the back of your King the better I'll like it.'

Álvaraz studied his boots for a moment, considering whether he should share his doubts. 'Sir Thomas, I do not think we will be riding for Portugal. The tide has turned against Don Pedro. Portugal will not be drawn into a conflict that sweeps across the whole of Spain.'

'You believe this? Despite his family connections?'

'I do.'

Blackstone knew that if Álvaraz was correct, then they were about to be surrounded by the French- and English-led routiers. 'Is there anywhere that remains loyal and holds their ground against them?'

'Only one place. The north. Galicia.'

'What route would we take?'

Álvaraz shrugged. 'If the Portuguese deny him, then we cannot ride in safety within their border. On this side there are towns defended by loyal troops. I do not know if Calveley and du Guesclin will give chase, but if we can reach Santiago de Compostela, then we are only hours from the coast.'

'How far to Santiago?'

Álvaraz sighed. 'Eleven, twelve days.'

'And in between?'

'If we can get beyond halfway – say, Salamanca – then we will have a chance.' He handed the lantern to Blackstone and, crouching, drew an outline of Spain in the dirt. He marked Seville and then scratched a line north and marked it with a stone. 'Salamanca holds out. Seven days from here, so it will be four or five days beyond that.' He placed another pebble near the northern coast. 'To Santiago. I do not think the routiers will follow us into Galicia. It is a difficult terrain of forests, mountains and rivers. No army would choose to fight there.'

Blackstone looked at the scratched dirt. 'We were only a few days from Corunna when we were at Burgos. Your King has damned us, Álvaraz. Can you see what will happen?'

Álvaraz looked at his crude map and shook his head.

Blackstone placed a stone north-east of Salamanca, and then another the same distance again. He pointed at the last stone he laid. 'Burgos.' He touched the first stone. 'Valladolid is halfway between Burgos and Salamanca.' He picked up the stone Álvaraz had laid down for Salamanca. 'Bertrand du Guesclin and Hugh Calveley will not pursue us south here to Seville, they will ride west from Burgos and strike us at Salamanca. They'll cut us off and array their men on open ground before we reach Galicia.'

Realization dawned on Álvaraz. 'Mother of God, Sir Thomas, we cannot get past them in time.'

They stood and gazed at the night shadows. 'Six or seven days from Seville to Salamanca. How many from Burgos?' said Blackstone.

'The same,' said Álvaraz.

Blackstone put himself in Calveley's place. 'They'll crown Henry King. He'll strip the city merchants and what's left of Pedro's wealth and pay off the skinners. So that buys us a few days. Three maybe. They'll be drunk and their purses will be heavy. Perhaps even four days.'

'The question is, would they come after Don Pedro? Is there any need?' said Álvaraz.

'His bastard half-brother would rather see him dead, that's one reason. Another is the French would like to see me dead with him.' Blackstone tossed away the stone. 'They'll come.'

CHAPTER FIFTY-NINE

Velasquita watched Blackstone's men go about their duties. They still looked no better than brigands but their swagger and contempt for pain and discomfort set them apart from other men. They often seemed close to brawling among themselves and she did not understand the insulting taunts they threw at each other, which often ended in laughter rather than violence. They were unlike the other Englishman, Ranulph de Hayle, a man easily bought, whose violence simmered skin deep, easily restrained through fear of the unknown. And to him, she was the unknown. That was not the case with Thomas Blackstone. His was a controlled violence that wielded ruthlessness when necessary.

She had used her guile to tempt him but it was Blackstone who had been the master in bed. She feared he could look into her as she did with others. He tempered his passion when they lay together, a man used to taking the lead in all things and whose relentless nature saw where and when to strike a floundering opponent. He was no different with her. When she thought she had heightened his pleasure and controlled the release of his passion, Blackstone held back and it was she who succumbed to the overwhelming tide that rendered her momentarily helpless.

She trembled. What caused her tremor? Was it the thought of his scarred body lying next to hers or the rising excitement as the vision of his death became ever clearer? To kill a man like Thomas Blackstone was no easy feat, but the devil had gifted him to her. She needed no soothsayer to interpret her dream's scattered images; the vision was as obvious as wiping steam from a window pane and seeing what lay beyond. It would not be long until Blackstone shuddered in death, helpless from her poison. Until then there were others who would die. When her journey with the King ended, Ranulph de Hayle would continue to do her bidding. She had already planned her escape. The final twist of fate that entrapped Blackstone and made him pursue her to his death had not yet been revealed to her. But that was just a small detail.

She noticed an urchin boy, a servant with one of Blackstone's men. De Hayle had told her that Blackstone was protecting the witness to the Queen's murder, but when de Hayle had searched the stables at Burgos, there had been no sign of the boy he'd captured when he fought the Bretons. So who was this lad she watched fetching and carrying? She turned to one of the King's servants.

'That boy. Do you see him?'

'My lady,' said the servant, acknowledging her.

'Do you know him?' she asked.

'He was with the English when they arrived at Burgos.'

Velasquita studied the boy a while longer. She had no recollection of him in her mind's eye. When de Hayle had delivered the severed head, she'd known immediately that it was not the witness. Could this be the boy? The one de Hayle had spoken of? Could he have missed him when he checked Blackstone's men in the stables at Burgos? If the boy they sought had been with Blackstone when de Hayle searched then he would have recognized him and reported to her. He had not. And yet something stirred in her. An unease.

'Go to him. Ask where he is from and when he joined the Englishmen.'

The servant scurried away. She watched as he tracked the boy doing his chores and then engaged him in conversation as he carried water to the men-at-arms. The servant returned.

'My lady. His name is Tello. He is from Pamplona. An orphan beggar. One of their soldiers took pity on him and made him a servant.'

She dismissed the informant with a curt nod. The ghost witness evaded her even as the King's flight was almost over. Don Pedro would soon be a pauper, his wealth stolen. He would make the journey to the English Prince as much a beggar as that boy. That much she knew. And then there would be another war, one that would ultimately destroy the English Prince. All of this knowledge had been gifted to her by a power even she did not understand. But if the witness could still be found and killed then suspicion would always be focused on the Spanish King: that it was he who murdered his wife. It would eat into the heart and soul of those who felt obliged to help him and weaken his cause. Suspicion was a slowly released poison. And who knew more about poison than Velasquita Alcón de Lugo?

She turned and felt a hammer blow in her chest. Blackstone stood watching her not ten paces away. Her thoughts had been too focused on the boy to be aware of his presence. She recovered her composure.

'You startled me. I didn't hear you.'

He had still not smiled in greeting and the thought came to her that if Thomas Blackstone did not want an enemy to hear his approach then it was likely that enemy would die.

'You were deep in thought,' he said. 'I didn't want to interrupt. Thinking of me, were you?' At last he smiled.

She went to him and laid a hand on his face. 'As a matter of fact, I was.'

'Good thoughts?'

'The future.'

'Ah, you mean where I die in your arms.'

'Is there a better way to die?'

He thought a moment and settled his stare on her. 'Killing my enemies.'

Once again she felt a mailed fist closing around her heart. If she was the devil's mistress, then was Thomas Blackstone his ill-begotten son? Did the Englishman have powers she had not bargained on? If he saw into her mind and heart, he would kill her and her prophecy would evaporate like campfire smoke into the night air. The devil only embraced those who did his bidding and succeeded in doing it.

He smiled again. 'After we have made love.'

Relief made her laugh.

'But first I must bathe.'

She placed a hand on his arm. 'There is no need.'

Lázaro reported to Beyard that one of the King's servants had questioned him. It had not happened at Burgos and no one had approached him on the journey. He assured Beyard that he had given the name Tello as had been agreed should any stranger ask.

'Then why now?' Beyard said when he told Killbere.

'He's been noticed by someone close to the King. It might have been innocent but we treat it otherwise,' said Killbere. 'The lad gave the false name and story as we told him?'

'He did.'

'Does his nerve hold?'

'He's been with us long enough to grow strong. It's second nature for him to be on his guard.' Beyard looked at the men settling down for the night. 'A servant talked to another servant – I don't think there's any danger. If there is they will seek him out once it's dark. They'll send more than one man to take him if they suspect anything.'

'Then we do nothing to draw suspicion. Carry on as usual. Keep him close. Warn your men someone was asking questions. I'll have Meulon and Renfred bring their men nearer to where you sleep.'

'Will you tell Sir Thomas they questioned the lad?'

'In good time. He's busy.'

A trickle of sweat crept down into the hollow of Velasquita's throat. Her skin, flushed with exertion and passion, welcomed the cool night breeze. She steadied her breathing, widening her eyes to focus on where she was, and then turned her head to where Blackstone lay on his side facing her. Her thumping heartbeat dislodged the pool of sweat, nudging it to trickle into the cleft of her breasts. Her loss of control from his lovemaking had once again alarmed her. Those final moments when passion cast her into a small death-like place, where she was aware of nothing except the acute spasm of her body which heightened the pleasure and lifted her from the living world. The lapping warmth of her emotions blunted her usually acute senses.

Blackstone placed a finger on her lips. She took it into her mouth and tasted his sweat, sucking on it like a child desperate for the teat. The desire to draw him into her, to consume him, eased when he blew gently onto her cheek. She took his hand and placed it on her breast.

'You possess me,' she whispered hoarsely.

'We find comfort together,' he said with a caress.

She sighed. 'I knew you would come into my life long before you arrived. I knew we would share moments like this. I was impatient for you.'

They lay face to face, the sweet scent of wine-perfumed breath brushing each other's lips. 'You know so much,' said Blackstone. 'And yet you reveal so little.'

'I have nothing to tell other than what I have already told you.'

Blackstone yawned lazily and pulled her to him so that she snuggled closer and half straddled him. He tugged the blanket across her lower back. He showed scant interest in his gently probing question or for her innocent reply. Her head nestled in his chest; his hand stroked her hair. 'But you know everything there is to know about the King and his court. So who do you think met Ranulph de Hayle the night before we left Burgos?'

There was an imperceptible moment as she held her breath. But she could not disguise it. Blackstone knew that to ask her straight out would yield no reaction. Her eyes would not flicker, her brow would not crease in feigned ignorance. She would lie cold and unemotional, giving nothing away. But now, pressed against his chest, he felt the brief hesitation and the brush of her eyelashes on his skin. Seduced, her guard was down for a heartbeat.

'Who?'

'An English routier who wishes me dead,' he said, keeping nothing but idle curiosity in his voice.

'I don't know him.'

'No, of course you don't,' he said as if believing her, 'but if anyone would know who it might have been then it would be you.'

'I don't,' she said without moving. An easy lie.

Blackstone kissed her forehead. A tenderness that said it didn't matter. That his idle thoughts were unimportant after their passion. She had expressed no surprise that a routier had been at Burgos, didn't ask why he wished Blackstone dead. Natural questions. Blackstone sighed. A deep sigh that signalled contentment, to ease any suspicion she might have about his gentle questioning.

His breathing settled as he drifted into sleep. There was no doubt in his mind. She was the enemy.

CHAPTER SIXTY

Blackstone had gathered his captains before they struck out for the ride to Seville. He shared his conviction that Velasquita was a danger to Lázaro. Blackstone believed she had had contact with Ranulph de Hayle. There was no direct proof, but he knew she had lied when asked.

'And we slipped a coin to the servant who questioned Lázaro. It was the witch who instructed him,' said Killbere.

It was evidence enough for everyone to believe it implicated her in the King's killing his wife.

'Maybe de Hayle was involved from the start?' said Killbere.

'If she was the one who met him that night at Burgos then what was she planning? Or was she sent by the King?' said John Jacob.

'If the King uses her to contact a killer like de Hayle, then he keeps his hands clean,' said Blackstone. 'What we cannot know is whether Don Pedro used de Hayle to kill his wife.'

'The King, the witch and the bastard,' said Will Longdon, chewing a strand of dry grass.

'But Lázaro did not say de Hayle was in the room when the Queen was murdered,' said Blackstone.

'It makes no sense to me why de Hayle is still around. He ambushed us and now he's where? He can't strike at us now that we have joined the Spanish and the Moors.'

'Will's right for once,' said Killbere. 'The bastard has no business with us now. He tried and failed to kill us. He searched for the boy and didn't find him. There's no reason for him to be here.'

'He might not even be close to us any more,' said Renfred.

Blackstone couldn't find a reason either. He scuffed the dirt with the toe of his boot. 'If he still thinks we have the witness to the Queen's murder then that's the only explanation. But she's involved, I'm sure of it.'

'Not in the Queen's killing, though. Lázaro didn't identify her being anywhere near her murder.'

'She's a go-between,' said Meulon. 'The King and de Hayle.'

A murmured agreement among them: they could find no other solution to Blackstone's suspicions.

'We make no changes to Lázaro's duties. His false story stands. But we keep watch. Ranulph de Hayle will not dare risk entering Seville. They would see him for what he is, a routier in the wrong place.'

Will Longdon spat out the grass. 'Aye, well, we're all likely to be in the wrong place if a few thousand skinners catch up with us.'

Blackstone and his men crested the hills and gazed down onto the Guadalquivir. Ships swayed on their moorings on the curving river beyond the semi-circular walled city of Seville. Others turned into the wind to anchor. At this distance their sails were little more than fluttering butterfly wings. An ancient Roman aqueduct signalled the city's heritage. Don Pedro summoned Blackstone to ride alongside him as they approached the city, following Sayyid al-Hakam's Moors, who cantered forward either side of the road. The city's Moorish guards, bearing shields and spears and clothed in richly dyed robes as colourful as any knight's pennon, held crowds back thirty yards and more. The crowd's roar swept across the

King's procession. Blackstone glanced left and right and saw the warriors pressing back the surge. The citizen's faces and raised voices seemed a less than warm welcome. But it was what lay at the end of the road that transfixed Blackstone. The Alcázar of Seville was breathtaking. Blackstone had never seen such architecture. Hundreds of arches divided by thin bands of green tiles fronted the walls. Ornamental stucco in interlacing arches gave the impression of a screen, extending forward of the main walls.

'We build on history, something your King Edward understands,' Don Pedro said, gesturing to the walls that stretched across their approach. 'Hundreds of years ago the Romans built their stronghold here and then the Moors and the Spanish continued. The Moors called it al-Qasr al-Mubarak; it means Palace of Good Fortune.'

Blackstone had never seen the Spanish King so animated or enthusiastic in his desire to share his knowledge.

Pedro turned to Blackstone. 'See there? We'll enter through the Lion's Gate. Even your great King has no palace like this. We have courtyards and gardens and cool pools of water. I am rebuilding and extending the façade. You see?' he repeated, pointing to the wooden scaffolding teeming with labourers, who dared to stop work and watch the King's arrival. He waved a hand across the imposing walls. His voice lowered as if in awe of his own achievements. 'I am humbled every time I come here.'

Blackstone restrained the mocking smile that threatened to insult the King of Castile. For a moment Pedro did genuinely appear humbled. Blackstone raised his eyes to the heights and realized there was a difference in the alternating Arabic texts inscribed between the first-floor doors and second-storey windows.

'What do those words mean?'

Pedro pointed at one inscription and then the other. '"The empire for God."' He crossed himself and kissed his fingers. 'And there it says, "There is no Conqueror but God."'

Blackstone saw the obvious sense of satisfaction on Pedro's face. It beamed with pride. Whatever fleeting moment of humility the King had experienced was gone.

'Built by Moors and Christians and peasants' sweat,' Blackstone said. The gentle rebuke made no impression on the King.

'And artisans,' Pedro emphasized, thinking Blackstone's comment was complimentary. 'Artisans the likes of which the Christian world have not seen unless they travel to Granada.' He smiled. 'And here.' They clattered under the vaulted entrance. Pedro pointed at the overhanging eave of wood. 'We call this *muqarnas*. It is Arabic. We honour Islamic architects who brought such beauty to a harsh world.'

Blackstone did not understand what the Arabic word meant but he appreciated the skill required to create the geometric decoration beneath the overhang. The King spurred his horse, eager to return to his most beloved of palaces: the Alcázar of Seville, a place whose magical name resonated with the promise of indulgent luxury.

Blackstone reined the bastard horse free from the procession. Álvaraz rode past. 'Follow me and my men. Our quarters lie in the courtyards beyond the gardens.'

Blackstone waited for Killbere and John Jacob.

'Did you see those crowds?' said Killbere. 'That was no joyous welcome for the King.'

'If a mob is forming they'll have to get past the Moors,' said John Jacob.

'If the city rises up they won't hold them,' said Blackstone. 'Álvaraz said the city can't be held if it's attacked. What he didn't consider is how quickly it will fall if there's an uprising.

There's no love lost between the King and his people. We should find our quarters and then prepare to leave Seville. And keep watch for the Lady Velasquita. Sooner or later she will try to cause us harm.' He spurred his horse deeper into the vaulted entrance. Such splendour could foster a man's vanity, lulling him into self-deception. If Don Pedro thought himself safe in this palace, then it would become the grandest tomb in Spain – unless Blackstone could convince him of the imminent danger.

Will Longdon had the archers billeted between William Ashford's and Meulon's men. The vast courtyard's green fringe of blossoming bushes and flowers was as luxuriant as a nobleman's embroidered cloak. Longdon wasted no time in having the men check their weapons. From what Blackstone had said they were not staying long.

Meulon strode across the square. 'Will, you see who our neighbours are?'

Will Longdon squinted through the glare at the distant speckled colours on the far side of the vast yard. 'Moors.'

'And on the other side Álvaraz's men. It's a place where tempers could flare. We need to keep the men in check. And your lads, especially the pagan Welsh, will fight if a fart carries on the wind.'

'My pagan Welsh archers can out-fart any of them bastards. Let them worry.'

'Merciful God, you don't see it. They carry bows. If a fight starts for any reason, their arrows will kill English and Welsh archers and this place will be a bloodbath.'

'Bows?' said Will Longdon, peering again into the distance. 'They have bowmen?'

'They're practising at the butts in the far corner,' said Meulon. 'Just keep your men in check. Feed and water them and bed them down with the horses.' He glared at the stocky archer. 'Keep your men away from them.'

'Aye, well, you tell William Ashford to keep his cut-throats in check. And Renfred and Beyard. Don't come here telling me how to control my men.'

'You've as much sense as a pig's arse. Where do you think I've been? Sir Gilbert had me tell all the captains.'

'Then consider your job done and let me get about my business.'

Meulon's scowl could sour milk. Will Longdon grinned. 'Meulon, you told me so I'd go over and make their acquaintance.'

Meulon glanced over his shoulder to check if Blackstone would hear him, but he was standing over two hundred yards away. He lowered his voice. 'They shoot fast. Quicker than you.'

Will Longdon's eyebrows arched. 'You bastard. You taunt me on purpose.'

Meulon's teeth appeared behind the heavy dark beard. 'Thought you might learn something.' He clapped a heavy hand on the archer's shoulder and sauntered to where Blackstone stood with Killbere and Álvaraz.

'Jack?' Will Longdon called to Halfpenny, who was sitting with his men as they checked and repaired arrow shafts. The young ventenar looked up.

'Bring your bow,' said Longdon.

Thirty Moors stood at the butts beyond the courtyard's far corner. A dozen archers stood in line pulling back on their curved bows while their companions waited their turn and fussed with their bow cords and fletchings, behaving no differently than Will Longdon's men. Archers nursed their weapons as tenderly as any mother caring for a child. Will Longdon and Jack Halfpenny stood watching until someone finally noticed them.

'All right, lads?' said Longdon with a smile. 'Me and Jack here thought we'd come and teach you how to shoot.'

Two of the Moors stepped towards them and said something. Their words weren't accompanied by a smile.

Will Longdon pulled a face and gestured, showing he did not understand. The Moors, now watched by their companions, talked to each other, glancing at the two rough-looking Englishmen. In contrast to the belted, robed Moors, Longdon and Halfpenny looked like vagabonds with their grease-streaked leather jerkins and grubby linen cowls.

'Give them something, Will,' said Halfpenny. 'They're the most miserable bastards I've seen all year. I've seen happier dead Frenchmen than this lot.'

Will Longdon rested his bow against his chest and rummaged in his jerkin. He came out with a small piece of dark meat and a half-eaten apple.

'You can't give them pig,' said Halfpenny. 'Their kind don't eat pig. Like the old Jew.'

'It's smoked boar meat,' said Will Longdon.

'That's the same as pig. It's swine. They don't eat swine. Give them the apple.'

'It's my last one.'

'Don't matter. Give it to them.' Halfpenny pushed forward Will Longdon's hand holding the apple. 'Smile. Tell them it's a gift.'

'I don't speak their language.'

'It's how you say it. Pretend you're paying a whore.'

'Then I'd have a face on me as sour as last week's latrine bucket.'

Halfpenny smiled at the fierce-looking tribesmen and nodded for them to take it. The two men accepted it and nodded their thanks, glanced at each other, said something and one pulled a fig from his robes. He freed a wicked-looking knife from his belt and cut the fig in half; then he then offered it to Longdon and Halfpenny, who studied the dark fruit.

'It's not an apple, and it's not an orange,' said Halfpenny.

'Might be dried horse turd,' said Longdon, looking uncertainly at the smiling Moor who gestured for him to eat.

Halfpenny took a bite. 'It's good. Try it.'

'I've never liked foreign food. I sucked one of their oranges back in Burgos and my gums stung for a day.'

Halfpenny shoved what was left of the fig into his mouth and nodded his thanks to the two men who watched his greed. The one muttered something, but his companion admonished him. Halfpenny made light work of Will Longdon's half.

Will Longdon pointed to one of the Moor's bows; after a moment's hesitation the man handed it to him. Longdon tested the pull. It was easier than the hefty pull on his own bow.

'Short range. Eighty, maybe a hundred yards,' he told Halfpenny, handing it to him so he could feel the pull weight.

Longdon bent his bow, nocked its cord and handed it to the Moor. The man studied its length – the bow was taller than him – and then he tried to pull it back, but managed only halfway despite his obvious strength. By now others had gravitated towards the four men. They passed Will Longdon's bow among them. A couple of men almost managed to pull its cord to their chest.

'A hundred-and-sixty-pound pull weight,' said Longdon, warming to their failure. 'Most of the lads have about a hundred and twenty or thirty, but me and Sir Thomas, we can pull the heaviest bows. I can pull more, truth be told.'

Halfpenny looked askance. 'You know damned well Sir Thomas could pull more than any of us.'

'They don't know that, do they? You told me it's how I say it that matters. Well, this is how I tell a yarn in an alehouse after a few jugs and everyone believes me, so they'll get the idea.'

They handed back his bow and beckoned the two archers to join them. The Moors became more animated and told their companions to draw and shoot at the targets eighty yards down the butts. The length and breadth of the square targets measured the same as an ash arrow with a bodkin point, a square yard fastened on a straw dummy the size of an average man.

'He's got that wrong,' said Halfpenny. 'Look how he's nocking his arrow.'

'Get that grin off your face, Jack, let's not make them look more foolish than they are,' Will said under his breath as the archer let the arrow settle on the wrong side of the bow. 'I reckon these aren't archers; they've been given these bows and told to learn to shoot.'

Both men were stunned into silence as the archers loosed three arrows in rapid succession, so fast that the action was a blur. All the targets had three arrow shafts sticking in them.'

'That don't make no damned sense,' said Halfpenny.

The Moors stood and waited.

'Do that again,' said Will Longdon and then gestured for the nearest man to shoot again. Longdon studied him. 'I'll be damned,' he said as the archer loosed another accurately aimed arrow. 'He uses his thumb instead of his fingers to pull back the cord. I see it now. You understand, Jack?'

Halfpenny shook his head. Will Longdon had gone to war with his bow since he was a boy. He knew how shafts flew in various weather conditions, understood distance and wind and his keen eye had shown him these expert bowmen's skill and technique. Had they been village idiots back in England and laid their shaft on the wrong side of an English longbow the arrow would have wavered and fluttered away like a broken-winged crow.

'They rest the shaft on the right-hand side of their bow and when they loose the cord with their thumb, it throws the arrow left. It's something to do with how the thumb twists the cord.' He stepped forward and lifted his war bow. 'Look here, lads, this is how we do it,' he said, ignoring the fact they didn't understand him. He waited until the men gathered closely around him and Halfpenny. He pulled an arrow from his belt, gripped the bow and laid the arrow left of the shaft on the top of his curled fist; then he showed them the first three fingers of his right hand, before laying them on the bowstring where the arrow's notch embraced the cord. The men muttered and grunted as the Englishmen showed their shooting technique. The Moors stepped aside and motioned for him to shoot at the targets. Will Longdon studied the yard-square targets then turned his back and walked towards the distant wall at the far end of the butts.

'Come on, Jack, let's show these heathen bastards how an Englishman shoots a war bow.'

When they reached 230 yards they could go no further because of a drainage ditch where water flowed from one yard to another. 'This'll do. One target together.'

'The middle one,' said Halfpenny.

The Moors stood between the Englishmen and the targets. None of them moved. To shuffle clear would show cowardice.

Will Longdon and Jack Halfpenny nocked an arrow and in unison pulled and loosed. The inch-thick ash ripped through the cooling air and struck the target a heartbeat apart punching through the square target on the straw man.

The Moors raised their voices in appreciation.

Blackstone, Álvaraz and Killbere turned from where they stood several hundred yards away as the roar sped across the enclosed courtyards.

'Trouble?' said Killbere.

Meulon grinned. 'I told Will the Moors were better archers. He's either convinced them otherwise or they've got his head on the end of a pole.'

Killbere grunted. 'It'll need to be a thick pole.'

CHAPTER SIXTY-ONE

Will Longdon beckoned the two Moors to follow him over to where Blackstone stood with Killbere. Álvaraz was walking towards one of the Alcázar's entrances. The two knights waited as Longdon ushered the men forward, despite their reticence.

'Thomas, Sir Gilbert. These are two of their archers. They'll benefit us. They don't drink, which makes friendship difficult, but we'll drink for them.' He pointed to the first man, who clasped his hands respectfully and bowed. 'This is Salam Lakum and I think this is his brother.' The second man followed his companion's gesture.

Blackstone addressed them. '*As-salāmu alaykum.*'

The men dipped their heads and spoke in unison. '*Alaykum as-salām.*'

Will Longdon looked from the men to Blackstone. 'You know them?'

Killbere lowered his voice. 'You damned village idiot. Tread carefully with these people. That's their greeting. You wish them peace and they do the same.'

'Well, you didn't see them shoot. Peace isn't their trade. We need Salam and his brother standing in line with me and the lads.'

Blackstone and Killbere stood in silence, unable to communicate with the two Moors. A man strode quickly towards Blackstone. It was the Moorish captain who had been saved by Will Longdon's arrows when they faced du

Guesclin's routiers. His snapped orders had the two Moors retreat towards the butts.

The veteran archer called after them: 'I'll see you later. You can try some of my lads' bows.' The men didn't turn around. Will Longdon looked at Blackstone and Killbere and the hawk-faced Moor who stood, hand on sword hilt, glaring at the stocky archer.

'It is not permitted to go among my men,' said the Moor.

'Oh, aye?' said Longdon, stepping aggressively forward, pointing a finger close to the man's chest. 'Then next time some routier bastard is going to shove his sword down your arrogant throat *I will not permit* my archers to save your sorry arse.'

Killbere put an arm between the two men. Provocation often put a sword or knife in a man's hand.

'What do you want?' said Blackstone.

The Moor took a step back when Blackstone faced him. 'My lord,' he said respectfully. 'You have asked to see the King. I am to escort you to him.'

Blackstone followed his escort through the voluminous corridors and ornate double archways towards the Lion's Gate entrance and the Hall of Justice. An angry swarming buzz carried on the breeze: a murmur of discontent from beyond the walls, exaggerated by the tiled floor and walls. His guide led him deeper into the cool chambers. The sound of trickling water from a rill echoed across a vast mosaic-decorated hall. Footfalls scuffed across the smooth floor as a delegation of three men, one man leading, two in attendance, crossed their path. The man who led them glanced at Blackstone. His finery told Blackstone he was someone of importance and the men's hurried pace made it obvious they were keen to leave the

Alcázar as soon as possible. Blackstone's escort turned into a passage and was blocked by Sayyid al-Hakam, who gave him a curt nod. The escort obeyed the silent command and walked away.

Sayyid al-Hakam stood six feet away from Blackstone, close enough that he could smell the Moor's breath, sweetened with the scent of something he had recently eaten or drunk.

'Go no further, Sir Thomas,' said Pedro's bodyguard.

Blackstone looked past the heavyset man; there was no one else in the shadows. If al-Hakam intended to challenge Blackstone, it would be a test of strength. He stared at the Moor. 'I'm to meet the King. You're in my way.'

'It was I who sent for you, Sir Thomas. And I used the one man I trust to bring you here. The King is inflamed with temper. You must not go close to him. Years ago he killed his brother while in such a rage. When it's unleashed we cannot tame his violence. If you go to him now one of you will die. And I know who that will be.' He paused and glanced over his shoulder. 'Your Prince would not look kindly on you killing a king.'

The confession surprised Blackstone. Loyalty to the King seemed absolute yet al-Hakam, the man closest to Don Pedro, had summoned him, using the King's name, to warn him. It was a grave risk the bodyguard had taken. He would know that if Blackstone told Don Pedro al-Hakam had warned him of his master's violence, then it would be the Moor's head on a spike.

'What has caused such rage in Don Pedro?' said Blackstone.

'He sent his treasury by ship down the Guadalquivir but it has been seized by his admiral, Boccanegra. The Portuguese ambassador delivered the news that the King's daughter's betrothal has been rejected and they will not offer him sanctuary. They are blockading the Guadalquivir.

No reinforcements from Granada can reach us and if there was ever a chance to escape by ship that is no longer a possibility.'

No wonder the delegation Blackstone saw scurrying away looked so nervous. A King crazed with fury had nothing to lose by killing messengers who bore bad news. They had run for their lives.

'You've seen his temper before: how long before we can talk sense into him?'

'Days. Now he insists on defending Seville.'

'If he does that, he'll die here. You hear that?' he said, meaning the rising sound beyond the walls. 'That's a mob. They know his half-brother's men are on our heels. Think about it. They storm the Alcázar and they gift the city to the skinners. You know what I mean by skinners? Mercenaries?'

'I understand,' al-Hakam said, 'but no one can enter the King's chambers. Not yet.'

'Where is Álvaraz?'

'He is guarding the entrances with my men.'

Blackstone nodded. 'He knew we would be trapped here.' Blackstone saw the danger that could soon swamp them. Leave it too late and the people of Seville would blockade the palace. It would take a bloodbath for an army to kill a whole city and make a fast escape. And Blackstone had no army. It was time to risk trusting the Moor. 'Álvaraz gave me men to go with my own and bring fresh horses.'

'The King's?'

Blackstone nodded. If such grand theft stirred the royal bodyguard's sense of duty, then he would order his men to stop Blackstone's.

'And now you also steal his wealth.'

'I use his wealth to save his life. We need fresh mounts. How will they be brought into the Alcázar?'

Al-Hakam hesitated. He and Blackstone were now conspirators together. He knew there was no longer any choice how best to serve Don Pedro. 'They'll bring them through the rear gates; they're narrow, easy to defend, and open to the farmland. I will see to it. It is a long ride north to the coast and that's now our only hope to deliver Don Pedro to your Prince.'

'We must persuade him, and quickly,' said Blackstone. 'I believe Bertrand du Guesclin will ride from Burgos and cut us off near Salamanca. Another army stands between us and the south.' He let the news sink in. 'You cannot get back to Granada and if you ride north with us, there is no place for Moors in northern Spain. You'll be hunted down. You and your men should stay here in Seville and strike a bargain with Henry of Trastámara. He will use you to negotiate a peace with Granada.'

'Sir Thomas, my people conquered and ruled Spain hundreds of years ago and when the Christian armies came together they pushed us south to the sea. My Lord Don Pedro already has a treaty with the Emirate. I am proof of that. Many of us will die for this King.' He smiled. 'Would it surprise you to know that you were to be abandoned here while we led him across the Portuguese border and then back into Granada? You were to fight the rearguard and die while we escaped.'

Blackstone remembered Velasquita's prophecy. 'What makes you confide in me now?'

'The man I sent to bring you here is my young brother. You saved his life that day against the French. We are both in your debt.'

'Then see the horses get safely to my men. Tell Sir Gilbert to ready them and we'll ride north and take this King of yours to safety whether he wants it or not.'

'How?'

'Where is the Lady Velasquita?'

Blackstone made his way into the Patio del Yeso through the intricately carved arches of the colonnade. The small courtyard's gardens flanked a rectangular pool where Velasquita sat dangling her feet in the water. She did not turn around when Blackstone entered beneath the arches and stood watching her for a moment.

'Do you hear the swarm outside the walls, Thomas?' she said. 'Discontent will soon become a roar.'

Blackstone wondered if she had seen him approach but realized she could not have from where she sat. Glancing around at the colonnade he realized that al-Hakam's voice might have carried along the corridors when he told Blackstone where she was. But that was unlikely given the distance. No matter how he tried to explain the woman's abilities to himself the answer always came back to her having second sight. She turned and smiled. The garden was half shaded as the sun settled lower in the sky. He looked up at the double storey walls surrounding the courtyard. The garden was a refuge from both heat and cold. In the height of summer the colonnade and walls would give shade and in winter the sun would bless the enclosure with warmth.

He walked to where she sat. 'This is my private place. I bathe here in summer. I swim naked while he watches.' She raised her face to the window on the upper storey.

'You tease him?' said Blackstone.

'I allow him the pleasure,' she answered.

Blackstone crouched next to her. She showed no sign of concern at the threat from the city. 'We cannot become trapped here, Velasquita. The King is in a violent rage. Portugal has abandoned him and his treasure has been seized by the admiral of the fleet, who has gone over to Trastámara. Don

Pedro seems determined to die here. I cannot allow that but I am not the one to convince him to leave.'

'There is no man in the kingdom who can convince him. No matter how powerful, strong, loyal or intelligent, not one of you can persuade this King what to do. Not one of you can calm him. Only a woman can do such a thing. And I am the only woman who can enter the royal quarters when he is so violent.'

'Why do you think I'm here?'

'Not to seduce me?'

The thought that she knew Ranulph de Hayle interrupted the moment. It was important to appear as if he still desired her. 'There isn't time.' Her look told him there was. Yet there was nothing more he needed from her except to prise the King out of Seville. 'The enemy is close and the door we escape through is closing.' She looked unperturbed. Did that mean she knew the outcome? 'What is it you see?' he asked, acknowledging her link with the unknown forces that hover between heaven and earth.

'Then you believe me and yet you are not afraid of me?'

'I deal in reality. I face whatever – or whoever – is trying to kill me, not distorted dreams or visions. But you were right about the King betraying me here – intending to escape and leave me and my men to defend the palace. Well, now his escape is blocked. If you want Don Pedro to live and reclaim Castile then you must get him to agree to ride north. There is no time. We must leave the city at first light.'

She picked up her sandals and rose to her feet. He stood next to her. She went on tiptoe and kissed him. Her smile was followed by a sigh. It was as if she was regretfully bidding him farewell. She turned and walked along the colonnade, suddenly merging into the shadows. Blackstone looked where her wet footprints had touched the hot clay tiles; they had already evaporated, as if she had never been there. Blackstone blinked in the glare but could not shake the sensation, questioning whether she had.

CHAPTER SIXTY-TWO

Álvaraz rode down the line of horsemen before bringing his men alongside the Moors ready to lead the King out of the Alcázar. Mobs had formed at the front gates, bellowing their rage, hurling stones and insults. Whatever Blackstone had done to get the King to agree to leave his beloved city, the Spanish captain was grateful. The King of Castile was leaving his palace through the back gate like a common labourer.

Don Pedro sat, stiff-backed, upright, staring directly ahead, boxed in the middle of the column for his protection. His glazed eyes appeared to be those of a man in a trance. They had abandoned everything of value. The supply horses carried only food; the King had with him just some clothing and personal jewellery. His reign was in tatters, as down at heel as the rough-looking Englishmen who had vowed to escort him to freedom so he might gather support and invade his own country from beyond the Pyrenees. When he had first arrived in the vast courtyard where the men waited, he commented to his High Steward that he had not remembered granting the horses to Blackstone's men. The High Steward lowered his voice so that no one could hear his reply, but whatever it was made the King look surprised but say nothing more.

Velasquita rode alone behind the King, flanked by neither courtiers nor cavalry. Blackstone had watched Don Pedro being guided to his horse and then helped to mount with the aid of a servant. Blackstone glanced at Velasquita, who stared back and then smiled. He knew the King's calm demeanour meant only one thing. She had drugged him.

Blackstone's men had seized the best horses from the King's stables. The bastard horse was as belligerent to the newcomers as it had been towards the old. Blackstone steered it clear of the column, accompanied by Killbere and John Jacob. The men had slept little, readying equipment and supplies throughout the night after Blackstone told them their route and what to expect.

Sayyid al-Hakam led four hundred cavalry and two hundred mounted archers through the narrow gate. Will Longdon called out to the two bowmen he had befriended.

'Salam, at the pace we'll be riding that nag will die under you and you'll be vulture bait. Before they pick your bones can I have your bow?'

The Moor smiled and raised a hand in farewell, unable to understand the archer but willing to believe his words were spoken in friendship.

'There, you see, Jack, that's how a man gets himself a souvenir.'

Halfpenny cleared his throat and spat. 'You're a thief in the night, Will Longdon. The poor bastard doesn't stand a chance with you around.'

Longdon watched the horsemen trot past. 'Young Salam, he's a good lad. A bit wet behind the ears but he's an archer and a half and if he ends up as maggot food then I'll have myself a nice war bow to trade with some tavern keeper in Santiago.'

Meulon and William Ashford drew up alongside as they led their men forward in the column. 'Santiago de Compostela is a place for the righteous. Even the taverns have daily prayers. There's little wine and plenty of callouses on your knees,' Meulon said.

'No tavern keeper in his right mind would do that,' said Longdon with a troubled look.

'Aye, I've heard that as well,' confirmed Halfpenny with a straight face.

'And thieves like you are beyond redemption,' the throat-cutter told him. 'So you're fucked. No wine or ale and damned as a sinner and a thief. That's Santiago for you.'

William Ashford took pity on him. 'Will, don't listen to them. They're squeezing your balls.'

Longdon grinned self-consciously. 'I knew that, William.'

'Once we ride into Santiago, the priests come into the street and question the captains and ask for their worst sinners so they can serve the pilgrims in the cathedral – you know, wash their feet like Our Lord did. Sir Thomas has told us it would be good for your soul if we all chose you.'

Before Longdon could close his gaping jaw and spit out a reply, Meulon and Ashford rode on, their laughter coming back to taunt him.

'You'll be laughing out your arse when you need us archers, you donkeys!' he yelled.

Meulon raised himself in the stirrups and bent his back, showing the centenar his backside.

Jack Halfpenny looked as bemused as his friends.

'And you watch yourself, Jack Halfpenny, or I'll give you a dozen of my Welsh archers to command. Those pagan bastards will drive a man to forsake drunkenness and whoring and beg to join the priesthood.'

Halfpenny slapped him on his shoulder. 'In that case, Will, you're a candidate for the Church yourself. I'll look for you having your head shaved and your arse kissed.' He spurred his horse away to join his men.

Killbere followed Blackstone and John Jacob as they trotted past towards the gate. 'Will! Then get those pagan

Welsh bastards in good order and join the column. This isn't a damned invitation,' he said.

Will Longdon curled the reins around his fist and turned in the saddle to face his archers. 'You're pagan bastards right enough, but you're my pagan bastards.'

He heeled his mount and followed the column out of the Alcázar, now abandoned to the mob and the enemy.

CHAPTER SIXTY-THREE

Blackstone pushed man and beast hard. On clear nights, when the moon rose and cast its light on the way ahead, he drove them long into the night. Don Pedro regained his temper and irritability by late on the first day but Sayyid al-Hakam stayed close to his master and his assurances assuaged the King's anger at having little recollection of being convinced to leave his beloved Alcázar in Seville.

The way to Salamanca and beyond was unknown to Blackstone and as a gesture he turned to the King for advice, but in reality depended on the Moor and the Spanish captain. He confirmed their suggestions of what route to take by sending out Renfred and his men to scout.

They crossed the Roman bridge at Salamanca, taking on more supplies from the city loyal to the King. Blackstone's men rode along the sandbanks below the bridge's several arches, screened by trees and brush, ensuring that the columns' full complement went unnoticed by the wary citizens who, despite professing their loyalty, might be tempted to pass such information to the King's enemies. The fewer men seen might help attract a smaller attack force when word of their numbers reached Bertrand du Guesclin, which it surely would.

'We skirted Salamanca, Thomas, but when the men returned with supplies, there were enough peasants with their hands out for silver to tell the French where we are,' said Killbere as they hunched over their small fire and dipped stale bread into the cooking pot simmering with pottage.

'They won't need to be told, Gilbert, they'll know. I'll wager du Guesclin is close. My prayer is that the King will do what we tell him.'

Killbere squinted through the fire's smoke towards the King's tent. 'He's been docile enough now that they have stripped him of his wealth and denied him sanctuary in Portugal.'

'Better for us if we could have crossed the border, but we need him to be elsewhere when the fight comes. If he's with us when the French strike we'll all die where we stand.'

The two veteran fighters fell silent. Killbere ran his tongue around his mouth to clear the saturated bread. 'You'll have to bed the woman again, you know that.'

Blackstone's quizzical look drew no smile from Killbere.

'Gilbert, I'll not deny I enjoyed it but there's no need for me to creep into her tent. I have my suspicions about her and that's enough.'

'You'd deny her her prophecy? It's not a bad way to die, y'know, Thomas. I can think of a worse death.'

Blackstone tossed the rest of the crust into the pot. 'You believe such nonsense?'

'Were it me I'd keep on testing what she said.' He wiped his greasy hands on his jerkin. 'You can't just stop seeing her; she'll think you suspect her. Best to stay close to an enemy.' He grinned. 'Closer the better.'

'I'll send you.'

'Oh no, my friend, I'll bed down whores and nuns and tavern maids, but witches need a braver man than me.'

'And I don't believe in twisted dreams that pass as prophecy so there's no need to crawl beneath her blankets again.'

'Thomas, if we are to fight the French then only she can make Don Pedro be elsewhere. He has death or glory written all over him and, like you said, when they come they'll come hard. We'll pay the price and it'll be costly to save his murderous skin but that's what they task us to do and we must do it no matter what. Let us not forget that by now Henry of Trastámara is crowned King of Castile. He's an enemy at our Prince's back. We must look beyond this arse-cracked arid place and get the bastard back to Aquitaine. So swallow your pride and bed the witch again and have her drug Pedro or fondle his balls or do whatever she has to do. We cannot win if he is in our midst because he will take command. He'll get in the way of the fight. We need to do what we do best.'

Blackstone knew his old friend spoke sense. 'It'll be me they'll want, Gilbert.'

'Aye, but they'll have to get past me and every captain and their men to reach you.' He grinned. 'The Frenchies won't like those odds.'

Stones from a tumbledown goat fold lay scattered on the hard ground. A canopy stretched across the half-walls gave Velasquita shelter from the chill wind. Servants had prepared a fire, cleared a place for her bedroll and served her food. She was, as always, separate from the King and his courtiers and distant enough from the common soldier to remain private. The remains of the stone walls were enough to keep the night air at bay as the breeze swirled around the firelight. She lay half propped against her saddle, her cloak wrapped around her as blankets and bedroll softened the harshness of what would otherwise be an inhospitable resting place. With or without the comfort of the bedroll, blankets and canopy, it would have been an enticing encounter with the sensuous woman. She gazed up at him.

'I thought you had abandoned me, Thomas. I've been cold in my blankets these past nights.'

Blackstone made no attempt to lie next to her but stood on the other side of the fire, letting it dance across her face. He saw the devil's smile emerging from the flames. 'You have the comfort of the souls of the dead, Velasquita. You draw them to you whenever you wish.' He paused, although the lure of the woman's passion was enticing. When the shadows danced across the ruin, it was easy to succumb to their illusion and let them draw him to her. His resolve kept him where he stood. 'I owe you a debt. You brought the King out of Seville.'

'I used a potion in his wine. Any man can be misled, Thomas, when his mind is befuddled.'

Was that what had happened to him? he wondered. He decided to play her game. Flattery was simply a sweet-sounding lie. 'My wine was not drugged, but my senses were overtaken with passion for you.'

'And you regret that?'

'How could any man?'

'Then lie with me tonight.'

'No. I must see to the King's safety tomorrow as well as yours. The French are close. My scouts have seen outriders. Another day and they'll be on us.' He stepped around the fire and crouched next to her, taking her hand to his lips. If he could convince her he was sincere, that he did not suspect her of knowing Ranulph de Hayle, then she would do as he asked. 'Velasquita, our time together is not ended but I must make you safe. You and the King must leave at dawn. Puebla de Sanabria is a day's ride, two at the most, north of here. A castle stronghold is there if you need it.'

She sat up. 'You abandon us, Thomas?'

'I hold back the French who expect us to run for the Portuguese border. We'll join you when the fight's over and then we ride for Santiago. The routiers won't follow us into Galicia. He'll be safe. Will you convince him?'

'Only if you ride with us.'

'I cannot. You know that.'

She laid her trap carefully. 'But afterward?'

Blackstone sensed her web enfolding him. He had no choice if he was to use her influence with the King. 'Then I'll come to you.'

A brazier warmed the King's comfortably furnished pavilion. He sat on a chair on an unfurled carpet with a side table of food close to hand. Despite the need to escape Seville in haste, Blackstone had not been able to convince the steward that pack horses should only carry essential supplies. A King does not sleep on stony ground or eat from a soldier's cooking pot was the response. More was the pity, Blackstone thought; a fighting man like the Prince of Wales would forsake comfort when a battle loomed. Sayyid al-Hakam and Álvaraz stood behind Don Pedro.

Álvaraz greeted Blackstone with a nod. The Englishman's tactics had prevailed so far and if there was any hope of success, then the Spaniard knew that it rested with Blackstone. The King glanced up and immediately lowered his head to his food again; but when the tent flap opened and closed once more, he raised his eyes. He wiped his mouth and smiled and nodded for Velasquita to come closer. She bent, kissed his proffered hand and allowed herself to be eased next to him to stand at his shoulder. Álvaraz scowled but Blackstone gave a gentle shake of his head. Stay quiet.

'Well?' said Don Pedro. 'We run like alley cats from feral dogs. Are you here to humiliate me further?' He wiped his hands on the linen cloth presented by the High Steward and waved away the food tray. A dutiful servant stepped forward and removed it.

'Your death is close, my lord,' said Blackstone.

Don Pedro's jaw dropped. Blackstone's words struck a shocked silence in the pavilion.

'You threaten or warn me?' said the King.

'Tomorrow the French routiers will swarm down the valley from Valladolid, south of Zamora, north of Salamanca. Once they see your banner they will keep coming until we are dead or captured.'

'Then it is time for me to make my stand,' said Don Pedro.

'It is time for you to be gone before we sight them. I have spoken to your captains: Álvaraz and al-Hakam. Bertrand du Guesclin and Hugh Calveley's routiers will expect us to have our backs to them as we run for the Portuguese border. Instead, we will have our backs to the mountains and stand across the river on the west bank of the Esla.'

The King looked at Álvaraz. 'Did you choose that place?' hissed the King.

Álvaraz did not cower before the King. 'I did.'

Don Pedro refrained from chastising his Spanish captain. He turned to Blackstone. 'And did Álvaraz tell you what that place is called?'

Blackstone saw no point in discussing geography. 'It makes no difference,' he said.

'El Campo del águila caída. In your language it means the Field of the Fallen Eagle. A thousand years ago a Roman cohort died there, trapped against the cliffs, slaughtered by tribes they sought to conquer. I am a superstitious man, Sir Thomas. Legends of the past are useful: they serve to inform us.'

'Legends are stories, my lord, and stories are for troubadours and minstrels. Fighting men seize the best opportunity they can to slow down and defeat an enemy. Do not let whispers from the past make us fearful of what must be done now. The

Romans left a better legacy. They built a bridge across the river so we will hold it. Once the French arrive, English routiers will be on their heels, and if the French haven't slaughtered us by then, then Hugh Calveley will cage and chain you and drag you through the streets and then your half-brother will have your head on a pole and your limbs severed and placed at crossroads. I warn you. We cannot beat the host that rides towards us, so you must not stay.'

Blackstone watched the bravado slip away from the King of Castile. He was already humiliated from the loss of his beloved Seville and the occupation of Burgos, and then the loss of his treasury. Physical degradation would be too deep a wound to contemplate. But then, to Blackstone's concern, he raised his head.

'I would rather die standing with my men than keep on running. I will fight at your side, Sir Thomas. I do not fear death.'

Álvaraz looked worried and stepped forward. 'Highness, the church at Puebla de Sanabria will give you sanctuary. It is only a day and a half ride on the far side of the river. If we hold the bridge long enough, then you will have a clear passage to Santiago and Corunna. Days, highness, only days and you will be with the English Prince.'

'No. I have run far enough.'

Velasquita took a pace forward. 'The King has a right to die where he chooses,' she said.

Blackstone and Álvaraz had not expected her to support Don Pedro.

'Woman, this council is no place for you,' said the High Steward.

'It is no place for those who are not prepared to face death. Are you?' she answered.

The taunt made the High Steward stand tall. 'As God wills.'

'Brave words, but when blades eviscerate you and you hold your innards watching your life ebb away, that is when we will test your courage.'

The King raised a hand to stop any further argument between the soothsayer and the steward. 'Velasquita, where shall I die? Tell me what you see so I may know the place and prepare myself.'

'My lord, I have seen your return to glory. I have seen your people rejoice. You will not die tomorrow or the next day or for many more thereafter, so you must not challenge Fate. Let others leave their blood in the sand. You must reach the English Prince. That is what I have seen. You have no choice. Spain is waiting for your victorious return.'

Don Pedro thought on it. He nodded. 'Very well. Puebla de Sanabria it shall be, and then on from there.'

'A wise choice, my lord,' said the High Steward with a hint of relief.

'God willing that bridge is held, Sir Thomas,' said Don Pedro.

'We will buy you time,' said Blackstone as Velasquita faced him, careful that no one else could see her raised eyebrows and triumphant smile. 'You take Álvaraz and your Spanish troops and Sayyid al-Hakam's men. We'll hold the bridge.'

The Moor lifted his sword blade an inch and slammed it back into its scabbard, enough to make everyone turn towards him.

'My Lord Pedro, we cannot do as Sir Thomas suggests,' he said. 'The French and their mercenaries must think you are among us. We should keep your pavilion and your banner and I and my men will stay behind with the English. The enemy knows that where we are then so too are you. Better that Álvaraz and his men ride as escort.'

'Master al-Hakam, you have light cavalry,' said Blackstone. 'You're ill equipped to fight so many.'

'And you, Sir Thomas, have even fewer men and yet you will stand your ground. Do you not see the truth? Where the King's royal guard is, then that is where the King would be. We stay.'

CHAPTER SIXTY-FOUR

Velasquita refrained from showing she had any association with Blackstone. The King's jealousy would have made him defy her advice, and then his desire for death or glory, whether imagined or real, would have made him stay and fight the fast-approaching Bertrand du Guesclin and his army.

It was an hour's ride from their camp to the River Esla and, as they clattered across the Roman bridge, she slowed her mount while the King and the courtiers galloped on. Blackstone drew alongside. Her cape's hood fell back from her face.

'Thomas, remember your promise and come to me.'

'If I live.'

'You still don't believe me, do you?'

'Perhaps at the end of today I will.'

She smiled. 'We will be at the Iglesia de Santa María del Azogue. It's the only church there is.' She gathered her reins. 'I won't pray for you.' She heeled the horse and rode off to catch up with the King's retinue.

Blackstone watched men stream across the bridge to where a legion had made their last stand. They guided the pack horses up towards the rocky cliffs. The Romans had built their bridge in one of the few accessible places. Elsewhere the craggy cliffs made the gorge too difficult even for Rome's engineers. This bridge spanned three hundred yards and Blackstone looked back to the far bank where the shore broadened into an open space above the high bank. The route leading away from the shoreline went east to the valleys that would bring the enemy from Burgos. Riverside shrubs, underwood and trees softened the breadth of the opposite shoreline. The river's current was strong enough to slow horsemen attempting to cross the shallower parts of the riverbed. Blackstone's captains were already dispersing the horses, leading them into protected shelter behind a cliff face that had been dug out and quarried, perhaps by these same Romans who used the stone to build the bridge. Time had not weakened their efforts and the bridge's several arches looked to be as strong as when first built.

'You looking at the masons' skill or being weaned from the witch?' said Killbere.

'Thinking how we'll stop them before they get to us. We can't destroy it and we can hold it for only so long. The French can't go up or downriver and outflank us because the cliffs are too steep. The cliffs at our backs protect us,' Blackstone pointed at the water breaking over rocks revealing shallower water. 'If they ford there, either side of the bridge, then we're outflanked.'

'Will and his lads can bring enough of them down to slow them but we don't have many arrows, Thomas, and they'll be hard pressed to hold the bastards back with sword and buckler.'

'We'll put al-Hakam's archers to good use,' said Blackstone, 'but even if we slow the skinners at the bridge, then we still need to stop them getting ashore from the shallows.'

Killbere studied the ground. They had five hundred yards from the river to the cliffs at their backs. Al-Hakam's men were erecting the King's pavilion and flying his banners. To an approaching enemy it would look like Don Pedro's camp. Men went about preparing the deception, gathering bundles of dry kindling and firewood. There would be a hundred

campfires lit that night dotted across the broad riverbank. If
the French routiers were as close as Blackstone thought, the
twinkling firelight would draw them like a moth to a flame. By
dawn the enemy would be across the river.

'Time is against us, Thomas. Best we get to what needs to
be done.'

The quarry was the strongest place to defend should they have
to fall back but it could also be a death trap if Blackstone's
men were overrun and their enemy scaled the cliff face
and shot down into them. Blackstone secured the bastard
horse's reins. Lázaro led his own and Beyard's horse into
the quarry. The boy had become an untiring ward of the
Gascon.

'Lázaro!' Blackstone called.

The lad changed direction and met Blackstone as he strode
towards him. 'My lord?'

'You know to keep clear of my horse?'

'I do, lord.'

'Good. Where has Beyard instructed you to be when the fight
comes?'

'Here with the horses. Some will not be used to sound of
battle so I will calm them as best as I can.'

'Not mine, remember.'

'I would not wish to go near yours, Sir Thomas.'

Blackstone stroked his hand down Beyard's horse's face.
'Lázaro, you have travelled the length of France and across
Spain with us and your courage has been noticed.'

The lad shrugged. 'I am with brave men, lord, how could I
not feel strong? But I still fear Ranulph de Hayle. Is he one of
the men coming to fight?'

'I don't know.'

'He will seize or kill me if he finds me. It is the person who killed the Queen who wants me. I cannot tell you who that person is, Sir Thomas. But I fear I will still die.'

'He won't get to you, Lázaro. If he is with the French and if every man here dies in battle, you can run. You go over that mountain and find any town or village and seek refuge. Take whatever you can carry. You have Beyard's blessing and mine to save yourself.'

The boy listened attentively. He touched the crucifix. 'My Queen prayed for my safety and her prayers were answered. I have prayed for my Lord Beyard and for you, Sir Thomas. You will win this fight and we will all go home together.'

A sharp screech echoed down into the quarry from the sky above. The horse shied but Lázaro held it easily enough. The hawk circled and then stooped away out of sight.

Lázaro smiled. 'You see, Sir Thomas, the hawk watches over us. She is our angel in the sky.'

Blackstone let the boy lead the horses away. Angel or demon? They would soon know.

'Salam!' Will Longdon called as Moors dragged dead wood from the river to impede horses clambering up the shallow bank. The Moor stopped and dropped the bleached tree trunk.

'English,' he said, addressing Longdon the only way he knew how.

Will Longdon looked across the open ground to where the Moors had hobbled their horses. They had nosebags tied on and stood compliant as the men worked around them. The archer was uncertain why the Moors' horses were not in the quarry. While his mind fought to find a way of asking, Salam pointed to the heaped river stones being placed by his bowmen.

'Stones,' said Longdon. He picked up a smooth rock and gestured for the Moor to watch him as he acted out what he was trying to say. 'Here and there, see?' He walked to where one archer had marked his place to fight. Arrows were jammed into the ground next to the river pebbles. Longdon held the rock in his fingers so his audience could see what he was doing and embellished his story with overwrought facial gestures. He plucked an arrow with one hand and held the stone with the other. 'Arrow – stone,' he said, showing each to the bemused Moor. Three more of his companions eased their efforts and watched the English archer. 'Arrows soon gone. Poof. See? Finished.' His gestures became more comical. The Moors were grinning at the unfolding act. 'Big fight. No more arrows. Stones. So you must gather.' He drew his arms together as if bundling sheaves of wheat. 'No arrows 'cause they're sticking in a skinner's gut. So with no arrows we have to kill them another way. Yes?' The ramble made no impression. Will Longdon looked at his bemused audience. Tucking the arrow behind his back so it was out of sight, he laid open his palm to show the rock again. 'Kill them with these.'

The man he called Salam spoke to his comrades to try to understand what the English archer was trying to tell them. There seemed to be some agreement. Salam bent, picked up a rock and hurled it towards the river to where their common enemy would attack.

'Rock,' he said.

'Yes, yes. Rock,' Longdon repeated, nodding happily. But then he shook his head. 'No throw. Not throw. See?' He tugged a slingshot from his belt, unfurled its arm-length cords, slipped his forefinger through the loop on one end and held the knot tied on the other end between his fingers. He pointed to a clump of rushes tall enough to be a man in the shallow part of the river fifty yards away. He placed the rock into the sling's pouch and then swung it rapidly. The stone swished through the air and tore into the target.

It impressed the Moors.

Longdon was frustrated. He wasn't showing his skills with a sling only to impress them; he was trying to tell them that the fight would be desperate and hard won and the Moors needed to adopt the same strategy.

Salam stepped forward, smiled and placed a hand on the Englishman's shoulder. He nodded, as if understanding all that had not been said. With a look of what could have been regret he looked to where their horses were. His voice was low, his meaning clear. They would die with their horses in the attack. The Moor turned back to his tasks, leaving Will Longdon with a premature sense of loss.

'They'll get slaughtered if they ride out,' Will Longdon told Blackstone. 'And the way Salam looked I reckon that's their plan.'

'Speak to the Moor, Thomas,' Killbere said.

Blackstone nodded. If his centenar's suspicion was correct, he was about to lose six hundred fighting men being led away from the battle lines. 'Will, you've got your lads ready?'

'Aye. They'll stand their ground as always.' He glanced behind him at the rugged cliffs. He grinned. 'No place else to go.' He walked away to join his archers, who were already in their ragged formation, ready to stand between the men-at-arms, and to join the fight when their arrows were exhausted.

'God's tears, Thomas, we will lose good men in this fight. More men than before, I reckon,' said Killbere. 'I'll fill my belly tonight and spend an hour at the latrines at dawn. Then I'll be ready for that arrogant Breton bastard. Damn the snivelling

French King for paying his ransom. I pray scabs form on him and peel him to the bone.'

'Gilbert, if your curses could save our day then the battle would already be won.'

'My curses? Merciful Mother of God, we need the damned witch to put a curse on these ravenous bastards that come for your head.'

'Then – with your help – I shall try and keep it.'

Blackstone made his way to where al-Hakam was speaking to some of his men. The Moor dismissed them when he saw Blackstone approaching.

'I had a mind to place boulders and anything else on the bridge to slow them. And when we kill them their bodies will hinder others. You have your horses being fed in the open. I'm no fool, Master al-Hakam, you intend to be across the river, don't you?'

'We kill those we can and once they get past us they will have little choice but to use the bridge. And there you can inflict many casualties on them,' said the Moor's commander. 'I have four hundred men with spear and sword and another two hundred archers. We fight on horseback, not like you English who stand and wait for the enemy to come to you.'

'Then you throw away your lives. Bertrand du Guesclin will have two thousand and more men with him. Hugh Calveley another thousand. You will die a useless death. Bring your men with mine. Stand next to us. We need you and your archers. We'll kill hundreds before they get across the bridge. They'll fall back and when they come again, we will kill them again. By the time their swords meet ours they will be weary from the effort. That is the best chance we have, al-Hakam. We have won many battles like this against even greater odds.'

'Sir Thomas, we know our fate. The treaty with the Emirate of Granada and this foul King is not of my doing. I am a soldier who follows orders. Don Pedro deserves to die in the gutter with his throat cut, but I am obliged to protect him because Allah is all-knowing and I am not. I cannot question why I die here. It is my destiny. As perhaps it is yours.'

Blackstone felt he had already lost the appeal. 'A warrior's duty is to kill the enemy and live so he may fight again and kill those who wish to kill him or those he serves. I beg you, stay on this side of the river. We are already heavily outnumbered.'

Sayyid al-Hakam looked around at the broad expanse of open ground between the cliffs and the river. 'You have chosen well, my friend. You will hold here long enough for Don Pedro to escape far enough into Galicia so as not to be followed. Your service to your Prince does you honour. Do not let me dishonour myself.'

'You would not.'

'The enemy would expect the royal bodyguard to stand between the King and his enemies. If we are to buy him time and convince them he is here so they do not ride upstream and find a crossing and pursue him, then they must see we are in their way. Then they will believe that Don Pedro is here with you.'

Blackstone saw there was no chance in changing the Moor's mind.

'I am a Nasrid Moor, Sir Thomas. Our blood will soak into the same soil as our ancestors who conquered this land. We die with honour. I will strike at them five hundred yards beyond the bridge. By the time they fight through us they will have their bodies and ours to slow them down.'

'I saw writing on the wall of the Alcázar: "*Wa la ghaliba illa Allah*" – "Here is no conqueror but God".'

Al-Hakam extended his hand. Blackstone grasped it.

'Peace be upon you, Sayyid al-Hakam.'

'And on you, Sir Thomas Blackstone.'

CHAPTER SIXTY-FIVE

Blackstone brought his captains together. The ground they would fight on was a crescent-shaped riverbank stretching five hundred yards from the bridge to the cliffs at their backs. Each flank was closed by a rock face that tumbled down onto the water's edge. The shallows in parts of the river were the most dangerous places for their enemy to storm across and it was there, once the routiers discovered the shallower water, that the archers had to kill as many of their attackers as possible. Once the assault across the bridge had been stopped then du Guesclin's men would have no choice but to attempt a river crossing. Meulon would hold the right flank, William Ashford the left. Between each of the men-at-arms, left and right, Will Longdon and Jack Halfpenny would sawtooth their archers. Blackstone scratched out the positions in the soft ground. He would position himself as the point of an arrowhead formation with Killbere and John Jacob at his shoulder.

'We're losing Sayyid al-Hakam and his men. They're going to cross the river to fight,' he told them.

'They'll kill a few hundred but not enough,' said William Ashford.

'And we'll hold our ground and stop the French at the top of the riverbank,' Blackstone said, pointing out the key areas along the river for his men to make their stand 'They'll breach our lines eventually. When they do we fall back across the horse traps we've dug.' He drew lines showing how the archers should withdraw to the cliff face while the men-at-arms formed a shield wall.

'They'll batter us down, Thomas,' said Killbere.

'Not before we make them bleed,' said Blackstone. 'Will, Jack, when you and your lads are down to half your arrows, use slings to buy time so we withdraw from the flanks. Then get behind us, form up and wait for my command. Once we're hard pressed we lower shields and you shoot.'

Will Longdon ground a finger in his ear, examined the congealed wax and wiped it on his hose. 'A half-dozen arrows is all each man will have left so we'll kill the first few ranks but they'll swarm over the bodies.'

'The dead will form a stumbling block, and those that live will be more exhausted than us. They'll have had to run several hundred yards, get across the river, up the bank and then stumble across their own dead.'

'And then?' said Renfred. 'If any of us survive?'

Killbere hawked and spat. 'Then we get as many of those who are still alive up the track and away, rejoin Don Pedro and reach the coast.'

It was a grim outlook for Blackstone's men but fighting against overwhelming odds added strength to a man's sword arm.

The captains broke off and went to their men. Meulon cursed quietly to himself. The ground between the river and the cliff was too soft for men to drive stakes into. All they could hope for was that the rocks and fallen trees they had dragged from the river and laid across its bank would slow an enemy riding hard across the shallows. The staggered slit trenches they had dug were a foot deep, wide enough for a man's boot or horse's hoof, sufficient to make a horse stumble if they got ashore. If the French had learnt their lessons from the past, then they would abandon their mounts and attack on foot. It made no difference: men on foot or horses would have to scramble over the traps before Blackstone's men killed them. Enemy dead would block the bridge once Will Longdon's archers had wreaked their violence but Meulon knew, as did every other man, that the weight of numbers would drive the routiers through their defences. Meulon's right flank and Ashford's left would push the attackers' centre onto Blackstone's arrowhead formation. Those routiers splashing across the shallows who survived Will Longdon's archers would face the lines of the men-at-arms, where they would be drawn in and smothered. The enemy's superior numbers would eventually drive Blackstone's ranks back and as they were diminished they would draw closer together to form a last pocket of resistance, backs against the cliffs, guarding the quarry entrance so that a handful of them could escape and warn Don Pedro. Someone had to tell the Prince of Wales that Thomas Blackstone and his men had died obeying his command at the Field of the Fallen Eagle.

They had faced overwhelming odds before and there was always a time to die. Meulon spat and kicked a stone. Godforsaken places were where fighting men found their courage. He dismissed any thought of defeat. Will Longdon and his archers were settled by their fires, using the light to check and fuss their arrowheads and fletchings. Every man had river pebbles and stones piled next to him.

The centenar looked up as Meulon loomed over him. 'Will, you'll be on my left so tell your men to keep their aim true because if we have to fight the skinners at the riverbank I don't want an arrow up my arse.'

Will Longdon passed him his wineskin. 'You keep your big arse out of my lads' way and you'll have no cause for complaint.'

Meulon drank and nudged his toe against the centenar, who had begun checking his arrows again. 'You take heed from what Sir Thomas said. If they overrun us you and your bowmen get back to the cliffs. That's your best chance.'

'Sword and buckler is the last chance any of us archers have.'

'Aye, well, if it comes to that the rest of us will be dead.'

'I can do without your good cheer, you oaf. Look to yourself and your lads and I'll do the same with mine. With Renfred on one side and you on the other it's best you don't get in our way. Your men-at-arms lumber around like bulls in a field looking for cows to mount.'

'Better to fight hand to hand, you humped-back dwarf, than sling stones that irritate no more than wasp stings.'

'I'll kill any man at forty yards with a sling and so too will my lads, so when you're being beaten senseless by a French bastard who takes a dislike to your ugly face then give a signal and we'll favour you with our aim.'

Meulon wiped his mouth and corked the wineskin, tossing it to the archer. 'Your wine's turning sour.'

Will Longdon grinned. 'That's why I gave it to you.'

Meulon belched. 'I shall keep you at my back when the fight starts so I can repay you with my farts.' He walked towards his own men, stepping around the archers' campfires.

Jack Halfpenny hunkered down as Meulon went on his way. 'What did he want?'

Will Longdon watched the departing man. 'To wish us luck,' he said without rancour.

*

Blackstone and Killbere walked the length of their defences. They spoke to their men, who, like the archers, were busying themselves preparing for the following day's battle. None of them grumbled or bemoaned their fate at being where they were. Their insults towards each other were tinged with the silent acknowledgement that the man they were taunting would be at their shoulder the next day. Killbere traded a few choice slurs himself with those he had known for years.

Renfred, the German captain, stood nonchalantly whittling a piece of wood. 'Sir Thomas, did you tell the Moors the French will be here soon after dawn?'

'I did.'

'You know they're fools to strike at them across the river. They'll kill a few hundred, if they're lucky, but they'll go down under French hooves.'

Killbere looked across the river. 'They sacrifice themselves for their honour, Renfred. They serve the King.'

'We all die for those we serve, Sir Gilbert, but honour? That's hard to find.'

'Did you or your men see any sign of Hugh Calveley?' said Blackstone.

Renfred shook his head. 'He will come a different way, I think. No, it was du Guesclin's advance party we saw. They bristle like a leafless forest.'

'Then we'll need to be woodcutters tomorrow,' Blackstone said.

The German looked at his whittled figure and then tossed it into the river. The carving was of no value; it had served its purpose, allowing the hardened man-at-arms and scout to concentrate his mind on the fight ahead.

Blackstone watched the scarred piece of wood float away in the moonlit current. 'Honour is standing firm to the man next to you,' he said. He clapped a hand on Renfred's shoulder. No more words needed.

When Blackstone and Killbere came to William Ashford's men on the far flank of the river one of them stood. 'Sir Thomas,' said Tom Brook, a man who had joined Blackstone's men when Ashford had been assigned to the Master of War. 'May I speak, lord?'

'Every man may speak if they are words worth listening to,' said Killbere, eyeing the fair-haired younger man.

'And even if they're not,' Blackstone added. 'We have time to hear them.'

The younger man, clearly not lacking in confidence, scratched in the dirt and pointed them out as being the battle lines. 'If we had a few mounted men at the quarry, they could hold there and when we are pushed back, they could then sweep across the skinners. That could give the lads on foot a chance to regroup or run for the quarry.'

Tom Brook looked no older than Blackstone's son, but he was already a veteran at twenty-two.

'And who would be the best men to do this?' said Blackstone.

Brook looked across to where al-Hakam's men camped. The Moors went without blankets on the cold night, draping them instead across their horses, keen for their mounts not to have stiff muscles when first light came and when, soon after, they'd ask them to drive hard at the enemy. 'They're horsemen like I've never seen before. I watched them back at Seville. They're tough and they're fearless. If they would give us twenty or thirty men on this side of the river it could turn things in our favour.'

'You make a good point, Tom,' said Killbere. 'But the Moors will not reduce their ranks for us.'

'Then will you ask Master Ashford if I can take a dozen men and lead them?'

'Tom, we need every man in the line,' said Blackstone. He looked across the open ground; he could see how the assault would take place and Tom Brook's idea had merit, but it would be costly to those who undertook its execution. 'I'll speak to William and ask him to choose a dozen of his best men. You will fight with me, and when the time comes I'll send you back to ready the horsemen. We'll have need of you, Tom, but I'll not think badly of you if you see it's too great a risk.'

'A greater risk than anyone else will take, Sir Thomas? We'll cut a wound into the bastards' hearts and they can choke on their own blood.'

The sky cleared. It appeared to be so close a man could lie in his blankets and reach up and seize a lifetime's wealth from the jewel-infused heaven, even as the accompanying night's chill seeped through men's clothing, burying itself deep in muscle and bone.

Beyard watched Lázaro murmur in his sleep, back pressed close to the river boulders edging the fire, which radiated warmth. Then he looked up from sharpening his knife. 'Hello, John. Doing your rounds?'

'Aye. Sir Thomas always goes among the men before a fight. You care for the blade as much as you do the boy,' said John Jacob, who had stepped next to Beyard's fire.

Beyard tested his thumb against the blade; then he slipped it into its scabbard. 'We look to him.'

'As Lázaro looks to you. The lad's come a long way.'

Beyard glanced again at the curled figure by the fire and tucked the blanket up around the boy's neck. 'He's found his voice and his courage over the months. How must it be for a lad his age enduring what he's gone through?'

'And tomorrow, where will he be?'

'With the horses.'

'Best place,' said John Jacob. He gazed across the camp. Both men were subdued. 'We need to kill ten of them for every one they kill of us.'

'It will be a long day,' said Beyard.

CHAPTER SIXTY-SIX

The dark blue sky began its slow retreat. The moon was chasing another night in another place as the first blade of a blood sun edged across the horizon. Men's breath whispered into the cold pre-dawn air. Blackstone's men had watched in silence as the Moors bent in prayer. Ignorance of the Muslims' customs did not impede their sense of respect for men bowing down in humility before going to their death.

The Moors went quietly to their horses, stroked their faces and blew gently into their nostrils as they murmured soothing words to them. Then they eased their blankets off them and one by one led their mounts across the ancient stone bridge. The gathered cavalrymen each waited on foot for their turn to go across the river. Sayyid al-Hakam watched a dozen of his archers carrying baskets of their arrows as they accompanied his brother to where Will Longdon stood. The man known to the centenar as Salam carried his own offering. They stopped in front of Longdon, and Sayyid's brother spoke.

'I am Abid al-Hakam. It was you who saved my life. I pray Allah will protect you this day.'

Salam and the men with him placed the baskets down in front of Longdon and Jack Halfpenny.

'My archers will have no need for more than half of their arrows. You understand?' said al-Hakam.

Will Longdon faced the men and knew they spoke of their own death. Their quiet courage and acceptance of their fate touched him and the battle-hardened archer felt tears sting his eyes. He nodded.

'This man,' said Abid, turning to Salam, 'his name is Najih bin Wālid. He wishes you to know this.'

Will Longdon's coarse life of soldiering served him well in this rare moment of emotion that he could not explain. He suppressed the inexplicable sadness he felt by plucking an arrow and examining it.

'These are fine arrows,' said Will Longdon, 'and we will kill many enemies with them.' He looked at the archer. 'And tell him I am glad to know his name and that it will be remembered.'

Abid al-Hakam told the man at his side.

'English,' bin Wālid said; he placed his hand across his chest in salute, and smiled.

They turned away.

By the time the Moors had led their horses across the bridge the sun had peeked over the distant hills. Sayyid al-Hakam was the last man to step onto the bridge. His men had formed up on the opposite bank in plain sight so that an approaching enemy could identify them, but their archers had filtered away into the trees on the left flank. Blackstone stood with the Moor as he looked back at the King's pavilion and Castile and León's standard next to Blackstone's banner.

'It is in a good place, far enough back for the French and their savages to fight through you, Sir Thomas.' He glanced at the sky. 'There is no wind now, but it will be here in an hour. You smell that? The breeze brings the scent of wild sage. The flags tremble. The wind will be at your back from the north-west. We will feel it and let it drive us into them. We kill as many as we can before they get past us.'

'You could still take a stand with us here. Several hundred men shoulder to shoulder stand a better chance,' Blackstone said.

'Sir Thomas, we are watched over by your God, our Rabbul Alamīn, He is the Nameless One who decides when it is we die. Now is our time. We choose how we die and we die as horsemen.'

Al-Hakam tugged the horse's trailing rein to lead it across the bridge. 'Fight well, Sir Thomas.'

'And you.'

The Moor took a couple of steps and then turned back. 'Don Pedro ordered me to protect the woman, Lady Velasquita, the night she met an English mercenary. This man, he showed her the head of a boy, but it was not the boy they hunted. Be careful. She is known to the devil, and he holds her close.'

Blackstone nodded his thanks and watched Sayyid al-Hakam take the long walk across the bridge as his men raised their voices to honour him. The Moor's final words had been offered in friendship between men who served and obeyed. The warning tarnished the woman further and strengthened Blackstone's suspicions. Whether she acted at the behest of Don Pedro or on her own volition, it meant Velasquita was involved with or party to the Queen's murder. He turned to where his men stood in position, listening to the Moors' voices reverberating against the cliffs.

'Beyard!' Blackstone beckoned the Gascon, who strode forward.

'Sir Thomas?'

'Who stands with you? Loys and Aicart?' he asked, naming two of the Gascons who had fought throughout Blackstone's campaigns.

'They command their own men at my side as always.'

'Will they stay with Lázaro? If the French overrun us I don't want him falling into their hands in case de Hayle rides with them.'

Beyard hesitated. His two men commanded loyalty among those they led. 'They would obey but I need them. I have told Lázaro to take my horse if the French break through.'

Blackstone knew it had been an unreasonable request. He recanted. 'So be it. The lad must ride for his life if the time comes. Tell him...' Blackstone had no proof Velasquita was the killer. Had she wanted the witness dead by the King's command or to protect herself? 'Tell him he must not trust the Lady Velasquita. Better to seek protection from Álvaraz the Spanish captain. If they defeat us, then Lázaro is abandoned again. I have brought him to great danger and we can no longer protect him.'

Beyard's concerned look reflected less the likelihood of them dying in battle than that Velasquita might be the Queen's murderer even though the boy had not identified her. 'I'll tell him.'

'Do it now before du Guesclin gets here.'

Beyard hurried towards the quarry entrance.

'Gilbert?' Blackstone called.

As always Killbere had staked his place to fight at Blackstone's shoulder, he on one side, John Jacob on the other. 'The lads are ready, Thomas.'

'The Moor tells me the wind will pick up. Get the men to build fires on the lip of the riverbank. As many as can be done in time. When al-Hakam's men can no longer hold the skinners, we stand upwind and let the smoke smother them. Do it now, Gilbert. Every other man in the line will have a torch ready. Use the night's fires for kindling. Have them readied. Take those blankets al-Hakam's men left.

Smother the wood with them. When they're lit, the smoke will choke the river.'

Killbere cast a doubtful look at the unblemished sky. 'And if the wind doesn't come?'

'It doesn't matter. It's one more obstacle for them to get around and horses panic when flames reach them. I should have thought of it before now.'

Killbere grinned. 'You must be getting old and forgetful.'

'If we live through today, I'll be grateful for that.'

Killbere strode away as Blackstone raised a hand to William Ashford, who stood with his men in formation. 'William, you are down the line at my left with Tom Brook behind me. You must protect Jack Halfpenny and his archers who stand between us.'

'Aye, Sir Thomas.'

'We must give Tom and those you've chosen time to get back to the horses.'

Ashford pointed to ten men who stood ready with shields. 'If God favours us and they live long enough, they'll cover Tom back.'

'Good. They need to judge when that time has come, William, because we'll be busy.'

Blackstone opened his stride to where Jack Halfpenny and his archers waited in formation between the men-at-arms on the left-hand side of where Blackstone would stand. 'Jack, you see Ashford's men back there? They'll give cover for Tom to reach the horses.'

The ventenar looked along the ranks, cast a look over his shoulder and shrugged. 'They'll not have a chance if the French get too close on our flank, Sir Thomas,' he said, already seeing how such a move might weaken the fighting line. 'Best I have half my lads turn and cover them.'

'Aye, Jack, best you do that,' said Blackstone. It was what he would have done in the young archer's place.

Men stacked dry wood and brush kindling chest high on the riverbank and draped the abandoned blankets over the pyres.

Blackstone looked at the preparations he had made. There was nothing else to be done.

He scanned the sky and saw the high dark shape of a hawk circling lazily on the rising warm air.

'They're here,' said Halfpenny.

CHAPTER SIXTY-SEVEN

Horses whinnied as the distant skyline altered shape. An indistinct wave was flooding towards them. The bristling banners and pennons spiked the air, wavering as the dark tide gathered pace like flotsam caught in a fast-moving river.

Blackstone strode to his position two hundred yards back from the bridge where John Jacob and Killbere stood ready. If they were overwhelmed they had another three hundred long strides to put their backs against the cliffs. Will Longdon had placed a pile of stones on the bridge wall at 350 yards from where his archers stood. That's where the routiers would first endure the storm of steel-tipped arrows.

'It's not Calveley,' said Killbere. 'It's the ugly Breton bastard du Guesclin and his paid skinners.'

The sun's rays slanted across the hillsides, throwing light onto the cloths' fluttering hues. The line of men spread across the valley, some riding haphazardly on their flanks across the lower slopes, then easing their mounts down to the main body of men. They soon choked the valley's breadth; their advance slowed and then stopped.

'Not just skinners,' said John Jacob. 'It looks as though every dispossessed Frenchman we've ever beaten in the past has joined du Guesclin. They must need the snivelling French King's money badly. His and the Pope's, that is.'

Killbere hawked and spat, leaning on his sword hilt as if idly watching a tournament's pageantry. 'It's more than that: it's business as usual, John. Their cocks harden at the thought of killing Thomas. Can we see who rides with the Breton? My eyes have become as weak as my bladder.'

The approaching host drew closer, their horses at the walk, until they reined in five hundred yards from Sayyid al-Hakam's men drawn up across the river front. The routiers' prize lay across the river beyond the Moors.

'D'Aubricourt's there, so too de Bourbon,' said Blackstone.

'Aye, well, he'll be out for revenge because we killed his father at Brignais. They're resentful bastards, these French,' said Killbere.

'I thought I saw Arnoul d'Audrehem's colours,' Blackstone said. 'He'll have scores to settle.'

Killbere shielded his eyes. 'Their arses are twitching now that they have to get past the Moors.'

An uneasy calm settled over the two forces facing each other. The routiers advanced slowly, caution guiding them. Bertrand du Guesclin's banner was back among the host, a dozen ranks and more between him and the front riders.

'Wait,' Blackstone said to himself. 'Another hundred yards and they'll be level with the trees... Just ... wait,' he muttered, willing al-Hakam to draw their enemy closer. There was no need. Sayyid al-Hakam was a veteran fighter. As the routiers' front ranks crossed the imaginary line the Moor raised himself in the saddle and lifted his sword. His men did not move, and the fact that they didn't charge momentarily confused the enemy. They pulled up their horses.

'God's tears!' Killbere spat as al-Hakam's mounted archers surged from the trees. It looked as though their horses were at full gallop from a standing start. Two hundred bowmen, shields on the same arm as their bows, stormed across the open ground. No sooner was the first man level with the routiers than they shot into the startled men. Not once, not twice, but repeated, rapid shooting. A dozen heartbeats saw them fell a hundred men and more. Screams shattered the morning air as routiers' horses panicked, trampling their fallen riders.

Will Longdon's archers bellowed their support.

Blackstone and every man around him stared in awe at al-Hakam's archers' speed and skill. Not only were their bow arms shielded, but the fingers on the hands that drew back the bowstring gripped the pommel of their sword hilts, with the long double-edged blade resting backwards across the crook of their draw arms. By the time the lead archers reached the end of the routiers' front line, their arrows were expended, the bow discarded and the sword fully gripped, ready to hack into the panicking routiers.

'Kill them! KILL THEM!' Will Longdon cried out.

Blackstone's men's blood was roused by the ferocity and skill of the mounted archers, who now slashed their way into the huddled ranks of mercenaries. Blackstone strode forward, knowing his men were fired with the lust to kill. He faced the ranks of men-at-arms and archers. 'Hold! We hold! They'll come soon enough!' He saw his captains control their men and then he turned and faced the far bank again where Sayidd al-Hakam held back his cavalry. His archers fought with sword and shield, driving their lightweight mounts into the enemy's heavy coursers even though the mercenaries showed no pity as they scythed into the courageous smaller horses.

Will Longdon choked back the tears of anger that threatened him. The man he had befriended would already be dead. He saw the routiers' sheer weight of numbers heave forward. And still al-Hakam held his men in check – until the skinners were two hundred yards from him, trying to skirt the fallen mounts, trampling their fallen comrades. Despite their numbers they could not yet get a clear run to spur their horses into a gallop.

And that's when Sayyid-al-Hakam bent low over his horse's withers and surged forward. Blackstone felt the ground tremble. Dust quivered and fell from the old stone bridge.

The French-led routiers had not learnt the lesson from Crécy and Poitiers and every engagement since when they fought the English. They stayed mounted. Bertrand du Guesclin and the French commanders with him remained steeped in their arrogance. Instead of withdrawing a half-mile, dismounting and setting up defensive positions on foot, they persisted in jostling forward, as eager as ever to claim honour and victory. But four hundred Moors on horseback, no matter how lightly armed, brought ferocity and fearlessness to the fight.

Al-Hakam's men hurled steel-tipped spears into the routiers and then, sword in hand, swarmed into the fray, leaving a trail of blood-soaked ground where man and horse writhed from the savagery inflicted on them. Further back in the French ranks, banners and pennons wavered, showing Blackstone that the Moors had penetrated deep into the enemy's ranks.

The battle on the far side of the river took two hours. It would soon be over.

Blackstone looked back at the King's pavilion. Al-Hakam's prediction was testament to his knowledge. The King's standard wavered amid dust swirling from the top of the cliffs as the backing wind picked up in strength. The standard of Castile and León snapped taut. The wind veered, Blackstone's banner crackled open, its blazon's mailed fist clasping the cruciform sword hilt and the banner's declaration: *Défiant à la Mort*.

The roar from Blackstone's men drowned the sounds of battle several hundred yards away. He looked left and right and saw Will Longdon and Jack Halfpenny ready their archers. They knew the French would soon trample over al-Hakam's dead in their eagerness to sweep across the river.

Tufts of weeds and detritus caught on the river's shallows served as distance markers for the archers once the attackers splashed across on both sides of the bridge, which would be choked with dead once the bowmen had loosed.

The routiers fought clear of the carnage at their feet and urged their horses forward. It was a mad charge for the bridge so that those first horsemen could strike rapidly into what they thought to be Don Pedro's lightly defended camp – believing that a race for the far bank meant the archers who stood in their ragged line between the men-at-arms would have insufficient time to shoot enough arrows to stop most of the attackers sweeping across.

'These bastards never learn,' said Will Longdon. Since arrows were scarce Longdon had briefed his men that they should shoot only once onto the bridge when the attack reached their halfway marker. Jack Halfpenny's men on the opposite flank would hold back for panicked riders who yanked reins and plunged down the bank, attempting to cross the river. The routiers did not yet know if the river ran deep or if there were shallows; that uncertainty would slow the concerted assault.

The bridge was wide enough for three horsemen abreast. The forty or so riders who led the charge were spread out, so that when they reached the bridge the first dozen horsemen had to rein in and jostle to cross, forcing those behind them to do the same. The bridge was choked and by the time the cursing riders had barged halfway across twenty horses jammed the bridge.

Will Longdon's archers' arrows were nocked. 'Draw!' he called. Bows creaked, backs arched. 'Loose!'

Blackstone's men-at-arms craned their necks to watch the dark storm rise up into the blue sky. The air shuddered and then, like an unseen giant smiting an enemy, those on the bridge died. Horses reared. Arrows pierced necks, blinded eyes; men tumbled with inch-thick ash shafts tearing through muscle and bone. The bridge's low walls crumbled as the horses' weight toppled the masonry, tumbling them into the river twenty feet below. Dead and dying clogged the bridge while on the far bank the assault slowed as the following ranks of du Guesclin's men turned chaotically this way and that, hauling on reins, raking spurs along their mounts' bloodied flanks. Horses whinnied and bellowed in pain.

Thirty horsemen on the far bank veered away from their fast approach to the bridge, lost control of their crazed horses and rode down the bank, splashing into the river. Half the riders fell from their saddles and were swept away as others brought their horses through the current and found the shallows. Will Longdon watched as Jack Halfpenny ordered a dozen of his men to shoot. The floundering routiers were as easy a target as shooting at the butts. Blood flowed as bodies spilled into the clear water. Loose-reined horses regained their footing, some turning back, a handful clambering up the bank, threatening havoc among Blackstone's ranks. There was no need for Blackstone to shout a command. Ashford's men hacked them down, cutting their legs from under them and finishing them off with sword thrusts.

Across the river, men bellowed commands. The swirling mass of routiers tried to reorganize but more than a thousand men needed a firm command to be turned into an efficient fighting force and routiers who had little reason to die needlessly galloped away across the low hills.

'That's a couple of hundred who'll live to drink and whore again,' said Killbere.

'If they listen to Bertrand du Guesclin and he convinces the French noblemen to dismount and attack, then they'll swarm like the plague over us,' said Blackstone, eyes on the surging enemy. 'If the arrogant bastards stay mounted, we'll kill a few hundred more before they get to us.'

Killbere looked along the ranks. 'Will and Jack's lads have no more than a sheaf of arrows apiece and whatever the Moors gave them. Let's hope the French see fighting on foot as beneath their dignity; it's easier to put man and horse on the ground.'

'Here they come,' said John Jacob. He smiled. 'Arrogant bastards to the end.'

The mass of horsemen had turned, urged on by those who commanded them. They would cross the river on either side of the bridge.

'Now it's up to Will and Jack,' said Blackstone.

Only the archers had drawn blood so far. Blackstone knew that if they stopped this surge then it would force even the French noblemen to listen to the Breton. Routiers spilled down the far bank. The jostling horses unseated some of their riders as others slid uncontrollably in the churned mud.

'Should we light the fires?' said one of the men carrying a burning torch, who stood with a dozen other men-at-arms behind Blackstone.

John Jacob half turned. 'They're not for the horsemen. Await the command.'

The surge of violence bellowed its malevolence as the avalanche of routiers pushed into the river. Some saw the shallows and urged their horses to find firm footing; others fought the chest-deep river's flow. The shallows gave the archers their next set of markers as determined riders forged onward. The attackers were too inflamed to hear the distant command to loose as they tried to control their horses and find a way across, pushed on by impatient men behind who shouted and cursed for more haste. Moments later the sound of a flock of birds flapping their wings became the terrifying flutter of bodkin-tipped ash shuddering through the air.

The current churned over bodies; eddies twisted around the corpses as blood discoloured the pristine mountain water. Those men who fell and were not trampled fought the current. The river swept the dead away. The dying clung to rocks and tufts of reeds until their strength gave way. Five times more Blackstone's archers lofted their arrows into the logjam of men and horses and then called a halt. Half their arrows were depleted and the main force had not yet committed to the attack.

Meulon turned to face the grim-faced Longdon from where he and his men stood beyond the archers. 'You slaughter so many you give the others a bridge to cross.'

'Let the scum trample their dead. There'll be enough for you to kill.'

A lull descended across the body-strewn battleground. The French and their routiers had suffered heavily. The bridge remained blocked with carcasses of men and horses. No one dared an attempt to clear a way across: Blackstone's archers had dissuaded anyone from trying. Blackstone and Killbere watched as the French banners wavered and then retreated. The main assault would have to come across the river.

'They'll dismount now,' said Killbere.

Blackstone stepped further forward and called to his centenar. 'Will?'

The archer raised his arms and formed a cross. They had used half their arrows.

Blackstone did the same with Jack Halfpenny and got the same answer.

'If it was me over there,' said John Jacob, 'I'd put crossbowmen on the other side to keep us back from the riverbank and then send the men-at-arms to get their feet wet.'

'We're barely in range, and the wind's against them,' said Killbere.

'But if they gain another thirty yards by going down to the bottom of the far bank then they might reach us and that would give cover for them to get across,' the squire replied.

Killbere shrugged. 'John's right, Thomas. We need to bring Will and Jack forward so they can shoot and kill their crossbowmen.'

It was two hundred paces to the rim of the riverbank from where Blackstone stood. He and Killbere strode forward, looked across at the corpses already littering the far bank and river shallows. Not one routier had made it past the halfway mark.

'We stop them as they clamber up the incline,' said Blackstone, 'but our archers need to kill their crossbowmen. Once their men-at-arms reach us here our backs will be against the cliffs.'

Killbere pointed across the river. 'They've listened to the ugly bastard du Guesclin.'

The French had dismounted and started their approach on foot. There was still five hundred yards before they reached the river and even then they were out of range for Blackstone's archers. As many of the French as possible had to be killed midstream before the survivors reached his side of the river.

'Will!' Blackstone summoned his centenar. Will Longdon ran to him. Blackstone pointed to the base of the far riverbank. 'If they put crossbowmen there they'll have the range to keep us back from the edge and that's where we have to stop the attack. They'll be able to give cover for the skinners and they'll get a foothold here.'

Will Longdon looked at the distance from their side of the river to where Blackstone pointed. 'We can't reach them from where we stand, we're too far back.' The centenar knew what Blackstone was asking of his vulnerable archers. They would be exposed to the crossbowmen before they could kill them in sufficient numbers. 'I'll bring my lads here to the edge. Keep Jack and his men on the far flank because we'll be using most of the arrows we have left, except for what the Moors gifted us.' He looked across the river to where a hundred crossbowmen ran towards the opposite bank. Without another word to Blackstone he summoned his archers with a sharp whistle. Who would get into position first? The crossbowmen were already slithering down the bank as Longdon's archers sprinted the two hundred yards from their positions. The mercenaries were readying to charge across once their bowmen were in place to cover them.

The routiers were veterans. Half of the hundred bowmen loosed their quarrels and as they reloaded the next fifty men shot high, sending their lethal bolts slamming into the bank where moments before Blackstone and Killbere had stood. Four of Will Longdon's archers were struck. There was no time to organize a line of defence; Longdon stopped and hauled back his bowstring and loosed as, seconds later, a dozen men at his side shot with him. No sooner had they loosed than the rest of his archers were running along the riverbank, stopping, turning side on and shooting in unison. Well-practised, disciplined, no one target being aimed for, but mass shooting into an enemy clustered close together. They sowed a ragged line of English ash but there were still enough crossbowmen shooting to bring down more of Longdon's men. It took another two deadly flights from his archers before the crossbowmen realized they were in range, panicked and began clambering back up the far bank. But the

Frenchmen's lethal shooting had allowed du Guesclin's men to swarm forward, splashing through the shallows or wading waist- and chest-deep, pushing aside fallen bodies, using them as shields against English arrows and howling with venom as they urged themselves forward.

Will Longdon's men now had a perfect killing zone. The French had crossed the halfway mark, well within range of his archers. They depressed their bow angle and shot into the skinners. There were too many. No matter how quickly they nocked and loosed they couldn't kill enough of them. It was time for Blackstone's men-at-arms to step forward. The archers had stopped the crossbowmen from covering the surging attack, which meant fewer men would reach their side of the river. For now.

'Back, lads!' Longdon shouted. He and those closest to him turned, but the soft ground gave way beneath their feet and they slid down the bank into the shoreline's lapping water. They were suddenly defenceless as the snarling routiers pushed hard towards them, an easy kill only yards away. They scrambled to their feet, too late to nock another arrow. Left with no choice, they grabbed their archer's knives, knowing a war bow and a misericord's narrow blade was no defence against mace- and sword-wielding men-at-arms. Someone barged at Will with such force he was flung aside. Meulon had thrown him clear and led a dozen of his men into the shallows.

'Get back, Will!' he yelled without turning, and striking an attacker with such force his blade cut beneath the man's neck into his chest, near enough severing his whole shoulder. The sudden violence from the men-at-arms made the attackers falter; they were at a disadvantage, knee-deep or worse in water, but these big men who came at them showed no concern for the stony riverbed or its current. Meulon's men stopped an initial insurgency of a few men but more were storming across beyond them.

A flight of arrows overhead told Meulon that Will Longdon's men had reached safety and were covering his withdrawal from the river. His men clambered over the rim and ran back into position.

'Clumsy bastard!' Meulon shouted at Longdon as he ran back with his men. The attack could not be stopped now no matter how many arrows were shot, and there were pitifully few of those left. Along the line archers kept shooting, but called out how many arrows remained.

'Save them!' Longdon yelled. They were down to the ten or twelve shafts gifted to each man by the Moors. He shoved them into his belt. All except one. He nocked it, drew back and thought of Najih bin Wālid and the man's courage as he shot it into a routier's chest.

'Now, John!' Blackstone said.

John Jacob strode forward and waved a pennon back and forth for all to see. Men ran from the ranks carrying burning torches to light the pyres. Now the enemy crossbowmen had been dealt with Blackstone stood less than ten yards from the riverbank's edge. The flames crackled, whipped by the wind at their back, and as the kindling and heavier dry wood flared, trapped beneath the abandoned damp blankets, thick smoke billowed across the river. The French and their routiers would be attacking blind.

Blackstone's men peered through the drifting smoke. Routiers attempted to shield their eyes as they tried to find their footing. Men cursed and bellowed in rage as Blackstone stood ready to kill the greed-driven mercenaries. He waited until the first stumbling men gained a foothold, eyes streaming, lungs heaving desperately for clean air, and then he killed four men in quick succession. On either side Killbere and John Jacob slashed and stabbed. The bodies fell back down the slope into the swell of men, who pulled aside the dead and scrambled over them. Blackstone's men-at-arms' line held until the dead began to fall before them. To kill their enemy efficiently, they stepped back a yard at a time as the bodies piled up. Dying men squirmed at their feet; blood soaked the defenders' boots; wounded attackers vomited in grievous pain, whimpering as they died.

So many men were swarming across the river that routiers on the far side were slowed by those ahead who waded, fell, scrambled and fought. As dull as any church bell, a death knell of clashing steel resounded against the cliff face. On William Ashford's flank, routiers found a way over bodies piled up in the shallow water. They stormed ahead, forcing Ashford's men back, shields raised, to protect the archers. The King's pavilion was overrun, but Beyard and his Gascons had snatched the King's standard and carried it into the centre of Blackstone's men. If the standard still flew, then it meant the King still lived and fought on.

Meulon and Renfred's line of defence edged closer together as men fell from their ranks. A new sound whirled through the air as slings' leather cords were whipped by the archers. At forty yards a hurled river pebble or ragged flint could stun a man, at twenty-five they smashed bones and killed. Will Longdon and Jack Halfpenny had stood their ground and waited until they could inflict the most damage at close quarters. A hailstorm lashed into the attackers, who'd thought themselves safe from archers since no arrow had been shot once Blackstone's men approached to defend the riverbank. Routiers raised their arms yet still stones broke bones in hands, they blinded men; sword and mace were dropped; teeth shattered; cheekbones crushed. The wounded men's courage drove them forward a few faltering steps where Meulon's men hamstrung them and plunged swords into throats. The carnage was at its most desperate.

Blackstone, slathered with blood, turned, searching for Tom Brook, but he lay dead. Killbere heaved for breath, his shield almost in tatters from the strikes against it. He spat blood from a blow to the face, half turned and rammed his sword's pommel into his attacker's eye, and as the man recoiled, he twisted on his heel slashing the blade between the man's ear and neck.

'Thomas!' he yelled. 'It's time!'

Blackstone's men were being forced back despite the toll they were taking on du Guesclin's men. 'William! Tom's dead.'

William Ashford took a pace back from his line of men. There was no need to question. He ran for the quarry.

'De Hayle? You see his blazon?' Blackstone said to Killbere, then rammed his shield against two men, braced his legs and forced them off balance; stepping forward, he kicked one fallen man in the face, snapping his neck, and lunged Wolf Sword into the other.

'He's not here, dammit!' Killbere said. They were being pushed back further now.

Blackstone saw his ranks closing. The archers had bought more time and slowed the advance over the riverbank's lip.

'Fall back!' Blackstone bellowed over the screaming horde. 'Will! Now! Get back now! John, give the signal.'

John Jacob bled like every other man, but he raised the pennon again and signalled for the men to fall back against the cliff face. They knew where the traps had been dug and their withdrawal gave the French added strength but ten yards later the staggered holes concealed by Blackstone's ranks snared their ankles. Stumbling headlong, they fell on defenders' blades. It was a temporary respite as Blackstone's shields came together, a half-circle of desperate men determined to fight to their last. The French and their routiers faltered. Exhaustion clawed at every fighter but the men who bore Blackstone's blazon still glared over the rim of their shields. The routiers sucked air, drank heavily from their wineskins, biding their time, waiting for more of their fellow mercenaries to breach the fallen and gather in strength.

The sun had arced across the sky and put Blackstone's men in the cliff's shade. The cool air refreshed them. The blood-soaked ground bore witness to the day-long battle.

'Be ready,' Blackstone called to Will Longdon and Jack Halfpenny, whose archers now stood with their backs against the rock face. He saw they had lost half their numbers. 'Will?'

'Aye, Thomas, but no man has more than a dozen shafts.'

'Then shoot as fast as the Moors. We'll only drop the shields once.'

They waited. Beyond the river hundreds of wounded men had dragged themselves back from the battle. Would they come again? Blackstone's resistance had defied everything they had thrown at the outnumbered men. French captains could be heard urging their troops to gather for one last effort to crush the beleaguered English. It boosted the mercenaries' courage and, with a low murmur soon whipped into a roar, they gathered a hundred paces back from where Blackstone's men huddled wearily behind their shields. The routiers chanted, beat swords against shields, forcing blood into tired muscles and failing courage. And then they charged.

'Wait,' said Blackstone. The routiers pounded forward. Seventy-five yards. They raised swords, bared teeth in a snarling hatred for the Englishmen who refused to die. Fifty yards. The weight of their attack would flatten the shield wall. 'Now!' Blackstone said.

The shield bearers dropped to one knee, exposing the attacking mercenaries to Blackstone's archers. The routiers died at thirty-five yards. Those behind stumbled but the archers shot again, and again. They loosed arrow shafts until they had no more. Blackstone's men raised their shields. The unexpected violence slowed the French but there were still men further back on the top of the riverbank.

The ground shuddered as William Ashford led a dozen horsemen from the quarry entrance and swept around the steadfast Englishmen, pressing aching shoulders against shields, blood knots biting into wrists, soaked from sweat and their enemy's gore. Ashford's horsemen rode through the routiers. They had no fight left in them. The final attack was broken. The French turned and scrambled across the blood-soaked riverbank.

Blackstone stepped forward over the fallen and watched the remnants of the army determined to kill him scatter in disarray. The distant flags and pennons of the French lords and that of the Breton commander were also turning away. But then the lowering sun caught the glint of mail and spear tip as an army of shadows crept across the distant hillside and rallied them. The French raised their banners and turned to face Blackstone's survivors once more. They would come again. The creeping darkness was Hugh Calveley and his thousand men, who swept across the broad expanse on the opposite bank. They formed up with Hugh Calveley at their head.

'Well, lads, we're done for now,' said Will Longdon.

Meulon turned from where he stood with his men. Blood dribbled down his neck into his congealed beard from a head wound. 'You must have left your brains in the shit pit, you fool. Did you think we would live through this?'

'You were never going to die drunk in a whore's bed with your hand on your cock trying to keep it up,' said Killbere. He wiped blood from his face and spat the foul taste from his throat.

A murmur of humour ran through the men.

'At least I would have had one to get my fist around. Now it'll be fed to the crows,' Longdon answered.

'Crows look for a meal not a morsel,' said Meulon.

They fell silent as Blackstone turned to face them. 'See here, lads. Calveley rides forward. He'll ask for our surrender. The Spanish and the French will have sport with us but if my head is to go on a spike outside Paris or Burgos then I reckon they must earn the right to take it.'

'I've not fought these bastards over the years to end up in a cage and be torn limb from limb for the entertainment of a mob of pig-shagging peasants. I'll not surrender to that,' said Killbere.

A cry went around the survivors. 'No surrender, Sir Thomas! No surrender!'

'Then so be it,' said Blackstone.

Hugh Calveley's horse had picked its way through the dead and waited at the far side of the bridge. Despite his aching body and gnawing wounds, Blackstone stepped over and around the corpses bristling with arrows and strode towards him.

He stopped ten yards from the mounted veteran whose side he had fought alongside at other battles in another time.

'Thomas, you should have taken my offer to join me after Auray.'

'I had other matters to attend to,' said Blackstone.

Hugh Calveley looked across the field of dead. 'Your banner still stands but few men left around it. Henry of Trastámara is king; we came for Don Pedro.'

'Then you're too late.'

'I thought as much. He's not here, is he? It was doubtful you'd let him fight against such odds. You held the ground so he might escape and reach the Prince.'

Blackstone made no reply. Hugh Calveley was one of the best field commanders and knew what options Blackstone had faced. Calveley gave a slight nod of his head towards the men waiting behind him. 'You caused Bertrand du Guesclin and the French heavy losses. But they want you, Thomas, more than anything in the world they want you, and now that we are here we can give them what they want.'

'There will be no surrender, Hugh.'

'And I would not ask it.'

'Then we have said all that needs to be said.'

Calveley leaned forward on his saddle's pommel. 'The French and their skinners are grievously hurt and without my men they will have no more stomach to fight. Thomas, I did not come here to kill our King's Master of War.' He wheeled the horse away.

Blackstone's exhaustion and relief threatened to put him on his knees. He faced his ragged handful of men, raised Wolf Sword above his head and heard their roar of victory.

CHAPTER SIXTY-EIGHT

It took two weary days of travel for Blackstone's men to reach Puebla de Sanabria where Don Pedro was waiting at the Iglesia de Santa María del Azogue. The town was spread across the top of a hillside within the bend of two rivers, a clear vantage point to observe any approaching enemy and a safe enough place for a fugitive King seeking refuge. They had carried their dead on horseback to the small town's church for burial. The routiers abandoned their own dead, leaving them to rot. Blackstone's losses were heavy. Twenty-seven archers had fallen and thirty-six men-at-arms. Their slow ride north took longer because of the men's wounds and exhaustion; in reality it was little more than a funeral procession that brought tears to those whose friends had died.

Lázaro had prayed hard during the battle and vowed to the Mother of Christ that he would serve his Lord Beyard if she spared the Gascon captain's life. Now on the journey, his prayers answered, he doubled his efforts to serve and attended Beyard and those of his Gascons who had survived. Aicart bore many small wounds, sword points' jabs through mail, Loys a gash to the bone across a forearm. Any man who rode at Beyard's side became the boy's charge. Lázaro was tireless – preparing food, boiling water to wash bloodied bandages and helping men tend their injuries. When he finished his day's work he attended to their horses, and when the moon was high he fuelled the fire and pushed his back against Beyard. Such comfort was the Holy Mother's reward for his faith in her.

And every night, when praying for those who had protected him, his final whispered invocation to the Almighty was for his dead Queen.

Don Pedro was not at Puebla de Sanabria. Álvaraz had left behind two of his men to explain that the distance between the battleground and the town meant the French and their mercenaries were too close. The King had gone deeper into Galicia, which remained loyal to him and where the enemy was unlikely to follow. He did not trust the priest at the church to uphold his sanctuary should the victorious French arrive.

'There's faith for you, Thomas,' said Killbere.

'He distrusts the Church,' Blackstone answered. 'And they know he's been excommunicated.'

'Not the Church, man, us. He had no faith that we could hold the bridge.'

'He's a king running for his life.'

'An ex-king with his tail between his legs,' said John Jacob.

'We paid a high price for his escape. We rest here a few days and bury our dead. We'll pay the priest to recite prayers for them for a month.'

They corralled their horses and found buildings to camp against whose walls faced the sun for much needed warmth in their muscles. Those townspeople who dared to venture from the safety of their homes brought food and wine once they realized these men were not there to cause them harm and paid for what meagre food they had. The women attended the wounded with skills learnt at their mother's knee.

The ancient fortress next to the church was in a continuous state of repair and expansion. The town's local lord was three days' ride away and seldom seen, sending his reeve once a month to check on progress and then yearly to collect taxes. Blackstone ordered the men from their scaffolds and had them bury his dead. Carpenters fashioned a cross for every man.

The priest told Blackstone that Don Pedro had taken their food stores without payment. He was their King and such a man did not recompense peasants, no matter that they swore loyalty to him.

'We have payment for you and we will take only what we need,' Blackstone assured him as he stood in the dank gloom of the old church. It was poorly lit, a single candle close to a crudely fashioned crucifix, hewn no doubt with reverence by a carpenter as poor as the man he sculpted. 'You have a blacksmith?'

'We have enough skilled men to sustain ourselves with the help and blessings of Lord Jesus,' he said, crossing himself and glancing at the crucified figure.

'Shoe my horses, sharpen our blades and tell us where we can find grazing.'

They took the horses back across the river where meadows were still rich with grass. The heavy rainfall in the area blessed the surrounding countryside with a plentiful supply of water and crops.

'He should have stayed here,' said John Jacob as he released his horse into the meadow.

'Perhaps we should all stay here,' Killbere said. 'The town has deep wells and grain stores; it would be a good place to spend next winter.'

Blackstone looked at him, knowing the truth of the matter.

'And the women have broad hips and are sturdy, not like city whores who spend their lives on their backs. These women can look after a man,' Killbere added.

'I leave you here long enough and what goodwill we have gained will be gone in days. Their men work in stone and timber, they haul rocks from the valley, they'd be hard men to fight once you and Will Longdon's lads invade their wives' beds.'

Killbere shrugged. 'I thought it a better proposal than chasing the shirt tails of a king on the run.'

'The weather will turn,' said John Jacob. 'Álvaraz's men say the storms come into the mountains from the sea.'

'Then we won't stay long before leaving to catch up to him – just give the men time to rest and eat. We're eight or nine days from Santiago at a steady pace, less if the going isn't hard. And neither Hugh Calveley nor Bertrand du Guesclin will come after us now.'

'And then?' said Killbere.

'Make sure Don Pedro gets on the ship for Aquitaine and leaves us to make our own way home.'

'I was thinking more about the woman, Velasquita,' said Killbere.

Blackstone looked across the idyllic meadow, the broad-leafed trees whose soft rustling accompanied the sound of water over rocks. A brief moment of tranquillity in the fighting men's lives. 'I wasn't,' he said.

CHAPTER SIXTY-NINE

The route to Santiago de Compostela meandered through valleys and deep forests, waterfalls tumbled from the heights and the further north they rode the more the sun's warmth diminished. They had gifted half the horses to the people at Puebla de Sanabria. They were good horse stock from a king's stables and valuable to trade. The remaining horses Blackstone's men trailed with them as replacements, not knowing what hardship might lie ahead and take a toll on their mounts. They were close now to the final days in their mission to secure passage of the deposed Spanish King to the safety and support of Edward, Prince of Wales.

They found Don Pedro's camp in a village three miles from Santiago de Compostela. Álvaraz rode out to greet them.

'Sir Thomas, you held the bridge,' he said, respect and surprise mingling in the compliment.

'At a cost,' said Blackstone.

Álvaraz looked at the riders and saw their depleted numbers. 'And al-Hakam?'

'The Moors took the fight to the French and fought like lions. Not one survived. They had more courage than most. I hope Don Pedro honours them.'

Álvaraz grimaced. 'All is not well, Sir Thomas. He refused to stay at Puebla de Sanabria for fear that the English and French mercenaries would find a way past you.'

'Your men who led us here told us,' said Killbere. 'What is it now? Does he have a fistula up his arse?'

DAVID GILMAN

Álvaraz smiled; he had missed the inherent disrespect the English held for those in authority. 'Sir Gilbert, the Archbishop has refused him entry to Santiago.'

'Galicia is loyal to the King,' said John Jacob.

'And the Archbishop is loyal to the Pope,' Álvaraz said. 'You know Don Pedro was excommunicated when he defied the Pope after aligning himself with the Moors.'

'Is that all? An archbishop can't stop him riding into the city,' Killbere said.

'Santiago throngs with pilgrims. People come to pray at the tomb of St James; they undertake an arduous journey to pray for loved ones who are stricken and for their own misdeeds to be forgiven. They come to request and behold blessings and miracles. The Archbishop can turn the city troops and militia against Don Pedro. How easy would it be to incite a mob, many of whom have committed violence in their lives? Don Pedro's own violence and acts of murder are well known. They will not permit him to ride into the city.'

Blackstone felt the weight of this King's reputation oppressing on him. 'God's tears, Álvaraz, I cannot wait to rid myself of this man.' He heaved a sigh. 'Very well, take us to him.'

Álvaraz laid a restraining hand on Blackstone's arm. 'Sir Thomas, his temper flares at the slightest mishap, the slightest. At any moment he could order every man in the room to be slain. The Moors would have done his bidding but my men will not carry out the orders of a man close to losing his reason. I will protect him as I must, but nothing more. He needs a strong hand now, Sir Thomas, a guiding hand that will not tolerate his excesses. A firm hand.'

No banners flew over the impoverished stone buildings where the King of Castile had taken refuge. They had not abandoned all comforts: a fire blazed, a table was laden with food. The High Steward looked as though he had spent a lifetime standing at his lord's shoulder. His face was more gaunt than when Blackstone last saw him, and it was obvious the journey had been arduous for the elderly man. Blackstone handed a folded banner to a servant. 'Your standard can fly again. Henry of Trastámara's forces never seized it. We held it safe.'

An agitated Don Pedro nodded to the servant to take away the standard of Castile and León as if it was of no importance.

'Lord, that is your kingdom's blazon,' said Blackstone.

'I no longer have a kingdom. I am deposed!' He threw a half-eaten apple into the fire. 'How much must a king endure? My personal wealth seized from my ships and then condemnation from the Archbishop here. I needed the plate and gold to secure my family's place in Aquitaine and it was imperative the Archbishop gave me his blessing as the rightful ruler of Castile. How can I return if my wealth is gone and the Archbishop himself declares me undesirable? All I have left of value is my name. Without that I am truly a pauper.'

'Greatness rears like the phoenix from the ruins of a man's misfortune, sire. My Prince recognizes you as the true King of Castile; no other authority is needed. No archbishop or thief can take that away. Ignore what has happened and ready yourself and your family.'

Don Pedro sulked. 'I expected you here sooner,' he said.

The vein in Blackstone's neck throbbed. Killbere knew the signs. To have lost so many men and then be treated with such contempt and self-pity put the King in danger. Killbere stepped forward and bowed before Blackstone could insult or, worse, threaten the King.

'There was a small matter of holding off a few thousand mercenaries and their French commanders,' said Killbere.

'Did they turn and run?'

'My lord?' said Killbere, uncertain if the King really was implying that the battle had been less fierce than their losses suggested.

'They were routiers. Paid to kill. If they saw their efforts were not worth what the French promised, then men like that run. Your losses, Sir Gilbert, might be because of your own poor fighting skills. Am I to grieve for not seeing for myself how the battle was fought?'

Killbere's fierce grip on Blackstone's arm could not stop him from breaking free and striding forward so rapidly he reached the King's table. Don Pedro recoiled. 'Guards!'

Killbere drew his sword and kept Álvaraz and two of his men at the entrance. Killbere shook his head at them. 'Leave it be, Álvaraz. It will only be the King's pride that will be wounded.'

Álvaraz shared the Englishmen's disdain for the man he served and was grateful that Killbere's blade at his throat made it look as though he was helpless to assist his master.

Blackstone slammed his fist on the table; beakers of wine spilled and food trembled. As did Don Pedro, but he reacted quickly and instinctively drew his knife. Blackstone's fist closed over the hand holding the blade and rammed it with such force into the table that half its length penetrated the wood. The sudden act of violence left Don Pedro speechless. The High Steward bravely took a step forward but Blackstone's glowering look halted him. Blackstone faced the King, who nursed his bruised hand.

'Six hundred of the bravest men I have ever seen in battle took the enemy head on. Sayyid al-Hakam's name should be honoured and remembered. He slowed the enemy so we could defend the bridge. I lost archers more precious than your jewels and men-at-arms more valuable than your damned kingdom. So I suggest you ride now for Corunna and the ship to Aquitaine – for that is the only place you will find salvation.'

The young King recoiled from Blackstone's assault. His breath came hard, sweat speckled his face, his speech faltered, disbelief and shock constricting his throat, swallowing the words. He lisped some kind of mumbled threat, and then slowly gathered his wits and his composure. Don Pedro did not lack intelligence. He knew his life and the future of regaining his kingdom rested squarely with the English King's Master of War. He steadied himself and swallowed his pride.

'I will honour the dead. I swear it. And I spoke hastily and without proper thought to those who defended my crown. I will offer prayers and beg forgiveness at the next church on our journey.' He spoke carefully so that his words calmed the threat that still hovered in the room. 'But,' he said, daring to take a step closer to Blackstone. 'It would be better for my act of contrition to be made in the cathedral at Santiago.'

'The place is unimportant,' said Blackstone.

'But the pilgrims who throng the city and the citizens of that revered place would acknowledge my piety once they see my standard flying again.'

'And see through it for what it is.'

Don Pedro's confidence grew. 'Sir Thomas, your fighting skills are beyond question, but politics is more than a blade with courage behind it. Galicia is the last province loyal to me. I must ride into its capital and receive the blessing and sacrament from the Archbishop and the acceptance of its people. It is better for me to meet your Prince knowing I have a province that will support and honour me because if we are to return in force and reclaim my throne then it might be through Galicia.'

Blackstone knew it was an argument to be considered. If the Prince of Wales put a rightful king back on his throne, no matter how unlikeable the man, he would have to bring an army either through the Pyrenees and the Kingdom of Navarre, which by now would have sided with the French and Henry of Trastámara, or land at a northern port in Galicia.

'King Edward's Master of War and the Prince's choice to save the Kingdom of Castile and León might hold sway with the Archbishop,' said Don Pedro.

The King had manoeuvred Blackstone into a corner. 'And if he still won't agree?'

'Then you have tried and I will ride to Corunna.' He paused for a moment, turning to warm himself at the fire. 'And by the time we return to Spain there might be another archbishop more willing to offer his support and blessings.'

CHAPTER SEVENTY

While Blackstone's men established camp their captains arranged food, clean cooking water and wine from the villagers. Once his men knew that he was to make an appeal to the Archbishop many wanted to ride with him. The cathedral gave them all a chance to be blessed and shriven in one of the most venerated places in Europe. Blackstone denied them their sudden desire for religion. Allowing war-weary, battle-hardened men into a city the size of Santiago de Compostela with its inns and prostitutes, merchants and money changers was a risk too far now that Blackstone was an emissary of the King.

Blackstone bathed as John Jacob attempted to clean his gambeson, cloak and hose.

'John and I will come with you, Thomas,' said Killbere. 'Religion has a strange way of slipping like sweat off a pilgrim's back when they see a knight who looks as though he carries a full purse.'

'Gilbert, this is no time for whoring and drink. What I told the men goes the same for you. We are there to seek an understanding.'

'And I give my word to stay at your side. Ride in, say what we must, and then ride out. I too want this business finished. I'm weary of it. If you can effect a reconciliation then I will be as thankful as the next man.' He scratched his armpit. 'If I'm to ride back to France then we'll need fresh clothes, so it might be worth buying fresh shirts in Santiago.'

It was obviously a roundabout attempt to spend time on the streets, spend money with merchants and ease into brothels and taverns.

Blackstone finished dressing. 'The village crones have a bathhouse for passing pilgrims. They'll wash your shirt and braies and scrub your back with fresh straw while you sit in a wooden tub of bathwater used by fifty travellers.'

Killbere shrugged. 'Then I shall itch in front of the Archbishop and apologize that I stink.'

'Why do you think they burn incense? It suffocates the stench of the unwashed and devours any disease carried in the air. You'll come back smelling sweet and disease free. I want to be back before nightfall and talking takes time.'

Killbere surrendered and walked to his tethered horse. 'The night is for witches,' he said with a suggestive smile.

Blackstone ignored him. He had not seen Velasquita since they arrived at the King's camp. There had been no time. And since Sayyid al-Hakam had told him she met a routier that night at Burgos he was even more cautious of her. That man had been Ranulph de Hayle, who would surely not lose sight of his prey. If Velasquita knew where he was then Blackstone would stay close to her.

Beyard walked towards him with Lázaro in tow. 'Sir Thomas, a word?'

Blackstone nodded for John Jacob to go to the horses; then he glanced towards the King's quarters and lowered his voice. 'Beyard, is everything all right with the boy? Has he remembered something?'

'Oh no, nothing, Sir Thomas, but he wants to ask a favour from you so I said I would bring him to you.' Beyard ushered the reluctant boy forward.

'Lázaro, what is it you ask?' said Blackstone.

'My lord, my Queen told me of this great place Santiago de Compostela, with its cathedral and the tomb of St James. She revered the place so much that she said one day she would undertake a pilgrimage here and allow me to go with her. I would beg you to let me go with you so I can pray for her and leave her crucifix on the saint's tomb. That way I will know that at last she has made her pilgrimage.'

Blackstone treated the boy's innocent simplicity and belief with heartfelt tenderness. 'Lázaro, I believe you to be the bravest boy I have ever known. Your Queen loved and trusted you and gave you her crucifix to protect you, but I am afraid I cannot take you with me today. This day is for the King's business.'

Lázaro's chin dropped, but he nodded his acceptance of Blackstone's ruling.

Blackstone lifted the boy's chin. 'But your courage and devotion should be rewarded, so I will speak to the Archbishop and ask if he will give you his personal blessing.'

The lad's eyes widened at the prospect.

'If the Archbishop agrees Beyard will take you tomorrow.'

Lázaro's joy overwhelmed him and, just as when he was first rescued and crushing fear made it difficult for him to speak, he could only stutter his gratitude.

Beyard's hand ruffled the boy's hair. 'Now, Lázaro, there is no need for your voice to desert you. We have spoken about this. Let your thoughts find the words and then your lips speak them.'

The boy's grin was a joy to behold for the men who cared for him. He calmed his stutter. 'From my heart I thank you, Sir Thomas.'

'And from mine I wish you joy and a long life in the service of this great captain. Now, I had best get to the Archbishop and arrange that meeting for you.'

Blackstone strode to where John Jacob and Killbere waited with the horses beneath a clump of trees. He untied the rein from the hitching post; the bastard horse's ears pricked forward, raising his head so quickly it took Blackstone by surprise. It did not, as expected, bare its yellow teeth and attempt to tear flesh from bone, but snuffled its soft muzzle against his shoulder.

Killbere and John Jacob were as startled as Blackstone.

'I'll be damned. If I didn't know better, I'd say that was a sign of affection,' said John Jacob.

'My arse,' said Killbere. 'Too much sweet grass and not enough oats is making it soft in the head. No different from us, John. Not enough meat in a man's belly and you see how quickly he starts simpering. Fighting men and their beasts need a diet that gives them strength and vigour.'

Blackstone turned the bastard horse. 'A leaf fell on my shoulder; it was after the berries.'

John Jacob laughed. 'For a moment there I thought there was hope.'

Killbere spat. 'Hope? John, that was washed away when our mothers sluiced us from their belly.' He spurred his horse onto the track leading to Santiago.

Blackstone and John Jacob followed. 'One day, Sir Gilbert will find some joy in his life,' said the squire.

'Oh, he has that already,' said Blackstone. 'He's a happy man when he's killing the French.'

CHAPTER SEVENTY-ONE

Santiago de Compostela was a spectacle to rival any bustling city. Pilgrimage was big business. Foot-weary and exhausted travellers had to eat and sleep somewhere and the citizens took full advantage of religious fervour to supply both food and bed and more besides. They sold scallop shells as tokens of successful completion of the arduous journey; silver and metal guilds employed smiths making bowls and other commemorative artefacts. Not every traveller's purse was empty, or soul bereft of hope for salvation. The wealthy travelled in comfort until the city was in sight and then piously walked the remaining few miles. Mostly, though, it was the poor who sought solace at the saint's tomb and a communal blessing in the cathedral from the Archbishop.

Blackstone, Killbere and John Jacob entered the fortified walls. Blackstone told the gate commander that he came to see the Archbishop in the name of the King of England and the Prince of Wales and Aquitaine. Killbere's questioning look once the lie had escaped Blackstone's lips earned him a shrug in reply. The closer they got to the cathedral the more street merchants and pilgrims jostled them. Their escort of soldiers cleared their passage.

They were led around the cathedral towards the Pórtico de la Gloria, the arched main gate into the cathedral entrance where lines of pilgrims were kept either side of the entrance, their garbled voices a pottage of different languages. Stewards and monks stripped the pilgrims of their clothing and tossed what were little more than rags into large braziers, handing every traveller a clean set of clothing.

'We need a safe place for our horses,' Blackstone told the escort.

'There is an alley beyond the plaza, lord. I will have my men guard them until your return.'

'Keep this horse separate,' he said, patting the bastard horse's neck. 'He is sent to test men's faith in God.'

The soldiers' eyes widened, but they nodded obediently.

'John, go with them. You handle my horse and then join us inside.'

'How will I find you?' said John Jacob as they dismounted.

'You'll hear the wailing of angels when men such as us enter a place such as this,' Killbere said.

Blackstone and Killbere followed their guide through the three arches, heavy with sculptures glorifying God and threatening the sinful with images of demons tearing out sinners' tongues. A monk greeted them and led them on.

'Makes you think, Thomas, a place as glorious as this,' Killbere whispered.

'Of what? Our lies and whoring?' Blackstone answered quietly.

'No, of how much they spent on it. They could have built a hundred taverns just from what those arches cost, and a more pleasurable place for a man to spend his time. These places are always so cold.'

'You never complain when you're shriven before battle.'

'Aye, well, that's different. My thoughts can't see my soul but my soul sees God. Better to be safe.'

The monk led them the length of the nave, the austere granite columns soaring to the high ceiling, belittling mankind's stature before the Almighty, but offering sanctuary to the very poor who could not afford lodgings at any price. They huddled to sleep along the side walls and in the upper gallery, while others lined up to confess their sins. The dull chanting of Latin echoed through the vast space as pilgrims sought indulgences.

They heard John Jacob's quick footfall behind them. 'A wonderment, isn't it?' he said, impressed by the spectacle, his face flushed from catching them up.

'Now that's a wonderment,' said Killbere as across the transept before them a silver censer, the size of a modest church bell, streamed forth incense. Eight robed men hauled a pulley and swung the heavy object back and forth at speed. Blackstone tapped the monk on the shoulder and pointed to the rapidly swinging censer, his look asking the question his lack of Spanish could not.

'*Botafumeiro*,' said the monk. Accustomed to those who travelled the French route into Spain, he went on in stumbling French: 'Charcoal and incense. It masks the pilgrims' stench and kills disease.'

'If it ever comes off that pulley it'll kill more than disease,' said Killbere.

'I told you there was no need to wash your shirt,' said Blackstone as they turned along the right-hand side of the transept, where the monk gestured for them to wait. The three men watched in quiet fascination, well clear of the hurtling censer, as hundreds of pilgrims knelt in prayer, or pressed their backs against the wall as the thick incense cloaked the pillars.

'Sir Thomas?' Blackstone turned when beckoned. The monk gestured for him to enter the room off the transept. Blackstone signalled Killbere and John Jacob to stay where they were. As he stepped inside the room, he saw it was the *antesacristia*. There, a man who appeared to be of some importance stood waiting while an older man in more elaborate ecclesiastical robes was being helped to dress for mass. The latter Blackstone guessed was the Archbishop of Santiago de Compostela.

Blackstone waited at a respectful distance, ignored by the Archbishop.

'I am Peralvarez, the dean here.'

'And I beg an audience with the Archbishop. I have travelled a great distance on the orders of the English Prince of Wales and Aquitaine.'

'Your name?'

'Sir Thomas Blackstone.'

'On request from the Prince?' said Peralvarez as if confirming the truth. 'His grace is soon to give the Most Holy Sacrifice of the mass. There is little time if you are here to seek indulgences or confession.'

The older man, who stood a few yards behind the dean, allowed his attendant to fuss over his vestments. 'I am Suero Gómez, Archbishop. What is it that brings you here?'

'Your grace, my Prince – who has the love and support of his father, Edward, King of England – has tasked me to save a man's life. The man whose bastard half-brother usurped his divine right to the throne of Castile and León.'

Archbishop Gómez looked up sharply. 'Don Pedro?'

Blackstone bowed his head in answer.

'I have ruled on this matter.'

Blackstone waited a moment before answering: 'The English King and his Prince are pious men who accept that it is God who has given them victory in battle. It is an ungodly act that the French have brought an army and mercenaries into Spain to seek and kill Don Pedro. They do this not to punish a man who has sinned but to put a bastard on the throne and an enemy at my Prince's back.'

Archbishop Gómez studied the tall, battle-scarred man who stood apparently obediently in front of him. 'So it is for fear of an enemy at your Prince's borders that you and your Prince plead for this murderer. A man who allies himself with heathens to fight other Christians; who murdered his Queen, his brother, his general. Don Pedro allows Jews and Muslims in his city only to usurp their wealth for his assaults on others. And you ask for this vile man, this excommunicate, to receive my blessings?'

'I do, your grace, for the sake of Spain. My Prince has demanded he take a Christian wife, turn his face to the Church and relent. And when he does these things he will return here with an army. Galicia is loyal to him.'

'Then let the peasants and the lords of the provinces be his friend. I will not.'

Blackstone knew he could make no further appeal on Don Pedro's behalf. 'I am grateful to you for allowing me an audience.'

'Pass my goodwill to your Prince. He is, as you say, a pious and devout man and he will need the Lord's strength and wisdom when dealing with Don Pedro.'

The audience was over. Blackstone bowed but did not leave the room. 'I have one more request.'

The look of irritation on Peralvarez's face was quickly dismissed by the Archbishop. 'Let him speak. This man is a loyal servant to his King, and I suspect has sacrificed many of his men to bring Don Pedro this far.'

'Your grace,' said Blackstone, 'when Queen Blanche was murdered there was a boy witness, a servant she took to her heart. She saved his life by hiding him.'

'He saw the killer?' Archbishop Gómez said hopefully, stepping closer to Blackstone.

'He did not see who was responsible, but he has travelled with us from northern France and across Spain in trying to identify those responsible. This boy has great courage: he has suffered hardship and lived in fear.'

'And your request?'

'The Queen gave him her crucifix moments before she died, and now he wishes to bring it here, receive your blessing and place the crucifix on St James's tomb.'

The Archbishop's compassion was plain to see. 'Tomorrow. Bring him through the Puerta de las Platerías.' He gestured to the right of where they stood. 'It is closest to here. I will receive the child and give thanks for his courage. He shall have his wish.'

'Your grace, he is guarded and cared for by my Gascon captain Beyard. Is it acceptable that he brings the boy to you?'

'Yes. What is this child's name?'

'Lázaro.'

CHAPTER SEVENTY-TWO

Álvaraz stood by the King's quarters, watching Blackstone and his companions return from the city. The Englishman's first duty should have been to attend the King; instead he sought one of his captains and the boy servant. Whatever he said to them caused the boy to bend his knee to Blackstone, who gently raised him up and put a hand on the boy's head. The smiling lad turned away as Blackstone continued to talk to the Gascon and finally strode towards the King.

'Is there news?' he asked Blackstone.

Blackstone shook his head. 'I might as well have told the Archbishop I was bringing plague into the city.'

Álvaraz's heart sank. 'Sir Thomas, I have served this King all my life. He is a bold and fearless fighter; he suffered when we abandoned you at the bridge. He did not wish others to fight his battles for him. Since then he has become increasingly torn in himself. I am not here to defend him, but he is still young and they have seized everything that is rightfully his. He has nothing. The Archbishop's approval was his last hope of recognition for his kingdom.'

'I can't help how he feels. I'm here to get him back to Aquitaine: beyond that I care nothing for him.'

Álvaraz had the look of a defeated man. 'He's had too much wine,' he warned.

'I don't give a damn. We leave for Corunna tomorrow,' said Blackstone. 'I'll tie him to his horse if I have to. Stay here.'

Blackstone stepped into the King's room. There was enough evidence of copious wine having been drunk and Blackstone saw no reason to disguise bad news with good manners. Without formality he told Don Pedro the result of his meeting with the Archbishop.

The turmoil within Don Pedro exploded. He bellowed, fuming with incoherent anger. The High Steward levelled his staff of office, keeping the servants out of harm's way as the King swept aside the contents of the table, the silver goblets and plates clattering across the floor. Servants retreated as he snatched at the nearest and beat him with his fists until blood spewed from a broken nose. The High Steward's eyes widened in horror as Blackstone strode across the room and restrained the King.

'Out!' the High Steward commanded the servants: an act that saved their lives. Don Pedro would never allow them to live had they witnessed the assault. The King stood quivering with doubt and fear as Blackstone pressed his weight against him, face to the wall, arms locked, his mouth close to the King's ear urging him to calm.

Don Pedro surrendered to Blackstone's quiet command, then shook himself free. He looked at the ashen-faced steward. 'Who witnessed this?'

'None, sire. I banished them from the room.'

'You will suffer the consequences for what you did,' he said to Blackstone.

'I restrained a king ready to commit murder. I saved you, highness, not the servant. My Prince would not tolerate such an act. I serve you in his name.'

A tense silence fell between the two men. A moment later the King nodded, regained his composure and calmed his breathing. Don Pedro smoothed his gambeson and resettled his belt.

'We are less than a day's ride to Corunna where there will be a ship to take you and your family to Bayonne. From there it's only a few hours' ride to Bordeaux,' Blackstone said. 'We are close to securing your safety and with my Prince's support the throne of Castile.'

Don Pedro glared at Blackstone. 'Enough has been said. Emotions are high. We have both suffered great loss of one sort or another. I will let what happened here pass.' He nodded to the High Steward, who summoned servants back into the room to re-lay the table and bring more wine. Ignoring Blackstone, he lifted the goblet to his lips. It was a simple dismissal. Blackstone turned on his heel and returned to his men.

As soon as the door closed there was an edge to the King's voice. 'This matter cannot go unpunished.'

'Blackstone, sire?' said a nervous High Steward. 'He is the Prince's favourite.'

'No, the Archbishop. Where is Velasquita?'

No sooner was the question asked than it was answered. The woman seemed to appear from nowhere. A simple explanation: she had been standing in the doorwell's deep shadow all along, but nonetheless her sudden appearance provoked a frisson of fear in the superstitious. The High Steward crossed himself.

'Out,' said Don Pedro.

The steward ushered away the servants and followed them out of the room. She waited and then pulled the hood of her cloak back from her face.

'You heard?'

She smiled. 'Of course.'

'I cannot be associated with what we must do. Suspicion will fall on you and the Englishman you use, de Hayle. You cannot return to me. Not yet.'

Her answer further eased his agitation. 'I will arrange a boat elsewhere. No one will know. You are free of all guilt. There will be no blemish on you. We have found no witness to the Queen's death. The way ahead is clear of all impediment.'

Don Pedro felt the authority of his birthright return; her soothing words had lulled his uncertainty. 'In time I will return to Castile with the English Prince's help. Be patient and come to me then.' He watched her; her demeanour was quiet, yet unsettling. 'And it would do no harm for Blackstone to become a martyr to his Prince,' he whispered.

She touched his face as a mother would comfort a child. She nodded.

'How?' he asked.

'As it is foretold.'

Velasquita slipped out through the servants' door where the High Steward waited dutifully to be summoned back to the King's presence. His gaunt features shrank as she stepped closer to him. He backed against the wall.

'The King will soon leave for the coast. You will arrange the supplies for the men.'

'Those who do my bidding attend to those matters.'

'And you are devoted to the King?'

'I am.'

'You have served him from the start.'

'I have.'

'He is an imperfect man, but he is king by divine right.'

The High Steward nodded. His mouth was dry.

'Whom do you love more? Our Lord Jesus or the devil?'

'Our blessed Lord, of course,' he answered, his voice so fearful it was barely a whisper.

'And whom do you fear the more?'

'The devil,' he whispered, crossing himself.

She held a thumb-sized leather-encased bottle in front of his face. 'The devil waits for you if you do not do as I tell you.'

The steward's throat constricted. He gasped out the words: 'I will cause no harm to the King.'

'But you will save the King and your soul if you put this into the Englishman's wineskin before they leave for the coast.'

CHAPTER SEVENTY-THREE

The dean had written a pass for Beyard and Lázaro, granting them access to the Archbishop, and they were accorded the privilege of an escort. They wound their way through the crowded streets accompanied by Beyard's Gascons, Aicart and Loys, eyes peeled for thieves in the crowds of pilgrims. Blackstone's gift to Lázaro, his own pilgrimage to the cathedral, was a reward for a resolute and loyal servant rescued all those months before. He had grown in confidence and his future was now more certain than it had ever been. Beyard had promised to find him service with his own powerful and influential lord, the Captal de Buch. Just as Jean de Grailly, the Captal, had gifted Beyard to serve Blackstone, now Beyard was ensuring the boy could serve one of the greatest lords in Gascony. Their journey would soon be at an end. Once they left Don Pedro at Corunna their ride along the coast would take three or four days and then they would be in Gascony.

Lázaro barely contained his excitement. 'And Sir Thomas spoke to the Archbishop himself? To ask him for a blessing?'

'Not just a blessing but a private one. Sir Thomas honoured you.'

'My lord, if God has seen fit to let me live despite what I witnessed then I will serve Him and your Lord de Grailly for as long as I live. Will I see the *botafumeiro*?'

'If luck favours us. Sir Gilbert said it was a thing of wonder.'

They approached the cathedral gates and watched pilgrims being given new clothes as their own were burnt. 'Must we undress?' said Lázaro.

'No, we are not pilgrims who have travelled for hundreds of miles; we ride with the English King's Master of War. You bathed, didn't you, as I told you to?'

'I did, and I put on a clean shirt.'

'Then you are free from lice and disease and we will be welcome. You have your Queen's crucifix?'

Lázaro nodded; his smile faded as he tugged it free and kissed it.

Beyard laid a comforting hand on the boy's shoulder. 'She would be proud of you. Ask the Archbishop to bless that as well.'

Their escort took them to the Puerta de las Platerías, forcing aside street hawkers selling silver trinkets. 'Through here to the *antesacristía*,' he explained. 'The dean will greet you. Your horses will be here.' Beyard led the way from the plaza's entrance and then through the double-arched door beneath the carved figures representing heaven and hell. The boy stopped, his gaze fixed on the figures shown on the tympanum. A half-dressed woman with a skull in her hands sat on two lions. A moment of fear stabbed at him.

'Lázaro?' said Beyard.

The boy drew his attention away, uncertain why the woman's image had made his heart jump a beat. He stepped into the cathedral's cool interior. He heard the undulating voices of hundreds of people in the nave but he and Beyard, with the Gascons, were in the transept's side entrance some distance from the clamouring pilgrims. Beyard held Lázaro back as the great censer was about to be swung in front of them.

'Lázaro, look, boy.'

All four stood transfixed by the censer's ever-increasing speed. Ropes creaked as it gained momentum, spewing clouds of burning incense. Lázaro gaped as it soared high, then flinched as it swooped so low it seemed it would strike the congregation.

'Come, we mustn't be late,' said Beyard, and ushered the boy along to where they would meet the Archbishop.

Aicart and Loys were almost at the *antesacristía*'s door when they heard voices raised in anger and then cries of pain.

Beyard pulled Lázaro behind him as Aicart drew his sword and eased the half-open door. Loys stood to one side, sword already in hand. The door swung fully open but there was no one in sight. The room was too gloomy for those outside to see what was happening within. But then a woman's voice said clearly, 'It is done.'

Lázaro clutched Beyard's arm. Fear struck him dumb. He mouthed something. Beyard, caught between the sinister cries that had emanated from the chapel and the boy's terror, turned his attention to Lázaro.

'What?' he hissed, shaking the boy. Lázaro stared at the man who protected him.

He found his voice. 'The assassin. The assassin,' he repeated. 'I heard those words when they killed the Queen. I remember now. It's what the killer said. I remember. It is her voice.'

No sooner had Lázaro spoken than Velasquita came out of the room followed by Ranulph de Hayle, bloodied sword in hand, four of his men behind him. The routiers stopped in their tracks as they saw Beyard and the two armed Gascons. Lázaro was pointing at Velasquita. She glared, caught unawares.

'It's her, my lord. She killed my Queen.'

Velasquita, face to face with the witness to the murder, did not hesitate. She pointed at the boy. 'Kill him.'

Ranulph de Hayle attacked. Lázaro encumbered Beyard by clinging to him. The Gascon captain pushed Lázaro behind him and struck at de Hayle as Aicart and Loys fought the men who accompanied him. Beyard blocked and parried, drew his knife with his free hand and slashed de Hayle's arm, forcing the mercenary back as Beyard took the fight to him.

Thick smoke from the charcoal-burning censer smothered the transept as de Hayle backed away under Beyard's onslaught. The Gascon saw past him into the room where the Archbishop and another man sprawled in blood. There was no doubt they were dead. De Hayle was hard pressed by Beyard, whose years of fighting at Blackstone's side gave him a single-minded focus on inflicting extreme violence on an enemy. Loys, still weakened from wounds sustained at the bridge, went down under two of de Hayle's men's swords. Aicart killed one of them, but another stabbed and slashed at him, wounding him. Despite his wounds Aicart rammed his blade into his attacker's throat. The two remaining routiers hurled themselves at Aicart. Beyard saw the fight had turned in de Hayle's favour.

Lázaro screamed. Beyard half turned and saw Velasquita drag a knife across the boy's throat. Beyard roared with grief and anger at the smiling woman and the startled look of surprise on the boy's face. And then Beyard's heart lurched. In the moment's distraction de Hayle had rammed his sword into the half-turned Gascon's back. Beyard reeled, twisted and struck hard. Aicart couldn't hold the others back.

'Go! Get Sir Thomas! Tell him! Tell him, Aicart!'

The loyal soldier held off two men a moment longer before, with a final, agonizing glance at the man he had followed for so many years, he turned to the side door and ran back into the square as Beyard fell under the blades of de Hayle and his swordsmen.

Beyard and Lázaro lay sprawled, their blood mingling on the cathedral floor.

CHAPTER SEVENTY-FOUR

News of Archbishop Suero Gómez's murder and that of his dean spread faster than the pestilence. Blackstone, Killbere and John Jacob rode hard once Aicart reached the King's camp. Santiago's stricken commander had his troops push panicked travellers away from the narrow streets and ushered Blackstone into the cathedral, now cleared of pilgrims. The incense and smell of acrid charcoal failed to disguise the stench of gore. Their friend's bodies lay where they had fallen. Smeared blood showed where the slain Archbishop and dean's bodies had been removed.

'Witnesses say your man here surprised the killers,' said the guard commander. He pointed to the bloodied footprints that led from the *antesacristía* to where Beyard and Lázaro lay in their congealed blood. The Gascon soldier Loys had fallen nearer the room's open door. 'I have sent for the bishop, who is visiting one of the outlying churches, but while we wait for his return, our priests will prepare for Peralvarez and the Archbishop's funeral.'

'My men and the boy...' Blackstone faltered. Losing Beyard and the boy was tearing at him; he felt no shame at the tears that fell. He bent and reached for Lázaro's hand and eased away the written pass that had brought them to their deaths. Blackstone looked at Killbere and John Jacob, their grief shared as they stood by helplessly. Blackstone wiped an arm across his tear-streaked face. He needed to think.

'We will take the bodies of our men and this boy to the monastery and bury them side by side.'

The city's guard commander saw the depth of the men's loss. 'I will have them made ready for you. Sir Thomas, do you know who did this?'

Blackstone shook his head. He didn't want a manhunt to deny him his revenge. With a final look at his fallen friends and their savage death, he turned away. John Jacob went to follow. Killbere put a hand out to stop him. 'No, John, let him be.'

When their friends' bodies had been taken to the monastery, Blackstone, Killbere and John Jacob, weeping no longer, sat huddled in the soft rain as clouds dragged from the forested mountains by a freshening breeze shrouded the city. No one tried to pass these hard-looking men who blocked the narrow passage, the *rúa* led to the monastery's side door and whatever business they had for being there it was their own and would go unchallenged. They squatted on the steps of a tavern, closed because of the Archbishop's murder but obliged to open and surrender a bottle of brandy to the insistent men who hammered on its doors.

'The King would not order the Archbishop's death,' said John Jacob. 'It would be madness. Álvaraz is loyal but he would not permit this to happen.'

'Ranulph de Hayle has followed us across Spain and the bitch has been the one paying him,' said Killbere.

'I failed to convince the Archbishop to give the King his blessing, so Don Pedro sent her. She had de Hayle waiting,' said Blackstone, 'and Beyard and Loys died trying to defend Lázaro. I'll cut the King's throat myself.'

Killbere drew breath before answering. Blackstone had retreated to a depth of anger he had not witnessed since an assassin had murdered his friend's wife and child. The cold manner in which he spoke hid the gathering storm within. And Killbere knew Blackstone was more than willing to kill a king no matter what the consequences. Years before, the French King John had come within a few determined strides from Blackstone and Wolf Sword's killing blow.

'Do that and we will have failed the Prince and dishonoured the men who died attempting to get him to Aquitaine,' Killbere said.

Blackstone drained the dregs and tossed the bottle into the gutter. 'We will bury and pray for our dead and I will have the truth from the bitch.'

The light was fading when they returned to the camp.

'Where is Don Pedro?' Blackstone asked the Spanish captain.

'At prayer,' said Álvaraz with undisguised contempt.

Killbere cursed. 'This bastard seeks redemption while our friend and the boy lie slain and cold in a grave.'

'The King was in a quiet mood,' said Álvaraz. 'I was pleased to have him gone. I cannot share your pain, Sir Thomas, but I have lost men close to me and I offer my prayers for your friends.'

Blackstone saw the High Steward watching from the King's quarters. He raised his voice. 'And did you see or hear anything of who might have committed these murders?'

The High Steward answered by lowering his eyes.

'Neither sees nor hears,' said Álvaraz. 'No royal steward ever would.'

Blackstone dismounted, his men gathering as he tied off the bastard horse. Aicart was with them, limping. The men were arguing how best to find the killers, emotions running high.

'Quiet, damn you,' Meulon bellowed. 'Sir Thomas is the only one to speak.'

Blackstone faced his chastised men. 'Beyard, Lázaro and Loys have been buried in the monastery in Santiago. They had gone for a blessing and found death instead. I have paid the monks to pray for them, and our grief and tears for them must now be cast aside.' He reached out to Killbere, who handed him a belted sheathed sword. 'Aicart, you served Beyard before either of you joined us. It is only right that you bear his sword now and remember the fortitude and courage he showed when it was in his hand.'

Aicart's eyes stung with tears. Renfred placed a hand on his arm and helped him step forward.

'I need no sword to remember him, Sir Thomas. It was you who put strength in his arm when he fought. These men know that as well as I do, but I thank you for the honour and I will wear it with pride.'

Blackstone addressed them. 'No man here is greater or lesser than the man next to him. We have shown that time and again. And now we are a day's ride from Corunna where we will deliver King Pedro of Castile and León to the ship that lies waiting to take him and his family to our Prince. We are honour bound to do this.'

'And when we get this King on his ship, what then?' said Will Longdon.

'Then we turn our backs on this place and we go home.' He looked from man to man, saw their uncertainty, anger and despair.

'And those who killed our friends and Lázaro?' said Jack Halfpenny.

'I will find them,' Blackstone said. 'I swear it. No matter how long it takes.'

Blackstone gave them time for their spirits to lift. They were battle-weary, having fought the length of France and then Spain. 'Make ready. Draw supplies. One day more, lads, only one more day and our duty is done.'

The men drifted away and Blackstone walked to where Álvaraz and his meagre escort of twenty men waited. 'Are your men ready to move?'

'Yes, Sir Thomas.'

'Be prepared to abandon your horses at Corunna. There won't be enough room on the ship.'

'When we reach the coast, I will secure the King's wellbeing and those with him, and then I abandon him. We will no longer serve him – and besides, I have no wish to live in Aquitaine and be told what to do by a King in exile and an English Prince who lavishes hospitality on him. I will find service for me and my men with an honourable lord.'

'Then I offer my thanks for standing at our side. Tell the High Steward to have the servants ready to move at first light.'

Blackstone went into the King's quarters where two servants stood patiently waiting against the far wall. A lantern hung on a hook and chain from the ceiling.

'Get out.' Blackstone's calm command made them scurry out of the back door. Blackstone heard a voice raised and then the High Steward entered, pushing the fearful servants back into the room. He recoiled when he saw the huge man standing in the room without permission, and quickly backed away when the King came in.

Don Pedro was unperturbed by Blackstone's presence. Blackstone made no move, did not bow, made no sign of honouring the rightful King of Spain.

'I was at prayer,' said Don Pedro, indicating he wanted wine. The steward poured and once more retreated as far back as he could.

'Get out,' said Blackstone again.

The frightened steward nearly tripped over himself in his attempt to escape. A look of alarm creased the King's face.

'Do not call for Álvaraz; he won't hear you,' said Blackstone.

Don Pedro was a seasoned hunter. He knew that when a predator fixed its attention on its prey, the way Blackstone looked at him, then it was as good as dead. 'I was offering prayers for the souls of your friend and the boy,' he said, keeping the edge of panic from his voice.

'You were praying for your miserable soul. Where is she?'

'You insult me? You have already dared to lay violent hands on a king.' His challenging tone was only momentarily that of a ruler; beneath his words was the fear of a man alone facing imminent violence.

'When you reach my warrior Prince you can whimper your misfortune to him and relate my disgust at sacrificing the best of men for you. Where is she?' Blackstone said again.

Don Pedro knew the Master of War might forsake his duty to his Prince and kill him if he remained loyal to Velasquita. 'I do not know. I do not control her actions. She fled. I don't know where,' he lied. 'I swear it.'

'You ordered the Archbishop's death, and the bitch used the Englishman Ranulph de Hayle to do the killing.'

'I have no association with him. They cannot hold me responsible.' Don Pedro suddenly realized the one person who could implicate him in the murders was already far away. He smirked. 'You have no proof.'

Blackstone leaned on the table. Don Pedro was tall, he had fought and killed at close quarters, but the size of the man who towered over him squeezed the breath from him.

'You are not my King. You are not worthy of being honoured as one. I should scrape you off my boot and let your bastard half-brother deal with your stench, but I promised my Prince to rescue you. You will be ready to ride for the coast at first light or by God I will deliver him your carcass.'

He turned for the door. 'Get back on your knees and pray I don't change my mind.'

CHAPTER SEVENTY-FIVE

Blackstone slept badly. The cold penetrating his bones beneath his blanket was more than the night's chill. He turned on his side, gazing into the fire's embers, seeing distorted images of death in their shifting colours. The figures of Beyard and Lázaro, lying together as if they were father and son, stung him. A searing reminder of his own wife and daughter slain by an assassin years before. The pain of the memory made him resolve to seek a closer relationship with his son and settle any differences between them. Thoughts of how they would reconcile calmed him and he drifted into a fitful sleep.

The biting morning air settled a fine down of mist on beards and cloaks. The men saddled their horses and made preparations for the final day's journey to the coast. The men's sullenness at the murder of their friends would cause others grief if for any reason Blackstone's men were attacked on this last leg of their journey.

In the distance a raptor screeched below the swirling mist and then flew out of sight.

Blackstone felt that same stab of uncertainty. 'The King had no falcons or hawks with him,' he said.

Álvaraz looked skyward. 'No. It'll be a peasant laying bird or squirrel traps scaring it from its high branches. I'll see to my men.'

Blackstone watched the mist's veil rising from the trees down the valley. The breeze veered, the clouds forced to abandon their tenacious hold on the treetops.

The apparition of a man emerged from the ghostly forest, a branch fashioned into a staff giving him support along the stone-laden track. He was wet and looked as though he had walked far. He was several hundred yards away. He stumbled, perhaps weak from hunger, but recovered and continued to make his way towards the camp.

'Jack?' Blackstone called. Halfpenny looked to where he pointed. 'An old man. A pilgrim. Looks as though he's lost. Going the wrong way if he's looking for Santiago. He's not on any pilgrim's route. Go and help him.' He whistled to draw Will Longdon's attention. 'Have one of your lads stoke a fire and ready hot food.'

By the time the men had tightened saddle girths and readied themselves to leave, daylight was creeping wider across the mountains. The old man sat by the comfort of a fire. He had said nothing but grunted hungrily as he slurped the bowl of pottage. He wiped a sleeve across the snot running from his nose. His home-sewn clothes were thick with moisture from the forest and his gnarled hands told them he was a man who knew hard labour. Blackstone allowed the man to finish the hot food ladled from the blackened cooking pot. Will Longdon, Halfpenny and the other captains watched him, asking questions: where he had come from? Why he was lost? Where he was going? He remained silent until the last mouthful, ran a palm across his beard and stared at the gathered men.

'I am grateful for your hospitality even though I am not on the Camino. My name is Gontrán.'

'Were you trying to trap food in the forest?' said Blackstone. 'You look hungry enough to eat the bark off a tree.'

'Hunt? No. I am a fisherman. Do I look like a hunter?' he said with a hint of self-mockery at his wiry body and tattered clothes.

'We saw the hawk rise up,' said Blackstone. 'Thought you might have tried to seize its breakfast. Raw rabbit or squirrel can keep a man going.'

Gontrán seemed an amiable fellow and gratefully accepted Meulon's wine flask. He swallowed and sighed with pleasure. He waved a hand in front of his face as if brushing away a fly. 'No, no, forests and wild animals: these are things a man must endure when he seeks redemption and pilgrimage, but I am no hunter, nor scavenger of carrion.'

'But you're a long way from the sea and the wrong direction from Santiago,' Renfred said.

Gontrán pointed vaguely away. 'I journey from the coast every year. You see those scallop shells they give to pilgrims? Eh? You know about them? I'm one of the fishermen who take them to the city every year.'

'Then you're from Corunna?' said Will Longdon.

Gontrán shook his head, extended his hand for the flask again and nodded his thanks when Meulon obliged. 'Northeast. Rugged country!' he emphasized. 'Corunna is too busy. Too many ships. My people know the meaning of a day's work.'

Blackstone crouched by the fire so he was level with the old man. 'If you came from that direction then you would have been on a direct route to Santiago and if you know the route well enough, you would not have missed the city.'

'You think I don't know that? I'm old but I'm not an idiot.' He glared defiantly at the men around him as if it were they whose minds were as flimsy as the forest mist.

Blackstone's instincts sensed there was more but the old man was reluctant to tell them.

Gontrán shrugged. 'I didn't know whether I was being brought into danger. There are villains who rob pilgrims.'

'And why do you say you were brought here?' Blackstone said. 'Who brought you?'

The men looked past him towards the forest but there was no sign of anyone else.

Gontrán hesitated, glancing around at the hard-faced men who stared at him. 'If you mock me, then I will leave with thanks for the warmth of the fire and food and for not causing me harm.'

'We will not mock you,' Blackstone assured him gently. 'What was it that brought you here?' he insisted.

'What? That hawk,' Gontrán said cautiously. 'It frightened me, I don't mind telling you. We are superstitious people in these parts.'

Blackstone saw the same look cross the faces of the gathered men. 'We have seen them circle high above us before battle. They can bring good fortune or bad, but that is every man's superstition,' he said. 'Now tell us why your courage brought you here.'

Gontrán nodded, encouraged by the compliment. 'I reached the outskirts of the city and heard the news that assassins had slain the Archbishop and others. Murdered them in cold blood. I turned away from that sacred place because I could not bear the thought of such violence being committed in a place of love and forgiveness. I was planning to return home but then I remembered seeing riders' – he shrugged – 'a few men, no more, cloaked and riding hard towards where I had journeyed from. Towards where I live. It is not a place people go to with any ease. Once through the valley and forests there is no place for horses. The cliffs are too steep; you have to go on foot. But to where, I asked myself? There are coves along the coast from my village where men smuggle. So I was frightened of returning in case these were the people who did the killing and were making their escape.' Gontrán seemed lost in a reverie as he put the pieces of his journey together. 'I prayed at a roadside shrine for the souls of the dead and begged to be kept safe and I swear' – he looked again at the attentive men – 'I swear when I opened my eyes the hawk was sitting on top of the shrine and glared at me. Have you seen a hawk's stare? It's as if it's ripping into your heart.'

Blackstone kept his eyes on the fisherman. He saw others cross themselves. He glanced at Killbere, whose concerned look told him he felt the same apprehension as himself.

Gontrán's voice lowered, reflecting his sense of awe at what he had seen. 'It flew low along the open path and then soared high. As if waiting for me. I turned my back on the way home, followed the path and into the forest. I kept hoping it would fly off, that my grief at the murders had twisted my mind. But every time I faltered, the hawk appeared.' He looked up at the silent men. 'And led me here, but I do not know why.'

CHAPTER SEVENTY-SIX

Blackstone thanked Gontrán, put coins in his calloused palm and told him to go into Santiago as he had intended, because it would be the prayers of the pilgrims who would restore the spiritual faith of the city.

Blackstone checked the bastard horse's girth, ever wary of it swinging its head and snapping with those yellowed teeth.

'No, Thomas, this is madness. You cannot go alone,' said Killbere.

Blackstone busied himself. 'The men are ready, Álvaraz knows the way, it is your job to protect Don Pedro and get him on that ship and then wait for me.'

'God's tears. Not one man will let you ride after the bastard de Hayle and the devil's whore alone. Not one of us!' Killbere's voice rose in a mixture of desperation and anger.

'There is no time to lose, Gilbert. I'll travel fast and I'll catch them up.'

'We will not do as you ask. Who knows how many the bitch has with her?'

'De Hayle had two left alive in the cathedral. I doubt he has more with him. We hurt him badly along the way. Most of those we didn't kill will have deserted him. He's done no raiding here; he has no money to pay more men. It is not a request, Gilbert,' said Blackstone, securing his shield to the saddle. 'You must command the men. Do not defy me, I beg you. Take this wretched King to his ship and send him to the

Prince.' He laid a hand on his friend's shoulder. 'Our honour demands it.'

Killbere's despair was plain to see. 'I cannot,' he pleaded.

'There are only a handful of men with her. They will be on foot once they reach the cliffs, and they are not us, Gilbert. We climb better than mountain goats and every one of them will lag behind the other. I'll kill them one by one.'

'One mistake, one fall – anything could happen and you'd lie dead on a mountainside. We can take this turd King to his ship and turn back and hunt them down.'

'You heard what the old man said. Why do you think they're avoiding the ports? They're going to a deserted part of the coast because they have a boat waiting in one of the coves. There is no time for us to hunt them. One man can track them. And that is my decision.'

Meulon, Renfred, Will Longdon and Jack Halfpenny followed John Jacob and William Ashford towards them.

'Sir Thomas,' said Meulon stepping forward, 'we have never disobeyed you but today we stand as one man and beg you to let us ride with you.'

Killbere threw his arm out. 'You see, Thomas, not one man will abandon you to this madness.'

Blackstone faced them. 'Our blazon says we are defiant unto death. Those words on our shields are there to confront our enemies, not to tear apart everything we have done together, the sacrifices we have made, or to dishonour our friends who died at our side. It was the Prince who gave us our blazon, who acknowledged our brotherhood. We swore an oath and I depend on every man here and those you command to honour it. I will take every one of you in my heart so I will not be alone, but I must give chase to the killers and deliver justice. Follow my orders and finish what our Prince asked of us.'

Blackstone's gentle persuasion gave his captains no means of reply.

'Wait for me,' he said, 'and then together we ride home.'

The captains returned to their men. Killbere rode at their head. Álvaraz's men cosseted the King, riding as close escort. By the end of the day they would be at the coast and their duty fulfilled.

'I am honoured to have been at your side,' said Álvaraz.

'And I yours,' said Blackstone.

'The map the old man drew for you is enough?'

'Even a single horseman leaves signs that a blind man could find. They won't expect anyone to be in pursuit.'

The two men clasped hands. 'I will pray God keeps you safe so you may inflict His punishment on them and cast them into hell,' Álvaraz said and wheeled his horse. The order to ride on was called and the column eased onto the road to Corunna.

Blackstone stared at Don Pedro as he rode past but the King sat upright, looking neither left nor right. Behind him the High Steward glanced at Blackstone and made the sign of the cross. A blessing or a curse? No one had treated his lord and master with such violence or contempt as the Englishman. Perhaps, Blackstone thought, the old patrician saw him as the devil's disciple.

John Jacob drew his horse next to Blackstone. 'I am your squire. I will ride with you as I always have. It is my obligation to accompany you. If I do not, then I am shamed.'

Blackstone smiled. 'Who could ever shame a man like you, John? I owe you so much. When you got Christiana and my children to safety all those years ago, that can never be repaid.'

'Sir Thomas, the past binds us all, but I have my duty. Shall we go?'

'No, my friend, not today. I have a greater duty for you. My son Henry has always looked to you with deep regard and affection. You were his guardian at a time I could not be his father. You taught him how to serve as a page and the discipline that entailed. If I do not return I ask you to take up that role again. You cannot be with me today in case he needs you tomorrow.'

CHAPTER SEVENTY-SEVEN

The old fisherman's description was correct. The road became a track and then petered out. The bastard horse had pulled up short a hundred yards from the blind bend, ears forward, muscles rippling, warning of other horses nearby. Blackstone eased him forward and saw two abandoned horses grazing. Riding closer, he looked along the base of the cliffs and the area between rock and forest. Another horse stood abandoned in the treeline, with loose reins and, like the others, still saddled. A fourth nudged it for companionship. Blackstone looked at the trampled grass and saw no more tracks.

He dismounted, slung his shield across his back and drank from his wineskin. He secured the small food sack on the saddle for his return and eased the bastard horse out of sight into a small glade in the trees. He hobbled it with enough rope to allow it to graze but not to wander and then searched for a route up the rock surface, slick with running water. Picking out an animal track that weaved its way to the summit, he bent his back into the hillside, which looked to be a thousand feet high or more. Despite the cold air, he was streaked with sweat when he reached the summit. His breathing was laboured. It felt unnatural. How many times before had he paced himself and the men on steeper hills than these?

He had kept watch on the sky, searching for the hawk that had brought Gontrán to their camp. If a man's mind could grasp that forces of nature existed other than those he could understand, then perhaps that was why men prayed.

He raised the Silver Wheel Goddess to his lips. An archer's token of protection from a pagan goddess was as good a reason to believe in such things as any other.

There was no sign of the hawk.

The undulating ground was broken with rock formations and tumbling water in a fast-flowing stream that began high up in the mountains and gushed across moss-laden boulders. The ice-cold water penetrated his boots, but he stumbled across the stream bed, instinct and good luck guiding him across the treacherous, ankle-snapping rocks beneath the surface. He clambered onto the far bank. The dense hillside forests swallowed the light. Blackstone felt his strength slipping away. He looked at his left hand and saw a slight tremor, a sign of weakness creeping throughout his body. How high had he climbed? He drank from the wineskin again, hoping the rough-tasting wine would warm and invigorate him. Blackstone pressed his hand against Wolf Sword's hilt and steadied himself against a boulder. His eyes followed the contour of the land, which bottomed out into a broad plateau, an uneven land of brutal mystery where waterfalls tumbled from increasing heights, their streams disappearing into the forest. The seething water swallowed any sound except the high-pitched keening of a hawk. Its sudden appearance made him cautious. Was it guide or bait? He raised his eyes to follow its passage on the thermal and felt dizziness claim him. He lifted Arianrhod to his lips again and asked the Celtic goddess to guide him to where Ranulph de Hayle and the witch had made their escape.

His years of fighting and trust in his instincts strengthened him. He concentrated on the wind rustling across the treetops, the same whispers that brought the hawk's call. Turning his head, he closed his eyes and let his mind's eye travel along the swirling breeze. Splashing water faded, the hawk's cry diminished. He stood motionless, waiting for the forest to yield its secrets. Like a man being swept out to sea on a rip tide, he surrendered to wind and water that bore him on their journey until he heard a sound that did not belong to nature. The slightest almost imperceptible resonance as metal clanged against rock. He opened his eyes. He was facing downstream. De Hayle was using the river to guide him to freedom. The routier had no skill at living in the forest, did not trust the ageless instincts of animals using a track to find their way. All that Blackstone understood. He ran into the trees. To follow de Hayle along the stream would expose him against the skyline. De Hayle would have left a crossbowman in ambush and the rocky terrain meant Blackstone would be unlikely to see him.

He pushed hard through the bracken, going deeper into the trees, instinct guiding him towards the bend in the river where he could cut off his quarry. The forest's gloom yielded to sunlight dancing this way and that as the treetops swayed, letting through the rays. His eyes went from tree to tree, penetrating ever deeper into the forest, searching for any sign of where the forest ended and the open ground began. He needed to be close to de Hayle and the temptress so he could kill them quickly. His lungs burned, but his mind forced him on. Every fifty paces he stopped, leaned against a tree and drew deep breaths, sucking air into failing lungs. He willed himself to beat back whatever the unknown weakness was that suddenly ailed him. To fight it and use his anger at the killings to put strength into his sword arm.

The forest's half-light caught the speckled camouflage of a deer's white tail as it ran from view. Had it been his presence that alerted it or something else? Bears would be hunting and if he stumbled on one grubbing in the high undergrowth, he would have little chance of surviving a sudden attack. He rested again. Sweat stung his eyes. Nausea rose up. His throat stung from its acid.

In that moment he saw the haunted face of the High Steward making the sign of the cross. And he knew the man had poisoned him. He hurled the wineskin away, forced his fingers down his throat and vomited. The more of the poison he could spew out the more chance he had of keeping death at bay.

As he raised his head a shadow swept through the trees. A shadow so fast he barely had time to snap his head back. The raptor caught his shoulder – was it a talon that slashed his neck, or had he stumbled back onto a ragged branch? The strike was as swift as a bodkin-tipped arrow's flight. The hawk's screech chilled him. It had already hurtled through the trees out of sight. Was it the witch? Had she been circling above in the form of a hawk? Watching his every movement? Seeing where he plunged into the forest to gain the advantage? Was her witchcraft so powerful that she took on other forms? The supernatural was as real as any man's belief in God. What proof was there that God existed? What proof was needed that devils and imps roamed the earth and witches took whatever form they needed to snare their victims? Fear of the unknown was more dangerous than facing men determined to kill you. Blackstone spat the sour phlegm from his throat. It was only fear. And fear could be despised and banished from a man's mind and heart. He pressed on with added determination. If he was to die alone in this harsh wilderness, he would strike down evil. Then he would fall into whomever's embrace awaited. God or the devil.

A cool trickle of blood from the tear on his neck settled beneath his collar. The hawk's strike had turned him away from his original route. He was disoriented. He pressed on and then faltered. A shape took form ahead in the forest. It was a broken-down hut, its caved-in roof smothered with moss and leaf mould. Some kind of shelter for wild men of the woods perhaps? Hermits or fugitives? Whoever had lived here was long gone.

He moved closer. The green growth of the forest floor had crept over any structure, including a circular mound in his path. He stepped forward and the ground gave way beneath his weight. He fell waist deep, his back slamming against the hard side of the pit, his shield ripped free. His boots crunched on something brittle. He pulled aside the weeds and growth. It was the remains of a charcoal pit. Layers of leaves would have been packed over a fire and then covered with soil until villagers reduced the burning timber to charcoal.

Blackstone rummaged beneath his feet and found chunks of blackened, crisp charcoal. Perhaps the hawk was not the witch but a guardian angel who had made him turn towards the abandoned charcoal burners' site. He bit into the charcoal, its crust clinging to the roof of his mouth. He swallowed and gagged, but, forcing spittle into his mouth, he ate more. The charcoal would help absorb the poison in his gut. He pushed a handful to sustain him beneath his jerkin and, clambering free, went back to the animal track that led towards the edge of the forest. He had gone thirty paces before realizing he had left his shield in the pit. Dizziness claimed him. He knelt, shook his head, felt his heart pounding.

The cloud-filtered sun had moved behind his right shoulder so he knew he had not travelled far before he smelled the chill of cold water and moss on the wind. The whooshing rhythm of water over rocks became more pronounced. He edged forward. The broken ground, pockmarked with boulders and rocks, embraced the stream. Thirst gripped him and he was a stride away from stumbling from the forest and gulping the clear mountain water, when the raptor's faint cry made him turn instinctively towards it. Had Arianrhod summoned her own guardian spirit to protect him? Ahead he saw the crossbowman huddled behind boulders, back to Blackstone, watching the worn ground next to the stream. The track would have led Blackstone directly into view barely thirty yards away as he crested the skyline.

There was no one else in sight. It was too risky creeping towards the unsuspecting bowman. He strode towards him, archer's knife in hand, the rushing water covering any footfall. The tall trees shifted in the wind, and as the low sun struck his back, his shadow loomed ahead of him. The man turned. Stiff from his cramped position, he moved slowly, but was quick enough to level the crossbow and loose a snap shot. The quarrel skimmed Blackstone's side, but his jerkin and mail offered enough protection for its wayward trajectory to glance off him. The bowman was on his feet, knife in hand, unafraid, lunging. A veteran of war, a man used to closing with the enemy. Except that the enemy had never been this scar-faced Englishman. Blackstone parried the right-handed strike and turned his fist so that the knife's pommel struck the bowman beneath his chin. His head snapped back and, legs buckling, he fell. Blackstone's weakened grip was still enough to keep the archer under his knife. The man's eyes blinked.

'De Hayle and the woman. Where are they?'

The bowman shook his head. Blood seeped between his teeth.

'Why would you be loyal to those who abandon you?' said Blackstone.

'I'm sworn to him. Death comes to us all,' spat the routier. An Englishman.

'Tell me and I won't kill you. You have my word.'

'A knight?' spluttered the pinned man.

'Thomas Blackstone.'

The bowman blinked, realizing who had bested him. He nodded. 'Towards the cliff. There's a path down. A boat's waiting.'

'How many more men?'

De Hayle's man shook his head. 'None. Him and the woman. Alone. We lost a man on the cliff face back there.'

Blackstone punched him unconscious and turned him over, slashing his knife across one leg. Blackstone had spared him. Hamstrung, he could not give chase or ever fight in a war again but, if he made it down the mountain, he would find a living begging somewhere with his one good leg and a crutch.

Blackstone raised his face to the wind. There was more than the damp smell of moss and water on the air. The wind brought the unmistakable tang of the sea.

And justice.

CHAPTER SEVENTY-EIGHT

Blackstone battled the paralysing waves threatening to engulf him. He knelt by the stream, forced himself to chew and swallow more charcoal and then plunged his head beneath the icy water, trying to wash the numbness from his mind. He cupped water and drank deeply. His mind taunted him: a ghost within warning he would soon die. That he was too weak to fight and win. But he would not let go, not now. His eye caught movement on the edge of the forest. His hunter's instinct kept him unmoving. The witch and de Hayle. The two killers he tracked were moving along the edge of the forest on the plateau between forest and clifftop. His archer's eye put them at twenty yards short of four hundred. The woman led the way towards the cliff and what must be a path down to the shore. Close to where the pair walked, the stream broadened as another tributary joined it in a display of power. White water smashed against boulders, calmed and then gathered pace and strength as it raced towards the cliff edge and fell as a waterfall to the beach far below.

Unyielding determination forced him to his feet. He banished the creeping fatigue and lengthened his stride. The uneven ground made it hard going; his ankle went from under him. He steadied himself, shaking away the sweat stinging his eyes. When he had covered half the distance, he stopped to gather his breath and drink more from the stream, lifting his heavy head again towards his goal. De Hayle and Velasquita had still not turned. They appeared to be in no hurry, confident perhaps that they would not be pursued by a man stricken with poison and who, if he still lived, was unlikely to get past a crossbowman.

Blackstone saw the sea beyond the cliff's edge. The vast expanse of horizon made him light-headed. He was in no condition to fight. Defeat settled over him like a coastal fog, seeping deep inside him. Like a drunk, he argued aloud with himself. Cursing his exhaustion. Berating his lack of defiance. Blackstone squeezed his eyes tight. He fled into the past, a fugitive from his own weakness. He saw the horde at Crécy; heard the cries of terror as man and horse fought and died; remembered how as a sixteen-year-old archer he had smashed and clawed his way through the tide of killing to try to save his brother. Voices in his memory from Poitiers cried out of the driving urge to kill the French King. The images fought to gain the upper hand. His mind swirled. He burst into the room at Meaux and saw his slaughtered wife and child. Blackstone stood still, blood and recollection surging through him. He raised his face to the sky and bellowed his rage.

He was downwind from those he pursued but de Hayle turned and saw him. The woman snarled, perhaps in surprise that Blackstone was still alive. She said something, her words snatched away by the wind. De Hayle unsheathed his sword and waited, a broad grin on his face that told the approaching Blackstone the routier was ready to kill his weakened opponent and would do it quickly.

Blackstone could not run. His legs refused to go any faster but he lengthened his stride to close with the murderous de Hayle, his determined approach showing he wanted nothing more than to gut the man from crotch to chin. Blackstone's foot caught a tuft of heavy grass. His leg almost gave way, but he recovered quickly. He heard de Hayle laugh.

'Come on, Blackstone, you're like a drunk who's spent a night in a whorehouse,' he taunted. 'I'll kill you quickly and then we can be on our way. I have a purse full of gold to spend.'

Blackstone concentrated on the man's face. It was a target to carry him forward over the tussocks. When he was twenty yards from the mercenary, he drew Wolf Sword. He looked at the woman, who stood unmoving thirty paces beyond de Hayle.

'You cannot live, Thomas,' she called. 'The poison is already in you. I'm surprised you made it this far. The more you labour the quicker it works. I should have given you a stronger dose. There is no need for you to suffer the humiliation of defeat or feel the pain of his blade. Sit by the stream and let the poison take you gently.'

Blackstone gripped Wolf Sword, wrapping his free hand over his fist, squeezing every bit of strength into both hands. He staggered, shaking his head to clear his blurred vision as he looked from one to the other.

De Hayle sneered. 'Over here, Blackstone. No good looking at her.' He opened his palm and waggled his fingers. 'Your Jew had fingers like a woman. I gave her his rings.' He took a couple of paces forward, weaving deliberately to distract Blackstone. 'I tried to give her the boy. Took his head to her. I thought that would have been the end of it.' He spat phlegm aside. 'Now it is.'

Blackstone thought of the gentle Halif ben Josef and the young guide Andrés. He squared his shoulders and called to Velasquita. 'When I've killed Ranulph de Hayle for the atrocities he committed, I will see you meet your unholy benefactor. I'll send you back to Satan.'

'For Christ's sake!' said de Hayle. 'Enough!' He strode forward, surefooted, sword in the high guard. Blackstone saw a bloodied rag tied around his left forearm. No doubt Beyard had caused his killer to bleed. If Blackstone did not have the strength to parry the blow, de Hayle would cleave him from neck to breastbone. De Hayle was a big man with a strength born from a lifetime of fighting. Fatigue would not come quickly to him.

Blackstone found firm ground and let him come. De Hayle roared and swept down his blade. Blackstone half turned, blocked it and felt the strike reverberate through the hardened steel into his weakened muscles. De Hayle was fast; with a quick change of stance, he put his weight on his left foot and, spinning on his ankle, he was already sweeping his sword low and fast towards Blackstone's legs. Blackstone could not parry the strike and blocked it by ramming Wolf Sword in the dirt; he clamped both hands on the pommel and felt the strike clang into his blade. Now de Hayle was off balance, the shuddering halt of his blade sending shock waves into his hands. Blackstone pulled Wolf Sword free but did not try to use its honed cutting edge. De Hayle was still half bent from his low strike. Blackstone took a step sideways and slammed the pommel into his face. Bone cracked. Blood spurted. It rocked De Hayle back on his heels. He spat blood but ignored the pain from his broken nose. He recovered his balance, one foot set well back against the other, sword sweeping through the air towards Blackstone's unguarded head. Blackstone ducked. The blade whispered through his hair: a finger's breadth lower and his skull would have split in two. The exertion had made him dizzy. He stumbled, legs failing.

De Hayle bore down on him with savage, unrelenting blows. It was all Blackstone could do to block them. He gripped the end of Wolf Sword's blade with his free hand and blocked the assault. The man's strength forced him back. Blackstone could barely stand now. He blinked. Sweat stung his eyes, blurring the relentless figure of de Hayle. His mind went blank. His ears rang from the clashing steel. He slipped and fell backwards. It took de Hayle by surprise but he rammed his blade towards Blackstone's face. Blackstone twisted, the blade's edge so close it nicked his cheek. The forward thrust forced de Hayle off balance again. He dropped forward, knees ramming Blackstone's chest. Pain shot through Blackstone but he kept Wolf Sword's blade across his chest.

'I'll kill you with my bare hands,' de Hayle spat, grabbing Blackstone's throat.

Blackstone bucked but could not throw the man clear. He choked. The stench of the man's fetid breath was nauseatingly close. Blackstone squirmed, found freedom with his right arm and shoulder, forced a half-roll and rammed Wolf Sword's cross piece into de Hayle's left eye. He screamed, released his hand and rolled clear. Blackstone clawed to his knees, sucked air into his belly and let de Hayle stumble a few paces away to retrieve his sword. Blackstone was desperate for respite. The poison was now racing through his body. De Hayle found his sword and wiped blood from his blinded eye.

Blackstone staggered uncertainly to his feet. He heard someone call his name. He looked left and right but there was no one. He was hallucinating. *Thomas! Come on, you lazy-arsed bastard! Be done with him! We have a battle to attend.* Blackstone turned and saw Killbere astride his horse not a hundred yards from where he fought. Blackstone's captains were with him in front of their men. John Jacob, Beyard, Meulon, Renfred, Jack Halfpenny and Will Longdon. *Shall I put a shaft of English ash through him, Sir Thomas?* called the archer.

Blackstone's puzzlement got the better of him. He shook his head. 'No. I can take him,' he muttered, but his grip barely held Wolf Sword. The strength had gone from his arm and hand.

'Blackstone!' De Hayle's sharp retort made him turn to the routier. 'Your mind has gone. Your strength with it. Throw down your sword and I'll finish it.'

Blackstone looked again to where the host of his men waited. He saw the army behind his captains. It was every man who had followed him into battle and fought at his side. Banners fluttered. Drums beat out their rhythm and trumpets blared. Killbere raised himself in the saddle. *Never yield! Rise up and carve a path to glory, Thomas. We've a fight on our hands. Rise up!* The men's roar thundered so loudly Blackstone took a step back. *RISE UP AND FIGHT!* came the bellowing chorus.

Blackstone felt blood-lust surge through his body. He clenched Wolf Sword, raised it and faced his men. The wind swept them and their battle cry away. He laughed. The poison's delusion had given him the means to win. He charged de Hayle, who was taken aback by his ferocity and suddenly forced on the defensive. Blackstone rained blows so hard that the routier took a dozen strikes on his weakening blade before regaining his strength. He fought back. Blackstone's head swirled. By luck the strike from de Hayle caught the side of Blackstone's head with the flat of his blade. It rattled Blackstone's teeth. He went down, rolled clear from the follow-up strike, snatched a handful of grass and hurled its muddy clod into de Hayle's good eye. It blinded the mercenary. He threw up his free hand to wipe the mud and grit away. Blackstone lunged from the ground with his last measure of strength and rammed Wolf Sword below de Hayle's breastbone. The force of the strike carried the blade through his chest and out the back of his neck. De Hayle dropped with the hardened steel embedded in bone and muscle.

Blackstone staggered. The killing had drained him. He slumped, then crawled towards the stream, desperate for its ice-cold shock. He was so weakened he could not cup his hands for water. Easing his chest over the shallow bank he sucked water like an animal. The current caught his shoulder and pulled him into the stream. He rolled, desperately keeping his head above water. His feet struck low rocks in the narrow stream bed and the force of water nudged him against the low sandy bank, his head resting on a smooth boulder. A place to slumber. A time to die.

He watched her approach. Velasquita looked down at him. She tossed aside her cloak, tugged at her dress and waded into the stream. He saw her draw a slim-bladed knife from her belt. He tried to move but could not. His fingers attempted to reach his archer's knife. He wedged his left shoulder slightly higher against the bank. Grunting with effort, he forced his left arm free but could raise it no higher to defend himself or deflect the knife blow he knew was coming. Her prophecy was true. His death was not a vision of the past when he lay in the river beneath Bergerac. And this time there was no Teutonic Knight to step out of the shadows and save him.

She bent at the waist to look at him. 'Thomas, no one has ever survived my poison before. Your strength brought you this far. You are dying now. Your exertions have helped me kill you. You die by your own efforts.'

The small tear-shaped pendant that swung free as she bent over him held his gaze, its enamelled green and gold polished stones catching the sun's dying rays. She paused as if in regret. 'I will embrace you and cut the vein in your neck and then you will drown and the prophecy is fulfilled. My blade will make sure you can no longer fight what tries so hard to kill you.' She smiled. 'Even legends die, Thomas.'

She bent lower, her arm reaching out with the blade. He saw the rings on her fingers. Anger lent strength to his arm but it was not enough to strike her. The hawk spiralled high above, its keening screech beckoning his soul, warning of imminent death. Velasquita looked up. The hawk distracted her as he forced his free hand to snatch at the hem of her dress. A surge of water gushed beneath his left leg, lifting the archer's knife within reach. She stumbled forward onto the blade, which slashed into her side. She fell across him, hands clutching the gash. Blood spiralling away in the eddies. She lay across his chest and right shoulder. Her face was so close he could have kissed her.

'I... did not see this,' she said, her face creased in pain. 'So I know I... will not die here,' she whispered and began forcing herself free of his feeble grip and the weight of water.

The pummelling undercurrent swept away the knife; using the stream's power to lift his shoulder, he rolled, finding hidden strength in his arm and hand. The bitterly cold water put iron into his fist. Clutching her throat, he forced her head beneath the clear water, saw her gasping, his hand tightening. Squeezing the life from her. Her eyes widened in panic. She fought him, but the thought of her victims gave him strength to hold her fast. She choked until she lay still. Lips parted in a macabre smile. Eyes wide, staring at him. Eyes never leaving his face.

He forced her neck between rocks and snatched at the pendant. Blackstone pressed his thumbnail beneath its cap and raised the small phial and whatever it held to his lips. He swallowed the bitter liquid and let the pendant be swept away. Was it the antidote or a final trick played by the witch? Was her prophecy fulfilled?

He lay, head resting on the boulder for how long he couldn't tell, but as the sun settled close to the far horizon, he felt warmth creep into his chest and then his arms and legs. He dragged himself free of the rushing water and tested his strength. From all fours on the bank, he stood and, as he heaved Wolf Sword from de Hayle's chest, he knew his power had returned. He kicked free the woman's trapped body. The current dragged her away. He watched her bob and slide through the water, nudged by boulders, until she disappeared to fall to the rocks below.

He walked to the cliff edge and looked down at Velasquita's shattered body. The dark-ruffled sea began to consume the sun's ball of fire. A ship's sails caught the wind and eased away from the shore.

'Legends never die,' he told the dead witch. 'Not until the wine barrels run dry.'

Killbere and the men were waiting. Blackstone turned for home.

He looked heavenward.

The hawk had flown.

AUTHOR'S NOTES

The War of the Breton Succession had raged for years between the French-backed claimant, Charles de Blois, and his adversary John IV de Montfort. Much of the Duchy of Brittany had been controlled by Edward III since 1342 when John de Montfort had been taken to England as an eight-year-old child as Edward's ward. Over the years Charles de Blois had fought hard to retain control of the duchy and when he was wounded and captured in June 1347, organized opposition to the English in Brittany was led by his wife, Jeanne de Penthièvre, who struggled with few resources in order to conserve what little power she had. Edward's main interest lay in denying the French a presence in western Brittany that could sever communications between England and Bordeaux and Gascony. Turmoil and poor governance continued for years and loyalties from regional lords changed sides during and after English success at Crécy and Poitiers. Various treaties followed and Brittany was legally a fief of the King of France, governed by Edward III in his ward's name.

When John de Montfort came of age in June 1362 Edward relinquished the duchy to him, but in practice it remained an English protectorate. When the King gave his son, the Prince of Wales, the Duchy of Aquitaine to govern, the Prince and the young de Montfort's close relationship and Brittany's geographical importance to the English Crown made it seem inevitable that the duchy would be secured for England and the decades-long civil war brought to a satisfactory conclusion.

When Charles de Blois raided across Brittany assisted by French captains, he successfully divided the duchy in two. The fuse was lit and de Montfort, no doubt with the King and Prince's encouragement, turned to English routiers for help.

Sir John Chandos and Sir Hugh Calveley were leading figures who joined de Montfort and formed the Anglo-Breton army. Prior to the battle, Charles de Blois and Breton lords who supported de Montfort tried to negotiate a peace but such was the English insistence that battle commence, any hope of reconciliation and division of the duchy was swept aside. When John de Montfort laid siege to Auray, Charles de Blois, well supported by French and Breton lords and mercenaries, hurried to trap de Montfort with his back to the sea, but on the day of the battle many of his Breton mercenaries deserted. When Charles de Blois was killed, and the battle won, it is recorded that English and Breton men-at-arms stuck their pennons and lances in a hedge and stripped off their armour and mail to cool down.

The Prince of Wales and Aquitaine needed safe borders for the Duchy of Aquitaine. He had charmed Gascon lords with his banquets and tourneys and when King Don Pedro I of Castile and León in Spain was threatened by a mercenary invasion led by French, Breton and English mercenaries, he knew the stated aim of waging a crusade against the Islamic Emirate of Granada, allies of Don Pedro lying south of Castile, was a pretext. The French intended to place Don Pedro's half-brother, the bastard Henry of Trastámara, on the throne. This French puppet would give the recently anointed French King, Charles V, a strategic advantage by placing an enemy at the Prince's back across the border. The duplicitous King of Navarre eventually played along with the French and closed his border to Gascony, which cut off any chance of Don Pedro escaping and avoiding death at his half-brother's hand. Don

Pedro's reputation was one of a licentious adulterer, a vicious King who slew hundreds, who embraced friendship with the Muslim South and was accused of having his young French bride, Blanche de Bourbon, murdered.

Don Pedro sent his Moors to slaughter his enemies with the threat that if they did not bring back their victims' heads, they would lose theirs. Despite such ruthlessness the Prince of Wales believed he was the legitimate King of Castile and that a bastard should not rule. Once Don Pedro had been denied sanctuary by his ally, the King of Portugal (his daughter's betrothal to the King's son was cancelled), Don Pedro had no choice but to escape to Aquitaine and beg assistance from the Prince of Wales. After fleeing to Seville he made his way to the province that remained loyal, Galicia, and then to Corunna, Galicia's northern port, where he took a ship to Bayonne. There is no record of what motivated him to murder the Archbishop of Santiago, Suero Gómez, and the dean of Santiago cathedral, Peralvarez, but I thought it reasonable to assume that as Don Pedro had already been excommunicated by the Pope that the Archbishop had made the King unwelcome and refused him entrance to the city and permission to attend communion.

The Jewish community had found sanctuary in Spain and Portugal and co-habited with Christians and Muslims. Castile and Navarre were safer for them than France and the rest of Europe. Most Spanish Jews preserved their Arabic language and nomenclature and remained extensively integrated into the Arab cultural terrain. Synagogues had many architectural and decorative similarities with mosques and were adorned with carvings of animals and vegetation and sacred verses in Hebrew lettering. However, discrimination still existed and complete integration was usually denied.

When Blackstone returned to Bordeaux with Halif ben Josef the Jewish physician, he found rooms on the street named as Arrua Judega which lay at the foot of the hill outside the city walls known as Mont Judaïque. This hill no longer exists and Arrua Judega is now named Rue Cheverus. When Bordeaux was under English rule the Jews were spared the expulsion orders that had been issued by the Kings of France, although various taxes were still levied, including the pepper tax. Charles of Navarre who, like Don Pedro of Castile, gave sanctuary to the Jews, levied a tax on wine but not on grapes. Halif ben Josef's home town, Estella-Lizarra still exists.

In order to take Blackstone on this particular journey through France and into Spain I compressed some of the time it took for historical events to unfold. Don Pedro had set up his headquarters at Burgos with the expectation that his enemies would strike from Saragossa. He was mistaken and was outflanked. The mercenaries attacked from the southeast, sweeping north through the valley of the River Ebro. The campaign against him was rapidly executed by, among others, Sir Hugh Calveley, who had agreed to fight with the Breton Bertrand du Guesclin on the condition Hugh would not fight against the English Crown. He was well rewarded for his success and given the title of Count of Carrión. Needless to say, the Jewish and Muslim communities abandoned by Don Pedro in Burgos and other Castilian cities soon had their property seized. Don Pedro's fate became ever more desperate and he ordered his treasury to be loaded onto a galley on the River Guadalquivir with orders for the ship to sail to a Portuguese port on the Atlantic coast. Gil Boccanegra, the Genoese Admiral of the Castilian Fleet, saw where his future lay and handed Don Pedro's treasury to the enemy. King Don Pedro I was now all but defeated and he had no choice but to escape and plan a return to Castile with the help of the Prince of Wales and Aquitaine.

The underground tunnels beneath Burgos Castle are 62 metres deep and the well is an impressive testament to the skill of medieval stonemasons. The spiral staircase descends around the well's walls to predetermined levels and then forms a passage to the opposite side of the well where the spiral staircase continues but in the opposite direction. This means those who used the staircase to reach the tunnels below don't have to descend in the same direction all the way down.

I am always appreciative of the help I receive from readers who have specialist knowledge and patiently listen to my queries so I can attempt to get historical elements as accurate as possible. I am grateful to Chris Verwijmeren in Holland, expert in medieval archery, for his help with advising me about the use of Saracen bows and for his videos of how the Moors' mounted archers balanced their swords on their bow arm ready for use. I also found the out-of-print book *Saracen Archery* by J. D. Latham, MA, DPhil (Oxon) & Lt Cdr W. F. Paterson, RN of great interest and help in my understanding of the skills of the Moors.

The steady hand of my ever-patient editor, Richenda Todd, guided this latest novel through the editing process, along with her usual keen eye and incisive comments.

Behind every author are the unsung heroes who do all the hard work. I am extremely lucky to have such a team at my publishers, Head of Zeus, who welcome every new Master of War volume with ongoing enthusiasm. Beavering away like monastic monks in a Blackstone novel, their efforts, along with Head of the Scriptorium Nic Cheetham's continual striving to find the perfect illumination for my book covers, has brought Master of War to a wide audience.

Blake Friedmann Literary Agency brings a world of experience and professional care to all aspects of my work. The arcane world of international rights, the contracts and all they entail are handled with what appears to be effortless calm under fire. My thanks to you all: James Pusey, Hana Murrell, Sian Ellis-Martin, Daisy Way, Lizzy Attree, Samuel Hodder, Tia Armstrong, Ane Reason, Louisa Minghella and Conrad Williams. I don't know how my agent, Isobel Dixon, finds the time to pay careful attention to my manuscripts and offer erudite and invaluable comments.

Thank you.

David Gilman
Devonshire, 2020

www.davidgilman.com
FB: @davidgilman.author
Twitter: @davidgilmanuk